**OXFORD **

SOUTH

ROBERT LOUIS STEVENSON, only child of Thomas Stevenson, engineer and lighthouse builder, and Margaret Balfour, daughter of a Scots minister, was born in Edinburgh in 1850. In 1871 he exchanged the study of engineering for the law. From 1876 he pursued a full-time literary career, beginning as an essayist and travel writer with the publication of *An Inland Voyage* (1878), *Edinburgh: Picturesque Notes* (1878), *Travels with a Donkey in the Cevennes* (1879), and *Virginibus Puerisque* (1881). He is probably best remembered for *Treasure Island* (his first widespread success, 1883), *Kidnapped* (1886), and *Dr Jekyll and Mr Hyde* (1886). Ill health prompted Stevenson to travel widely on the Continent and in the South Seas, where he settled in 1889–90 until his death in Samoa on 3 December 1894.

ROSLYN JOLLY is a lecturer in the School of English at the University of New South Wales. She is the author of *Henry James: History, Narrative, Fiction* (Oxford, 1993).

OXFORD WORLD'S CLASSICS

For over 100 years Oxford World's Classics have brought readers closer to the world's great literature. Now with over 700 titles—from the 4,000-year-old myths of Mesopotamia to the twentieth century's greatest novels—the series makes available lesser-known as well as celebrated writing.

The pocket-sized hardbacks of the early years contained introductions by Virginia Woolf, T. S. Eliot, Graham Greene, and other literary figures which enriched the experience of reading. Today the series is recognized for its fine scholarship and reliability in texts that span world literature, drama and poetry, religion, philosophy and politics. Each edition includes perceptive commentary and essential background information to meet the changing needs of readers.

OXFORD WORLD'S CLASSICS

ROBERT LOUIS STEVENSON

South Sea Tales

Edited with an Introduction and Notes by
ROSLYN JOLLY

OXFORD
UNIVERSITY PRESS

OXFORD
UNIVERSITY PRESS

Great Clarendon Street, Oxford OX2 6DP

Oxford University Press is a department of the University of Oxford.
It furthers the University's objective of excellence in research, scholarship,
and education by publishing worldwide in

Oxford New York

Athens Auckland Bangkok Bogotá Buenos Aires Calcutta
Cape Town Chennai Dar es Salaam Delhi Florence Hong Kong Istanbul
Karachi Kuala Lumpur Madrid Melbourne Mexico City Mumbai
Nairobi Paris São Paulo Singapore Taipei Tokyo Toronto Warsaw

with associated companies in Berlin Ibadan

Oxford is a registered trade mark of Oxford University Press
in the UK and in certain other countries

Published in the United States
by Oxford University Press Inc., New York

First published as a World's Classics paperback 1996
Reissued as an Oxford World's Classics paperback 1999
Reissued 2008

British Library Cataloguing in Publication Data

Data available

Library of Congress Cataloging in Publication Data

Stevenson, Robert Louis, 1850–1894.
South Sea tales / Robert Louis Stevenson, edited with an introduction by Roslyn Jolly.
p. cm.—(Oxford world's classics)
Includes bibliographical references.
Contents: The beach of Falesá—The bottle imp—The isle of voices—The
ebb-ride—The cart-horses and the saddle-horse—Something in it.
1. South Pacific Ocean—Social life and customs—Fiction. 2. Oceania—Social life and
customs—Fiction. I. Jolly, Roslyn. II. Title. III. Series.
PR5481.J65 1996 823'.8—dc20 95–52207

ISBN 978–0–19–953608–5

17

Printed in Great Britain by
Clays Ltd, Elcograf S.p.A.

ACKNOWLEDGEMENTS

Manuscript material in the Edwin J. Beinecke Robert Louis Stevenson Collection is quoted by permission of the Beinecke Rare Book and Manuscript Library, Yale University. Items from this collection are indicated by the reference 'Beinecke' and the catalogue number in George L. McKay, *A Stevenson Library: Catalogue of a Collection of Writings by and about Robert Louis Stevenson Formed by Edwin J. Beinecke*, 6 vols. (New Haven: Yale University Press, 1951–64). Quotations from Stevenson's autograph 'Vailima Letters' are published by permission of the Houghton Library, Harvard University. Quotations from the manuscript of 'The Beach of Falesá' (Huntington Library, HM 2391) are published by permission of the Huntington Library, San Marino, California.

CONTENTS

INTRODUCTION

> Awfully nice man here to-night. Public servant—New Zealand. Telling us all about the South Sea Islands till I was sick with desire to go there; beautiful places, green for ever; perfect climate; perfect shapes of men and women, with red flowers in their hair; and nothing to do but to study oratory and etiquette, sit in the sun, and pick up the fruits as they fall. Navigator's Island is the place; absolute balm for the weary.
>
> Stevenson, letter of spring 1875[1]

WHEN Stevenson went to make his permanent home in Samoa (also called the Navigator Islands) in 1890, the New Zealander's visit of 1875 was to the fore of his mind. He represented his transplantation to Samoa in the light of an invitation long deferred but finally accepted, or even a prophecy fulfilled, and the islands as a kind of promised land: 'and now in 1890, I (or what is left of me) go at last to the Navigator Islands. God go with us! It is but a Pisgah sight when all is said; I go there only to grow old and die' (*Letters*, iii. 315).[2] Before he died, though, Stevenson was to make a substantial contribution to the literature of the region. He had been in the Pacific since 1888, coming in search of health and with a commission to write a series of travel articles for syndication to American and English newspapers. In three cruises from 1888 to 1890 he had traversed the ocean from Hawaii in the north to Australia in the south, from the Marquesas in the east to the Marshall Islands in the west. He was never to return to Europe, but died at his home, Vailima,

[1] R. L. Stevenson, *The Letters of Robert Louis Stevenson*, ed. Sidney Colvin, 5 vols. (London: Heinemann, 1924), i. 235. Subsequent references to this edition of the letters (vols. xxxi–xxxv of the *Tusitala Edition* of Stevenson's works) are included in the text with the abbreviation *Letters*, i–v.

[2] Having led the Israelites out of captivity, Moses was not allowed to enter the promised land, only to see it from the top of Mt. Pisgah. See Deut. 3: 23–7; 34: 1–4.

in Samoa, in December 1894. During the last six years of his life he produced a significant body of work on Pacific subjects: a novel, *The Wrecker,* and novella, *The Ebb-Tide* (both written in collaboration with Lloyd Osbourne), two works of non-fiction (*In the South Seas* and *A Footnote to History*), a volume of short stories (*Island Nights' Entertainments,* consisting of 'The Beach of Falesá', 'The Bottle Imp', and 'The Isle of Voices'), and various poems, public letters, pamphlets, and fables. This volume collects all of Stevenson's shorter Pacific fiction.[3]

In *In the South Seas* Stevenson wrote: 'The first experience can never be repeated. The first love, the first sunrise, the first South Sea island, are memories apart, and touched a virginity of sense.'[4] Yet, as his letters show, while only one island could be the first, every island represented a new beginning for the visitor, an unknown world with its own people, landscape, culture, and possibilities of engagement. Stevenson revelled in the sense of perpetual discovery, the opening out of a new world with every new island visited. He wrote to Henry James in 1889: 'this precious deep is filled with islands, which we may still visit; and though the sea is a deathful place, I like to be there, and like squalls (when they are over); and to draw near to a new island, I cannot say how much I like' (*Letters,* iii. 241). Writing to James Payn, he expanded on the same theme: 'My good news is a health astonishingly reinstated. This climate; these voyagings; these landfalls at dawn; new islands peaking from the morning bank; new forested

[3] I do not classify as fiction the unpublished 'Talofa, Togarewa!', introduced by Stevenson as 'the true story of an island' (Beinecke 6958); this is really an essay warning the Samoans of the consequences of harbouring lepers and, though cast in narrative form, contains no characterization. The fictional letter, 'Plain John Wiltshire on the Situation' (HM 2409, Huntington Library, San Marino, California) has not been included as it is not a story, but a polemic directed by Stevenson against the British High Commissioner for the Western Pacific. I do not count as works by Stevenson the 'Two Tahitian Legends' published over his name in Andrew Lang's column 'At the Sign of the Ship' in *Longman's Magazine,* 19 (1892), 568–72, in which Stevenson has merely 'slavishly reproduced' local tales told him in Tahiti (p. 571).

[4] Stevenson, *The Works of Robert Louis Stevenson, Tusitala Edition,* 35 vols. (London: Heinemann, 1923–4), xx. 4. Subsequent references to this edition are included in the text with the abbreviation *Tusitala.*

harbours; new passing alarms of squalls and surf; new interests of gentle natives,—the whole tale of my life is better to me than any poem' (*Letters*, iii. 262). The sense of the allure, for a European, of a new Pacific island, is captured in two of the stories in this collection. 'The Beach of Falesá' begins with a landfall at dawn, narrated by the trader Wiltshire:

I saw that island first when it was neither night nor morning. The moon was to the west, setting, but still broad and bright. To the east, and right amidships of the dawn, which was all pink, the daystar sparkled like a diamond. The land breeze blew in our faces, and smelt strong of wild lime and vanilla: other things besides, but these were the most plain; and the chill of it set me sneezing. I should say I had been for years on a low island near the line, living for the most part solitary among natives. Here was a fresh experience: even the tongue would be quite strange to me; and the look of these woods and mountains, and the rare smell of them, renewed my blood. (p. 3)

Another island landfall marks a turning-point in the action of *The Ebb-Tide*:

The isle—the undiscovered, the scarce-believed in—now lay before them and close aboard; and Herrick thought that never in his dreams had he beheld anything more strange and delicate. The beach was excellently white, the continuous barrier of trees inimitably green; the land perhaps ten feet high, the trees thirty more. Every here and there, as the schooner coasted northward, the wood was intermitted; and he could see clear over the inconsiderable strip of land (as a man looks over a wall) to the lagoon within—and clear over that again to where the far side of the atoll prolonged its pencilling of trees against the morning sky. He tortured himself to find analogies. The isle was like the rim of a great vessel sunken in the waters; it was like the embankment of an annular railway grown upon with wood: so slender it seemed amidst the outrageous breakers, so frail and pretty, he would scarce have wondered to see it sink and disappear without a sound, and the waves close smoothly over its descent. (pp. 187–8)

In each case the new island is an object of desire, but desire takes different forms in the two landfalls, as it does throughout the two stories. Wiltshire's island meets him with an appeal to the senses, setting the tone for the story of how his sensual attachment to his native wife, Uma, transmutes into love. The description of the island is intensely physical, as is the plot which unfolds, initiated by sex and resolved through violence. The appeal of Herrick's island in *The Ebb-Tide* is much more intellectual, prompting speculation about truth and illusion and the force of analogies, speculation which takes its place within the story's broader concern with presenting the world as a stage and meaning as a parable. Emerging from the ocean like a mirage in a desert, the island offers an image for the novella's concern with the deceptiveness of desire. The two island landfalls suggest in miniature two accounts of what Europeans seek in the Pacific: in Wiltshire's case, trade, goods, sex, and physical adventure; in Herrick's, meaning, redemption or, failing that, self-obliteration.

As Stevenson prolonged his stay in the Pacific, and especially after he settled in Samoa, the traveller's interest in new islands began to give way to—or to be contextualized within—the resident's interest in the complex society of which he had become a member. Increasingly Stevenson realized that not only did each island offer itself, individually, as a new world for experience and for fiction, but that the whole Pacific was itself a new world, hardly known in Europe and barely represented in literature. 'I am going on with a lot of island work, exulting in the knowledge of a new world, "a new created world" and new men', he wrote in 1891; 'I have a whole world in my head, a whole new society to work' (*Letters*, iv. 57, 94). The keynote of this world was contrast and unexpected juxtaposition: 'The Pacific is a strange place; the nineteenth century only exists there in spots; all round, it is a no man's land of the ages, a stir-about of epochs and races, barbarisms and civilisations, virtues and crimes' (*Letters*, iii. 261). The juxtaposition of 'barbarisms and civilisations' was nowhere more apparent than in the confrontation of Polynesians and Europeans, and what made Stevenson's Pacific work controversial as well as novel was that, more often than not, the 'barbarisms' belonged to his European characters while his Polynesian characters were shown to be the inheritors of 'civilisations' unsuspected by his Western readers.

As early as 1889 Stevenson was drawing contrasts between

native and expatriate society, in favour of the former. He wrote to his friend Charles Baxter of a week spent in a native village on the Kona coast of Hawaii, 'a lovely week among God's best—at least God's sweetest works—Polynesians' and regretted his return to 'vile Honolulu, where I am always out of sorts, amidst heat and cold and cesspools and beastly *haoles*. What is a haole? You are one; and so, I am sorry to say, am I. After so long a dose of whites, it was a blessing to get among Polynesians again even for a week' (*Letters*, iii. 251). Comments such as this offended the white residents of the Pacific and led to accusations that Stevenson betrayed a 'prejudice against civilized men' and an 'indiscriminate love for Polynesians' whom he misguidedly romanticized.[5] In fact, he described the Samoans as 'like other folk, false enough, lazy enough, not heroes, not saints—ordinary men damnably misused' (*Letters*, iv. 97). Left to themselves the Samoans were, he believed, 'a healthy and happy people', unlike the Europeans who wished to control them, and he came to regard European civilization in general as 'a hollow fraud' and the European administration of Samoa in particular as 'this dance of folly and injustice and unconscious rapacity' (*Letters*, iii. 314; iv. 94).

The native crew of the schooner *Farallone* are led a similar dance by the white characters in *The Ebb-Tide*. Although it focuses on the experience of Europeans in the Pacific, this work draws the clearest picture found in Stevenson's fiction of the abuse of Pacific islanders by the representatives of a supposedly superior civilization. Herrick and his two companions, whom he met 'on the beach' or down and out in Tahiti, have stolen a ship and plan to sell its cargo of champagne. As his friends abandon responsibility for sailing the ship in favour of drinking their way through the cargo, Herrick draws closer to the native crew. One old man tells him 'his simple and hard story of exile, suffering, and injustice among cruel whites' (p. 167); this includes the tale of the ship's last cruise, on which the white captain and mate, also engaged in

[5] Arthur Johnstone, *Recollections of Robert Louis Stevenson in the Pacific* (London: Chatto & Windus, 1905), 9.

a fraudulent voyage, 'entered on a career of drunkenness', lost their position, and sailed aimlessly while, 'seeing themselves lost on the huge deep with their insane conductors, the natives had drunk deep of terror' (p. 169). The ship is a microcosm of imperialist society, directed by greedy but incompetent whites, the labour supplied by long-suffering natives who fulfil their duties without orders and are true to the missionary faith which the Europeans make no pretence of respecting. 'It was thus a cutting reproof to compare the islanders and the whites aboard the *Farallone*' (p. 168).

'The Bottle Imp' and 'The Isle of Voices' are not explicitly concerned with imperialism or the relations between whites and natives; using Polynesians as protagonists, the stories depict a contemporary Pacific world obviously marked by European contact, but in which white characters appear only peripherally. Yet when they do appear, whites are often depicted negatively. In 'The Bottle Imp', the magic bottle which brings power and riches, but also damnation, is sold to the Hawaiian Keawe by an American who tricks him into buying it. The bottle passes out of the story at the end in the possession of an 'old brutal Haole' (p. 98) who damns himself through his arrogance and rapacity, to the regret of no one. 'The Isle of Voices' is peppered with expressions of the Hawaiian protagonist's poor opinion of white men. Meanwhile in the fable 'The Cart-Horses and the Saddle-Horse' the horses from 'the colonies' (that is, Australia and New Zealand) rebuff the friendly overtures of the 'Kanaka' horse from Samoa, thereby revealing their own small-mindedness and insecurities. But it is 'The Beach of Falesá' which offers perhaps the most interesting account of the relations between white and native society in the Pacific. Without making the abuse of natives by whites an explicit topic, as it is in *The Ebb-Tide*, and without drawing such a stark moral contrast between the two groups, the story nevertheless subverts European assumptions of superiority. The tale traces the narrator Wiltshire's transfer of allegiance from the whites of 'the beach' to his native wife. At the beginning of the story he colludes with the leader of 'the beach', Case, to trick the young girl Uma into a fraudulent marriage; when he discovers he has been tabooed by the people of Falesá he seeks advice not from his wife ('it's a bad idea to set natives up with any notion of consulting them' (p. 21) but from Case. However, as it becomes apparent that Case has engineered both taboo and marriage to deprive his rival of trade, Wiltshire finds that his emotional attachment to the girl outweighs his desire for profit and, rather than abandoning her, he legitimates the marriage and works with her to outmanoeuvre Case. The native characters in the story are not romanticized, indeed some are presented as foolish or cynically opportunistic; even Uma, while highly courageous and faithful, is not above manipulating what she knows of the white man's character: as she offers to leave Wiltshire and free him of the taboo which bars him from the copra (coconut-meat) trade, 'She looked at [him] sidelong with a smile. "You see, you get copra," she said, the same as you might offer candies to a child' (p. 28). The natives are presented as humanly imperfect, but the whites, Case and Randall, are the sources of evil and objects of disgust: as Stevenson wrote of the story to his friend and literary adviser, Sidney Colvin, 'will you please to observe that almost all that is ugly is in the whites?' (*Letters*, iv. 182). Certainly Wiltshire observes it, yet cannot abandon the racist assumptions which permeate his narrative. This makes the story particularly interesting as a first-person narrative: Stevenson foreshadows Conrad in his use of a narrator who is partly complicit with, partly critical of, and not fully conscious of his own place within, imperialism. Wiltshire works to end Case's suzerainty over Falesá, yet still says, of Europeans in the Pacific, 'It would be a strange thing if we came all this way and couldn't do what we pleased' (p. 24). After all his experience of the duplicity and corruption of white men in the islands he writes, of the need to find husbands for his half-caste daughters, 'I can't reconcile my mind to their taking up with Kanakas, and I'd like to know where I'm to find the whites?' (p. 71). Wiltshire's lack of self-awareness and his refusal to modify his preconceptions in the light of his experience make his narrative an unconscious satire on the assumptions of racial and cultural superiority held by most of Stevenson's European contemporaries.

In Stevenson's Pacific stories, such a lack of self-knowledge on the part of Europeans is matched by their lack of knowledge of the new world around them. When one of the crew of the *Farallone* gives his name, Captain Davis dismisses it as 'gibberish' (p. 156) and gives him instead the insulting nickname 'Uncle Ned'; we later learn that, because of his ignorance of island pronunciation, Davis has failed to recognize 'Taveeta' as the Christian name David—as Taveeta scornfully says, 'no savvy nothing' (p. 168). Taveeta links Davis's ignorance to that of Wiseman and Wishart, the captain and mate on the *Farallone*'s previous voyage, whose inability to read the signs of sickness and death in a native village leads to their contracting small-pox. Their fate may be compared with that of the brutal white mate who torments Keola in 'The Isle of Voices': he arrives at an island at 'the beginning of the sickly season in that isle, when the fish of the lagoon are poisonous, and all who eat of them swell up and die. The mate was told of it . . . but he was a fool of a white man, who would believe no stories but his own, and he caught one of these fish, cooked it and ate it, and swelled up and died, which was good news to Keola' (p. 116). The idea that 'white men are like children and only believe their own stories' (p. 112) is the theme of the fable 'Something in It'. Secure in the belief that 'my stories are the true ones' (p. 255), a missionary breaks a local taboo and is forced to acknowledge that there is 'something in' the native lore and mythologies he has always discounted. The reader is asked to consider with him, 'if these tales are true, I wonder what about my tales!' (p. 256).

'Something in It' is one expression of Stevenson's ambivalence towards the missionaries who were such an important part of South Sea life in the nineteenth century. In the fable, the missionary's 'stories' and 'taboos' are all proved to be baseless, yet his stubborn loyalty to his own moral teachings saves him from destruction by the Samoan devils whose existence he has been forced to acknowledge. It is unclear how much he may have learned from or been changed by his experience, and the verse 'moral' at the end of the fable leaves us hesitating whether to praise or condemn the narrow but unshakeable moral foundation on which the missionary stands. The South Sea setting of the fable which provides its central conflict between Polynesian and Christian religious 'stories' allows Stevenson to explore an ambivalence about religious faith which long pre-dated his arrival in the Pacific. His rebellion against his strict Presbyterian upbringing is well documented in his letters, yet his continuing fascination with his 'Covenanting' (radical Scots Protestant) heritage is also evident throughout his writings. These conflicting impulses led to the kind of mixed response to Christianity found in a letter of 1891, where Stevenson wrote: 'mind you, I am a child of the Covenanters—whom I do not love, but they are mine after all, my father's and my mother's—and they had their merits, too, and their ugly beauties, and grotesque heroisms, that I love them for, the while I laugh at them' (*Letters*, iv. 79). The missionary in 'Something in It' is a figure through whom Stevenson explores the ways in which personal faith, always full (like the sentence just quoted) of self-contradiction, fares when also contradicted by an alien religious system. But missionaries in the South Seas in the era of imperialism were not simply representatives of a personal faith, as Stevenson well knew; their presence and their practices were bound up with various institutional and political forces. Always wary of missionaries who tried to bind the islanders to European cultural norms of behaviour and dress, Stevenson was openly critical of those who went further and made themselves the agents of European or American political interests in the Pacific: his 'Father Damien' pamphlet (1890) and *A Footnote to History* (1892) include scathing denunciations of Protestant missionaries and their political interests in Hawaii and Samoa respectively. Nevertheless, Stevenson liked and respected many missionaries, both Protestant and Catholic; he called the Revd James Chalmers, working in New Guinea for the London Missionary Society, 'the most attractive, simple, brave, and interesting man in the whole Pacific' (*Letters*, iv. 38–9), and his admiration for Father Damien, the 'leper priest of Molokai', led him to risk a libel suit by attacking one of the priest's detractors.[6] What Stevenson most objected to in missionary work was its hidden—or not so hidden—agenda

[6] See *Father Damien: An Open Letter to the Reverend Doctor Hyde of Honolulu from Robert Louis Stevenson* (London: Chatto & Windus, 1890); *Tusitala*, xxi. 25–42.

of cultural imperialism. He wrote in *In the South Seas* that some missionaries, by deriding and violating native customs and substituting European ones unsuitable to the circumstances, 'have rendered life in a more or less degree unliveable to their converts' (*Tusitala*, xx. 37). A similar impatience with missionary work as cultural domestication is expressed by Stevenson's most extraordinary missionary character, Attwater of *The Ebb-Tide*: 'They go the wrong way to work; they are too parsonish, too much of the old wife, and even the old apple-wife. *Clothes, clothes*, are their idea; but clothes are not Christianity, any more than they are the sun in heaven, or could take the place of it! They think a parsonage with roses, and church bells, and nice old women bobbing in the lanes, are part and parcel of religion' (pp. 203–4). This lack of imagination on the part of conventional missionaries diminishes the 'interest in missions' (p. 203) which, in part, drew Attwater to the South Seas; nevertheless, although he lacks (and scorns) institutional authorization, Attwater is indeed a missionary, an impassioned evangelist, as well as a trader and personal empire-builder. In Attwater Stevenson combined a scorn for the bourgeois trappings of religion which he himself shared; the kind of religious fanaticism (like that of the Covenanters) which was prepared to kill or die for faith, and which had always alternately attracted and repelled him; and late nineteenth-century notions of racial supremacy and the will to power, which he abhorred. The result was a character who 'intrigued, puzzled, dazzled, enchanted and revolted' (p. 207). Visionary, enigmatic, and sinister, Attwater is a precursor for Conrad's more famous character Kurtz as a figure embodying the contradictions and corruptions at the heart of imperialism.

Attwater is a monster: with his black cat on his shoulder, or extorting repentance at the end of a Winchester rifle, he is a figure of parable, of demonology, as much as of realist fiction. In quite another key is the character of Mr Tarleton, the missionary in 'The Beach of Falesá'. Like all the characters in the story, Mr Tarleton is presented through the eyes of the narrator, Wiltshire, and must gradually emerge in his true character from the preconceptions and prejudices through which Wiltshire at first views him. These prejudices shed an interesting light on class and race relations in the Pacific world:

This was the first time, in all my years in the Pacific, I had ever exchanged two words with any missionary, let alone asked one for a favour. I didn't like the lot, no trader does; they look down upon us, and make no concealment; and, besides, they're partly Kanakaized, and suck up with natives instead of with other white men like themselves. (p. 34)

[Uma] and Mr Tarleton called each other by name, and he was very civil to her seemingly. But I thought little of that; they can always find civility for a Kanaka, it's us white men they lord it over. (p. 36)

Missionaries infuriate Wiltshire because they do not recognize the (to him) obvious superiority of all white men over natives and, however unintentionally, remind him of his inferiority in terms of class, education, and the doubtful legitimacy of his trading and sexual practices among the islanders. However, Wiltshire comes to find in Mr Tarleton an invaluable ally against his enemy Case, while to the reader the missionary emerges as a conscientious man, harrassed by unscrupulous whites, unwillingly embroiled in petty local intrigues, but 'as anxious to do well for these islands as [Wiltshire] can be to please and to protect [his] pretty wife' (p. 40).

Wiltshire's 'pretty wife' was a new departure for Stevenson. He wrote to Sidney Colvin in 1891 that 'The Beach of Falesá' was '(for once in my works) rendered pleasing by the presence of a heroine who is pretty. Miss Uma is pretty; a fact. All my other bitches have been as ugly as sin'.[7] Stevenson's earlier fiction had been anomolous within the strongly feminine English novel tradition because of its presentation of exclusively or predominantly masculine worlds, an oddity often noted by contemporary reviewers. 'The Beach of Falesá' offered a rare thing in Stevenson's works, a courtship plot, but in such an unusual form that it flouted rather than obeyed

[7] Stevenson, letter to Sidney Colvin, 29 April 1891, 'Vailima Letters', Widener Collection, Houghton Library, Harvard University (*HEW 10.13 21); modified version published in *Letters*, iv. 75.

novelistic convention; and if the author thought the story would be 'rendered pleasing' to his publishers by the presence of Uma, he soon discovered he was mistaken. Clement Shorter, editor of the *Illustrated London News*, in which the story was to appear as a serial, objected to the fraudulent marriage certificate used to seduce Uma:

> This is to certify that Uma daughter of Fa'avao of Falesá island of ——, is illegally married to Mr John Wiltshire for one night, and Mr John Wiltshire is at liberty to send her to hell next morning. (p. 11)

Stevenson resisted the demand that the document be omitted—'The plaintive request sent to me, to make the young folks married properly before "that night", I refused; you will see what would be left of the yarn, had I consented' (*Letters*, iv. 149)—but the magazine went ahead and censored the certificate anyway, thereby rendering impenetrable much of the plot that follows. When Cassell's came to publish the story in book form the firm suggested a compromise designed to shield the sensibilities of its readers, although it is difficult to see exactly how; this time Stevenson gave in: 'Well, well, if the dears prefer a week, why, I'll give them ten days, but the real document, from which I have scarcely varied, ran for one night' (*Letters*, iv. 182; see also note to p. 11). The episode threw some light on Stevenson's celebrated avoidance of female characters as, like so many of his fellow late nineteenth-century novelists, he complained about the prudery that ruled the publishing world: 'This is a poison bad world for the romancer, this Anglo-Saxon world; I usually get out of it by not having any women in it at all' (*Letters*, iv. 149). As he wrote in connection with another story on which he was working at this time, 'with all my romance, I am a realist and a prosaist, and a most fanatical lover of plain physical sensations plainly and expressly rendered' (*Letters*, iv. 184); 'If I have got to kill a man, I kill him good; and if my characters have to go to bed to each other—well, I want them to go.'[8] Stevenson's publishers could

[8] Stevenson, letter to Sidney Colvin, 19 May 1892, 'Vailima Letters', Widener Collection, Houghton Library, Harvard University (*HEW 10.13 21); omitted from *Letters*, iv. 184.

isolate and censor the scandalous marriage contract, but they could not rid Wiltshire's narrative of the strong impulse of sexual desire, plainly expressed, that runs as a motive force through the story. The powerful sexual bond between Keawe and Kokua in 'The Bottle Imp' is also evident, although less explicitly rendered, while 'The Isle of Voices' is quite matter-of-fact about sexual needs: Keola takes a second wife while on the cannibal island and although the missionary in Hawaii is 'very sharp on him' for it (p. 122), no one else in the story, including the narrator, seems particularly concerned.

What is interesting about the female characters in these stories is not just that they break up the traditionally all-male world of Stevensonian fiction and allow Stevenson to write about love and sex, but that they are such positive representations of native women and such powerful forces within the plots. In all three stories that make up *Island Nights' Entertainments* a husband is rescued by his wife's resourcefulness and courage. In 'The Isle of Voices' Lehua defies her powerful and sinister father and steals his magic to rescue Keola from the cannibals' island. Uma braves Case's rifle and the devils she believes to haunt the bush to warn Wiltshire of his enemy's pursuit; Wiltshire, 'one of those most opposed to any nonsense about native women' (p. 12), not only loses his head over her sexually, but discovers she is 'a trump' (p. 64). Kokua, in 'The Bottle Imp', is one of the most attractive of all Stevenson's characters. When she learns that Keawe has mortgaged his soul to the devil to have her, she energetically sets about solving the predicament that seems to him hopeless: 'You know nothing . . . I was educated in a school in Honolulu; I am no common girl. And I tell you, I shall save my lover' (p. 92). She is brave as well as intelligent, and when her ingenious scheme appears to have failed, she dares hell's fire herself to save her husband.

It was unusual at this time for a European writing about the Pacific to create native protagonists and to look at the Pacific world through their eyes; the effort shows Stevenson attempting to write not only about, but also from within and through, other cultures. Stevenson's South Sea tales present the Pacific world from many different points of view, Polynesian and

European, and they closely link differences in perspective to differences in language. Stevenson was acutely aware of the nineteenth-century Pacific as a great linguistic melting-pot, in which many different kinds of speech met and modified each other. The many 'voices' of trade and imperialism figure in 'The Isle of Voices', in which the systematic international plunder of the Pacific region in the nineteenth century is translated into a fantastic plot involving sorcerers of many nations: having seen the money made by the sorcerers, Keola thinks 'it is clear that all the new coin in all the world is gathered on these sands' (p. 119), and we are told that '[a]ll tongues of the earth were spoken there; the French, the Dutch, the Russian, the Tamil, the Chinese' (p. 119). The sentence inevitably calls to mind the image of the Tower of Babel, which indeed is used by Wiltshire to describe his linguistic confusion as, finding that English is spoken little in Falesá, he tries to learn 'native and French at the same time' under the tutelage of an old priest who 'muddled [him] up with foreign languages worse than the tower of Babel' (p. 44). The problems created by linguistic diversity in the Pacific were solved by the evolution of a *lingua franca*, described by Stevenson in *In the South Seas* as 'an efficient pidgin, what is called to the westward "Beach-la-Mar"', which 'may be called, and will almost certainly become, the tongue of the Pacific' (*Tusitala*, xx. 10).[9] Beach-la-Mar is used by Taveeta to talk to Herrick in *The Ebb-Tide*, and is also presumably the form of English used by Sally Day in the same story to communicate with the rest of the crew of the *Farallone* (p. 168); a native of 'some far western island' (p. 155), his home would fall outside the zone of cognate languages in the eastern Pacific which allows the Hawaiian characters in 'The Bottle Imp' and 'The Isle of Voices' to understand easily the speech of Tahiti or the Paumotus. A 'compromise' or 'contact' language, Beach-la-Mar is the vehicle for Wiltshire's conversations with his wife, and is thus woven into the narrative style of 'The Beach of Falesá', described by Stevenson as 'trader's talk, which is a strange conglomerate of literary expressions and

[9] Also called 'beach-de-mar'; see note to p. 30.

English and American slang, and Beach de Mar, or native English' (*Letters*, iv. 101).

Pidgin is a form of English which includes as many speakers as possible and erases distinctions between them; other language-styles of the South Seas worked through definition and exclusion of speakers. The speech map of the Pacific could be traced by class and profession as well as by race or nationality, and *The Ebb-Tide* makes great use of speech patterns which work to empower or disempower different groups of English speakers. 'For heaven's sake, tell me some of the words,' Herrick begs of Davis as he attempts to pass himself off as a trained seaman (p. 156). The line between landsman and sailor is crossed with relative ease as Herrick 'overhauled his reminiscences of sea romance for some appropriate words' and learns to imitate 'that precise and cut-and-dry English which prevails on board a ship' (p. 155); however, the barrier between social classes, also expressed in languages, proves impassable. As the story progresses, Davis and Huish (an American and a Cockney) and Herrick and Attwater (one educated at Oxford, the other at Cambridge) are shown to inhabit two distinct language zones. The first is distinguished by slang and references to popular culture (songs, advertisements), while the second is the product of a classical education. Herrick is, whether he likes it or not, bound to Attwater by this world of shared reference, and concomitantly alienated from his companions by their exclusion from it. As well as demonstrating the durability of class distinctions, even in a new environment and amidst the seemingly democratizing effects of poverty and desperation, the delineation of Herrick's and Attwater's linguistic world offers an important commentary on the relations between language, education, and empire. Herrick carries a copy of the *Aeneid* about with him, and dips into it randomly (as some people do the Bible) seeking clues about the future:

> And if the oracle (as is the way of oracles) replied with no very certain nor encouraging voice, visions of England at least would throng upon the exile's memory: the busy schoolroom, the green playing-fields, holidays at home, and the perennial roar of London, and the fireside, and the white head of his father. For it is the destiny of those

grave, restrained and classic writers, with whom we make enforced and often painful acquaintanceship at school, to pass into the blood and become native in the memory; so that a phrase of Virgil speaks not so much of Mantua or Augustus, but of English places and the student's own irrevocable youth. (pp. 124–5)

For the English, as for the Romans, Virgil's *Aeneid* is part of a discourse of imperialism: not, as in Roman civilization, because of its direct exhortation to found an empire, but because it comes indirectly to represent a class interest, a way of life, and a set of values that form the basis of a nationalism so deeply rooted as to be almost unconsciously held. Thus when Herrick finds himself automatically completing Attwater's quotation from Virgil (p. 202) he is acknowledging institutional and cultural bonds which are just as powerful as his more personal reaction of horror at the man's empire-building methods. To see the Pacific through the language of Virgil, as Attwater does and as Herrick is half-inclined to do, is to assimilate it to a mission of English cultural imperialism far more subtle, and therefore far more insidious, than that of the Protestant missionaries and their bourgeois preoccupation with clothing the natives. Filtered through the language of a classical education, the Pacific looks a very different place from that described in Taveeta's pidgin.

Stevenson's sensitivity to the linguistic diversity of the South Seas means that his stories contain many different styles of speech, and characterization works to a great extent through the relations between these different styles. As an author, Stevenson was also interested in exploring the Pacific world through different styles of writing. The generic diversity of his Pacific work is evident in this volume, but the self-consciousness with which that diversity was pursued is even more apparent when the extant work is placed in the context of the projected works—for, sadly, much of what Stevenson planned to write about the South Seas was not completed, or even begun, before his death in 1894.

'The Beach of Falesá' was one of a series of stories which Stevenson planned to set on an imaginary island called Ulufanua (*Letters*, iv. 94). While the island was imaginary, the stories were grounded in Stevenson's experience of contemporary Samoan life: one, 'The Bloody Wedding', was to be 'founded on fact—very possibly true, being an attempt to read a murder case—not yet months old, in this very place and house where I now write', he wrote from Pago-Pago, now in American Samoa (*Letters*, iv. 64); another, 'The Labour Slave', was to be 'a political story' (*Letters*, iv. 94) drawing on Stevenson's knowledge of the Samoan plantations that used imported, virtually slave, labour from the western Pacific. These three realistic stories were to make up a volume called *Beach de Mar* (*Letters*, iv. 182)—the title reveals their common concern with pidgin culture, with experience taking place in the space of transactions between Europeans and Polynesians. However, 'The Labour Slave' became absorbed into a longer plantation novel set in Tahiti, *Sophia Scarlet*, which was planned but not written; 'The Bloody Wedding', similarly, never progressed beyond the initial planning stage. This meant that 'The Beach of Falesá' had to be published in another volume, *Island Nights' Entertainments*, which Stevenson had always intended as a collection of '*Märchen*' (*Letters*, v. 5), folk tales and supernatural stories, of which 'The Bottle Imp' was to be the '*pièce de résistance*' (*Letters*, iv. 268). This volume, which would also include 'The Isle of Voices' and for which Stevenson had planned to write more stories, was a generically inappropriate home for 'The Beach of Falesá', which the author called 'the child of a quite different inspiration' (*Letters*, iv. 269); however, the compromise volume was produced in the interests of publishing expediency. Meanwhile, *The Ebb-Tide* (originally called *The Pearl Fisher*) was initially intended to be one of three novel-length 'South Sea Yarns', all to be written in collaboration with Stevenson's stepson, Lloyd Osbourne. An aspirant writer who had already published one novel (*The Wrong Box*) with his stepfather, Osbourne accompanied the Stevensons on their Pacific cruises and settled with them in Samoa. The first of the proposed collaborative South Sea series, *The Wrecker*, was completed and was published in 1892. *The Pearl Fisher*, conceived as a similarly 'huge' novel (*Letters*, iii. 309) was set aside in the early stages of writing; Stevenson later resumed the project alone, completing the story in a much more condensed form as a novella.[10] The third in the series, *The Beachcombers*, was never written at all.[11] The key-notes of the projected 'South Sea Yarns' series seem to have been a realistic style embracing grotesque situations and violent incidents, and a broad social sweep depicting the 'strange ways of life' and 'hot-bed of strange characters and incidents' (*Letters*, iii. 269) associated with white men adrift in the Pacific world.

While none of Stevenson's larger projects of Pacific writing was carried out as planned, the completed short fiction collected in this volume bears the marks of the diverse generic impulses around which he planned his South Sea work: the domestic realism of the *Beach de Mar* volume is evident in 'The Beach of Falesá', the strange mixture of epic and naturalistic impulses of the 'South Sea Yarns' characterizes *The Ebb-Tide*, while 'The Bottle Imp' and 'The Isle of Voices' embody the compact folk-tale structures and supernatural elements intended to distinguish *Island Nights' Entertainments*. Meanwhile, the two fables belong to yet another kind of writing: the short fiction cast as moral allegory or debate, which derives from the intellectual impulse that produced the longer and more circumstantial fable, *Strange Case of Dr Jekyll and Mr Hyde*, as well as the many meditations on morality and behaviour Stevenson wrote in essay form.

Generic diversity had always been the hallmark of Stevenson's career as a writer; he had always produced many kinds and styles of writing—too many, indeed, for the comfort of critics who wished to pigeon-hole him. What was new about his Pacific writing was its movement towards the realistic depiction of contemporary life. Although he also wrote children's stories, travel works, and fantasy literature, Stevenson's name had been particularly associated with historical

[10] Osbourne made a significant contribution only to the first four or five chapters. Stevenson explained: 'Up to the discovery of the champagne, the tale was all planned between us and drafted by Lloyd; from that moment he has had nothing to do with it except talking it over' (*Letters*, v. 79). The chapters originally drafted by Osbourne were also revised by Stevenson. For more detail on the process of composition, see Roger G. Swearingen, *The Prose Writings of Robert Louis Stevenson: A Guide* (Hamden: Archon Books, 1980), 183–7.

[11] Swearingen, *Prose Writings*, 143–4, 184.

romance; the new interest in contemporary realism was therefore a significant shift in focus. Stevenson was aware that his fiction was changing, as is evident in a letter he wrote to Charles Baxter about *The Wrecker*: 'it is certainly well nourished with facts; no realist can touch me there; for by this time I do begin to know something of life in the XIXth century' (*Letters*, iv. 117). The real turning-point was 'The Beach of Falesá', which Stevenson saw as a ground-breaking work, in terms both of the fiction of the Pacific and of his own stylistic development. He wrote to Sidney Colvin that the story was 'extraordinarily *true*; it's sixteen pages of the South Seas; their essence' (*Letters*, iv. 95), and explained:

> It is the first realistic South Sea story; I mean with real South Sea character and details of life. Everybody else who has tried, that I have seen, got carried away by the romance, and ended in a kind of sugar candy sham epic, and the whole effect was lost—there was no etching, no human grin, consequently no conviction. Now I have got the smell and look of the thing a good deal. You will know more about the South Seas after you have read my little tale than if you had read a library. (*Letters*, iv. 100–1)

The story's realism works, at one level, through Stevenson's predeliction for 'plain physical sensations plainly and expressly rendered' (*Letters*, iv. 184): one thinks immediately of the narration of Wiltshire's stabbing of Case, in which the blood comes over his hands 'hot as tea' (p. 68). Perhaps a more important indicator of the story's realism, though, is its handling of the manners of a contemporary society; for, unusually for a Stevenson work up to this point, the plot—the 'adventure'—of 'The Beach of Falesá' is far less important than its representation of the manners of various social groups in an outpost of empire at the end of the nineteenth century. Although it challenges the usual understanding of the term, 'The Beach of Falesá' is, essentially, a novel of manners. For all its folk-tale structure and use of supernatural elements, 'The Bottle Imp' is also, like 'The Beach of Falesá', 'well fed with facts' and 'true to the manners' of the society it depicts (*Letters*, iv. 75). It is set solidly in the contemporary world of the Pacific islands, filled with references to real people, real buildings, real ships which Stevenson knew from his time spent in Hawaii and Tahiti.

'The Bottle Imp', in its extreme circumstantiality, reflects Stevenson's new interest in representing the contemporary social life he saw around him in the Pacific; at the same time it retains the charm and lightness of touch on which much of Stevenson's popularity rested. Not so *The Ebb-Tide*, whose gritty naturalistic style and frequently sordid subject-matter startled its readers and challenged the current vogue for imperial romances. The narrative's uncompromisingly unromantic view of imperialism is established in the first sentence:

> Throughout the island world of the Pacific, scattered men of many European races and from almost every grade of society carry activity and disseminate disease. (p. 123)

Stevenson expressed great ambivalence about the tale while writing it, at times recording his enthusiasm, at other times condemning it as too 'grim' and 'grimy' (*Letters*, v. 35). On rereading it in print he pronounced it 'excellent' (*Letters*, v. 114), but the work baffled its critics. Most were unwilling to applaud, yet unable wholly to condemn, what they saw as the confrontational nature of the work. An unsigned review in the *Speaker* was typically both affronted and challenged by the story:

> It is strong with a strength that is almost, if not absolutely, savage. There is a directness of speech which startles the ordinary reader, and a vivid force of character-painting that astounds him ... Of grace, virtue, beauty, we get no glimpse. All that we have in exchange is a picture of the fag ends of certain useless and degraded lives.[12]

The reviewer acknowledged the power of the work, but recoiled from its violence and grotesqueness, what Sidney Colvin called its 'general revoltingness'.[13] Like others who looked to Stevenson to offer an alternative to Zolaesque

[12] Unsigned review, *Speaker*, 29 September 1894; repr. Paul Maixner (ed.), *Robert Louis Stevenson: The Critical Heritage* (London: Routledge & Kegan Paul, 1981), 458.

[13] Sidney Colvin, letter to R. L. Stevenson, 20 February 1894 (Beinecke 4397).

naturalism and pessimistic psychological analysis in late nineteenth-century fiction, the anonymous reviewer found *The Ebb-Tide* disconcerting: 'This is not the Stevenson we love'.[14]

Stevenson's popularity rested on the charm of the *New Arabian Nights*, the adventure of *Kidnapped*, the romance of *Treasure Island*, the fantasy of *Dr Jekyll and Mr Hyde*. In the literary debates on romance and realism that took place in England in the 1880s and 1890s, champions of romance such as Andrew Lang and George Saintsbury enlisted Stevenson under their banner.[15] He lent theoretical as well as practical authority to their cause, writing the debate's most intelligent and technically astute defences of romance and critiques of realism in essays such as 'A Gossip on Romance' (1882), 'A Note on Realism' (1883), and the masterly 'A Humble Remonstrance' (1884).[16] It was generally expected that Stevenson would continue producing the kinds of romances and fantasies with which he had won his fame; when he did not, readerly reactions were mostly negative. Oscar Wilde asked for Stevenson's historical romances—*The Master of Ballantrae*, *Kidnapped*, *Treasure Island*—to be sent to him in gaol, but was disappointed by the *Vailima Letters*, and commented upon Stevenson's immersion in the contemporary life around him in Samoa: 'I see that romantic surroundings are the worst surroundings possible for a romantic writer. In Gower Street Stevenson could have written a new *Trois Mousquetaires*. In Samoa he wrote letters to *The Times* about Germans.'[17] Wilde was flippant about Stevenson's swerve in style and subject-matter, but others, like Sidney Colvin, were

[14] Maixner, *Critical Heritage*, 459.

[15] Andrew Lang, 'Realism and Romance', *Contemporary Review*, 52 (1887), 690–1; George Saintsbury, 'The Present State of the Novel', *Fortnightly Review*, 42 (1887), 411, 415.

[16] 'A Gossip on Romance' (1882), repr. *Memories and Portraits* (London: Chatto & Windus, 1887), *Tusitala*, xxix. 119–31; 'A Note on Realism' (1883), repr. *Essays in the Art of Writing* (London: Chatto & Windus, 1905), *Tusitala*, xxviii. 69–75; 'A Humble Remonstrance' (1884), repr. *Memories and Portraits*, *Tusitala*, xxix. 132–43.

[17] Oscar Wilde, *The Letters of Oscar Wilde*, ed. Rupert Hart-Davis (London: Hart-Davis, 1962), 520. The requests for the Stevenson works, sent from Holloway Prison and Reading Prison, are on pp. 394 and 423.

personally and professionally distressed. 'I wish he had worked at any thing else but this,' Colvin wrote to Charles Baxter of *The Ebb-Tide*, and even wanted to have the book publication of the tale suppressed, fearing it would damage Stevenson's reputation.[18]

Colvin's fears were unfounded: *The Ebb-Tide* did not damage Stevenson's reputation, because it was left out of the count by most critics when they came to reckon up Stevenson's achievements after his death. This was true not just of *The Ebb-Tide*, but of all the South Sea tales. It was as if this body of work simply did not exist. The reasons for this neglect are not hard to find. The disturbing subject-matter and realistic manner of *The Ebb-Tide* and 'The Beach of Falesá' undoubtedly contributed to it. Furthermore, the anti-imperialistic and pro-native sentiments of all the stories clashed with the romance of imperialism being played out in English public consciousness and popular literature at the end of the century—a romance with which Stevenson could be assimilated only against the evidence of the stories themselves. But the most important reason for the critical neglect into which these works almost immediately fell was the unfamiliarity of the world they presented; unlike the India depicted by Kipling, to which British culture and society were closely bound by an immense apparatus of colonizing institutions, the Pacific world seemed to readers too marginal, too eccentric, to be the setting for important literature.

The critical silence about this work, the inability to find a place for it in a summing-up of Stevenson's career, was the product of the kind of metropolitan assumptions expressed by Edmund Gosse, responding in 1891 to Stevenson's *Ballads* (which dealt with South Sea subjects) and to the travel letters that were to become *In the South Seas*: 'The fact seems to be that it is very nice to *live* in Samoa, but not healthy to *write* there. Within a three-mile radius of Charing Cross is the literary atmosphere, I suspect.'[19] Henry James's Eurocentrism was just as deeply rooted, though more subtly expressed. He

[18] Sidney Colvin, letters to Charles Baxter, 27 June 1893 (Beinecke 4253) and 20 July 1893 (Beinecke 4255).

[19] Maixner, *Critical Heritage*, 375.

argued that because it was healthy for Stevenson to live in Samoa, it was by definition healthy for him to write there—but only about Scotland: 'Samoa was susceptible of no "style" . . . save the demonstration of its rightness for life; and this left the field abundantly clear for the Border, the Great North Road and the eighteenth century.'[20] James's retrospective study of Stevenson, published in 1900, follows an already established pattern in which criticism of Stevenson's late period focused exclusively on the historical novels set in Scotland—*Catriona*, and the unfinished *Weir of Hermiston* and *St Ives*—on which he had worked, alongside his Pacific fiction, during his years in Samoa. Meanwhile other critics, less sophisticated than James, sensationalized Samoa as the exotic backdrop against which Stevenson played out a romance of exile, the only meaningful reference point for which was, again, Scotland. Investing his life in Samoa with the glamour of a 'barbaric king, story-teller in chief to the islanders',[21] they resolutely ignored what he wrote about the Pacific, and the myth of 'Tusitala' (the teller of tales, as the Samoans called him) successfully displaced any consideration of the tales actually told.

An exception to this kind of critical response was the work of Stephen Gwynn. In two fine essays on Stevenson in 1894 and 1898[22] Gwynn acknowledged the importance of the Pacific fiction, in terms both of the new subject-matter being placed before English readers and of the new narrative style Stevenson was developing here. Gwynn predicted that Stevenson's name would become permanently identified with this body of fiction:

> What Mr Kipling has done for British India, Mr Stevenson is doing for the Southern Seas. He is peopling a definite field in our

[20] Henry James, *Literary Criticism: Essays on Literature, American Writers, English Writers,* ed. Leon Edel and Mark Wilson (New York: Library of America, 1984), 1271.

[21] J. A. MacCulloch, 'R. L. Stevenson: Characteristics', *Westminster Review,* 149 (1898), 646.

[22] Stephen Gwynn, 'Mr Robert Louis Stevenson: A Critical Study', *Fortnightly Review,* os 62 (1894), 776–92, and 'The Posthumous Works of Robert Louis Stevenson', *Fortnightly Review,* os 69 (1898), 561–75.

imaginations; there at least his work takes root in life; and, if I mistake not, to future generations his name and personality will suggest these islands of the Pacific, as Smollett makes us think of a ship, Fielding of the fleet or an inn, Thackeray of London, Scott of the Border, George Eliot of the Midland Counties.[23]

Instead of producing a biographical or mythological account of Stevenson's 'exile' organized around the motif of romance (as so many of his contemporaries did), Gwynn analysed the fiction Stevenson produced in Samoa and pointed out that he had made Pacific society an object of realistic depiction, 'peopling a definite field in [his readers'] imaginations'. He argued that '[i]t was only after Stevenson went to Samoa that his work became closely and obviously related to his own experiences; first, to his material environment; lastly, and in its highest development, to the spiritual adventures which had left their marks upon his youth.'[24] Gwynn cites 'The Beach of Falesá' as the text which shows Stevenson mastering a new body of material, and argues that in *The Ebb-Tide* 'the new material found for itself a new manner'[25]—terse, direct, concentrated—which was then ready for use in *Weir of Hermiston,* at the time widely regarded as Stevenson's unfinished masterpiece.

Writing at the end of the nineteenth century, Gwynn focused on what then seemed the most important aspect of Stevenson's Pacific work: its realism. From our perspective, a century later, we can identify two other important features of the work which Gwynn was not in a position, historically, to recognize: its modernism, and its insights into the emergence of twentieth-century global culture. 'The Beach of Falesá' displays a modernist's interest in the '"subjective" adventure' (to use Henry James's term)[26] and the limited narrator, while *The Ebb-Tide* shows how Stevenson preceded Conrad in working out a narrative mode that overlaid extreme realism with

[23] Gwynn, 'Mr Robert Louis Stevenson', 778.
[24] Gwynn, 'Posthumous Works', 563.
[25] Gwynn, 'Posthumous Works', 565.
[26] Henry James, *Literary Criticism: French Writers, Other European Writers, the Prefaces to the New York Edition,* (ed.) Leon Edel and Mark Wilson (New York: Library of America, 1984), 1170.

symbolism and a kind of dreamlike imagistic excess to explore the nightmare of imperialism. As Conrad, Kipling, Waugh, and Camus were to do after him, Stevenson in *The Ebb-Tide* used the edges of empire as the setting for a modern and modernist existential drama. But Stevenson does not use the colonial setting as a stage on which to play out purely European concerns; nor does he focus only on the horrors of imperialism. Rather, his stories capture the sense of a multicultural world in which diverse forms of encounter and exchange take place between Europeans, Americans, white-settler colonials, and members of various island societies. The stories collected here are the product of Stevenson's exposure to both the indigenous and the imperialist cultures of the Pacific, and they demonstrate the inseparability of these two elements in the cultural constitution of the region. Their subject-matter places Stevenson as an important witness both to nineteenth-century imperialism and to the creation of the modern post-colonial world. As, in the late twentieth century, we struggle to come to terms with the legacies of imperialism—the creation of the 'third world', immigration, multiculturalism—these works offer valuable insights into the transformation of nineteenth-century imperial culture into twentieth-century global culture, a transformation which was taking place in the Pacific region as Stevenson was writing. If, as Gwynn predicted, Stevenson's name as an author of fiction becomes primarily associated with the Pacific, it will suggest not a region of vague romance, but the complex reality of modern, post-colonial, global society.

NOTE ON THE TEXTS

THE texts of the stories are those of the first English book editions, with emendations as cited below.

'The Beach of Falesá' has a complicated and controversial textual history. The story was first published in the *Illustrated London News* in six instalments between 2 July and 6 August 1892, under the title 'Uma; or The Beach of Falesá (Being the Narrative of a South-Sea Trader)'. In January 1892 Stevenson had received a request from those handling the serialization of the story that the narrative be altered 'to make the young folks married properly before "that night"' (*Letters*, iv. 149). Stevenson refused, but the editor of the *Illustrated London News*, Clement Shorter, proceeded to censor the story anyway by omitting the illegal marriage certificate from chapter 1. When Stevenson saw the serial version in print, he was appalled both by this censorship and by the 'misprints abominable' (*Letters*, iv. 229). He insisted that the marriage contract be restored in the book publication of the story (*Letters*, iv. 229), although he had already reluctantly agreed to a compromise with his publishers, Cassell's, altering the terms of the contract (*Letters*, iv. 182). Copyright of the story had been protected by printing the serial text in book form, but in late 1892 Stevenson was sent another version of the text, the so-called trial issue (Beinecke 564), for his consideration. Many of the misprints and omissions of the serial version had already been corrected in the trial issue, to which Stevenson added further corrections. The corrected text of the story was published by Cassell's in England in April 1893 in the volume *Island Nights' Entertainments*; in the same month Scribner's published an American edition based on an uncorrected text.

The Cassell text of 1893 has been selected as the copy-text for this edition, on the grounds that it represents the latest version of the story corrected by the author. Of the other available texts of the story, the serial and copyright versions are clearly corrupt. Galley proofs produced by the *Illustrated London News* have been regarded by some as authoritative, on the basis of a note by Edmund Gosse claiming that they constitute 'the sole genuine text of the story' (Beinecke 562A, Note by Edmund Gosse appended to galley proofs of R. L. Stevenson's 'The Beach of Falesá'). This is clearly not the case, as the (uncorrected) galleys are filled with misprints which were then carried into the serial text, many of which Stevenson later complained about in letters and corrected on the trial issue. Indeed, one must conclude from the evidence that Stevenson never saw the galleys, and that they therefore have no textual authority.

The other text which commands attention is, of course, the manuscript. I have decided not to take the manuscript as the copy-text for this edition, because while it represents the text Stevenson originally wrote, it does not represent the text he finally passed for publication. To rate the authority of the manuscript above the authority of the final text corrected by the author is to assume that none of the changes introduced by the text's various editors has any authority, even though they were accepted by the author; this seems to me an untenable assumption, given that Stevenson had the opportunity to correct the text used by Cassell's and did, indeed, make many alterations which suggest a close and careful reading. Nevertheless, the manuscript represents an important alternative text of 'The Beach of Falesá', and contains material such as Case's 'yarn' which was omitted from published versions of the story. I have included this, and what seem to me the other most interesting and significant variants between the manuscript and the Cassell edition, in the explanatory notes. Readers who are interested in making a full comparison between the two texts should consult Barry Menikoff's edition of *The Beach of Falesá* (Stanford: Stanford University Press, 1987), which is based on the manuscript.

The Cassell edition faithfully incorporates all of Stevenson's corrections to the trial issue, except for two changes in punctuation, one of which is partly crossed out, suggesting the author changed his mind, and the other of which does not make sense and has been altered to do so. Apart from standardizing the practice of italicizing Samoan words, the only other discrepancy between the Cassell text and Stevenson's corrected text is the introduction of an unauthorized change ('low-down' substituted for 'low') on p. 35; here I have used the wording of the trial issue. The only other part of the Cassell text which we know does not represent the author's intentions is the marriage certificate on p. 11, the alterations to which Stevenson accepted only unwillingly. I have emended the text of the certificate using the uncensored manuscript version, though retaining the spelling 'Fa'avao' standard throughout the Cassell edition. I have also used the manuscript to correct an incoherence in the text on p. 39, where the trial issue omits a key phrase which Stevenson then restores in a position that makes little sense. The remaining emendations have been made on the grounds of consistency and sense: 'towards' is emended to 'toward' on p. 23 to conform with the other use of the word on that page; 'Damn' on p. 28 is spelt out in full, as is 'God-damned' on p. 35; 'came' is corrected to 'come' on p. 38; the spelling of 'Johnny', 'Galoshes', 'cocoanuts', 'cocoa-palms', and 'flying-foxes' has been standardized.

'The Bottle Imp' was published serially in the New York *Herald* 8 February–1 March 1891 and in England in *Black and White* 28 March and 4 April 1891; translated into Samoan by the Revd Arthur E. Claxton, it appeared under the title 'O Le Fagu Aitu' in the Samoan missionary magazine *O Le Sulu Samoa* May–December 1891. The story was paired with 'The Beach of Falesá' in the trial issue sent to Stevenson in late 1892 (see above), to which the author made numerous corrections. Cassell's published the story in the volume *Island Nights' Entertainments* (1893), using the corrected text of the trial issue; in the American edition of *Island Nights' Entertainments* (Scribner's, 1893) 'The Bottle Imp' was set from an uncorrected text. The Cassell edition, which incorporates all of Stevenson's corrections to the trial issue, is reprinted here.

'The Isle of Voices' was published serially in the *National Observer* 4–25 February 1893. Stevenson did not have the opportunity to correct proofs of the story before it was published in *Island Nights' Entertainments* in April 1893. The text reprinted here is that of the Cassell edition of *Island*

Nights' Entertainments. I have corrected four obvious misprints: 'its' is corrected to 'it's' (p. 113), the name 'Donat-Kimaran' to 'Donat-Rimarau' (p. 117, see note), 'feel' to 'fell' (p. 119), and 'free' to 'flee' (p. 121).

The Ebb-Tide was published serially in *To-day* 11 November 1893–3 February 1894 and in *McClure's Magazine* February–July 1894. The novella was published as a complete volume under the title *The Ebb-Tide: A Trio and Quartette* by Heinemann in 1894 (book publication in America by Stone & Kimball, 1894). The text reprinted here is the Heinemann edition, with the following emendations made on the basis of sense and consistency: 'But' to 'Bet' (p. 131); 'wy' to 'w'y' on p. 131; semicolon replaced with comma after 'plank' (p.137); the island names are corrected to 'Raraka' and 'Katiu' (p. 170, see note); 'stone houses' to 'store-houses' (p. 201, see note); 'islands' to 'islanders' (p. 205); 'done' to 'down' (p. 216); question mark deleted after 'house' (p. 225); '*situytion*' to '*situyation*' (p. 241); 'B.-and-S.' hyphenated (p. 243); 'cries' to 'cried' (p. 251). The spelling 'busses' has been corrected to 'buses' on p. 131. Obvious misprints, such as the misspelling of characters' names, have been corrected. Stevenson's inconsistent use of 'O' and 'Oh' has been retained.

Stevenson's fables, on which he worked for twenty years, were not published until after his death. Journal publication was in *Longman's Magazine*, 26 (1895), 362–79, 472–89; first book publication was in *The Strange Case of Dr Jekyll and Mr Hyde with Other Fables* (London: Longmans, Green, & Company, 1896); the *Fables* were also published by Scribner's in America later in 1896. The texts of 'The Cart-Horses and the Saddle-Horse' and 'Something in It' published here are reprinted from the first (English) book edition.

Hyphenated forms such as 'to-day' and 'common-sense' have been modernized, and the spelling '-ise' has been emended to '-ize'. Missing and misplaced quotation marks have been restored.

SELECT BIBLIOGRAPHY

BIBLIOGRAPHY

McKay, George L., *A Stevenson Library: Catalogue of a Collection of Writings by and about Robert Louis Stevenson Formed by Edwin J. Beinecke*, 6 vols. (New Haven: Yale University Press, 1951–64).

Prideaux, W. F., *A Bibliography of the Works of Robert Louis Stevenson*, rev. edn. (London: Hollings, 1917).

Swearingen, Roger G., *The Prose Writings of Robert Louis Stevenson: A Guide* (Hamden: Archon Books, 1980).

WORKS BY STEVENSON

The Works of Robert Louis Stevenson, Tusitala Edition, 35 vols. (London: Heinemann, 1923–4). References to this edition are indicated by the abbreviation *Tusitala* and the appropriate volume number.

The Ebb-Tide: A Trio and Quartette, written in collaboration with Lloyd Osbourne (London: Heinemann, 1894); *Tusitala*, xiv.

Father Damien: An Open Letter to the Reverend Doctor Hyde of Honolulu from Robert Louis Stevenson (London: Chatto & Windus, 1890); *Tusitala*, xxi.

A Footnote to History: Eight Years of Trouble in Samoa (London: Cassell, 1892); *Tusitala*, xxi.

In the South Seas: Being an Account of Experiences and Observations in the Marquesas, Paumotus and Gilbert Islands in the Course of Two Cruises, on the Yacht 'Casco' (1888) and the Schooner 'Equator' (1889) (London: Chatto & Windus, 1900); *Tusitala*, xx.

Island Nights' Entertainments (London: Cassell, 1893); *Tusitala*, xiii.

The Wrecker, written in collaboration with Lloyd Osbourne (London: Cassell, 1892); *Tusitala*, xii.

LETTERS

Henry James and Robert Louis Stevenson: A Record of Friendship and Criticism, ed. Janet Adam Smith (London: Hart-Davis, 1948).

The Letters of Robert Louis Stevenson, ed. Bradford A. Booth and Ernest Mehew, 8 vols. (New Haven: Yale University Press, 1994–5). Incomplete at the time of preparing the present volume, this work will undoubtedly be the standard edition of Stevenson's letters.

The Letters of Robert Louis Stevenson, ed. Sidney Colvin, 5 vols. (London: Heinemann, 1924); *Tusitala*, xxxi–xxxv.

R. L. S.: Stevenson's Letters to Charles Baxter, ed. DeLancey Ferguson and Marshall Waingrow (New Haven: Yale University Press, 1956).

BIOGRAPHY

Balfour, Graham, *The Life of Robert Louis Stevenson*, 2 vols. (London: Methuen, 1901).

Furnas, J. C., *Voyage to Windward: The Life of Robert Louis Stevenson* (London: Faber, 1952).

McLynn, Frank, *Robert Louis Stevenson: A Biography* (London: Hutchinson, 1993).

Rankin, Nicholas, *Dead Man's Chest: Travels After Robert Louis Stevenson* (London: Faber, 1987).

HISTORICAL AND BIOGRAPHICAL SOURCES ON STEVENSON AND THE PACIFIC

Field, Isobel, *This Life I've Loved* (London: Michael Joseph, 1937).

Fraser, Marie, *In Stevenson's Samoa* (London: Smith, Elder, 1895).

Johnstone, Arthur, *Recollections of Robert Louis Stevenson in the Pacific* (London: Chatto & Windus, 1905).

Knight, Alanna (ed.), *R. L. S. in the South Seas: An Intimate Photographic Record* (Edinburgh: Mainstream, 1986).

McGaw, Martha Mary, *Stevenson in Hawaii* (Honolulu: University of Hawaii Press, 1950).

Moors, H. J., *With Stevenson in Samoa* (London: Fisher Unwin, 1910).

Osbourne, Lloyd, 'Stevenson at Thirty-Nine', *Tusitala*, vol. xiv, pp. vii–xv.

—— 'Stevenson at Forty', *Tusitala*, vol. xii, pp. vii–xiv.

Stevenson, Mrs R. L. [Fanny], *The Cruise of the 'Janet Nichol' among the South Sea Islands* (London: Chatto & Windus, 1915).

—— 'Prefatory Note' to *Island Nights' Entertainments, Tusitala*, vol. xiii, pp. xi–xiv.

—— 'Prefatory Note' to *The Wrecker, Tusitala*, vol. xii, pp. xv–xxiv.

Stevenson, Fanny and Robert Louis, *Our Samoan Adventure*, ed. Charles Neider (London: Weidenfeld & Nicolson, 1956).

Stevenson, M. I., *From Saranac to the Marquesas and Beyond*, ed. Marie Clothilde Balfour (London: Methuen, 1903).

—— *Letters from Samoa 1891–1895*, ed. Marie Clothilde Balfour (London: Methuen, 1906).

CRITICISM

Eigner, Edwin M., *Robert Louis Stevenson and Romantic Tradition* (Princeton: Princeton University Press, 1966).

Gilmour, Peter, 'Robert Louis Stevenson: Forms of Evasion', in *Robert Louis Stevenson*, ed. Andrew Noble (London: Vision; Totowa: Barnes & Noble, 1983), 188–201.

Hillier, Robert Irwin, *The South Seas Fiction of Robert Louis Stevenson*, American University Studies Series IV, vol. xci (New York: Peter Lang, 1989).

Kiely, Robert, *Robert Louis Stevenson and the Fiction of Adventure* (Cambridge, Mass.: Harvard University Press, 1964).

Linehan, Katherine Bailey, 'Taking Up With Kanakas: Stevenson's Complex Social Criticism in "The Beach of Falesá" ', *English Literature in Transition 1880–1920*, 33 (1990), 407–22.

Maixner, Paul (ed.), *Robert Louis Stevenson: The Critical Heritage* (London: Routledge & Kegan Paul, 1981).

Menikoff, Barry, *Robert Louis Stevenson and 'The Beach of Falesá': A Study in Victorian Publishing* (Stanford: Stanford University Press, 1984).

Sandison, Alan, 'Robert Louis Stevenson: A Modernist in the South Seas', *Durham University Journal*, 83 (1991), 45–51.

A CHRONOLOGY OF ROBERT LOUIS STEVENSON

1850 Born in Edinburgh, 13 November.

1862–3 Excursions with his parents to Germany, the Riviera and Italy.

1867 Enters Edinburgh University to study engineering.

1871 Makes decision to abandon engineering and study law.

1872 Passes preliminary examinations for the Scottish Bar.

1873 Crisis with his father over his agnosticism; following this, and a bout of ill health, goes to Suffolk to stay with his Balfour cousins. Meets Frances Sitwell, one of the most important influences on his life until his marriage. Beginning of his friendship with Sidney Colvin. Further ill health sends R.L.S. south to France at the end of the year.

1874 At Menton in France. Returns to Edinburgh in May and resumes reading for the Bar. Contributes to the *Cornhill Magazine.*

1875 Meets W. E. Henley in Edinburgh. Called to the Scottish Bar but does not practise as a barrister. Visits France and joins his cousin, Bob Stevenson, at the artists' colony at Barbizon, Fontainebleau (1875–6); contributes to *Vanity Fair* and the *Academy.*

1876 Makes a canoe trip around the canals of northern France, later to be recorded in *An Inland Voyage.* Meets Fanny Osbourne, a married woman with two children, from Indiana.

1877 Divides year between Edinburgh, London and Fontainebleau.

1878 Fanny returns to her husband in California and, eventually, divorce proceedings begin. R.L.S. goes on travels with his donkey, Modestine, in the Cévennes. Publication of *An Inland Voyage* and *Edinburgh: Picturesque Notes.*

1879 Divides time between London, Scotland and France. Very ill in March and April. Sets off on journey to join Fanny in America. *Travels with a Donkey* published.

1880 Marries Fanny in San Francisco in May. They stay in the Californian mountains and then return to Scotland. Publication of *Deacon Brodie,* R.L.S.'s first play in collaboration with W. E. Henley.

1881 At Braemar, writes 15 chapters of *Treasure Island.* Visits Davos in Switzerland where *Treasure Island* is completed (serialized in *Young Folks* October 1881–January 1882). Publication of *Virginibus Puerisque* (includes 'The English Admirals').

1882 At Davos, then R.L.S. and Fanny move to Hyères, France, their main home from March 1883–July 1884. Publication of *Familiar Studies of Men and Books* and *New Arabian Nights.*

1883 Publication of *The Silverado Squatters* and *Treasure Island.* Serialization of *The Black Arrow* in *Young Folks* (June–October).

1884 Illness at Nice in January and further serious ill health in May. The Stevensons return to England at about the same time as an outbreak of cholera at Hyères. They go to Bournemouth, their home from September of this year until August 1887. Publication of *Austin Guinea* and *Beau Austin,* both in collaboration with W. E. Henley. Henry James publishes 'The Art of Fiction' in September; Stevenson's rejoinder, 'A Humble Remonstrance', is published in December.

1885 Moves to 'Skerryvore', Bournemouth (the house was a wedding present from Thomas Stevenson to his daughter-in-law). Henry James pays a long visit to Bournemouth. Publication of *A Child's Garden of Verses*; *Prince Otto*; *More New Arabian Nights*; *The Dynamiter,* with Fanny Stevenson; *Macaire,* with W. E. Henley.

1886 Publication of *Strange Case of Dr Jekyll and Mr Hyde,* Stevenson's first large-scale British and American success, and *Kidnapped* (previously serialized in *Young Folks,* May–July 1886).

1887 Thomas Stevenson dies in May. In August, R.L.S. sails for America with his mother, Fanny, and stepson Lloyd. For reasons of health stays at Saranac in the Adirondack Mountains. Publication of *The Merry Men and Other Tales and Fables*; *Underwoods*; *Memories and Portraits*; and *A Memoir of Fleeming Jenkin.*

1888 Pacific voyage made possible by commission to produce a series of travel articles on the South Seas for newspaper syndication. R.L.S. and family sail on the yacht *Casco* to the Marquesas, Paumotus, Tahiti and Hawaii. Publication of *The Black Arrow.*

1889 Mrs Thomas Stevenson returns to Scotland. In June, R.L.S., Fanny and Lloyd sail from Honolulu on the trading schooner *Equator* to the Gilbert Islands and on to Samoa, arriving in December. R.L.S. immediately begins to gather information on Samoan politics for *A Footnote to History.*

1890 Buys Vailima estate near Apia on the island of Upolu, Samoa. Visits Sydney while work begins on clearing the estate and building a house. From Sydney begins third Pacific voyage with Fanny and Lloyd, in the trading steamer *Janet Nicoll*, visiting the Tokelau, Gilbert and Marshall Islands. Further ill health, including a serious haemorrhage, leads the Stevensons to realize that R.L.S. can never again leave a tropical climate. In October they take up residence at Vailima. R.L.S. begins work on 'The Beach of Falesá'. Publication of *Ballads.*

1891 Newspaper publication of South Sea letters (later published as *In the South Seas*, 1896). Serial publication of 'The Bottle Imp' in *Black and White* and (in Samoan) in *O Le Sulu Samoa.*

1892 Deepens involvement in Samoan politics. Fears of deportation from Samoa as the British High Commissioner for the Western Pacific issues *A Regulation for the Maintenance of Peace and Good Order in Samoa*, clearly designed to stop Stevenson's interventions in Samoan affairs. 'The Beach of Falesá' appears in the *Illustrated London News.* Publication of *A Footnote to History*, *Across the Plains*, and *The Wrecker.*

1893 Works on *The Ebb-Tide.* 'The Isle of Voices' appears in the *National Observer.* Outbreak of war in Samoa; Stevenson supports Mataafa. Visits Honolulu. Publication of *Island Nights' Entertainments* and *Catriona.* Serial publication of *The Ebb-Tide* begins.

1894 Followers of Mataafa build 'The Road of Loving Hearts' in gratitude to R.L.S. for helping their cause. Book publication of *The Ebb-Tide.* R.L.S. dies on 3 December of cerebral haemorrhage.

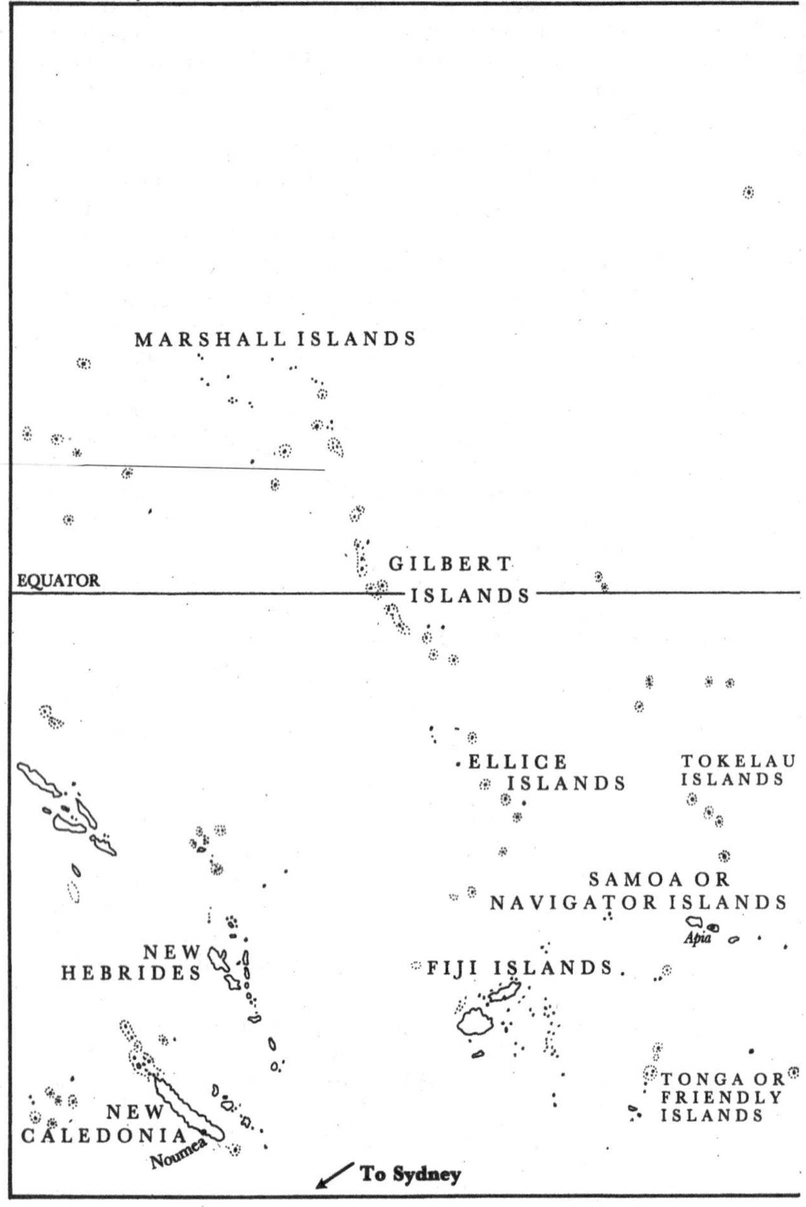

A MAP OF THE SOUTH SEAS

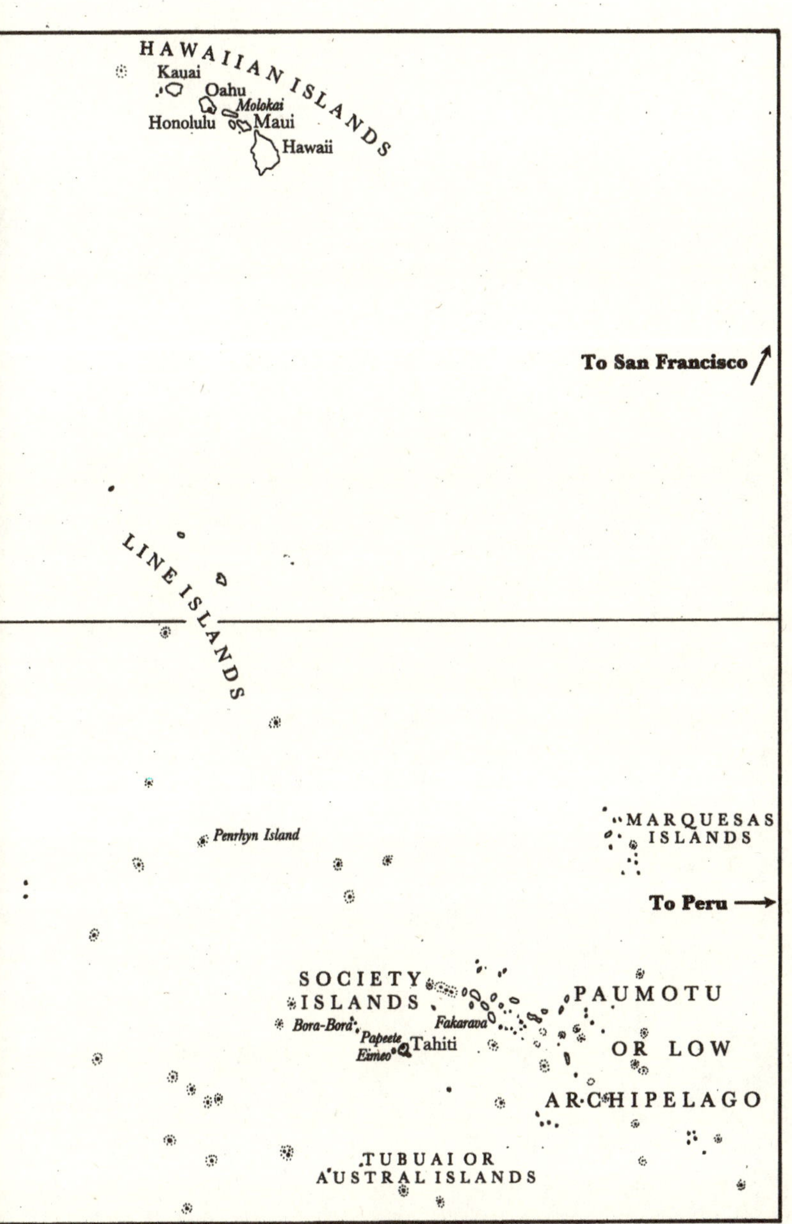

Place-names are those used in Stevenson's writings

SOUTH SEA
TALES

THE BEACH OF FALESÁ

CHAPTER I

A SOUTH SEA BRIDAL

I SAW that island first when it was neither night nor morning. The moon was to the west, setting, but still broad and bright. To the east, and right amidships of the dawn, which was all pink, the daystar sparkled like a diamond. The land breeze blew in our faces, and smelt strong of wild lime and vanilla: other things besides, but these were the most plain; and the chill of it set me sneezing. I should say I had been for years on a low island near the line,* living for the most part solitary among natives. Here was a fresh experience: even the tongue would be quite strange to me; and the look of these woods and mountains, and the rare smell of them, renewed my blood.

The captain blew out the binnacle lamp.*

'There!' said he, 'there goes a bit of smoke, Mr Wiltshire, behind the break of the reef. That's Falesá, where your station is, the last village to the east; nobody lives to windward—I don't know why. Take my glass, and you can make the houses out.'

I took the glass; and the shores leaped nearer, and I saw the tangle of the woods and the breach of the surf, and the brown roofs and the black insides of houses peeped among the trees.

'Do you catch a bit of white there to the east'ard?' the captain continued. 'That's your house. Coral built, stands high, verandah you could walk on three abreast; best station in the South Pacific. When old Adams saw it, he took and shook me by the hand. "I've dropped into a soft thing here," says he.—"So you have," says I, "and time too!" Poor Johnny! I never saw him again but the once, and then he had changed his tune—couldn't get on with the natives, or the whites, or something; and the next time we came round there he was dead and buried. I took and put up a bit of a stick to him: "John Adams, *obit* eighteen and sixty-eight. Go thou and do likewise." I missed that man. I never could see much harm in Johnny.'

'What did he die of?' I inquired.

'Some kind of sickness,' says the captain. 'It appears it took him sudden. Seems he got up in the night, and filled up on Pain-Killer and Kennedy's Discovery.* No go: he was booked beyond Kennedy. Then he had tried to open a case of gin. No go again: not strong enough. Then he must have turned to and run out on the verandah, and capsized over the rail. When they found him, the next day, he was clean crazy—carried on all the time about somebody watering his copra.* Poor John!'

'Was it thought to be the island?' I asked.

'Well, it was thought to be the island, or the trouble, or something,' he replied. 'I never could hear but what it was a healthy place. Our last man, Vigours, never turned a hair. He left because of the beach*—said he was afraid of Black Jack and Case and Whistling Jimmie, who was still alive at the time, but got drowned soon afterward when drunk. As for old Captain Randall, he's been here any time since eighteen-forty, forty-five. I never could see much harm in Billy, nor much change. Seems as if he might live to be Old Kafoozleum.* No, I guess it's healthy.'

'There's a boat coming now,' said I. 'She's right in the pass; looks to be a sixteen-foot whale; two white men in the stern sheets.'*

'That's the boat that drowned Whistling Jimmie!' cried the Captain; 'let's see the glass. Yes, that's Case, sure enough, and the darkie. They've got a gallows bad reputation, but you know what a place the beach is for talking. My belief, that Whistling Jimmie was the worst of the trouble; and he's gone to glory, you see. What'll you bet they ain't after gin? Lay you five to two they take six cases.'

When these two traders came aboard I was pleased with the looks of them at once, or, rather, with the looks of both, and the speech of one. I was sick for white neighbours after my four years at the line, which I always counted years of prison;

getting tabooed,* and going down to the Speak House* to see and get it taken off; buying gin and going on a break, and then repenting; sitting in the house at night with the lamp for company; or walking on the beach and wondering what kind of a fool to call myself for being where I was. There were no other whites upon my island, and when I sailed to the next, rough customers made the most of the society. Now to see these two when they came aboard was a pleasure. One was a negro, to be sure; but they were both rigged out smart in striped pyjamas and straw hats, and Case would have passed muster in a city. He was yellow and smallish, had a hawk's nose to his face, pale eyes, and his beard trimmed with scissors. No man knew his country, beyond he was of English speech; and it was clear he came of a good family and was splendidly educated. He was accomplished too; played the accordion first-rate; and give him a piece of string or a cork or a pack of cards, and he could show you tricks equal to any professional. He could speak, when he chose, fit for a drawing-room; and when he chose he could blaspheme worse than a Yankee boatswain, and talk smart* to sicken a Kanaka.* The way he thought would pay best at the moment, that was Case's way, and it always seemed to come natural, and like as if he was born to it. He had the courage of a lion and the cunning of a rat; and if he's not in hell today, there's no such place. I know but one good point to the man: that he was fond of his wife, and kind to her. She was a Samoa woman, and dyed her hair red, Samoa style; and when he came to die (as I have to tell of) they found one strange thing—that he had made a will, like a Christian, and the widow got the lot: all his, they said, and all Black Jack's, and the most of Billy Randall's in the bargain, for it was Case that kept the books. So she went off home in the schooner *Manu'a*, and does the lady to this day in her own place.

But of all this on that first morning I knew no more than a fly. Case used me like a gentleman and like a friend, made me welcome to Falesá, and put his services at my disposal, which was the more helpful from my ignorance of the native. All the better part of the day* we sat drinking better acquaintance in the cabin, and I never heard a man talk more to the point.

There was no smarter trader, and none dodgier, in the islands.* I thought Falesá seemed to be the right kind of a place; and the more I drank the lighter my heart. Our last trader had fled the place at half an hour's notice, taking a chance passage in a labour ship from up west.* The captain, when he came, had found the station closed, the keys left with the native pastor, and a letter from the runaway, confessing he was fairly frightened of his life. Since then the firm had not been represented, and of course there was no cargo. The wind, besides, was fair, the captain hoped he could make his next island by dawn, with a good tide, and the business of landing my trade was gone about lively. There was no call for me to fool with it, Case said; nobody would touch my things, everyone was honest in Falesá, only about chickens or an odd knife or an odd stick of tobacco; and the best I could do was to sit quiet till the vessel left, then come straight to his house, see old Captain Randall, the father of the beach, take pot-luck, and go home to sleep when it got dark. So it was high noon, and the schooner was under way before I set my foot on shore at Falesá.

I had a glass or two on board; I was just off a long cruise, and the ground heaved under me like a ship's deck. The world was like all new painted; my foot went along to music; Falesá might have been Fiddler's Green,* if there is such a place, and more's the pity if there isn't! It was good to foot the grass, to look aloft at the green mountains, to see the men with their green wreaths and the women in their bright dresses, red and blue. On we went, in the strong sun and the cool shadow, liking both; and all the children in the town came trotting after with their shaven heads and their brown bodies, and raising a thin kind of a cheer in our wake, like crowing poultry.

'By-the-bye,' says Case, 'we must get you a wife.'

'That's so,' said I; 'I had forgotten.'

There was a crowd of girls about us, and I pulled myself up and looked among them like a Bashaw.* They were all dressed out for the sake of the ship being in; and the women of Falesá are a handsome lot to see. If they have a fault, they are a trifle broad in the beam; and I was just thinking so when Case touched me.

'That's pretty,' says he.

I saw one coming on the other side alone. She had been fishing; all she wore was a chemise, and it was wetted through.* She was young and very slender for an island maid, with a long face, a high forehead, and a shy,* strange, blindish look, between a cat's and a baby's.

'Who's she?' said I. 'She'll do.'

'That's Uma,' said Case, and he called her up and spoke to her in the native. I didn't know what he said; but when he was in the midst she looked up at me quick and timid, like a child dodging a blow, then down again, and presently smiled. She had a wide mouth, the lips and the chin cut like any statue's; and the smile came out for a moment and was gone. Then she stood with her head bent, and heard Case to an end, spoke back in the pretty Polynesian voice, looking him full in the face, heard him again in answer, and then with an obeisance started off. I had just a share of the bow, but never another shot of her eye, and there was no more word of smiling.

'I guess it's all right,' said Case. 'I guess you can have her. I'll make it square with the old lady. You can have your pick of the lot for a plug of tobacco,' he added, sneering.

I suppose it was the smile stuck in my memory, for I spoke back sharp. 'She doesn't look that sort,' I cried.

'I don't know that she is,' said Case. 'I believe she's as right as the mail. Keeps to herself, don't go round with the gang, and that. O no, don't you misunderstand me—Uma's on the square.' He spoke eager, I thought, and that surprised and pleased me. 'Indeed,' he went on, 'I shouldn't make so sure of getting her, only she cottoned to the cut of your jib.* All you have to do is to keep dark and let me work the mother my own way; and I'll bring the girl round to the captain's for the marriage.'

I didn't care for the word marriage, and I said so.

'Oh, there's nothing to hurt in the marriage,' says he. 'Black Jack's the chaplain.'

By this time we had come in view of the house of these three white men; for a negro is counted a white man, and so is a Chinese! a strange idea, but common in the islands. It was a board house with a strip of rickety verandah. The store was to the front, with a counter, scales, and the poorest possible display of trade: a case or two of tinned meats; a barrel of hard bread; a few bolts of cotton stuff, not to be compared with mine; the only thing well represented being the contraband, firearms and liquor. 'If these are my only rivals,' thinks I, 'I should do well in Falesá.' Indeed, there was only the one way they could touch me, and that was with the guns and drink.

In the back room was old Captain Randall, squatting on the floor native fashion, fat and pale, naked to the waist, grey as a badger, and his eyes set with drink. His body was covered with grey hair and crawled over by flies; one was in the corner of his eye—he never heeded; and the mosquitoes hummed about the man like bees. Any clean-minded man would have had the creature out at once and buried him; and to see him, and think he was seventy, and remember he had once commanded a ship, and come ashore in his smart togs, and talked big in bars and consulates, and sat in club verandahs, turned me sick and sober.

He tried to get up when I came in, but that was hopeless; so he reached me a hand instead, and stumbled out some salutation.

'Papa's[1] pretty full this morning,' observed Case. 'We've had an epidemic here; and Captain Randall takes gin for a prophylactic—don't you, Papa?'

'Never took such a thing in my life!' cried the captain indignantly. 'Take gin for my health's sake, Mr Wha's-ever-your-name—'s a precautionary measure.'

'That's all right, Papa,' said Case. 'But you'll have to brace up. There's going to be a marriage—Mr Wiltshire here is going to get spliced.'

The old man asked to whom.

'To Uma,' said Case.

'Uma!' cried the captain. 'Wha's he want Uma for? 's he come here for his health, anyway? Wha' 'n hell 's he want Uma for?'

'Dry up, Papa,' said Case. ''Tain't you that's to marry her. I guess you're not her godfather and godmother. I guess Mr Wiltshire's going to please himself.'

[1] Please pronounce *pappa* throughout.

With that he made an excuse to me that he must move about the marriage, and left me alone with the poor wretch that was his partner and (to speak truth) his gull. Trade and station belonged both to Randall; Case and the negro were parasites; they crawled and fed upon him like the flies, he none the wiser. Indeed, I have no harm to say of Billy Randall beyond the fact that my gorge rose at him, and the time I now passed in his company was like a nightmare.

The room was stifling hot and full of flies; for the house was dirty and low and small, and stood in a bad place, behind the village, in the borders of the bush, and sheltered from the trade.* The three men's beds were on the floor, and a litter of pans and dishes. There was no standing furniture; Randall, when he was violent, tearing it to laths. There I sat and had a meal which was served us by Case's wife; and there I was entertained all day by that remains of man, his tongue stumbling among low old jokes and long old stories, and his own wheezy laughter always ready, so that he had no sense of my depression. He was nipping gin all the while. Sometimes he fell asleep, and awoke again, whimpering and shivering, and every now and again he would ask me why I wanted to marry Uma.* 'My friend,' I was telling myself all day, 'you must not come to be an old gentleman like this.'

It might be four in the afternoon, perhaps, when the back door was thrust slowly open, and a strange old native woman crawled into the house almost on her belly. She was swathed in black stuff to her heels; her hair was grey in swatches; her face was tattooed, which was not the practice in that island; her eyes big and bright and crazy. These she fixed upon me with a rapt expression that I saw to be part acting. She said no plain word, but smacked and mumbled with her lips, and hummed aloud, like a child over its Christmas pudding. She came straight across the house, heading for me, and, as soon as she was alongside, caught up my hand and purred and crooned over it like a great cat. From this she slipped into a kind of song.

'Who the devil's this?' cried I, for the thing startled me.

'It's Fa'avao,' says Randall; and I saw he had hitched along the floor into the farthest corner.

'You ain't afraid of her?' I cried.

'Me 'fraid!' cried the captain. 'My dear friend, I defy her! I don't let her put her foot in here, only I suppose 's different today, for the marriage. 's Uma's mother.'

'Well, suppose it is; what's she carrying on about?' I asked, more irritated, perhaps more frightened, than I cared to show; and the captain told me she was making up a quantity of poetry in my praise because I was to marry Uma. 'All right, old lady,' says I, with rather a failure of a laugh, 'anything to oblige. But when you're done with my hand, you might let me know.'

She did as though she understood; the song rose into a cry, and stopped; the woman crouched out of the house the same way that she came in, and must have plunged straight into the bush, for when I followed her to the door she had already vanished.

'These are rum manners,' said I.

''s a rum crowd,' said the captain, and, to my surprise, he made the sign of the cross on his bare bosom.

'Hillo!' says I, 'are you a Papist?'

He repudiated the idea with contempt. 'Hard-shell Baptis',' * said he. 'But, my dear friend, the Papists got some good ideas too; and tha' 's one of 'em. You take my advice, and whenever you come across Uma or Fa'avao or Vigours, or any of that crowd, you take a leaf out o' the priests, and do what I do. Savvy?' says he, repeated the sign, and winked his dim eye at me. 'No, *sir*!' he broke out again, 'no Papists here!' and for a long time entertained me with his religious opinions.

I must have been taken with Uma from the first, or I should certainly have fled from that house, and got into the clean air, and the clean sea, or some convenient river—though, it's true, I was committed to Case; and, besides, I could never have held my head up in that island if I had run from a girl upon my wedding-night.

The sun was down, the sky all on fire, and the lamp had been some time lighted, when Case came back with Uma and the negro. She was dressed and scented; her kilt was of fine tapa,* looking richer in the folds than any silk; her bust, which was of the colour of dark honey, she wore bare only for some half a dozen necklaces of seeds and flowers; and behind her ears and in her hair she had the scarlet flowers of the hibiscus. She showed the best bearing for a bride conceivable, serious and still; and I thought shame to stand up with her in that mean house and before that grinning negro. I thought shame, I say; for the mountebank was dressed with a big paper collar, the book he made believe to read from was an odd volume of a novel, and the words of his service not fit to be set down. My conscience smote me when we joined hands; and when she got her certificate I was tempted to throw up the bargain and confess. Here is the document. It was Case that wrote it, signatures and all, in a leaf out of the ledger:

This is to certify that Uma daughter of Fa'avao of Falesá island of ——, is illegally married to Mr John Wiltshire for one night, and Mr John Wiltshire is at liberty to send her to hell next morning.

John Blackamoor
Chaplain to the Hulks.

Extracted from the register
by William T. Randall
Master Mariner.

A nice paper to put in a girl's hand and see her hide away like gold. A man might easily feel cheap for less. But it was the practice in these parts,* and (as I told myself) not the least the fault of us white men, but of the missionaries. If they had let the natives be, I had never needed this deception, but taken all the wives I wished, and left them when I pleased, with a clear conscience.

The more ashamed I was, the more hurry I was in to be gone; and our desires thus jumping together, I made the less remark of a change in the traders. Case had been all eagerness to keep me; now, as though he had attained a purpose, he seemed all eagerness to have me go. Uma, he said, could show me to my house, and the three bade us farewell indoors.

The night was nearly come; the village smelt of trees and flowers and the sea and breadfruit-cooking; there came a fine roll of sea from the reef, and from a distance, among the woods and houses, many pretty sounds of men and children. It did me good to breathe free air; it did me good to be done with the captain and see, instead, the creature at my side. I felt for all the world as though she were some girl at home in the Old Country, and, forgetting myself for the minute, took her hand to walk with. Her fingers nestled into mine, I heard her breathe deep and quick, and all at once she caught my hand to her face and pressed it there. 'You good!' she cried, and ran ahead of me, and stopped and looked back and smiled, and ran ahead of me again, thus guiding me through the edge of the bush, and by a quiet way to my own house.

The truth is, Case had done the courting for me in style—told her I was mad to have her, and cared nothing for the consequence; and the poor soul, knowing that which I was still ignorant of, believed it, every word, and had her head nigh turned with vanity and gratitude. Now, of all this I had no guess; I was one of those most opposed to any nonsense about native women, having seen so many whites eaten up by their wives' relatives, and made fools of in the bargain; and I told myself I must make a stand at once, and bring her to her bearings. But she looked so quaint and pretty as she ran away and then awaited me, and the thing was done so like a child or a kind dog, that the best I could do was just to follow her whenever she went on, to listen for the fall of her bare feet, and to watch in the dusk for the shining of her body. And there was another thought came in my head. She played kitten with me now when we were alone; but in the house she had carried it the way a countess might, so proud and humble. And what with her dress—for all there was so little of it, and that native enough—what with her fine tapa and fine scents, and her red flowers and seeds, that were quite as bright as jewels, only larger—it came over me she was a kind of countess really, dressed to hear great singers at a concert, and no even mate for a poor trader like myself.

She was the first in the house; and while I was still without I saw a match flash and the lamplight kindle in the windows. The station was a wonderful fine place, coral built, with quite a wide verandah, and the main room high and wide. My chests and cases had been piled in, and made rather of a mess; and there, in the thick of the confusion, stood Uma by the table, awaiting me. Her shadow went all the way up behind her into the hollow of the iron roof; she stood against it bright, the lamplight shining on her skin. I stopped in the door, and she looked at me, not speaking, with eyes that were eager and yet daunted; then she touched herself on the bosom.

'Me—your wifie,' she said. It had never taken me like that before; but the want of her took and shook all through me, like the wind in the luff* of a sail.

I could not speak if I had wanted; and if I could, I would not. I was ashamed to be so much moved about a native, ashamed of the marriage too, and the certificate she had treasured in her kilt; and I turned aside and made believe to rummage among my cases. The first thing I lighted on was a case of gin, the only one that I had brought; and, partly for the girl's sake, and partly for horror of the recollections of old Randall, took a sudden resolve. I prized the lid off. One by one I drew the bottles with a pocket corkscrew, and sent Uma out to pour the stuff from the verandah.

She came back after the last, and looked at me puzzled like.*

'No good,' said I, for I was now a little better master of my tongue. 'Man he drink, he no good.'

She agreed with this, but kept considering. 'Why you bring him?'* she asked presently. 'Suppose you no want drink, you no bring him, I think.'

'That's all right,' said I. 'One time I want drink too much; now no want. You see, I no savvy I get one little wifie. Suppose I drink gin, my little wifie he 'fraid.'

To speak to her kindly was about more than I was fit for; I had made my vow I would never let on to weakness with a native, and I had nothing for it but to stop.

She stood looking gravely down at me where I sat by the open case. 'I think you good man,' she said. And suddenly she had fallen before me on the floor. 'I belong you all-e-same pig!' she cried.

CHAPTER II

THE BAN

I CAME on the verandah just before the sun rose on the morrow. My house was the last on the east; there was a cape of woods and cliffs behind that hid the sunrise. To the west, a swift cold river ran down, and beyond was the green of the village, dotted with cocoa-palms and breadfruits and houses. The shutters were some of them down and some open; I saw the mosquito bars still stretched, with shadows of people new-awakened sitting up inside; and all over the green others were stalking silent, wrapped in their many-coloured sleeping clothes like Bedouins in Bible pictures. It was mortal still and solemn and chilly, and the light of the dawn on the lagoon was like the shining of a fire.

But the thing that troubled me was nearer hand. Some dozen young men and children made a piece of a half-circle, flanking my house: the river divided them, some were on the near side, some on the far, and one on a boulder in the midst; and they all sat silent, wrapped in their sheets, and stared at me and my house as straight as pointer dogs. I thought it strange as I went out. When I had bathed and come back again, and found them all there, and two or three more along with them, I thought it stranger still. What could they see to gaze at in my house, I wondered, and went in.

But the thought of these starers stuck in my mind, and presently I came out again. The sun was now up, but it was still behind the cape of woods. Say a quarter of an hour had come and gone. The crowd was greatly increased, the far bank of the river was lined for quite a way—perhaps thirty grown folk, and of children twice as many, some standing, some squatted on the ground, and all staring at my house. I have seen a house in a South Sea village thus surrounded, but then a trader was thrashing his wife inside, and she singing out. Here was nothing: the stove was alight, the smoke going up in a Christian manner; all was shipshape and Bristol fashion.* To be sure, there was a stranger come, but they had a chance to see that stranger yesterday, and took it quiet enough. What ailed them now? I leaned my arms on the rail and stared back. Devil a wink* they had in them! Now and then I could see the children chatter, but they spoke so low not even the hum of their speaking came my length. The rest were like graven images: they stared at me, dumb and sorrowful, with their bright eyes; and it came upon me things would look not much different if I were on the platform of the gallows, and these good folk had come to see me hanged.

I felt I was getting daunted, and began to be afraid I looked it, which would never do. Up I stood, made believe to stretch myself, came down the verandah stair, and strolled towards the river. There went a short buzz from one to the other, like what you hear in theatres when the curtain goes up; and some of the nearest gave back the matter of a pace. I saw a girl lay one hand on a young man and make a gesture upward with the other; at the same time she said something in the native with a gasping voice. Three little boys sat beside my path, where I must pass within three feet of them. Wrapped in their sheets, with their shaved heads and bits of top-knots, and queer faces, they looked like figures on a chimney-piece. Awhile they sat their ground, solemn as judges. I came up hand over fist, doing my five knots, like a man that meant business; and I thought I saw a sort of a wink and gulp in the three faces. Then one jumped up (he was the farthest off) and ran for his mammy. The other two, trying to follow suit, got foul, came to ground together bawling, wriggled right out of their sheets mother-naked, and in a moment there were all three of them scampering for their lives and singing out like pigs. The natives, who would never let a joke slip, even at a burial, laughed and let up, as short as a dog's bark.

They say it scares a man to be alone. No such thing. What scares him in the dark or the high bush is that he can't make sure, and there might be an army at his elbow. What scares him worst is to be right in the midst of a crowd, and have no guess of what they're driving at. When that laugh stopped, I stopped too. The boys had not yet made their offing, they were still on the full stretch going the one way, when I had already gone about ship and was sheering off the other. Like a fool I had come out, doing my five knots; like a fool I went back again. It must have been the funniest thing to see, and what knocked me silly, this time no one laughed; only one old woman gave a kind of pious moan, the way you have heard Dissenters* in their chapels at the sermon.

'I never saw such fools of Kanakas* as your people here,' I said once to Uma, glancing out of the window at the starers.

'Savvy nothing,' says Uma, with a kind of disgusted air that she was good at.

And that was all the talk we had upon the matter, for I was put out, and Uma took the thing so much as a matter of course that I was fairly ashamed.

All day, off and on, now fewer and now more, the fools sat about the west end of my house and across the river, waiting for the show, whatever that was—fire to come down from heaven, I suppose, and consume me, bones and baggage. But by evening, like real islanders, they had wearied of the business, and got away, and had a dance instead in the big house of the village, where I heard them singing and clapping hands till, maybe, ten at night, and the next day it seemed they had forgotten I existed. If fire had come down from heaven or the earth opened and swallowed me, there would have been nobody to see the sport or take the lesson, or whatever you like to call it. But I was to find they hadn't forgot either, and kept an eye lifting for phenomena over my way.

I was hard at it both these days getting my trade in order and taking stock of what Vigours had left. This was a job that made me pretty sick, and kept me from thinking on much else. Ben* had taken stock the trip before—I knew I could trust Ben—but it was plain somebody had been making free in the meantime. I found I was out by what might easily cover six months' salary and profit, and I could have kicked myself all round the village to have been such a blamed ass, sitting boozing with that Case instead of attending to my own affairs and taking stock.

However, there's no use crying over spilt milk. It was done now, and couldn't be undone. All I could do was to get what was left of it, and my new stuff (my own choice) in order, to go round and get after the rats and cockroaches, and to fix up that store regular Sydney style.* A fine show I made of it; and the third morning when I had lit my pipe and stood in the doorway and looked in, and turned and looked far up the mountain and saw the cocoanuts waving and posted up the tons of copra, and over the village green and saw the island dandies and reckoned up the yards of print they wanted for their kilts and dresses, I felt as if I was in the right place to make a fortune, and go home again and start a public-house. There was I, sitting in that verandah, in as handsome a piece of scenery as you could find, a splendid sun, and a fine fresh healthy trade that stirred up a man's blood like sea-bathing; and the whole thing was clean gone from me, and I was dreaming England, which is, after all, a nasty, cold, muddy hole, with not enough light to see to read by; and dreaming the looks of my public, by a cant* of a broad high-road like an avenue, and with the sign on a green tree.

So much for the morning, but the day passed and the devil anyone looked near me, and from all I knew of natives in other islands I thought this strange. People laughed a little at our firm and their fine stations, and at this station of Falesá in particular; all the copra in the district wouldn't pay for it (I had heard them say) in fifty years, which I supposed was an exaggeration. But when the day went, and no business came at all, I began to get downhearted; and, about three in the afternoon, I went out for a stroll to cheer me up. On the green I saw a white man coming with a cassock on, by which and by the face of him I knew he was a priest. He was a good-natured old soul to look at, gone a little grizzled, and so dirty you could have written with him on a piece of paper.

'Good day, sir,' said I.

He answered me eagerly in native.

'Don't you speak any English?' said I.

'French,'* says he.

'Well,' said I, 'I'm sorry, but I can't do anything there.'

He tried me awhile in the French, and then again in native, which he seemed to think was the best chance. I made out he was after more than passing the time of day with me, but had something to communicate, and I listened the harder. I heard the names of Adams and Case and of Randall—Randall the oftenest—and the word 'poison', or something like it, and a native word that he said very often. I went home, repeating it to myself.

'What does fussy-ocky* mean?' I asked of Uma, for that was as near as I could come to it.

'Make dead,' said she.

'The devil it does!' says I. 'Did ever you hear that Case had poisoned Johnny Adams?'

'Every man he savvy that,' says Uma, scornful-like. 'Give him whites sand—bad sand. He got the bottle still. Suppose he give you gin, you no take him.'

Now I had heard much the same sort of story in other islands, and the same white powder always to the front, which made me think the less of it. For all that, I went over to Randall's place to see what I could pick up, and found Case on the doorstep, cleaning a gun.

'Good shooting here?' says I.

'A 1,' says he. 'The bush is full of all kinds of birds. I wish copra was as plenty,' says he—I thought, slyly—'but there don't seem anything doing.'

I could see Black Jack in the store, serving a customer.

'That looks like business, though,' said I.

'That's the first sale we've made in three weeks,' said he.

'You don't tell me?' says I. 'Three weeks? Well, well.'

'If you don't believe me,' he cries, a little hot, 'you can go and look at the copra-house. It's half empty to this blessed hour.'

'I shouldn't be much the better for that, you see,' says I. 'For all I can tell, it might have been whole empty yesterday.'

'That's so,' says he, with a bit of a laugh.

'By-the-bye,' I said, 'what sort of a party is that priest? Seems rather a friendly sort.'

At this Case laughed right out loud. 'Ah!' says he, 'I see what ails you now. Galuchet's been at you.' *Father Galoshes* was the name he went by most, but Case always gave it the French quirk, which was another reason we had for thinking him above the common.

'Yes, I have seen him,' I says. 'I made out he didn't think much of your Captain Randall.'

'That he don't!' says Case. 'It was the trouble about poor Adams. The last day, when he lay dying, there was young Buncombe round. Ever met Buncombe?'

I told him no.

'He's a cure,* is Buncombe!' laughs Case. 'Well, Buncombe took it in his head that, as there was no other clergyman about, bar Kanaka pastors, we ought to call in Father Galuchet, and have the old man administered and take the sacrament. It was all the same to me, you may suppose; but I said I thought Adams was the fellow to consult. He was jawing away about watered copra and a sight of foolery. "Look here," I said, "you're pretty sick. Would you like to see Galoshes?" He sat right up on his elbow. "Get the priest," says he, "get the priest; don't let me die here like a dog!" He spoke kind of fierce and eager, but sensible enough. There was nothing to say against that, so we sent and asked Galuchet if he would come. You bet he would. He jumped in his dirty linen at the thought of it. But we had reckoned without Papa. He's a hard-shell Baptist, is Papa; no Papists need apply. And he took and locked the door. Buncombe told him he was bigoted, and I thought he would have had a fit. "Bigoted!" he says. "Me bigoted? Have I lived to hear it from a jackanapes like you?" And he made for Buncombe, and I had to hold them apart; and there was Adams in the middle, gone luny again, and carrying on about copra like a born fool. It was good as the play, and I was about knocked out of time with laughing, when all of a sudden Adams sat up, clapped his hands to his chest, and went into the horrors.* He died hard, did John Adams,' says Case, with a kind of a sudden sternness.

'And what became of the priest?' I asked.

'The priest?' says Case. 'O! he was hammering on the door outside, and crying on the natives to come and beat it in, and singing out it was a soul he wished to save, and that. He was in a rare taking,* was the priest. But what would you have? Johnny had slipped his cable; no more Johnny in the market; and the administration racket clean played out. Next thing, word came to Randall the priest was praying upon Johnny's grave. Papa was pretty full, and got a club, and lit out straight for the place, and there was Galoshes on his knees, and a lot of natives looking on. You wouldn't think Papa cared that much about anything, unless it was liquor; but he and the priest stuck to it two hours, slanging each other in native, and every time Galoshes tried to kneel down Papa went for him with the club. There never were such larks in Falesá. The end of it was that Captain Randall knocked over with some kind of a fit or stroke, and the priest got in his goods after all. But he was the angriest priest you ever heard of, and complained to the chiefs about the outrage, as he called it. That was no account, for our chiefs are Protestant here; and, anyway, he had been making trouble about the drum for morning school, and they were glad to give him a wipe. Now he swears old Randall gave Adams poison or something, and when the two meet they grin at each other like baboons.'

He told this story as natural as could be, and like a man that enjoyed the fun; though, now I come to think of it after so long, it seems rather a sickening yarn. However, Case never set up to be soft, only to be square and hearty, and a man all round; and, to tell the truth, he puzzled me entirely.

I went home and asked Uma if she were a Popey, which I had made out to be the native word for Catholics.

'*E le ai!*' says she. She always used the native when she meant 'no' more than usually strong, and, indeed, there's more of it. 'No good Popey,' she added.

Then I asked her about Adams and the priest, and she told me much the same yarn in her own way. So that I was left not much farther on, but inclined, upon the whole, to think the bottom of the matter was the row about the sacrament, and the poisoning only talk.

The next day was a Sunday, when there was no business to be looked for. Uma asked me in the morning if I was going to 'pray'; I told her she bet not, and she stopped home herself with no more words. I thought this seemed unlike a native, and a native woman, and a woman that had new clothes to show off; however, it suited me to the ground, and I made the less of it. The queer thing was that I came next door to going to church after all, a thing I'm little likely to forget. I had turned out for a stroll, and heard the hymn tune up. You know how it is. If you hear folk singing, it seems to draw you; and pretty soon I found myself alongside the church. It was a little long low place, coral built, rounded off at both ends like a whale-boat, a big native roof on the top of it, windows without sashes and doorways without doors. I stuck my head into one of the windows, and the sight was so new to me—for things went quite different in the islands I was acquainted with—that I stayed and looked on. The congregation sat on the floor on mats, the women on one side, the men on the other, all rigged out to kill—the women with dresses and trade hats, the men in white jackets and shirts. The hymn was over; the pastor, a big buck Kanaka, was in the pulpit, preaching for his life; and by the way he wagged his hand, and worked his voice, and made his points, and seemed to argue with the folk, I made out he was a gun at the business. Well, he looked up suddenly and caught my eye, and I give you my word he staggered in the pulpit; his eyes bulged out of his head, his hand rose and pointed at me like as if against his will, and the sermon stopped right there.

It isn't a fine thing to say for yourself, but I ran away; and if the same kind of a shock was given me, I should run away again tomorrow. To see that palavering Kanaka struck all of a heap at the mere sight of me gave me a feeling as if the bottom had dropped out of the world. I went right home, and stayed there, and said nothing. You might think I would tell Uma, but that was against my system. You might have thought I would have gone over and consulted Case; but the truth was I was ashamed to speak of such a thing, I thought everyone would blurt out laughing in my face. So I held my tongue, and thought all the more; and the more I thought, the less I liked the business.

By Monday night I got it clearly in my head I must be tabooed. A new store to stand open two days in a village and not a man or woman come to see the trade was past believing.

'Uma,' said I, 'I think I'm tabooed.'

'I think so,' said she.

I thought awhile whether I should ask her more, but it's a bad idea to set natives up with any notion of consulting them, so I went to Case. It was dark, and he was sitting alone, as he did mostly, smoking on the stairs.

'Case,' said I, 'here's a queer thing. I'm tabooed.'

'O, fudge!' says he; ''tain't the practice in these islands.'

'That may be, or it mayn't,' said I. 'It's the practice where I was before. You can bet I know what it's like; and I tell it you for a fact, I'm tabooed.'

'Well,' said he, 'what have you been doing?'

'That's what I want to find out,' said I.

'O, you can't be,' said he; 'it ain't possible. However, I'll tell you what I'll do. Just to put your mind at rest, I'll go round and find out for sure. Just you waltz in and talk to Papa.'

'Thank you,' I said, 'I'd rather stay right out here on the verandah. Your house is so close.'

'I'll call Papa out here, then,' says he.

'My dear fellow,' I says, 'I wish you wouldn't. The fact is, I don't take to Mr Randall.'

Case laughed, took a lantern from the store, and set out into the village. He was gone perhaps a quarter of an hour, and he looked mighty serious when he came back.

'Well,' said he, clapping down the lantern on the verandah steps, 'I would never have believed it. I don't know where the impudence of these Kanakas 'll go next; they seem to have lost all idea of respect for whites. What we want is a man-of-war—a German, if we could—they know how to manage Kanakas.'*

'I *am* tabooed, then?' I cried.

'Something of the sort,' said he. 'It's the worst thing of the kind I've heard of yet. But I'll stand by you, Wiltshire, man to man. You come round here tomorrow about nine, and we'll have it out with the chiefs. They're afraid of me, or they used to be; but their heads are so big by now, I don't know what to think. Understand me, Wiltshire; I don't count this your quarrel,' he went on, with a great deal of resolution, 'I count it all of our quarrel, I count it the White Man's Quarrel, and I'll stand to it through thick and thin, and there's my hand on it.'

'Have you found out what's the reason?' I asked.

'Not yet,' said Case. 'But we'll fix them down tomorrow.'

Altogether I was pretty well pleased with his attitude, and almost more the next day, when we met to go before the chiefs, to see him so stern and resolved. The chiefs awaited us in one of their big oval houses, which was marked out to us from a long way off by the crowd about the eaves, a hundred strong if there was one—men, women, and children. Many of the men were on their way to work and wore green wreaths, and it put me in thoughts of the 1st of May at home. This crowd opened and buzzed about the pair of us as we went in, with a sudden angry animation. Five chiefs were there; four mighty stately men, the fifth old and puckered. They sat on mats in their white kilts and jackets; they had fans in their hands, like fine ladies; and two of the younger ones wore Catholic medals, which gave me matter of reflection. Our place was set, and the mats laid for us over against these grandees, on the near side of the house; the midst was empty; the crowd, close at our backs, murmured and craned and jostled to look on, and the shadows of them tossed in front of us on the clean pebbles of the floor. I was just a hair put out by the excitement of the commons, but the quiet civil appearance of the chiefs reassured me, all the more when their spokesman began and made a long speech in a low tone of voice, sometimes waving his hand toward Case, sometimes toward me, and sometimes knocking with his knuckles on the mat. One thing was clear: there was no sign of anger in the chiefs.

'What's he been saying?' I asked, when he had done.

'O, just that they're glad to see you, and they understand by me you wish to make some kind of complaint, and you're to fire away, and they'll do the square thing.'

'It took a precious long time to say that,' said I.

'O, the rest was sawder* and *bonjour* and that,' said Case. 'You know what Kanakas are.'

'Well, they don't get much *bonjour* out of me,' said I. 'You tell them who I am. I'm a white man, and a British subject, and no end of a big chief at home; and I've come here to do them good, and bring them civilization; and no sooner have I got my trade sorted out than they go and taboo me, and no one dare come near my place! Tell them I don't mean to fly in the face of anything legal; and if what they want's a present, I'll do what's fair. I don't blame any man looking out for himself, tell them, for that's human nature; but if they think they're going to come any of their native ideas over me, they'll find themselves mistaken. And tell them plain that I demand the reason of this treatment as a white man and a British subject.'

That was my speech. I know how to deal with Kanakas: give them plain sense and fair dealing, and—I'll do them that much justice—they knuckle under every time. They haven't any real government or any real law, that's what you've got to knock into their heads; and even if they had, it would be a good joke if it was to apply to a white man. It would be a strange thing if we came all this way and couldn't do what we pleased. The mere idea has always put my monkey up,* and I rapped my speech out pretty big. Then Case translated it—or made believe to, rather—and the first chief replied, and then a second, and a third, all in the same style, easy and genteel, but solemn underneath. Once a question was put to Case, and he answered it, and all hands (both chiefs and commons) laughed out aloud, and looked at me. Last of all, the puckered old fellow and the big young chief that spoke first started in to put Case through a kind of catechism. Sometimes I made out that Case was trying to fence, and they stuck to him like hounds, and the sweat ran down his face, which was no very pleasant sight to me, and at some of his answers the crowd moaned and murmured, which was a worse hearing. It's a cruel shame I knew no native, for (as I now believe) they were asking Case about my marriage, and he must have had a tough job of it to clear his feet. But leave Case alone; he had the brains to run a parliament.

'Well, is that all?' I asked, when a pause came.

'Come along,' says he, mopping his face; 'I'll tell you outside.'

'Do you mean they won't take the taboo off?' I cried.

'It's something queer,' said he. 'I'll tell you outside. Better come away.'

'I won't take it at their hands,' cried I. 'I ain't that kind of a man. You don't find me turn my back on a parcel of Kanakas.'

'You'd better,' said Case.

He looked at me with a signal in his eye; and the five chiefs looked at me civilly enough, but kind of pointed; and the people looked at me and craned and jostled. I remembered the folks that watched my house, and how the pastor had jumped in his pulpit at the bare sight of me; and the whole business seemed so out of the way that I rose and followed Case. The crowd opened again to let us through, but wider than before, the children on the skirts running and singing out, and as we two white men walked away they all stood and watched us.

'And now,' said I, 'what is all this about?'

'The truth is I can't rightly make it out myself. They have a down on you,' says Case.

'Taboo a man because they have a down on him!' I cried. 'I never heard the like.'

'It's worse than that, you see,' said Case. 'You ain't tabooed—I told you that couldn't be. The people won't go near you, Wiltshire, and there's where it is.'

'They won't go near me? What do you mean by that? Why won't they go near me?' I cried.

Case hesitated. 'Seems they're frightened,' says he, in a low voice.

I stopped dead short. 'Frightened?' I repeated. 'Are you gone crazy, Case? What are they frightened of?'

'I wish I could make out,' Case answered, shaking his head. 'Appears like one of their tomfool superstitions. That's what I don't cotton to,' he said. 'It's like the business about Vigours.'

'I'd like to know what you mean by that, and I'll trouble you to tell me,' says I.

'Well, you know, Vigours lit out and left all standing,' said he. 'It was some superstition business—I never got the hang of it; but it began to look bad before the end.'

'I've heard a different story about that,' said I, 'and I had better tell you so. I heard he ran away because of you.'

'O! well, I suppose he was ashamed to tell the truth,' says Case; 'I guess he thought it silly. And it's a fact that I packed him off. "What would you do, old man?" says he. "Get," says I, "and not think twice about it." I was the gladdest kind of man to see him clear away. It ain't my notion to turn my back on a mate when he's in a tight place, but there was that much trouble in the village that I couldn't see where it might likely end. I was a fool to be so much about with Vigours. They cast it up to me today. Didn't you hear Maea—that's the young chief, the big one—ripping out about "Vika"? That was him they were after. They don't seem to forget it, somehow.'

'This is all very well,' said I, 'but it don't tell me what's wrong; it don't tell me what they're afraid of—what their idea is.'

'Well, I wish I knew,' said Case. 'I can't say fairer than that.'

'You might have asked, I think,' says I.

'And so I did,' says he. 'But you must have seen for yourself, unless you're blind, that the asking got the other way. I'll go as far as I dare for another white man; but when I find I'm in the scrape myself, I think first of my own bacon. The loss of me is I'm too good-natured. And I'll take the freedom of telling you you show a queer kind of gratitude to a man who's got into all this mess along of your affairs.'

'There's a thing I am thinking of,' said I. 'You were a fool to be so much about with Vigours. One comfort, you haven't been much about with me. I notice you've never been inside my house. Own up now; you had word of this before?'

'It's a fact I haven't been,' said he. 'It was an oversight, and I am sorry for it, Wiltshire. But about coming now, I'll be quite plain.'

'You mean you won't?' I asked.

'Awfully sorry, old man, but that's the size of it,' says Case.

'In short, you're afraid?' says I.

'In short, I'm afraid,' says he.

'And I'm still to be tabooed for nothing?' I asked.

'I tell you you're not tabooed,' said he. 'The Kanakas won't go near you, that's all. And who's to make 'em? We traders have a lot of gall, I must say; we make these poor Kanakas take back their laws, and take up their taboos, and that, whenever it happens to suit us. But you don't mean to say you expect a law obliging people to deal in your store whether they want to or not? You don't mean to tell me you've got the gall for that? And if you had, it would be a queer thing to propose to me. I would just like to point out to you, Wiltshire, that I'm a trader myself.'

'I don't think I would talk of gall if I was you,' said I. 'Here's about what it comes to, as well as I can make out: None of the people are to trade with me, and they're all to trade with you. You're to have the copra, and I'm to go to the devil and shake myself. And I don't know any native, and you're the only man here worth mention that speaks English, and you have the gall to up and hint to me my life's in danger, and all you've got to tell me is you don't know why!'

'Well, it *is* all I have to tell you,' said he. 'I don't know—I wish I did.'

'And so you turn your back and leave me to myself! Is that the position?' says I.

'If you like to put it nasty,' says he. 'I don't put it so. I say merely, "I'm going to keep clear of you; or, if I don't, I'll get in danger for myself."'

'Well,' says I, 'you're a nice kind of a white man!'

'O, I understand; you're riled,' said he. 'I would be myself. I can make excuses.'

'All right,' I said, 'go and make excuses somewhere else. Here's my way, there's yours!'

With that we parted, and I went straight home, in a hot temper,* and found Uma trying on a lot of trade goods like a baby.

'Here,' I said, 'you quit that foolery! Here's a pretty mess to have made, as if I wasn't bothered enough anyway! And I thought I told you to get dinner!'

And then I believe I gave her a bit of the rough side of my tongue, as she deserved. She stood up at once, like a sentry to his officer; for I must say she was always well brought up, and had a great respect for whites.

'And now,' says I, 'you belong round here, you're bound to understand this. What am I tabooed for, anyway? Or, if I ain't tabooed, what makes the folks afraid of me?'

She stood and looked at me with eyes like saucers.

'You no savvy?' she gasps at last.

'No,' said I. 'How would you expect me to? We don't have any such craziness where I come from.'

'Ese no tell you?' she asked again.

(*Ese* was the name the natives had for Case; it may mean

foreign, or extraordinary; or it might mean a mummy apple;* but most like it was only his own name misheard and put in a Kanaka spelling.)

'Not much,' said I.

'Damn Ese!' she cried.

You might think it funny to hear this Kanaka girl come out with a big swear. No such thing. There was no swearing in her—no, nor anger; she was beyond anger, and meant the word simple and serious. She stood there straight as she said it. I cannot justly say that I ever saw a woman look like that before or after, and it struck me mum. Then she made a kind of an obeisance, but it was the proudest kind, and threw her hands out open.

'I 'shamed,' she said. 'I think you savvy. Ese he tell me you savvy, he tell me you no mind, tell me you love me too much. Taboo belong me,' she said, touching herself on the bosom, as she had done upon our wedding-night. 'Now I go 'way, taboo he go 'way too. Then you get too much copra. You like more better, I think. *Tofá, alii,*' says she in the native—'Farewell, chief!'

'Hold on!' I cried. 'Don't be in such a hurry.'*

She looked at me sidelong with a smile. 'You see, you get copra,' she said, the same as you might offer candies to a child.

'Uma,' said I, 'hear reason. I didn't know, and that's a fact; and Case seems to have played it pretty mean upon the pair of us. But I do know now, and I don't mind; I love you too much. You no go 'way, you no leave me, I too much sorry.'

'You no love me,' she cried, 'you talk me bad words!' And she threw herself in a corner of the floor, and began to cry.

Well, I'm no scholar, but I wasn't born yesterday, and I thought the worst of that trouble was over. However, there she lay—her back turned, her face to the wall—and shook with sobbing like a little child, so that her feet jumped with it. It's strange how it hits a man when he's in love; for there's no use mincing things—Kanaka and all, I was in love with her, or just as good. I tried to take her hand, but she would none of that. 'Uma,' I said, 'there's no sense in carrying on like this. I want you stop here, I want my little wifie, I tell you true.'

'No tell me true,' she sobbed.

'All right,' says I, 'I'll wait till you're through with this.' And I sat right down beside her on the floor, and set to smooth her hair with my hand. At first she wriggled away when I touched her; then she seemed to notice me no more; then her sobs grew gradually less, and presently stopped; and the next thing I knew, she raised her face to mine.

'You tell me true? You like me stop?' she asked.

'Uma,' I said, 'I would rather have you than all the copra in the South Seas,' which was a very big expression, and the strangest thing was that I meant it.

She threw her arms about me, sprang close up, and pressed her face to mine in the island way of kissing, so that I was all wetted with her tears, and my heart went out to her wholly. I never had anything so near me as this little brown bit of a girl. Many things went together, and all helped to turn my head. She was pretty enough to eat; it seemed she was my only friend in that queer place; I was ashamed that I had spoken rough to her: and she was a woman, and my wife, and a kind of a baby besides that I was sorry for; and the salt of her tears was in my mouth. And I forgot Case and the natives; and I forgot that I knew nothing of the story, or only remembered it to banish the remembrance; and I forgot that I was to get no copra, and so could make no livelihood; and I forgot my employers, and the strange kind of service I was doing them, when I preferred my fancy to their business; and I forgot even that Uma was no true wife of mine, but just a maid beguiled, and that in a pretty shabby style. But that is to look too far on. I will come to that part of it next.

It was late before we thought of getting dinner. The stove was out, and gone stone-cold; but we fired up after a while, and cooked each a dish, helping and hindering each other, and making a play of it like children. I was so greedy of her nearness that I sat down to dinner with my lass upon my knee, made sure of her with one hand, and ate with the other. Ay, and more than that. She was the worst cook I suppose God made; the things she set her hand to it would have sickened an honest horse to eat of; yet I made my meal that day on Uma's cookery, and can never call to mind to have been better pleased.

I didn't pretend to myself, and I didn't pretend to her. I saw I was clean gone; and if she was to make a fool of me, she must. And I suppose it was this that set her talking, for now she made sure that we were friends. A lot she told me, sitting in my lap and eating my dish, as I ate hers, from foolery—a lot about herself and her mother and Case, all which would be very tedious, and fill sheets if I set it down in Beach de Mar,* but which I must give a hint of in plain English, and one thing about myself, which had a very big effect on my concerns, as you are soon to hear.

It seems she was born in one of the Line Islands;* had been only two or three years in these parts,* where she had come with a white man, who was married to her mother and then died; and only the one year in Falesá. Before that they had been a good deal on the move, trekking about after the white man, who was one of those rolling stones that keep going round after a soft job. They talk about looking for gold at the end of a rainbow; but if a man wants an employment that'll last him till he dies, let him start out on the soft-job hunt. There's meat and drink in it too, and beer and skittles, for you never hear of them starving, and rarely see them sober; and as for steady sport, cock-fighting isn't in the same county with it. Anyway, this beachcomber* carried the woman and her daughter all over the shop, but mostly to out-of-the-way islands, where there were no police, and he thought, perhaps, the soft job hung out. I've my own view of this old party; but I was just as glad he had kept Uma clear of Apia and Papeete and these flash towns.* At last he struck Fale-alii* on this island, got some trade—the Lord knows how!—muddled it all away in the usual style, and died worth next to nothing, bar a bit of land at Falesá that he had got for a bad debt, which was what put it in the minds of the mother and daughter to come there and live. It seems Case encouraged them all he could, and helped to get their house built. He was very kind those days, and gave Uma trade, and there is no doubt he had his eye on her from the beginning. However, they had scarce settled, when up turned a young man, a native, and wanted to marry her. He was a small chief, and had some fine mats and old songs in his family, and was 'very pretty', Uma said; and, altogether, it was an extraordinary match for a penniless girl and an out-islander.

At the first word of this I got downright sick with jealousy. 'And you mean to say you would have married him?' I cried.

'*Ioe*, yes,' said she. 'I like too much!'

'Well!' I said. 'And suppose I had come round after?'

'I like you more better now,' said she. 'But, suppose I marry Ioane, I one good wife. I no common Kanaka. Good girl!' says she.

Well, I had to be pleased with that; but I promise you I didn't care about the business one little bit. And I liked the end of that yarn no better than the beginning. For it seems this proposal of marriage was the start of all the trouble. It seems, before that, Uma and her mother had been looked down upon, of course, for kinless folk and out-islanders, but nothing to hurt; and, even when Ioane came forward, there was less trouble at first than might have been looked for. And then, all of a sudden, about six months before my coming, Ioane backed out and left that part of the island, and from that day to this Uma and her mother had found themselves alone. None called at their house, none spoke to them on the roads. If they went to church, the other women drew their mats away and left them in a clear place by themselves. It was a regular excommunication, like what you read of in the Middle Ages; and the cause or sense of it beyond guessing. It was some *tala pepelo*, Uma said, some lie, some calumny; and all she knew of it was that the girls who had been jealous of her luck with Ioane used to twit her with his desertion, and cry out, when they met her alone in the woods, that she would never be married. 'They tell me no man he marry me. He too much 'fraid,' she said.

The only soul that came about them after this desertion was Master Case. Even he was chary of showing himself, and turned up mostly by night; and pretty soon he began to table his cards and make up to Uma. I was still sore about Ioane, and when Case turned up in the same line of business I cut up downright rough.

'Well,' I said, sneering, 'and I suppose you thought Case "very pretty" and "liked too much"?'

'Now you talk silly,' said she. 'White man, he come here, I marry him all-e-same Kanaka; very well then, he marry me all-e-same white woman. Suppose he no marry, he go 'way, woman he stop. All-e-same thief, empty hand, Tonga-heart*—no can love! Now you come marry me. You big heart—you no 'shamed island-girl. That thing I love you for too much. I proud.'

I don't know that ever I felt sicker all the days of my life. I laid down my fork, and I put away 'the island-girl'; I didn't seem somehow to have any use for either, and I went and walked up and down in the house, and Uma followed me with her eyes, for she was troubled, and small wonder! But troubled was no word for it with me. I so wanted, and so feared, to make a clean breast of the sweep* that I had been.

And just then there came a sound of singing out of the sea; it sprang up suddenly clear and near, as the boat turned the headland, and Uma, running to the window, cried out it was 'Misi'* come upon his rounds.

I thought it was a strange thing I should be glad to have a missionary; but, if it was strange, it was still true.

'Uma,' said I, 'you stop here in this room, and don't budge a foot out of it till I come back.'

CHAPTER III

THE MISSIONARY

As I came out on the verandah, the mission boat was shooting for the mouth of the river. She was a long whale-boat painted white; a bit of an awning astern; a native pastor crouched on the wedge of the poop, steering; some four-and-twenty paddles flashing and dipping, true to the boat-song; and the missionary under the awning, in his white clothes, reading in a book, and set him up!* It was pretty to see and hear; there's no smarter sight in the islands than a missionary boat with a good crew and a good pipe to them; and I considered it for half a minute, with a bit of envy perhaps, and then strolled down towards the river.

From the opposite side there was another man aiming for the same place, but he ran and got there first. It was Case; doubtless his idea was to keep me apart from the missionary, who might serve me as interpreter; but my mind was upon other things. I was thinking how he had jockeyed us about the marriage, and tried his hand on Uma before; and at the sight of him rage flew into my nostrils.

'Get out of that, you low, swindling thief!' I cried.

'What's that you say?' says he.

I gave him the word again, and rammed it down with a good oath. 'And if ever I catch you within six fathoms of my house,' I cried, 'I'll clap a bullet in your measly carcase.'

'You must do as you like about your house,' said he, 'where I told you I have no thought of going; but this is a public place.'

'It's a place where I have private business,' said I. 'I have no idea of a hound like you eavesdropping, and I give you notice to clear out.'

'I don't take it, though,' says Case.

'I'll show you, then,' said I.

'We'll have to see about that,' said he.

He was quick with his hands, but he had neither the height

nor the weight, being a flimsy creature alongside a man like me, and, besides, I was blazing to that height of wrath that I could have bit into a chisel. I gave him first the one and then the other, so that I could hear his head rattle and crack, and he went down straight.

'Have you had enough?' cried I. But he only looked up white and blank, and the blood spread upon his face like wine upon a napkin. 'Have you had enough?' I cried again. 'Speak up, and don't lie malingering there, or I'll take my feet to you.'

He sat up at that, and held his head—by the look of him you could see it was spinning—and the blood poured on his pyjamas.

'I've had enough for this time,' says he, and he got up staggering, and went off by the way that he had come.

The boat was close in; I saw the missionary had laid his book to one side, and I smiled to myself. 'He'll know I'm a man, anyway,' thinks I.

This was the first time, in all my years in the Pacific, I had ever exchanged two words with any missionary, let alone asked one for a favour. I didn't like the lot, no trader does; they look down upon us, and make no concealment; and, besides, they're partly Kanakaized, and suck up with natives instead of with other white men like themselves. I had on a rig of clean striped pyjamas—for, of course, I had dressed decent to go before the chiefs; but when I saw the missionary step out of this boat in the regular uniform, white duck clothes, pith helmet, white shirt and tie, and yellow boots to his feet, I could have bunged stones at him. As he came nearer, queering me* pretty curious (because of the fight, I suppose), I saw he looked mortal sick, for the truth was he had a fever on, and had just had a chill in the boat.

'Mr Tarleton, I believe?' says I, for I had got his name.

'And you, I suppose, are the new trader?' says he.

'I want to tell you first that I don't hold with missions,' I went on, 'and that I think you and the likes of you do a sight of harm, filling up the natives with old wives' tales and bumptiousness.'

'You are perfectly entitled to your opinions,' says he, looking a bit ugly, 'but I have no call to hear them.'

'It so happens that you've got to hear them,' I said. 'I'm no missionary, nor missionary lover; I'm no Kanaka, nor favourer of Kanakas—I'm just a trader; I'm just a common, low, God-damned white man and British subject, the sort you would like to wipe your boots on. I hope that's plain!'

'Yes, my man,' said he. 'It's more plain than creditable. When you are sober, you'll be sorry for this.'

He tried to pass on, but I stopped him with my hand. The Kanakas were beginning to growl. Guess they didn't like my tone, for I spoke to that man as free as I would to you.

'Now, you can't say I've deceived you,' said I, 'and I can go on. I want a service—I want two services, in fact; and, if you care to give me them, I'll perhaps take more stock in what you call your Christianity.'

He was silent for a moment. Then he smiled. 'You are rather a strange sort of man,' says he.

'I'm the sort of man God made me,' says I. 'I don't set up to be a gentleman,' I said.

'I am not quite so sure,' said he. 'And what can I do for you, Mr ——?'

'Wiltshire,' I says, 'though I'm mostly called Welsher;* but Wiltshire is the way it's spelt, if the people on the beach could only get their tongues about it. And what do I want? Well, I'll tell you the first thing. I'm what you call a sinner—what I call a sweep—and I want you to help me make it up to a person I've deceived.'

He turned and spoke to his crew in the native. 'And now I am at your service,' said he, 'but only for the time my crew are dining. I must be much farther down the coast before night. I was delayed at Papa-Malulu* till this morning, and I have an engagement in Fale-alii tomorrow night.'

I led the way to my house in silence, and rather pleased with myself for the way I had managed the talk, for I like a man to keep his self-respect.

'I was sorry to see you fighting,' says he.

'O, that's part of the yarn I want to tell you,' I said. 'That's service number two. After you've heard it you'll let me know whether you're sorry or not.'

We walked right in through the store, and I was surprised to find Uma had cleared away the dinner things. This was so unlike her ways that I saw she had done it out of gratitude, and liked her the better. She and Mr Tarleton called each other by name, and he was very civil to her seemingly. But I thought little of that; they can always find civility for a Kanaka, it's us white men they lord it over. Besides, I didn't want much Tarleton just then. I was going to do my pitch.

'Uma,' said I, 'give us your marriage certificate.' She looked put out. 'Come,' said I, 'you can trust me. Hand it up.'

She had it about her person, as usual; I believe she thought it was a pass to heaven, and if she died without having it handy she would go to hell. I couldn't see where she put it the first time, I couldn't see now where she took it from; it seemed to jump into her hand like that Blavatsky business in the papers.* But it's the same way with all island women, and I guess they're taught it when young.

'Now,' said I, with the certificate in my hand, 'I was married to this girl by Black Jack the negro. The certificate was wrote by Case, and it's a dandy piece of literature, I promise you. Since then I've found that there's a kind of cry in the place against this wife of mine, and so long as I keep her I cannot trade. Now, what would any man do in my place, if he was a man?' I said. 'The first thing he would do is this, I guess.' And I took and tore up the certificate and bunged the pieces on the floor.

'*Aué!*'[2] cried Uma, and began to clap her hands; but I caught one of them in mine.

'And the second thing that he would do,' said I, 'if he was what I would call a man and you would call a man, Mr Tarleton, is to bring the girl right before you or any other missionary, and to up and say: "I was wrong married to this wife of mine, but I think a heap of her, and now I want to be married to her right." Fire away, Mr Tarleton. And I guess you'd better do it in native; it'll please the old lady,' I said, giving her the proper name of a man's wife upon the spot.

So we had in two of the crew for to witness, and were spliced in our own house; and the parson prayed a good bit, I must

[2] Alas!

say—but not so long as some—and shook hands with the pair of us.

'Mr Wiltshire,' he says, when he had made out the lines and packed off the witnesses, 'I have to thank you for a very lively pleasure. I have rarely performed the marriage ceremony with more grateful emotions.'

That was what you would call talking. He was going on, besides, with more of it, and I was ready for as much taffy* as he had in stock, for I felt good. But Uma had been taken up with something half through the marriage, and cut straight in.

'How your hand he get hurt?' she asked.

'You ask Case's head, old lady,' says I.

She jumped with joy, and sang out.

'You haven't made much of a Christian of this one,' says I to Mr Tarleton.

'We didn't think her one of our worst,' says he, 'when she was at Fale-alii; and if Uma bears malice I shall be tempted to fancy she has good cause.'

'Well, there we are at service number two,' said I. 'I want to tell you our yarn, and see if you can let a little daylight in.'

'Is it long?' he asked.

'Yes,' I cried; 'it's a goodish bit of a yarn!'

'Well, I'll give you all the time I can spare,' says he, looking at his watch. 'But I must tell you fairly, I haven't eaten since five this morning, and, unless you can let me have something I am not likely to eat again before seven or eight tonight.'

'By God, we'll give you dinner!' I cried.

I was a little caught up at my swearing, just when all was going straight; and so was the missionary, I suppose, but he made believe to look out of the window, and thanked us.

So we ran him up a bit of a meal. I was bound to let the old lady have a hand in it, to show off, so I deputized her to brew the tea. I don't think I ever met such tea as she turned out. But that was not the worst, for she got round with the salt-box, which she considered an extra European touch, and turned my stew into sea-water. Altogether, Mr Tarleton had a devil of a dinner of it; but he had plenty entertainment by the way, for all the while that we were cooking, and afterwards, when he was making believe to eat, I kept posting him up on Master Case and the beach of Falesá, and he putting questions that showed he was following close.

'Well,' said he at last, 'I am afraid you have a dangerous enemy. This man Case is very clever and seems really wicked. I must tell you I have had my eye on him for nearly a year, and have rather had the worst of our encounters. About the time when the last representative of your firm ran so suddenly away, I had a letter from Namu, the native pastor, begging me to come to Falesá at my earliest convenience, as his flock were all "adopting Catholic practices". I had great confidence in Namu; I fear it only shows how easily we are deceived. No one could hear him preach and not be persuaded he was a man of extraordinary parts. All our islanders easily acquire a kind of eloquence, and can roll out and illustrate, with a great deal of vigour and fancy, second-hand sermons; but Namu's sermons are his own, and I cannot deny that I have found them means of grace. Moreover, he has a keen curiosity in secular things, does not fear work, is clever at carpentering, and has made himself so much respected among the neighbouring pastors that we call him, in a jest which is half serious, the Bishop of the East. In short, I was proud of the man; all the more puzzled by his letter, and took an occasion to come this way. The morning before my arrival, Vigours had been sent on board the *Lion*, and Namu was perfectly at his ease, apparently ashamed of his letter, and quite unwilling to explain it. This, of course, I could not allow, and he ended by confessing that he had been much concerned to find his people using the sign of the cross, but since he had learned the explanation his mind was satisfied. For Vigours had the Evil Eye, a common thing in a country of Europe called Italy, where men were often struck dead by that kind of devil, and it appeared the sign of the cross was a charm against its power.

'"And I explain it, Misi," said Namu, "in this way: The country in Europe is a Popey country, and the devil of the Evil Eye may be a Catholic devil, or, at least, used to Catholic ways. So then I reasoned thus: if this sign of the cross were used in a Popey manner it would be sinful, but when it is used only to protect men from a devil, which is a thing harmless in itself, the sign too must be harmless. For the sign is neither good nor bad, even as a bottle is neither good nor bad. But if the bottle be full of gin, the gin is bad; and if the sign be made in idolatry, so is the idolatry bad." And, very like a native pastor, he had a text apposite about the casting out of devils.

'"And who has been telling you about the Evil Eye?" I asked.

'He admitted it was Case. Now, I am afraid you will think me very narrow, Mr Wiltshire, but I must tell you I was displeased, and cannot think a trader at all a good man to advise or have an influence upon my pastors. And, besides, there had been some flying talk in the country of old Adams and his being poisoned, to which I had paid no great heed; but it came back to me at the moment.

'"And is this Case a man of a sanctified life?" I asked.

'He admitted he was not; for, though he did not drink, he was profligate with women, and had no religion.

'"Then," said I, "I think the less you have to do with him the better."

'But it is not easy to have the last word with a man like Namu. He was ready in a moment with an illustration. "Misi," said he, "you have told me there were wise men, not pastors, not even holy, who knew many things useful to be taught—about trees for instance, and beasts, and to print books, and about the stones that are burned to make knives of. Such men teach you in your college, and you learn from them, but take care not to learn to be unholy. Misi, Case is my college."

'I knew not what to say. Mr Vigours had evidently been driven out of Falesá by the machinations of Case and with something not very unlike the collusion of my pastor. I called to mind it was Namu who had reassured me about Adams and traced the rumour to the ill-will of the priest. And I saw I must inform myself more thoroughly from an impartial source. There is an old rascal of a chief here, Faiaso, whom I dare say you saw today at the council; he has been all his life turbulent and sly, a great fomenter of rebellions, and a thorn in the side of the mission and the island. For all that he is very shrewd, and, except in politics or about his own misdemeanours, a teller of the truth. I went to his house, told him what I had heard, and besought him to be frank. I do not think I had ever a more painful interview. Perhaps you will understand me, Mr Wiltshire, if I tell you that I am perfectly serious in these old wives' tales with which you reproached me, and as anxious to do well for these islands as you can be to please and to protect your pretty wife. And you are to remember that I thought Namu a paragon, and was proud of the man as one of the first ripe fruits of the mission. And now I was informed that he had fallen in a sort of dependence upon Case. The beginning of it was not corrupt; it began, doubtless, in fear and respect, produced by trickery and pretence; but I was shocked to find that another element had been lately added, that Namu helped himself in the store, and was believed to be deep in Case's debt. Whatever the trader said, that Namu believed with trembling. He was not alone in this; many in the village lived in a similar subjection; but Namu's case was the most influential, it was through Namu Case had wrought most evil; and with a certain following among the chiefs, and the pastor in his pocket, the man was as good as master of the village. You know something of Vigours and Adams, but perhaps you have never heard of old Underhill, Adams' predecessor. He was a quiet, mild old fellow, I remember, and we were told he had died suddenly: white men die very suddenly in Falesá. The truth, as I now heard it, made my blood run cold. It seems he was struck with a general palsy, all of him dead but one eye, which he continually winked. Word was started that the helpless old man was now a devil, and this vile fellow Case worked upon the natives' fears, which he professed to share, and pretended he durst not go into the house alone. At last a grave was dug, and the living body buried at the far end of the village. Namu, my pastor, whom I had helped to educate, offered up a prayer at the hateful scene.*

'I felt myself in a very difficult position. Perhaps it was my duty to have denounced Namu and had him deposed. Perhaps I think so now, but at the time it seemed less clear. He had a great influence, it might prove greater than mine. The natives are prone to superstition; perhaps by stirring them up I might but ingrain and spread these dangerous fancies. And

Namu besides, apart from this novel and accursed influence, was a good pastor, an able man, and spiritually minded. Where should I look for a better? How was I to find as good? At that moment, with Namu's failure fresh in my view, the work of my life appeared a mockery; hope was dead in me. I would rather repair such tools as I had than go abroad in quest of others that must certainly prove worse; and a scandal is, at the best, a thing to be avoided when humanly possible. Right or wrong, then, I determined on a quiet course. All that night I denounced and reasoned with the erring pastor, twitted him with his ignorance and want of faith, twitted him with his wretched attitude, making clean the outside of the cup and platter,* callously helping at a murder, childishly flying in excitement about a few childish, unnecessary, and inconvenient gestures; and long before day I had him on his knees and bathed in the tears of what seemed a genuine repentance. On Sunday I took the pulpit in the morning, and preached from First Kings, nineteenth, on the fire, the earthquake, and the voice, distinguishing the true spiritual power,* and referring with such plainness as I dared to recent events in Falesá. The effect produced was great, and it was much increased when Namu rose in his turn and confessed that he had been wanting in faith and conduct, and was convinced of sin. So far, then, all was well; but there was one unfortunate circumstance. It was nearing the time of our "May" in the island, when the native contributions to the missions are received; it fell in my duty to make a notification on the subject, and this gave my enemy his chance, by which he was not slow to profit.

'News of the whole proceedings must have been carried to Case as soon as church was over, and the same afternoon he made an occasion to meet me in the midst of the village. He came up with so much intentness and animosity that I felt it would be damaging to avoid him.

' "So," says he, in native, "here is the holy man. He has been preaching against me, but that was not in his heart. He has been preaching upon the love of God; but that was not in his heart, it was between his teeth. Will you know what was in his heart?" cries he. "I will show it you!" And, making a snatch at my head, he made believe to pluck out a dollar, and held it in the air.

'There went that rumour through the crowd with which Polynesians receive a prodigy. As for myself, I stood amazed. The thing was a common conjuring trick which I have seen performed at home a score of times; but how was I to convince the villagers of that? I wished I had learned legerdemain instead of Hebrew, that I might have paid the fellow out with his own coin. But there I was; I could not stand there silent, and the best I could find to say was weak.

' "I will trouble you not to lay hands on me again," said I.

' "I have no such thought," said he, "nor will I deprive you of your dollar. Here it is," he said, and flung it at my feet. I am told it lay where it fell three days.'

'I must say it was well played,' said I.

'O! he is clever,' said Mr Tarleton, 'and you can now see for yourself how dangerous. He was a party to the horrid death of the paralytic; he is accused of poisoning Adams; he drove Vigours out of the place by lies that might have led to murder; and there is no question but he has now made up his mind to rid himself of you. How he means to try we have no guess; only be sure, it's something new. There is no end to his readiness and invention.'

'He gives himself a sight of trouble,' says I. 'And after all, what for?'

'Why, how many tons of copra may they make in this district?' asked the missionary.

'I daresay as much as sixty tons,' says I.

'And what is the profit to the local trader?' he asked.

'You may call it three pounds,' said I.

'Then you can reckon for yourself how much he does it for,' said Mr Tarleton. 'But the more important thing is to defeat him. It is clear he spread some report against Uma, in order to isolate and have his wicked will of her. Failing of that, and seeing a new rival come upon the scene, he used her in a different way. Now, the first point to find out is about Namu. Uma, when people began to leave you and your mother alone, what did Namu do?'

'Stop away all-e-same,' says Uma.

'I fear the dog has returned to his vomit,' said Mr Tarleton. 'And now what am I to do for you? I will speak to Namu, I will warn him he is observed; it will be strange if he allow anything to go on amiss when he is put upon his guard. At the same time, this precaution may fail, and then you must turn elsewhere. You have two people at hand to whom you might apply. There is, first of all, the priest, who might protect you by the Catholic interest; they are a wretchedly small body, but they count two chiefs. And then there is old Faiaso. Ah! if it had been some years ago you would have needed no one else; but his influence is much reduced, it has gone into Maea's hands, and Maea, I fear, is one of Case's jackals. In fine, if the worst comes to the worst, you must send up or come yourself to Fale-alii, and, though I am not due at this end of the island for a month, I will just see what can be done.'

So Mr Tarleton said farewell; and half an hour later the crew were singing and the paddles flashing in the missionary-boat.

CHAPTER IV

DEVIL-WORK

NEAR a month went by without much doing. The same night of our marriage Galoshes called round, and made himself mighty civil, and got into a habit of dropping in about dark and smoking his pipe with the family. He could talk to Uma, of course, and started to teach me native and French at the same time. He was a kind old buffer, though the dirtiest you would wish to see, and he muddled me up with foreign languages worse than the tower of Babel.

That was one employment we had, and it made me feel less lonesome; but there was no profit in the thing, for though the priest came and sat and yarned, none of his folks could be enticed into my store; and if it hadn't been for the other occupation I struck out, there wouldn't have been a pound of copra in the house. This was the idea: Fa'avao (Uma's mother) had a score of bearing trees. Of course we could get no labour, being all as good as tabooed, and the two women and I turned to and made copra with our own hands. It was copra to make your mouth water when it was done—I never understood how much the natives cheated me till I had made that four hundred pounds of my own hand—and it weighed so light I felt inclined to take and water it myself.

When we were at the job a good many Kanakas used to put in the best of the day looking on, and once that nigger turned up. He stood back with the natives and laughed and did the big don and the funny dog,* till I began to get riled.

'Here, you nigger!' says I.

'I don't address myself to you, Sah,' says the nigger. 'Only speak to gen'le'um.'

'I know,' says I, 'but it happens I was addressing myself to you, Mr Black Jack. And all I want to know is just this: did you see Case's figure-head about a week ago?'

'No, Sah,' says he.

'That's all right, then,' says I; 'for I'll show you the

own brother to it, only black, in the inside of about two minutes.'

And I began to walk towards him, quite slow, and my hands down; only there was trouble in my eye, if anybody took the pains to look.

'You're a low, obstropulous* fellow, Sah,' says he.

'You bet!' says I.

By that time he thought I was about as near as convenient, and lit out so it would have done your heart good to see him travel. And that was all I saw of that precious gang until what I am about to tell you.

It was one of my chief employments these days to go pot-hunting in the woods, which I found (as Case had told me) very rich in game. I have spoken of the cape which shut up the village and my station from the east. A path went about the end of it, and led into the next bay. A strong wind blew here daily, and as the line of the barrier reef stopped at the end of the cape, a heavy surf ran on the shores of the bay. A little cliffy hill cut the valley in two parts, and stood close on the beach; and at high water the sea broke right on the face of it, so that all passage was stopped. Woody mountains hemmed the place all round; the barrier to the east was particularly steep and leafy, the lower parts of it, along the sea, falling in sheer black cliffs streaked with cinnabar;* the upper part lumpy with the tops of the great trees. Some of the trees were bright green, and some red, and the sand of the beach as black as your shoes. Many birds hovered round the bay, some of them snow-white; and the flying-fox (or vampire)* flew there in broad daylight, gnashing its teeth.

For a long while I came as far as this shooting, and went no farther. There was no sign of any path beyond, and the cocoa-palms in the front of the foot of the valley were the last this way. For the whole 'eye' of the island, as natives call the windward end, lay desert. From Falesá round about to Papamalulu, there was neither house, nor man, nor planted fruit-tree; and the reef being mostly absent, and the shores bluff, the sea beat direct among crags, and there was scarce a landing-place.

I should tell you that after I began to go in the woods,

although no one offered to come near my store, I found people willing enough to pass the time of day with me where nobody could see them; and as I had begun to pick up native, and most of them had a word or two of English, I began to hold little odds and ends of conversation, not to much purpose to be sure, but they took off the worst of the feeling, for it's a miserable thing to be made a leper of.

It chanced one day towards the end of the month, that I was sitting in this bay in the edge of the bush, looking east, with a Kanaka. I had given him a fill of tobacco, and we were making out to talk as best we could; indeed, he had more English than most.

I asked him if there was no road going eastward.

'One time one road,' said he. 'Now he dead.'

'Nobody he go there?' I asked.

'No good,' said he. 'Too much devil he stop there.'

'Oho!' says I, 'got-um plenty devil, that bush?'

'Man devil, woman devil; too much devil,' said my friend. 'Stop there all-e-time. Man he go there, no come back.'

I thought if this fellow was so well posted on devils and spoke of them so free, which is not common, I had better fish for a little information about myself and Uma.

'You think me one devil?' I asked.

'No think devil,' said he soothingly. 'Think all-e-same fool.'

'Uma, she devil?' I asked again.

'No, no; no devil. Devil stop bush,' said the young man.

I was looking in front of me across the bay, and I saw the hanging front of the woods pushed suddenly open, and Case, with a gun in his hand, step forth into the sunshine on the black beach. He was got up in light pyjamas, near white, his gun sparkled, he looked mighty conspicuous; and the land-crabs scuttled from all round him to their holes.

'Hullo, my friend!' says I, 'you no talk all-e-same true. Ese he go, he come back.'

'Ese no all-e-same; Ese *Tiapolo*,' says my friend; and, with a 'Good-bye', slunk off among the trees.

I watched Case all round the beach, where the tide was low; and let him pass me on the homeward way to Falesá. He was in deep thought, and the birds seemed to know it, trotting quite near him on the sand, or wheeling and calling in his ears. When he passed me I could see by the working of his lips that he was talking to himself, and what pleased me mightily, he had still my trade mark on his brow. I tell you the plain truth: I had a mind to give him a gunful in his ugly mug, but I thought better of it.

All this time, and all the time I was following home, I kept repeating that native word, which I remembered by 'Polly, put the kettle on and make us all some tea', tea-a-pollo.

'Uma,' says I, when I got back, 'what does *Tiapolo* mean?'

'Devil,' says she.

'I thought *aitu* was the word for that,' I said.

'*Aitu* 'nother kind of devil,' said she; 'stop bush, eat Kanaka. Tiapolo big chief devil, stop home; all-e-same Christian devil.'

'Well then,' said I, 'I'm no farther forward. How can Case be Tiapolo?'

'No all-e-same,' said she. 'Ese belong Tiapolo; Tiapolo too much like; Ese all-e-same his son. Suppose Ese he wish something, Tiapolo he make him.'

'That's mighty convenient for Ese,' says I. 'And what kind of things does he make for him?'

Well, out came a rigmarole of all sorts of stories, many of which (like the dollar he took from Mr Tarlcton's head) were plain enough to me, but others I could make nothing of; and the thing that most surprised the Kanakas was what surprised me least—namely, that he would go in the desert among all the *aitus*. Some of the boldest, however, had accompanied him, and had heard him speak with the dead and give them orders, and, safe in his protection, had returned unscathed. Some said he had a church there, where he worshipped Tiapolo, and Tiapolo appeared to him; others swore that there was no sorcery at all, that he performed his miracles by the power of prayer, and the church was no church, but a prison, in which he had confined a dangerous *aitu*. Namu had been in the bush with him once, and returned glorifying God for these wonders. Altogether, I began to have a glimmer of the man's position, and the means by which he had acquired it, and, though I saw he was a tough nut to crack, I was noways cast down.

'Very well,' said I, 'I'll have a look at Master Case's place of worship myself, and we'll see about the glorifying.'

At this Uma fell in a terrible taking; if I went in the high bush I should never return; none could go there but by the protection of Tiapolo.

'I'll chance it on God's,' said I. 'I'm a good sort of a fellow, Uma, as fellows go, and I guess God'll con me through.'

She was silent for a while. 'I think,' said she, mighty solemn—and then, presently—'Victoreea, he big chief?'

'You bet!' said I.

'He like you too much?' she asked again.

I told her, with a grin, I believed the old lady was rather partial to me.

'All right,' said she. 'Victoreea he big chief, like you too much. No can help you here in Falesá; no can do—too far off. Maea he small chief—stop here. Suppose he like you—make you all right. All-e-same God and Tiapolo. God he big chief—got too much work. Tiapolo he small chief—he like too much make-see, work very hard.'

'I'll have to hand you over to Mr Tarleton,' said I. 'Your theology's out of its bearings, Uma.'

However, we stuck to this business all the evening, and, with the stories she told me of the desert and its dangers, she came near frightening herself into a fit. I don't remember half a quarter of them, of course, for I paid little heed; but two come back to me kind of clear.

About six miles up the coast there is a sheltered cove they call *Fanga-anaana*—'the haven full of caves'. I've seen it from the sea myself, as near as I could get my boys to venture in; and it's a little strip of yellow sand. Black cliffs overhang it, full of the black mouths of caves; great trees overhang the cliffs, and dangle-down lianas;* and in one place, about the middle, a big brook pours over in a cascade. Well, there was a boat going by here, with six young men of Falesá, 'all very pretty', Uma said, which was the loss of them. It blew strong, there was a heavy head sea, and by the time they opened Fanga-anaana, and saw the white cascade and the shady beach, they were all tired and thirsty, and their water had run out. One proposed to land and get a drink, and, being reckless fellows, they were all of the same mind except the youngest. Lotu was his name; he was a very good young gentleman, and very wise; and he held out that they were crazy, telling them the place was given over to spirits and devils and the dead, and there were no living folk nearer than six miles the one way, and maybe twelve the other. But they laughed at his words, and, being five to one, pulled in, beached the boat, and landed. It was a wonderful pleasant place, Lotu said, and the water excellent. They walked round the beach, but could see nowhere any way to mount the cliffs, which made them easier in their mind; and at last they sat down to make a meal on the food they had brought with them. They were scarce set, when there came out of the mouth of one of the black caves six of the most beautiful ladies ever seen: they had flowers in their hair, and the most beautiful breasts, and necklaces of scarlet seeds; and began to jest with these young gentlemen, and the young gentlemen to jest back with them, all but Lotu. As for Lotu, he saw there could be no living woman in such a place, and ran, and flung himself in the bottom of the boat, and covered his face, and prayed. All the time the business lasted Lotu made one clean break of prayer, and that was all he knew of it, until his friends came back, and made him sit up, and they put to sea again out of the bay, which was now quite desert, and no word of the six ladies. But, what frightened Lotu most, not one of the five remembered anything of what had passed, but they were all like drunken men, and sang and laughed in the boat, and skylarked. The wind freshened and came squally, and the sea rose extraordinary high; it was such weather as any man in the islands would have turned his back to and fled home to Falesá; but these five were like crazy folk, and cracked on all sail and drove their boat into the seas. Lotu went to the bailing; none of the others thought to help him, but sang and skylarked and carried on, and spoke singular things beyond a man's comprehension, and laughed out loud when they said them. So the rest of the day Lotu bailed for his life in the bottom of the boat, and was all drenched with sweat and cold sea-water; and none heeded him. Against all expectation, they came safe in a dreadful tempest to Papamalulu, where the palms were singing out, and the cocoanuts flying like cannon-balls about the village green; and the same night the five young gentlemen sickened, and spoke never a reasonable word until they died.

'And do you mean to tell me you can swallow a yarn like that?' I asked.

She told me the thing was well known, and with handsome young men alone it was even common;* but this was the only case where five had been slain the same day and in a company by the love of the women-devils; and it had made a great stir in the island, and she would be crazy if she doubted.

'Well, anyway,' says I, 'you needn't be frightened about me. I've no use for the women-devils. You're all the women I want, and all the devil too, old lady.'

To this she answered there were other sorts, and she had seen one with her own eyes. She had gone one day alone to the next bay, and, perhaps, got too near the margin of the bad place. The boughs of the high bush overshadowed her from the cant of the hill, but she herself was outside on a flat place, very stony and growing full of young mummy-apples four and five feet high. It was a dark day in the rainy season, and now there came squalls that tore off the leaves and sent them flying, and now it was all still as in a house. It was in one of these still times that a whole gang of birds and flying-foxes came pegging out of the bush like creatures frightened. Presently after she heard a rustle nearer hand, and saw, coming out of the margin of the trees, among the mummy-apples, the appearance of a lean grey old boar. It seemed to think as it came, like a person; and all of a sudden, as she looked at it coming, she was aware it was no boar but a thing that was a man with a man's thoughts. At that she ran, and the pig after her, and as the pig ran it holla'd aloud, so that the place rang with it.

'I wish I had been there with my gun,' said I. 'I guess that pig would have holla'd so as to surprise himself.'

But she told me a gun was of no use with the like of these, which were the spirits of the dead.

Well, this kind of talk put in the evening, which was the best of it; but of course it didn't change my notion, and the next day, with my gun and a good knife, I set off upon a voyage of discovery. I made, as near as I could, for the place where I had seen Case come out; for if it was true he had some kind of establishment in the bush I reckoned I should find a path. The beginning of the desert was marked off by a wall, to call it so, for it was more of a long mound of stones. They say it reaches right across the island, but how they know it is another question, for I doubt if anyone has made the journey in a hundred years, the natives sticking chiefly to the sea and their little colonies along the coast, and that part being mortal high and steep and full of cliffs. Up to the west side of the wall, the ground has been cleared, and there are cocoa-palms and mummy-apples and guavas, and lots of sensitive.* Just across, the bush begins outright: high bush at that, trees going up like the masts of ships, and ropes of liana hanging down like a ship's rigging, and nasty orchids growing in the forks like funguses. The ground where there was no underwood looked to be a heap of boulders. I saw many green pigeons which I might have shot, only I was there with a different idea. A number of butterflies flopped up and down along the ground like dead leaves; sometimes I would hear a bird calling, sometimes the wind overhead, and always the sea along the coast.

But the queerness of the place it's more difficult to tell of, unless to one who has been alone in the high bush himself. The brightest kind of a day it is always dim down there. A man can see to the end of nothing; whichever way he looks the wood shuts up, one bough folding with another like the fingers of your hand; and whenever he listens he hears always something new—men talking, children laughing, the strokes of an axe a far way ahead of him, and sometimes a sort of a quick, stealthy scurry near at hand that makes him jump and look to his weapons. It's all very well for him to tell himself that he's alone, bar trees and birds; he can't make out to believe it; whichever way he turns the whole place seems to be alive and looking on. Don't think it was Uma's yarns that put me out; I don't value native talk a fourpenny-piece; it's a thing that's natural in the bush, and that's the end of it.*

As I got near the top of the hill, for the ground of the wood goes up in this place steep as a ladder, the wind began to sound straight on, and the leaves to toss and switch open and let in the sun. This suited me better; it was the same noise all the time, and nothing to startle. Well, I had got to a place where there was an underwood of what they call wild cocoa-nut—mighty pretty with its scarlet fruit—when there came a sound of singing in the wind that I thought I had never heard the like of. It was all very fine to tell myself it was the branches; I knew better. It was all very fine to tell myself it was a bird; I knew never a bird that sang like that. It rose and swelled, and died away and swelled again; and now I thought it was like someone weeping, only prettier; and now I thought it was like harps; and there was one thing I made sure of, it was a sight too sweet to be wholesome in a place like that. You may laugh if you like; but I declare I called to mind the six young ladies that came, with their scarlet necklaces, out of the cave at Fanga-anaana, and wondered if they sang like that. We laugh at the natives and their superstitions; but see how many traders take them up, splendidly educated white men, that have been bookkeepers (some of them) and clerks in the old country. It's my belief a superstition grows up in a place like the different kind of weeds; and as I stood there and listened to that wailing I twittered in my shoes.

You may call me a coward to be frightened; I thought myself brave enough to go on ahead. But I went mighty carefully, with my gun cocked, spying all about me like a hunter, fully expecting to see a handsome young woman sitting somewhere in the bush, and fully determined (if I did) to try her with a charge of duck-shot. And sure enough, I had not gone far when I met with a queer thing. The wind came on the top of the wood in a strong puff, the leaves in front of me burst open, and I saw for a second something hanging in a tree. It was gone in a wink, the puff blowing by and the leaves closing. I tell you the truth: I had made up my mind to see an *aitu*; and if the thing had looked like a pig or a woman, it wouldn't have given me the same turn. The trouble was that it seemed kind of square, and the idea of a square thing that was alive and sang knocked me sick and silly. I must have stood quite a while; and I made pretty certain it was right out of the same tree that the singing came. Then I began to come to myself a bit.

'Well,' says I, 'if this is really so, if this is a place where there are square things that sing, I'm gone up anyway. Let's have my fun for my money.'

But I thought I might as well take the off chance of a prayer being any good; so I plumped on my knees and prayed out loud; and all the time I was praying the strange sounds came out of the tree, and went up and down, and changed, for all the world like music, only you could see it wasn't human—there was nothing there that you could whistle.

As soon as I had made an end in proper style, I laid down my gun, stuck my knife between my teeth, walked right up to that tree, and began to climb. I tell you my heart was like ice. But presently, as I went up, I caught another glimpse of the thing, and that relieved me, for I thought it seemed like a box; and when I had got right up to it I near fell out of the tree with laughing.

A box it was, sure enough, and a candle-box at that, with the brand upon the side of it; and it had banjo strings stretched so as to sound when the wind blew. I believe they call the thing a Tyrolean[3] harp, whatever that may mean.*

'Well, Mr Case,' said I, 'you've frightened me once, but I defy you to frighten me again,' I says, and slipped down the tree, and set out again to find my enemy's head office, which I guessed would not be far away.

The undergrowth was thick in this part; I couldn't see before my nose, and must burst my way through by main force and ply the knife as I went, slicing the cords of the lianas and slashing down whole trees at a blow. I call them trees for the bigness, but in truth they were just big weeds, and sappy to cut through like carrot. From all this crowd and kind of vegetation, I was just thinking to myself, the place might have once been cleared, when I came on my nose over a pile of stones, and saw in a moment it was some kind of a work of man. The Lord knows when it was made or when deserted, for this part of the island has lain undisturbed since long before the whites

[3] Æolian.

came. A few steps beyond I hit into the path I had been always looking for. It was narrow, but well beaten, and I saw that Case had plenty of disciples. It seems, indeed, it was a piece of fashionable boldness to venture up here with the trader, and a young man scarce reckoned himself grown till he had got his breech tattooed, for one thing, and seen Case's devils for another. This is mighty like Kanakas; but, if you look at it another way, it's mighty like white folks too.

A bit along the path I was brought to a clear stand, and had to rub my eyes. There was a wall in front of me, the path passing it by a gap; it was tumbledown and plainly very old, but built of big stones very well laid; and there is no native alive today upon that island that could dream of such a piece of building. Along all the top of it was a line of queer figures, idols or scarecrows, or what not. They had carved and painted faces ugly to view, their eyes and teeth were of shell, their hair and their bright clothes blew in the wind, and some of them worked with the tugging. There are islands up west where they make these kind of figures till today; but if ever they were made in this island, the practice and the very recollection of it are now long forgotten. And the singular thing was that all these bogies were as fresh as toys out of a shop.

Then it came in my mind that Case had let out to me the first day that he was a good forger of island curiosities, a thing by which so many traders turn an honest penny. And with that I saw the whole business, and how this display served the man a double purpose: first of all, to season his curiosities, and then to frighten those that came to visit him.

But I should tell you (what made the thing more curious) that all the time the Tyrolean harps were harping round me in the trees, and even while I looked, a green-and-yellow bird (that, I suppose, was building) began to tear the hair off the head of one of the figures.

A little farther on I found the best curiosity of the museum. The first I saw of it was a longish mound of earth with a twist to it. Digging off the earth with my hands, I found underneath tarpaulin stretched on boards, so that this was plainly the roof of a cellar. It stood right on the top of the hill, and the entrance was on the far side, between two rocks, like the entrance to a cave. I went as far in as the bend, and, looking round the corner, saw a shining face. It was big and ugly, like a pantomime mask, and the brightness of it waxed and dwindled, and at times it smoked.

'Oho!' says I, 'luminous paint!'*

And I must say I rather admired the man's ingenuity. With a box of tools and a few mighty simple contrivances he had made out to have a devil of a temple. Any poor Kanaka brought up here in the dark, with the harps whining all round him, and shown that smoking face in the bottom of a hole, would make no kind of doubt but he had seen and heard enough devils for a lifetime. It's easy to find out what Kanakas think. Just go back to yourself any way round from ten to fifteen years old, and there's an average Kanaka. There are some pious, just as there are pious boys; and the most of them, like the boys again, are middling honest and yet think it rather larks to steal, and are easy scared and rather like to be so. I remember a boy I was at school with at home who played the Case business. He didn't know anything, that boy; he couldn't do anything; he had no luminous paint and no Tyrolean harps; he just boldly said he was a sorcerer, and frightened us out of our boots, and we loved it. And then it came in my mind how the master had once flogged that boy, and the surprise we were all in to see the sorcerer catch it and bum* like anybody else. Thinks I to myself, 'I must find some way of fixing it so for Master Case.' And the next moment I had my idea.

I went back by the path, which, when once you had found it, was quite plain and easy walking; and when I stepped out on the black sands, who should I see but Master Case himself. I cocked my gun and held it handy, and we marched up and passed without a word, each keeping the tail of his eye on the other; and no sooner had we passed than we each wheeled round like fellows drilling, and stood face to face. We had each taken the same notion in his head, you see, that the other fellow might give him the load of his gun in the stern.

'You've shot nothing,' says Case.

'I'm not on the shoot today,' said I.

'Well, the devil go with you for me,' says he.

'The same to you,' says I.

But we stuck just the way we were; no fear of either of us moving.

Case laughed. 'We can't stop here all day, though,' said he.

'Don't let me detain you,' says I.

He laughed again. 'Look here, Wiltshire, do you think me a fool?' he asked.

'More of a knave, if you want to know,' says I.

'Well, do you think it would better me to shoot you here, on this open beach?' said he. 'Because I don't. Folks come fishing every day. There may be a score of them up the valley now, making copra; there might be half a dozen on the hill behind you, after pigeons; they might be watching us this minute, and I shouldn't wonder. I give you my word I don't want to shoot you. Why should I? You don't hinder me any. You haven't got one pound of copra but what you made with your own hands, like a negro slave. You're vegetating—that's what I call it—and I don't care where you vegetate, nor yet how long. Give me your word you don't mean to shoot me, and I'll give you a lead and walk away.'

'Well,' said I, 'you're frank and pleasant, ain't you? And I'll be the same. I don't mean to shoot you today. Why should I? This business is beginning; it ain't done yet, Mr Case. I've given you one turn already; I can see the marks of my knuckles on your head to this blooming hour, and I've more cooking for you. I'm not a paralee, like Underhill. My name ain't Adams, and it ain't Vigours; and I mean to show you that you've met your match.'

'This is a silly way to talk,' said he. 'This is not the talk to make me move on with.'

'All right,' said I; 'stay where you are. I ain't in any hurry, and you know it. I can put in a day on this beach and never mind. I ain't got any copra to bother with. I ain't got any luminous paint to see to.'

I was sorry I said that last, but it whipped out before I knew. I could see it took the wind out of his sails, and he stood and stared at me with his brow drawn up. Then I suppose he made up his mind he must get to the bottom of this.

'I take you at your word,' says he, and turned his back, and walked right into the devil's bush.

I let him go, of course, for I had passed my word. But I watched him as long as he was in sight, and after he was gone lit out for cover as lively as you would want to see, and went the rest of the way home under the bush, for I didn't trust him sixpence-worth. One thing I saw, I had been ass enough to give him warning, and that which I meant to do I must do at once.

You would think I had had about enough excitement for one morning, but there was another turn waiting me. As soon as I got far enough round the cape to see my house I made out there were strangers there; a little farther, and no doubt about it. There was a couple of armed sentinels squatting at my door. I could only suppose the trouble about Uma must have come to a head, and the station been seized. For aught I could think, Uma was taken up already, and these armed men were waiting to do the like with me.

However, as I came nearer, which I did at top speed, I saw there was a third native sitting on the verandah like a guest, and Uma was talking with him like a hostess. Nearer still I made out it was the big young chief, Maea, and that he was smiling away and smoking. And what was he smoking? None of your European cigarettes fit for a cat, not even the genuine big, knock-me-down native article that a fellow can really put in the time with if his pipe is broke—but a cigar, and one of my Mexicans at that, that I could swear to. At sight of this my heart started beating, and I took a wild hope in my head that the trouble was over, and Maea had come round.

Uma pointed me out to him as I came up, and he met me at the head of my own stairs like a thorough gentleman.

'Vilivili,' said he, which was the best they could make of my name, 'I pleased.'

There is no doubt when an island chief wants to be civil he can do it. I saw the way things were from the word go. There was no call for Uma to say to me: 'He no 'fraid Ese now, come bring copra.' I tell you I shook hands with that Kanaka like as if he was the best white man in Europe.

The fact was, Case and he had got after the same girl; or Maea suspected it, and concluded to make hay of the trader on the chance. He had dressed himself up, got a couple of his retainers cleaned and armed to kind of make the thing more public, and, just waiting till Case was clear of the village, came round to put the whole of his business my way. He was rich as well as powerful. I suppose that man was worth fifty thousand nuts per annum. I gave him the price of the beach and a quarter cent better, and as for credit, I would have advanced him the inside of the store and the fittings besides, I was so pleased to see him. I must say he bought like a gentleman: rice and tins and biscuits enough for a week's feast, and stuffs by the bolt. He was agreeable besides; he had plenty fun to him; and we cracked jests together, mostly through the interpreter,* because he had mighty little English, and my native was still off colour. One thing I made out: he could never really have thought much harm of Uma; he could never have been really frightened, and must just have made believe from dodginess, and because he thought Case had a strong pull in the village and could help him on.

This set me thinking that both he and I were in a tightish place. What he had done was to fly in the face of the whole village, and the thing might cost him his authority. More than that, after my talk with Case on the beach, I thought it might very well cost me my life. Case had as good as said he would pot me if ever I got any copra; he would come home to find the best business in the village had changed hands; and the best thing I thought I could do was to get in first with the potting.

'See here, Uma,' says I, 'tell him I'm sorry I made him wait, but I was up looking at Case's Tiapolo store in the bush.'

'He want savvy if you no 'fraid?' translated Uma.

I laughed out. 'Not much!' says I. 'Tell him the place is a blooming toy-shop! Tell him in England we give these things to the kids to play with.'

'He want savvy if you hear devil sing?' she asked next.

'Look here,' I said, 'I can't do it now because I've got no banjo-strings in stock; but the next time the ship comes round I'll have one of these same contraptions right here in my verandah, and he can see for himself how much devil there is to it. Tell him, as soon as I can get the strings I'll make one for his picaninnies. The name of the concern is a Tyrolean harp; and you can tell him the name means in English that nobody but dam-fools give a cent for it.'

This time he was so pleased he had to try his English again. 'You talk true?' says he.

'Rather!' said I. 'Talk all-e-same Bible. Bring out a Bible here, Uma, if you've got such a thing, and I'll kiss it. Or, I'll tell you what's better still,' says I, taking a header,* 'ask him if he's afraid to go up there himself by day.'

It appeared he wasn't; he could venture as far as that by day and in company.

'That's the ticket, then!' said I. 'Tell him the man's a fraud and the place foolishness, and if he'll go up there tomorrow he'll see all that's left of it. But tell him this, Uma, and mind he understands it: If he gets talking, it's bound to come to Case, and I'm a dead man! I'm playing his game, tell him, and if he says one word my blood will be at his door and be the damnation of him here and after.'

She told him, and he shook hands with me up to the hilt, and, says he: 'No talk. Go up tomollow. You my friend?'

'No, sir,' says I, 'no such foolishness. I've come here to trade, tell him, and not to make friends. But, as to Case, I'll send that man to glory!'

So off Maea went, pretty well pleased, as I could see.

CHAPTER V

NIGHT IN THE BUSH

WELL, I was committed now; Tiapolo had to be smashed up before next day, and my hands were pretty full, not only with preparations, but with argument. My house was like a mechanics' debating society:* Uma was so made up that I shouldn't go into the bush by night, or that, if I did, I was never to come back again. You know her style of arguing: you've had a specimen about Queen Victoria and the devil; and I leave you to fancy if I was tired of it before dark.

At last I had a good idea. What was the use of casting my pearls before her? I thought; some of her own chopped hay would be likelier to do the business.

'I'll tell you what, then,' said I. 'You fish out your Bible, and I'll take that up along with me. That'll make me right.'

She swore a Bible was no use.

'That's just your Kanaka ignorance,'* said I. 'Bring the Bible out.'

She brought it, and I turned to the title-page, where I thought there would likely be some English, and so there was. 'There!' said I. 'Look at that! "*London: Printed for the British and Foreign Bible Society, Blackfriars*",* and the date, which I can't read, owing to its being in these X's. There's no devil in hell can look near the Bible Society, Blackfriars. Why, you silly!' I said, 'how do you suppose we get along with our own *aitus* at home? All Bible Society!'

'I think you no got any,' said she. 'White man, he tell me you no got.'

'Sounds likely, don't it?' I asked. 'Why would these islands all be chock full of them and none in Europe?'

'Well, you no got breadfruit,' said she.

I could have torn my hair. 'Now, look here, old lady,' said I, 'you dry up, for I'm tired of you. I'll take the Bible, which 'll put me as straight as the mail, and that's the last word I've got to say.'

The night fell extraordinary dark, clouds coming up with sundown and overspreading all; not a star showed; there was only an end of a moon, and that not due before the small hours. Round the village, what with the lights and the fires in the open houses, and the torches of many fishers moving on the reef, it kept as gay as an illumination; but the sea and the mountains and woods were all clean gone. I suppose it might be eight o'clock when I took the road, laden like a donkey. First there was that Bible, a book as big as your head, which I had let myself in for by my own tomfoolery. Then there was my gun, and knife, and lantern, and patent matches, all necessary. And then there was the real plant of the affair in hand, a mortal weight of gunpowder, a pair of dynamite fishing-bombs, and two or three pieces of slow match that I had hauled out of the tin cases and spliced together the best way I could; for the match was only trade stuff, and a man would be crazy that trusted it. Altogether, you see, I had the materials of a pretty good blow-up! Expense was nothing to me; I wanted that thing done right.

As long as I was in the open, and had the lamp in my house to steer by, I did well. But when I got to the path, it fell so dark I could make no headway, walking into trees and swearing there, like a man looking for the matches in his bedroom. I knew it was risky to light up, for my lantern would be visible all the way to the point of the cape, and as no one went there after dark, it would be talked about, and come to Case's ears. But what was I to do? I had either to give the business over and lose caste with Maea, or light up, take my chance, and get through the thing the smartest I was able.

As long as I was on the path I walked hard, but when I came to the black beach I had to run. For the tide was now nearly flowed; and to get through with my powder dry between the surf and the steep hill, took all the quickness I possessed. As it was, even, the wash caught me to the knees, and I came near falling on a stone. All this time the hurry I was in, and the free air and smell of the sea, kept my spirits lively; but when I was once in the bush and began to climb the path I took it easier. The fearsomeness of the wood had been a good bit rubbed off for me by Master Case's banjo-strings and graven images, yet I thought it was a dreary walk, and guessed, when the disciples went up there, they must be badly scared. The light of the lantern, striking among all these trunks and forked branches and twisted rope-ends of lianas, made the whole place, or all that you could see of it, a kind of a puzzle of turning shadows. They came to meet you, solid and quick like giants, and then span off and vanished; they hove up over your head like clubs, and flew away into the night like birds. The floor of the bush glimmered with dead wood, the way the matchbox used to shine after you had struck a lucifer.* Big, cold drops fell on me from the branches overhead like sweat. There was no wind to mention; only a little icy breath of a land-breeze that stirred nothing; and the harps were silent.

The first landfall I made was when I got through the bush of wild cocoanuts, and came in view of the bogies on the wall. Mighty queer they looked by the shining of the lantern, with their painted faces and shell eyes, and their clothes and their hair hanging. One after another I pulled them all up and piled them in a bundle on the cellar roof, so as they might go to glory with the rest. Then I chose a place behind one of the big stones at the entrance, buried my powder and the two shells, and arranged my match along the passage. And then I had a look at the smoking head, just for good-bye. It was doing fine.

'Cheer up,' says I. 'You're booked.'

It was my first idea to light up and be getting homeward; for the darkness and the glimmer of the dead wood and the shadows of the lantern made me lonely. But I knew where one of the harps hung; it seemed a pity it shouldn't go with the rest; and at the same time I couldn't help letting on to myself that I was mortal tired of my employment, and would like best to be at home and have the door shut. I stepped out of the cellar and argued it fore and back. There was a sound of the sea far down below me on the coast; nearer hand not a leaf stirred; I might have been the only living creature this side of Cape Horn. Well, as I stood there thinking, it seemed the bush woke and became full of little noises. Little noises they were, and nothing to hurt—a bit of a crackle, a bit of a rush—but the breath jumped right out of me and my throat went as dry as a biscuit. It wasn't Case I was afraid of, which would have been common sense; I never thought of Case; what took me, as sharp as the colic, was the old wives' tales, the devil-women and the man-pigs. It was the toss of a penny whether I should run: but I got a purchase on myself, and stepped out, and held up the lantern (like a fool) and looked all round.

In the direction of the village and the path there was nothing to be seen; but when I turned inland it's a wonder to me I didn't drop. There, coming right up out of the desert and the bad bush—there, sure enough, was a devil-woman, just as the way I had figured she would look. I saw the light shine on her bare arms and her bright eyes, and there went out of me a yell so big that I thought it was my death.

'Ah! No sing out!' says the devil-woman, in a kind of a high whisper. 'Why you talk big voice? Put out light! Ese he come.'

'My God Almighty, Uma, is that you?' says I.

'*Ioe*,'[4] says she. 'I come quick. Ese here soon.'

'You come alone?' I asked. 'You no 'fraid?'

'Ah, too much 'fraid!' she whispered, clutching me. 'I think die.'

'Well,' says I, with a kind of a weak grin, 'I'm not the one to laugh at you, Mrs Wiltshire, for I'm about the worst scared man in the South Pacific myself.'

She told me in two words what brought her. I was scarce gone, it seems, when Fa'avao came in, and the old woman had met Black Jack running as hard as he was fit from our house to Case's. Uma neither spoke nor stopped, but lit right out to come and warn me. She was so close at my heels that the lantern was her guide across the beach, and afterwards, by the glimmer of it in the trees, she got her line up hill. It was only when I had got to the top or was in the cellar that she wandered Lord knows where! and lost a sight of precious time, afraid to call out lest Case was at the heels of her, and falling in the bush, so that she was all knocked and bruised. That must have been when she got too far to the southward, and how she came to take me in the flank at last and frighten me beyond what I've got the words to tell of.

[4] Yes.

Well, anything was better than a devil-woman, but I thought her yarn serious enough. Black Jack had no call to be about my house, unless he was set there to watch; and it looked to me as if my tomfool word about the paint, and perhaps some chatter of Maea's, had got us all in a clove hitch.* One thing was clear: Uma and I were here for the night; we daren't try to go home before day, and even then it would be safer to strike round up the mountain and come in by the back of the village, or we might walk into an ambuscade. It was plain, too, that the mine should be sprung immediately, or Case might be in time to stop it.

I marched into the tunnel, Uma keeping tight hold of me, opened my lantern and lit the match. The first length of it burned like a spill of paper, and I stood stupid, watching it burn, and thinking we were going aloft with Tiapolo, which was none of my views. The second took to a better rate, though faster than I cared about; and at that I got my wits again, hauled Uma clear of the passage, blew out and dropped the lantern, and the pair of us groped our way into the bush until I thought it might be safe, and lay down together by a tree.

'Old lady,' I said, 'I won't forget this night. You're a trump, and that's what's wrong with you.'

She humped herself close up to me. She had run out the way she was, with nothing on her but her kilt; and she was all wet with the dews and the sea on the black beach, and shook straight on with cold and the terror of the dark and the devils.

'Too much 'fraid,' was all she said.

The far side of Case's hill goes down near as steep as a precipice into the next valley. We were on the very edge of it, and I could see the dead wood shine* and hear the sea sound far below. I didn't care about the position, which left me no retreat, but I was afraid to change. Then I saw I had made a worse mistake about the lantern, which I should have left lighted, so that I could have had a crack at Case when he stepped into the shine of it. And even if I hadn't had the wit to do that, it seemed a senseless thing to leave the good lantern to blow up with the graven images. The thing belonged to me, after all, and was worth money, and might come in handy. If I could have trusted the match, I might have run in still and rescued it. But who was going to trust the match? You know what trade is. The stuff was good enough for Kanakas to go fishing with, where they've got to look lively anyway, and the most they risk is only to have their hand blown off. But for anyone that wanted to fool around a blow-up like mine that match was rubbish.

Altogether the best I could do was to lie still, see my shot-gun handy, and wait for the explosion. But it was a solemn kind of a business. The blackness of the night was like solid; the only thing you could see was the nasty bogy glimmer of the dead wood, and that showed you nothing but itself; and as for sounds, I stretched my ears till I thought I could have heard the match burn in the tunnel, and that bush was as silent as a coffin. Now and then there was a bit of a crack; but whether it was near or far, whether it was Case stubbing his toes within a few yards of me, or a tree breaking miles away, I knew no more than the babe unborn.

And then, all of a sudden, Vesuvius went off. It was a long time coming; but when it came (though I say it that shouldn't) no man could ask to see a better. At first it was just a son of a gun of a row, and a spout of fire, and the wood lighted up so that you could see to read. And then the trouble began. Uma and I were half buried under a wagonful of earth, and glad it was no worse, for one of the rocks at the entrance of the tunnel was fired clean into the air, fell within a couple of fathoms of where we lay, and bounded over the edge of the hill, and went pounding down into the next valley. I saw I had rather undercalculated our distance, or overdone the dynamite and powder, which you please.

And presently I saw I had made another slip. The noise of the thing began to die off, shaking the island; the dazzle was over; and yet the night didn't come back the way I expected. For the whole wood was scattered with red coals and brands from the explosion; they were all round me on the flat; some had fallen below in the valley, and some stuck and flared in the tree-tops. I had no fear of fire, for these forests are too wet to kindle. But the trouble was that the place was all lit up—not very bright, but good enough to get a shot by; and the way the coals were scattered, it was just as likely Case might have the advantage as myself. I looked all round for his white face, you may be sure; but there was not a sign of him. As for Uma, the life seemed to have been knocked right out of her by the bang and blaze of it.

There was one bad point in my game. One of the blessed graven images had come down all afire, hair and clothes and body, not four yards away from me. I cast a mighty noticing glance all round; there was still no Case, and I made up my mind I must get rid of that burning stick before he came, or I should be shot there like a dog.

It was my first idea to have crawled, and then I thought speed was the main thing, and stood half up to make a rush. The same moment from somewhere between me and the sea there came a flash and a report, and a rifle bullet screeched in my ear. I swung straight round and up with my gun, but the brute had a Winchester,* and before I could as much as see him his second shot knocked me over like a ninepin. I seemed to fly in the air, then came down by the run and lay half a minute, silly; and then I found my hands empty, and my gun had flown over my head as I fell. It makes a man mighty wide awake to be in the kind of box that I was in. I scarcely knew where I was hurt, or whether I was hurt or not, but turned right over on my face to crawl after my weapon. Unless you have tried to get about with a smashed leg you don't know what pain is, and I let out a howl like a bullock's.

This was the unluckiest noise that ever I made in my life. Up to then Uma had stuck to her tree like a sensible woman, knowing she would be only in the way; but as soon as she heard me sing out, she ran forward. The Winchester cracked again, and down she went.

I had sat up, leg and all, to stop her; but when I saw her tumble I clapped down again where I was, lay still, and felt the handle of my knife. I had been scurried and put out before. No more of that for me. He had knocked over my girl, I had got to fix him for it; and I lay there and gritted my teeth, and footed up the chances. My leg was broke, my gun was gone. Case had still ten shots in his Winchester. It looked a kind of hopeless business. But I never despaired nor thought upon despairing: that man had got to go.

For a goodish bit not one of us let on. Then I heard Case

begin to move nearer in the bush, but mighty careful. The image had burned out; there were only a few coals left here and there, and the wood was main dark, but had a kind of a low glow in it like a fire on its last legs. It was by this that I made out Case's head looking at me over a big tuft of ferns, and at the same time the brute saw me and shouldered his Winchester. I lay quite still, and as good as looked into the barrel: it was my last chance, but I thought my heart would have come right out of its bearings. Then he fired. Lucky for me it was no shot-gun, for the bullet struck within an inch of me and knocked the dirt in my eyes.

Just you try and see if you can lie quiet, and let a man take a sitting shot at you and miss you by a hair. But I did, and lucky too. A while Case stood with the Winchester at the port-arms;* then he gave a little laugh to himself, and stepped round the ferns.

'Laugh!' thought I. 'If you had the wit of a louse you would be praying!'

I was all as taut as a ship's hawser* or the spring of a watch, and as soon as he came within reach of me I had him by the ankle, plucked the feet right out from under him, laid him out, and was upon the top of him, broken leg and all, before he breathed. His Winchester had gone the same road as my shot-gun; it was nothing to me—I defied him now. I'm a pretty strong man anyway, but I never knew what strength was till I got hold of Case. He was knocked out of time by the rattle he came down with, and threw up his hands together, more like a frightened woman, so that I caught both of them with my left. This wakened him up, and he fastened his teeth in my forearm like a weasel. Much I cared. My leg gave me all the pain I had any use for, and I drew my knife and got it in the place.

'Now,' said I, 'I've got you; and you're gone up, and a good job too! Do you feel the point of that? That's for Underhill! And there's for Adams! And now here's for Uma, and that's going to knock your blooming soul right out of you!'

With that I gave him the cold steel for all I was worth. His body kicked under me like a spring sofa; he gave a dreadful kind of a long moan, and lay still.

'I wonder if you're dead? I hope so!' I thought, for my head was swimming. But I wasn't going to take chances; I had his own example too close before me for that; and I tried to draw the knife out to give it him again. The blood came over my hands, I remember, hot as tea; and with that I fainted clean away, and fell with my head on the man's mouth.

When I came to myself it was pitch dark; the cinders had burned out; there was nothing to be seen but the shine of the dead wood, and I couldn't remember where I was nor why I was in such pain nor what I was all wetted with. Then it came back, and the first thing I attended to was to give him the knife again a half-a-dozen times up to the handle. I believe he was dead already, but it did him no harm and did me good.

'I bet you're dead now,' I said, and then I called to Uma.

Nothing answered, and I made a move to go and grope for her, fouled my broken leg, and fainted again.

When I came to myself the second time the clouds had all cleared away, except a few that sailed there, white as cotton. The moon was up—a tropic moon. The moon at home turns a wood black, but even this old butt-end of a one showed up that forest as green as by day. The night birds—or, rather, they're a kind of early morning bird—sang out with their long, falling notes like nightingales. And I could see the dead man, that I was still half resting on, looking right up into the sky with his open eyes, no paler than when he was alive; and a little way off Uma tumbled on her side. I got over to her the best way I was able, and when I got there she was broad awake, and crying and sobbing to herself with no more noise than an insect. It appears she was afraid to cry out loud, because of the *aitus.* Altogether she was not much hurt, but scared beyond belief; she had come to her senses a long while ago, cried out to me, heard nothing in reply, made out we were both dead, and had lain there ever since, afraid to budge a finger. The ball had ploughed up her shoulder, and she had lost a main quantity of blood; but I soon had that tied up the way it ought to be with the tail of my shirt and a scarf I had on, got her head on my sound knee and my back against a trunk, and settled down to wait for morning. Uma was for neither use nor ornament, and could only clutch hold of me and shake and cry. I don't suppose there was ever anybody worse scared, and, to do her justice, she had had a lively night of it. As for me, I was in a good bit of pain and fever, but not so bad when I sat still; and every time I looked over to Case I could have sung and whistled. Talk about meat and drink! To see that man lying there dead as a herring filled me full.

The night birds stopped after a while; and then the light began to change, the east came orange, the whole wood began to whirr with singing like a musical box, and there was the broad day.

I didn't expect Maea for a long while yet; and, indeed, I thought there was an off-chance he might go back on the whole idea and not come at all. I was the better pleased when, about an hour after daylight, I heard sticks smashing and a lot of Kanakas laughing and singing out to keep their courage up. Uma sat up quite brisk at the first word of it; and presently we saw a party come stringing out of the path, Maea in front, and behind him a white man in a pith helmet. It was Mr Tarleton, who had turned up late last night in Falesá, having left his boat and walked the last stage with a lantern.

They buried Case upon the field of glory, right in the hole where he had kept the smoking head. I waited till the thing was done; and Mr Tarleton prayed, which I thought tomfoolery, but I'm bound to say he gave a pretty sick view of the dear departed's prospects, and seemed to have his own ideas of hell. I had it out with him afterwards, told him he had scamped his duty, and what he had ought to have done was to up like a man and tell the Kanakas plainly Case was damned, and a good riddance; but I never could get him to see it my way. Then they made me a litter of poles and carried me down to the station. Mr Tarleton set my leg, and made a regular missionary splice of it, so that I limp to this day. That done, he took down my evidence, and Uma's, and Maea's, wrote it all out fine, and had us sign it; and then he got the chiefs and marched over to Papa Randall's to seize Case's papers.

All they found was a bit of a diary, kept for a good many years, and all about the price of copra, and chickens being stolen, and that; and the books of the business and the will I told you of in the beginning, by both of which the whole thing (stock, lock, and barrel) appeared to belong to the Samoa woman. It was I that bought her out at a mighty reasonable figure, for she was in a hurry to get home. As for Randall and the black, they had to tramp; got into some kind of a station on the Papa-malulu side; did very bad business, for the truth is neither of the pair was fit for it, and lived mostly on fish, which was the means of Randall's death. It seems there was a nice shoal in one day, and papa went after them with the dynamite; either the match burned too fast, or papa was full, or both, but the shell went off (in the usual way) before he threw it, and where was papa's hand? Well, there's nothing to hurt in that; the islands up north are all full of one-handed men, like the parties in the 'Arabian Nights';* but either Randall was too old, or he drank too much, and the short and the long of it was that he died. Pretty soon after, the nigger was turned out of the island for stealing from white men, and went off to the west, where he found men of his own colour, in case he liked that, and the men of his own colour took and ate him at some kind of a corroborree,* and I'm sure I hope he was to their fancy!

So there was I, left alone in my glory at Falesá; and when the schooner came round I filled her up, and gave her a deck-cargo half as high as the house. I must say Mr Tarleton did the right thing by us; but he took a meanish kind of a revenge.

'Now, Mr Wiltshire,' said he, 'I've put you all square with everybody here. It wasn't difficult to do, Case being gone; but I have done it, and given my pledge besides that you will deal fairly with the natives. I must ask you to keep my word.'

Well, so I did. I used to be bothered about my balances, but I reasoned it out this way: We all have queerish balances, and the natives all know it, and water their copra in a proportion so that it's fair all round; but the truth is, it did use to bother me, and, though I did well in Falesá, I was half glad when the firm moved me on to another station, where I was under no kind of a pledge and could look my balances in the face.

As for the old lady, you know her as well as I do. She's only the one fault. If you don't keep your eye lifting she would give away the roof off the station. Well, it seems it's natural in Kanakas. She's turned a powerful big woman now, and could throw a London bobby over her shoulder. But that's natural in Kanakas too, and there's no manner of doubt that she's an A 1 wife.

Mr Tarleton's gone home, his trick being over.* He was the best missionary I ever struck, and now, it seems, he's parsonizing down Somerset way. Well, that's best for him; he'll have no Kanakas there to get luny over.

My public-house? Not a bit of it, nor ever likely. I'm stuck here, I fancy. I don't like to leave the kids, you see: and—there's no use talking—they're better here than what they would be in a white man's country, though Ben took the eldest up to Auckland, where he's being schooled with the best. But what bothers me is the girls. They're only half-castes, of course; I know that as well as you do, and there's nobody thinks less of half-castes than I do; but they're mine, and about all I've got. I can't reconcile my mind to their taking up with Kanakas, and I'd like to know where I'm to find the whites?*

Note—Any student of that very unliterary product, the English drama of the early part of the century, will here recognize the name and the root idea of a piece once rendered popular by the redoubtable O. Smith.* The root idea is there and identical, and yet I hope I have made it a new thing. And the fact that the tale has been designed and written for a Polynesian audience* may lend it some extraneous interest nearer home.—R.L.S.

THE BOTTLE IMP

THERE was a man of the Island of Hawaii,* whom I shall call Keawe; for the truth is, he still lives, and his name must be kept secret; but the place of his birth was not far from Honaunau, where the bones of Keawe the Great lie hidden in a cave.* This man was poor, brave, and active; he could read and write like a schoolmaster; he was a first-rate mariner besides, sailed for some time in the island steamers, and steered a whaleboat on the Hamakua coast.* At length it came in Keawe's mind to have a sight of the great world and foreign cities, and he shipped on a vessel bound to San Francisco.

This is a fine town, with a fine harbour, and rich people uncountable; and, in particular, there is one hill which is covered with palaces.* Upon this hill Keawe was one day taking a walk with his pocket full of money, viewing the great houses upon either hand with pleasure. 'What fine houses these are!' he was thinking, 'and how happy must those people be who dwell in them, and take no care for the morrow!' The thought was in his mind when he came abreast of a house that was smaller than some others, but all finished and beautified like a toy; the steps of that house shone like silver, and the borders of the garden bloomed like garlands, and the windows were bright like diamonds; and Keawe stopped and wondered at the excellence of all he saw. So stopping, he was aware of a man that looked forth upon him through a window so clear that Keawe could see him as you see a fish in a pool upon the reef. The man was elderly, with a bald head and a black beard; and his face was heavy with sorrow, and he bitterly sighed. And the truth of it is, that as Keawe looked in upon the man, and the man looked out upon Keawe, each envied the other.

All of a sudden, the man smiled and nodded, and beckoned Keawe to enter, and met him at the door of the house.

'This is a fine house of mine,' said the man, and bitterly sighed. 'Would you not care to view the chambers?'

So he led Keawe all over it, from the cellar to the roof, and there was nothing there that was not perfect of its kind, and Keawe was astonished.

'Truly,' said Keawe, 'this is a beautiful house; if I lived in the like of it, I should be laughing all day long. How comes it, then, that you should be sighing?'

'There is no reason,' said the man, 'why you should not have a house in all points similar to this, and finer, if you wish. You have some money, I suppose?'

'I have fifty dollars,' said Keawe; 'but a house like this will cost more than fifty dollars.'

The man made a computation. 'I am sorry you have no more,' said he, 'for it may raise you trouble in the future; but it shall be yours at fifty dollars.'

'The house?' asked Keawe.

'No, not the house,' replied the man; 'but the bottle. For, I must tell you, although I appear to you so rich and fortunate, all my fortune, and this house itself and its garden, came out of a bottle not much bigger than a pint. This is it.'

And he opened a lockfast place, and took out a round-bellied bottle with a long neck; the glass of it was white like milk, with changing rainbow colours in the grain. Withinsides something obscurely moved, like a shadow and a fire.

'This is the bottle,' said the man; and, when Keawe laughed, 'You do not believe me?' he added. 'Try, then, for yourself. See if you can break it.'

So Keawe took the bottle up and dashed it on the floor till he was weary; but it jumped on the floor like a child's ball, and was not injured.

'This is a strange thing,' said Keawe. 'For by the touch of it, as well as by the look, the bottle should be of glass.'

'Of glass it is,' replied the man, sighing more heavily than ever; 'but the glass of it was tempered in the flames of hell. An imp lives in it, and that is the shadow we behold there moving: or so I suppose. If any man buy this bottle the imp is at his command; all that he desires—love, fame, money, houses like this house, ay, or a city like this city—all are his at the word uttered. Napoleon had this bottle, and by it he grew to be the king of the world; but he sold it at the last, and fell. Captain

Cook had this bottle, and by it he found his way to so many islands; but he, too, sold it, and was slain upon Hawaii.* For, once it is sold, the power goes and the protection; and unless a man remain content with what he has, ill will befall him.'

'And yet you talk of selling it yourself?' Keawe said.

'I have all I wish, and I am growing elderly,' replied the man. 'There is one thing the imp cannot do—he cannot prolong life; and, it would not be fair to conceal from you, there is a drawback to the bottle; for if a man die before he sells it, he must burn in hell forever.'

'To be sure, that is a drawback and no mistake,' cried Keawe. 'I would not meddle with the thing. I can do without a house, thank God; but there is one thing I could not be doing with one particle, and that is to be damned.'

'Dear me, you must not run away with things,' returned the man. 'All you have to do is to use the power of the imp in moderation, and then sell it to someone else, as I do to you, and finish your life in comfort.'

'Well, I observe two things,' said Keawe. 'All the time you keep sighing like a maid in love, that is one; and, for the other, you sell this bottle very cheap.'

'I have told you already why I sigh,' said the man. 'It is because I fear my health is breaking up; and, as you said yourself, to die and go to the devil is a pity for anyone. As for why I sell so cheap, I must explain to you there is a peculiarity about the bottle. Long ago, when the devil brought it first upon earth, it was extremely expensive, and was sold first of all to Prester John* for many millions of dollars; but it cannot be sold at all, unless sold at a loss. If you sell it for as much as you paid for it, back it comes to you again like a homing pigeon. It follows that the price has kept falling in these centuries, and the bottle is now remarkably cheap. I bought it myself from one of my great neighbours on this hill, and the price I paid was only ninety dollars. I could sell it for as high as eighty-nine dollars and ninety-nine cents, but not a penny dearer, or back the thing must come to me. Now, about this there are two bothers. First, when you offer a bottle so singular for eighty odd dollars, people suppose you to be jesting. And second—but there is no hurry about that—and I need not go into it. Only remember it must be coined money that you sell it for.'

'How am I to know that this is all true?' asked Keawe.

'Some of it you can try at once,' replied the man. 'Give me your fifty dollars, take the bottle, and wish your fifty dollars back into your pocket. If that does not happen, I pledge you my honour I will cry off the bargain and restore your money.'

'You are not deceiving me?' said Keawe.

The man bound himself with a great oath.

'Well, I will risk that much,' said Keawe, 'for that can do no harm.' And he paid over his money to the man, and the man handed him the bottle.

'Imp of the bottle,' said Keawe, 'I want my fifty dollars back.' And sure enough he had scarce said the word before his pocket was as heavy as ever.

'To be sure this is a wonderful bottle,' said Keawe.

'And now good-morning to you, my fine fellow, and the devil go with you for me!' said the man.

'Hold on,' said Keawe, 'I don't want any more of this fun. Here, take your bottle back.'

'You have bought it for less than I paid for it,' replied the man, rubbing his hands. 'It is yours now; and, for my part, I am only concerned to see the back of you.' And with that he rang for his Chinese servant, and had Keawe shown out of the house.

Now, when Keawe was in the street, with the bottle under his arm, he began to think. 'If all is true about this bottle, I may have made a losing bargain,' thinks he. 'But perhaps the man was only fooling me.' The first thing he did was to count his money; the sum was exact—forty-nine dollars American money, and one Chili piece.* 'That looks like the truth,' said Keawe. 'Now I will try another part.'

The streets in that part of the city were as clean as a ship's decks, and though it was noon, there were no passengers. Keawe set the bottle in the gutter and walked away. Twice he looked back, and there was the milky, round-bellied bottle where he left it. A third time he looked back, and turned a corner; but he had scarce done so, when something knocked upon his elbow, and behold! it was the long neck sticking up;

and as for the round belly, it was jammed into the pocket of his pilot-coat.

'And that looks like the truth,' said Keawe.

The next thing he did was to buy a corkscrew in a shop, and go apart into a secret place in the fields. And there he tried to draw the cork, but as often as he put the screw in, out it came again, and the cork as whole as ever.

'This is some new sort of cork,' said Keawe, and all at once he began to shake and sweat, for he was afraid of that bottle.

On his way back to the port-side, he saw a shop where a man sold shells and clubs from the wild islands, old heathen deities, old coined money, pictures from China and Japan, and all manner of things that sailors bring in their sea-chests. And here he had an idea. So he went in and offered the bottle for a hundred dollars. The man of the shop laughed at him at the first, and offered him five; but, indeed, it was a curious bottle—such glass was never blown in any human glassworks, so prettily the colours shone under the milky white, and so strangely the shadow hovered in the midst; so, after he had disputed awhile after the manner of his kind, the shop-man gave Keawe sixty silver dollars for the thing, and set it on a shelf in the midst of his window.

'Now,' said Keawe, 'I have sold that for sixty which I bought for fifty—or, to say truth, a little less, because one of my dollars was from Chili. Now I shall know the truth upon another point.'

So he went back on board his ship, and, when he opened his chest, there was the bottle, and had come more quickly than himself. Now Keawe had a mate on board whose name was Lopaka.

'What ails you?' said Lopaka, 'that you stare in your chest?'

They were alone in the ship's forecastle, and Keawe bound him to secrecy, and told all.

'This is a very strange affair,' said Lopaka; 'and I fear you will be in trouble about this bottle. But there is one point very clear—that you are sure of the trouble, and you had better have the profit in the bargain. Make up your mind what you want with it; give the order, and if it is done as you desire, I will buy the bottle myself; for I have an idea of my own to get a schooner, and go trading through the islands.'

'That is not my idea,' said Keawe; 'but to have a beautiful house and garden on the Kona Coast,* where I was born, the sun shining in at the door, flowers in the garden, glass in the windows, pictures on the walls, and toys and fine carpets on the tables, for all the world like the house I was in this day—only a storey higher, and with balconies all about like the King's palace; and to live there without care and make merry with my friends and relatives.'

'Well,' said Lopaka, 'let us carry it back with us to Hawaii; and if all comes true, as you suppose, I will buy the bottle, as I said, and ask a schooner.'

Upon that they were agreed, and it was not long before the ship returned to Honolulu, carrying Keawe and Lopaka, and the bottle. They were scarce come ashore when they met a friend upon the beach, who began at once to condole with Keawe.

'I do not know what I am to be condoled about,' said Keawe.

'Is it possible you have not heard,' said the friend, 'your uncle—that good old man—is dead, and your cousin—that beautiful boy—was drowned at sea?'

Keawe was filled with sorrow, and, beginning to weep and to lament, he forgot about the bottle. But Lopaka was thinking to himself, and presently, when Keawe's grief was a little abated, 'I have been thinking,' said Lopaka. 'Had not your uncle lands in Hawaii, in the district of Kaü?'*

'No,' said Keawe, 'not in Kaü; they are on the mountain side—a little way south of Hookena.'*

'These lands will now be yours?' asked Lopaka.

'And so they will,' says Keawe, and began again to lament for his relatives.

'No,' said Lopaka, 'do not lament at present. I have a thought in my mind. How if this should be the doing of the bottle? For here is the place ready for your house.'

'If this be so,' cried Keawe, 'it is a very ill way to serve me by killing my relatives. But it may be, indeed; for it was in just such a station that I saw the house with my mind's eye.'

'The house, however, is not yet built,' said Lopaka.

'No, nor like to be!' said Keawe; 'for though my uncle has some coffee and ava* and bananas, it will not be more than will keep me in comfort; and the rest of that land is the black lava.'

'Let us go to the lawyer,' said Lopaka; 'I have still this idea in my mind.'

Now, when they came to the lawyer's, it appeared Keawe's uncle had grown monstrous rich in the last days, and there was a fund of money.

'And here is the money for the house!' cried Lopaka.

'If you are thinking of a new house,' said the lawyer, 'here is the card of a new architect, of whom they tell me great things.'

'Better and better!' cried Lopaka. 'Here is all made plain for us. Let us continue to obey orders.'

So they went to the architect, and he had drawings of houses on his table.

'You want something out of the way,' said the architect. 'How do you like this?' and he handed a drawing to Keawe.

Now, when Keawe set eyes on the drawing, he cried out aloud, for it was the picture of his thought exactly drawn.

'I am in for this house,' thought he. 'Little as I like the way it comes to me, I am in for it now, and I may as well take the good along with the evil.'

So he told the architect all that he wished, and how he would have that house furnished, and about the pictures on the wall and the knick-knacks on the tables; and he asked the man plainly for how much he would undertake the whole affair.

The architect put many questions, and took his pen and made a computation; and when he had done he named the very sum that Keawe had inherited.

Lopaka and Keawe looked at one another and nodded.

'It is quite clear,' thought Keawe, 'that I am to have this house, whether or no. It comes from the devil, and I fear I will get little good by that; and of one thing I am sure, I will make no more wishes as long as I have this bottle. But with the house I am saddled, and I may as well take the good along with the evil.'

So he made his terms with the architect, and they signed a

paper; and Keawe and Lopaka took ship again and sailed to Australia; for it was concluded between them they should not interfere at all, but leave the architect and the bottle imp to build and to adorn that house at their own pleasure.

The voyage was a good voyage, only all the time Keawe was holding in his breath, for he had sworn he would utter no more wishes, and take no more favours from the devil. The time was up when they got back. The architect told them that the house was ready, and Keawe and Lopaka took a passage in the *Hall*,* and went down Kona way to view the house, and see if all had been done fitly according to the thought that was in Keawe's mind.

Now, the house stood on the mountain side, visible to ships. Above, the forest ran up into the clouds of rain; below, the black lava fell in cliffs, where the kings of old lay buried.* A garden bloomed about that house with every hue of flowers; and there was an orchard of papaia on the one hand and an orchard of breadfruit on the other, and right in front, toward the sea, a ship's mast had been rigged up and bore a flag. As for the house, it was three storeys high, with great chambers and broad balconies on each. The windows were of glass, so excellent that it was as clear as water and as bright as day. All manner of furniture adorned the chambers. Pictures hung upon the wall in golden frames: pictures of ships, and men fighting, and of the most beautiful women, and of singular places; nowhere in the world are there pictures of so bright a colour as those Keawe found hanging in his house. As for the knick-knacks, they were extraordinary fine; chiming clocks and musical boxes, little men with nodding heads, books filled with pictures, weapons of price from all quarters of the world, and the most elegant puzzles to entertain the leisure of a solitary man. And as no one would care to live in such chambers, only to walk through and view them, the balconies were made so broad that a whole town might have lived upon them in delight; and Keawe knew not which to prefer, whether the back porch, where you got the land breeze, and looked upon the orchards and the flowers, or the front balcony, where you could drink the wind of the sea, and look down the steep wall of the mountain and see the *Hall* going by once a week or so between Hookena and the hills of Pele, or the schooners plying up the coast for wood and ava and bananas.

When they had viewed all, Keawe and Lopaka sat on the porch.

'Well,' asked Lopaka, 'is it all as you designed?'

'Words cannot utter it,' said Keawe. 'It is better than I dreamed, and I am sick with satisfaction.'

'There is but one thing to consider,' said Lopaka; 'all this may be quite natural, and the bottle imp have nothing whatever to say to it. If I were to buy the bottle, and got no schooner after all, I should have put my hand in the fire for nothing. I gave you my word, I know; but yet I think you would not grudge me one more proof.'

'I have sworn I would take no more favours,' said Keawe. 'I have gone already deep enough.'

'This is no favour I am thinking of,' replied Lopaka. 'It is only to see the imp himself. There is nothing to be gained by that, and so nothing to be ashamed of; and yet, if I once saw him, I should be sure of the whole matter. So indulge me so far, and let me see the imp; and, after that, here is the money in my hand, and I will buy it.'

'There is only one thing I am afraid of,' said Keawe. 'The imp may be very ugly to view; and if you once set eyes upon him you might be very undesirous of the bottle.'

'I am a man of my word,' said Lopaka. 'And here is the money betwixt us.'

'Very well,' replied Keawe. 'I have a curiosity myself. So come, let us have one look at you, Mr Imp.'

Now as soon as that was said, the imp looked out of the bottle, and in again, swift as a lizard; and there sat Keawe and Lopaka turned to stone. The night had quite come, before either found a thought to say or voice to say it with; and then Lopaka pushed the money over and took the bottle.

'I am a man of my word,' said he, 'and had need to be so, or I would not touch this bottle with my foot. Well, I shall get my schooner and a dollar or two for my pocket; and then I will be rid of this devil as fast as I can. For to tell you the plain truth, the look of him has cast me down.'

'Lopaka,' said Keawe, 'do not you think any worse of me than you can help; I know it is night, and the roads bad, and the pass by the tombs an ill place to go by so late, but I declare since I have seen that little face, I cannot eat or sleep or pray till it is gone from me. I will give you a lantern, and a basket to put the bottle in, and any picture or fine thing in all my house that takes your fancy;—and be gone at once, and go sleep at Hookena with Nahinu.'*

'Keawe,' said Lopaka, 'many a man would take this ill; above all, when I am doing you a turn so friendly, as to keep my word and buy the bottle; and for that matter, the night and the dark, and the way by the tombs, must be all tenfold more dangerous to a man with such a sin upon his conscience, and such a bottle under his arm. But for my part, I am so extremely terrified myself, I have not the heart to blame you. Here I go then; and I pray God you may be happy in your house, and I fortunate with my schooner, and both get to heaven in the end in spite of the devil and his bottle.'

So Lopaka went down the mountain; and Keawe stood in his front balcony, and listened to the clink of the horse's shoes, and watched the lantern go shining down the path, and along the cliff of caves where the old dead are buried; and all the time he trembled and clasped his hands, and prayed for his friend, and gave glory to God that he himself was escaped out of that trouble.

But the next day came very brightly, and that new house of his was so delightful to behold that he forgot his terrors. One day followed another, and Keawe dwelt there in perpetual joy. He had his place on the back porch; it was there he ate and lived, and read the stories in the Honolulu newspapers; but when anyone came by they would go in and view the chambers and the pictures. And the fame of the house went far and wide; it was called *Ka-Hale Nui*—the Great House*—in all Kona; and sometimes the Bright House, for Keawe kept a Chinaman, who was all day dusting and furbishing; and the glass, and the gilt, and the fine stuffs, and the pictures, shone as bright as the morning. As for Keawe himself, he could not walk in the chambers without singing, his heart was so enlarged; and when ships sailed by upon the sea, he would fly his colours on the mast.

So time went by, until one day Keawe went upon a visit as far as Kailua* to certain of his friends. There he was well feasted; and left as soon as he could the next morning, and rode hard, for he was impatient to behold his beautiful house; and, besides, the night then coming on was the night in which the dead of old days go abroad in the sides of Kona;* and having already meddled with the devil, he was the more chary of meeting with the dead. A little beyond Honaunau, looking far ahead, he was aware of a woman bathing in the edge of the sea; and she seemed a well-grown girl, but he thought no more of it. Then he saw her white shift flutter as she put it on, and then her red holoku;* and by the time he came abreast of her she was done with her toilet, and had come up from the sea, and stood by the track-side in her red holoku, and she was all freshened with the bath, and her eyes shone and were kind. Now Keawe no sooner beheld her than he drew rein.

'I thought I knew everyone in this country,' said he. 'How comes it that I do not know you?'

'I am Kokua,* daughter of Kiano,' said the girl, 'and I have just returned from Oahu.* Who are you?'

'I will tell you who I am in a little,' said Keawe, dismounting from his horse, 'but not now. For I have a thought in my mind, and if you knew who I was, you might have heard of me, and would not give me a true answer. But tell me, first of all, one thing: Are you married?'

At this Kokua laughed out aloud. 'It is you who ask questions,' she said. 'Are you married yourself?'

'Indeed, Kokua, I am not,' replied Keawe, 'and never thought to be until this hour. But here is the plain truth. I have met you here at the roadside, and I saw your eyes, which are like the stars, and my heart went to you as swift as a bird. And so now, if you want none of me, say so, and I will go on to my own place; but if you think me no worse than any other young man, say so, too, and I will turn aside to your father's for the night, and tomorrow I will talk with the good man.'

Kokua said never a word, but she looked at the sea and laughed.

'Kokua,' said Keawe, 'if you say nothing, I will take that for the good answer; so let us be stepping to your father's door.'

She went on ahead of him, still without speech; only

sometimes she glanced back and glanced away again, and she kept the strings of her hat in her mouth.

Now, when they had come to the door, Kiano came out on his verandah, and cried out and welcomed Keawe by name. At that the girl looked over, for the fame of the great house had come to her ears; and, to be sure, it was a great temptation. All that evening they were very merry together; and the girl was as bold as brass under the eyes of her parents, and made a mock of Keawe, for she had a quick wit. The next day he had a word with Kiano, and found the girl alone.

'Kokua,' said he, 'you made a mock of me all the evening; and it is still time to bid me go. I would not tell you who I was, because I have so fine a house, and I feared you would think too much of that house and too little of the man that loves you. Now you know all, and if you wish to have seen the last of me, say so at once.'

'No,' said Kokua; but this time she did not laugh, nor did Keawe ask for more.

This was the wooing of Keawe; things had gone quickly; but so an arrow goes, and the ball of a rifle swifter still, and yet both may strike the target. Things had gone fast, but they had gone far also, and the thought of Keawe rang in the maiden's head; she heard his voice in the breach of the surf upon the lava, and for this young man that she had seen but twice she would have left father and mother and her native islands. As for Keawe himself, his horse flew up the path of the mountain under the cliff of tombs, and the sound of the hoofs, and the sound of Keawe singing to himself for pleasure, echoed in the caverns of the dead. He came to the Bright House, and still he was singing. He sat and ate in the broad balcony, and the Chinaman wondered at his master, to hear how he sang between the mouthfuls. The sun went down into the sea, and the night came; and Keawe walked the balconies by lamp-light, high on the mountains, and the voice of his singing startled men on ships.

'Here am I now upon my high place,' he said to himself. 'Life may be no better; this is the mountain top; and all shelves about me toward the worse. For the first time I will light up the chambers, and bathe in my fine bath with the hot water and the cold, and sleep alone in the bed of my bridal chamber.'

So the Chinaman had word, and he must rise from sleep and light the furnaces; and as he wrought below, beside the boilers, he heard his master singing and rejoicing above him in the lighted chambers. When the water began to be hot the Chinaman cried to his master; and Keawe went into the bathroom; and the Chinaman heard him sing as he filled the marble basin; and heard him sing, and the singing broken, as he undressed; until of a sudden, the song ceased. The Chinaman listened, and listened; he called up the house to Keawe to ask if all were well, and Keawe answered him 'Yes,' and bade him go to bed; but there was no more singing in the Bright House; and all night long, the Chinaman heard his master's feet go round and round the balconies without repose.

Now the truth of it was this: as Keawe undressed for his bath, he spied upon his flesh a patch like a patch of lichen on a rock, and it was then that he stopped singing. For he knew the likeness of that patch, and knew that he was fallen in the Chinese Evil.[1]

Now, it is a sad thing for any man to fall into this sickness. And it would be a sad thing for anyone to leave a house so beautiful and so commodious, and depart from all his friends to the north coast of Molokai between the mighty cliff and the sea-breakers.* But what was that to the case of the man Keawe, he who had met his love but yesterday, and won her but that morning, and now saw all his hopes break, in a moment, like a piece of glass?

Awhile he sat upon the edge of the bath; then sprang, with a cry, and ran outside; and to and fro, to and fro, along the balcony, like one despairing.

'Very willingly could I leave Hawaii, the home of my fathers,' Keawe was thinking. 'Very lightly could I leave my house, the high-placed, the many-windowed, here upon the mountains. Very bravely could I go to Molokai, to Kalaupapa* by the cliffs, to live with the smitten and to sleep there, far

[1] Leprosy.

from my fathers. But what wrong have I done, what sin lies upon my soul, that I should have encountered Kokua coming cool from the sea-water in the evening? Kokua, the soul ensnarer! Kokua, the light of my life! Her may I never wed, her may I look upon no longer, her may I no more handle with my loving hand; and it is for this, it is for you, O Kokua! that I pour my lamentations!'

Now you are to observe what sort of a man Keawe was, for he might have dwelt there in the Bright House for years, and no one been the wiser of his sickness; but he reckoned nothing of that, if he must lose Kokua. And again, he might have wed Kokua even as he was; and so many would have done, because they have the souls of pigs; but Keawe loved the maid manfully, and he would do her no hurt and bring her in no danger.

A little beyond the midst of the night, there came in his mind the recollection of that bottle. He went round to the back porch, and called to memory the day when the devil had looked forth; and at the thought ice ran in his veins.

'A dreadful thing is the bottle,' thought Keawe, 'and dreadful is the imp, and it is a dreadful thing to risk the flames of hell. But what other hope have I to cure my sickness or to wed Kokua? What!' he thought, 'would I beard the devil once, only to get me a house, and not face him again to win Kokua?'

Thereupon he called to mind it was the next day the *Hall* went by on her return to Honolulu. 'There must I go first,' he thought, 'and see Lopaka. For the best hope that I have now is to find that same bottle I was so pleased to be rid of.'

Never a wink could he sleep; the food stuck in his throat; but he sent a letter to Kiano, and about the time when the steamer would be coming, rode down beside the cliff of the tombs. It rained; his horse went heavily; he looked up at the black mouths of the caves, and he envied the dead that slept there and were done with trouble; and called to mind how he had galloped by the day before, and was astonished. So he came down to Hookena, and there was all the country gathered for the steamer as usual. In the shed before the store they sat and jested and passed the news; but there was no matter of speech in Keawe's bosom, and he sat in their midst and looked without on the rain falling on the houses, and the surf beating among the rocks, and the sighs arose in his throat.

'Keawe of the Bright House is out of spirits,' said one to another. Indeed, and so he was, and little wonder.

Then the *Hall* came, and the whaleboat carried him on board. The after-part of the ship was full of Haoles[2] who had been to visit the volcano, as their custom is; and the midst was crowded with Kanakas,* and the fore-part with wild bulls from Hilo* and horses from Kaü; but Keawe sat apart from all in his sorrow, and watched for the house of Kiano. There it sat, low upon the shore in the black rocks, and shaded by the cocoa palms, and there by the door was a red holoku, no greater than a fly, and going to and fro with a fly's busyness. 'Ah, queen of my heart,' he cried, 'I'll venture my dear soul to win you!'

Soon after, darkness fell, and the cabins were lit up, and the Haoles sat and played at the cards and drank whiskey as their custom is; but Keawe walked the deck all night; and all the next day, as they steamed under the lee of Maui* or of Molokai, he was still pacing to and fro like a wild animal in a menagerie.

Towards evening they passed Diamond Head,* and came to the pier of Honolulu. Keawe stepped out among the crowd and began to ask for Lopaka. It seemed he had become the owner of a schooner—none better in the islands—and was gone upon an adventure as far as Pola-Pola or Kahiki;* so there was no help to be looked for from Lopaka. Keawe called to mind a friend of his, a lawyer in the town (I must not tell his name), and inquired of him. They said he was grown suddenly rich, and had a fine new house upon Waikiki* shore; and this put a thought in Keawe's head, and he called a hack and drove to the lawyer's house.

The house was all brand new, and the trees in the garden no greater than walking-sticks, and the lawyer, when he came, had the air of a man well pleased.

'What can I do to serve you?' said the lawyer.

[2] Whites.

'You are a friend of Lopaka's,' replied Keawe, 'and Lopaka purchased from me a certain piece of goods that I thought you might enable me to trace.'

The lawyer's face became very dark. 'I do not profess to misunderstand you, Mr Keawe,' said he, 'though this is an ugly business to be stirring in. You may be sure I know nothing, but yet I have a guess, and if you would apply in a certain quarter I think you might have news.'

And he named the name of a man, which, again, I had better not repeat. So it was for days, and Keawe went from one to another, finding everywhere new clothes and carriages, and fine new houses and men everywhere in great contentment, although, to be sure, when he hinted at his business their faces would cloud over.

'No doubt I am upon the track,' thought Keawe. 'These new clothes and carriages are all the gifts of the little imp, and these glad faces are the faces of men who have taken their profit and got rid of the accursed thing in safety. When I see pale cheeks and hear sighing, I shall know that I am near the bottle.'

So it befell at last that he was recommended to a Haole in Beritania Street.* When he came to the door, about the hour of the evening meal, there were the usual marks of the new house, and the young garden, and the electric light shining in the windows; but when the owner came, a shock of hope and fear ran through Keawe; for here was a young man, white as a corpse, and black about the eyes, the hair shedding from his head, and such a look in his countenance as a man may have when he is waiting for the gallows.

'Here it is, to be sure,' thought Keawe, and so with this man he noways veiled his errand. 'I am come to buy the bottle,' said he.

At the word, the young Haole of Beritania Street reeled against the wall.

'The bottle!' he gasped. 'To buy the bottle!' Then he seemed to choke, and seizing Keawe by the arm carried him into a room and poured out wine in two glasses.

'Here is my respects,' said Keawe, who had been much

about with Haoles in his time. 'Yes,' he added, 'I am come to buy the bottle. What is the price by now?'

At that word the young man let his glass slip through his fingers, and looked upon Keawe like a ghost.

'The price,' says he; 'the price! You do not know the price?'

'It is for that I am asking you,' returned Keawe. 'But why are you so much concerned? Is there anything wrong about the price?'

'It has dropped a great deal in value since your time, Mr Keawe,' said the young man, stammering.

'Well, well, I shall have the less to pay for it,' says Keawe. 'How much did it cost you?'

The young man was as white as a sheet. 'Two cents,' said he.

'What?' cried Keawe, 'two cents? Why, then, you can only sell it for one. And he who buys it—' The words died upon Keawe's tongue; he who bought it could never sell it again, the bottle and the bottle imp must abide with him until he died, and when he died must carry him to the red end of hell.

The young man of Beritania Street fell upon his knees. 'For God's sake buy it!' he cried. 'You can have all my fortune in the bargain. I was mad when I bought it at that price. I had embezzled money at my store; I was lost else; I must have gone to jail.'

'Poor creature,' said Keawe, 'you would risk your soul upon so desperate an adventure, and to avoid the proper punishment of your own disgrace; and you think I could hesitate with love in front of me. Give me the bottle, and the change which I make sure you have all ready. Here is a five-cent piece.'

It was as Keawe supposed; the young man had the change ready in a drawer; the bottle changed hands, and Keawe's fingers were no sooner clasped upon the stalk than he had breathed his wish to be a clean man. And, sure enough, when he got home to his room, and stripped himself before a glass, his flesh was whole like an infant's. And here was the strange thing: he had no sooner seen this miracle, than his mind was changed within him, and he cared naught for the Chinese Evil, and little enough for Kokua; and had but the one thought, that here he was bound to the bottle imp for time and for eternity, and had no better hope but to be a cinder for ever in the flames of hell. Away ahead of him he saw them blaze with his mind's eye, and his soul shrank, and darkness fell upon the light.

When Keawe came to himself a little, he was aware it was the night when the band played at the hotel. Thither he went, because he feared to be alone; and there, among happy faces, walked to and fro, and heard the tunes go up and down, and saw Berger beat the measure,* and all the while he heard the flames crackle, and saw the red fire burning in the bottomless pit. Of a sudden the band played *Hiki-ao-ao*; that was a song that he had sung with Kokua, and at the strain courage returned to him.

'It is done now,' he thought, 'and once more let me take the good along with the evil.'

So it befell that he returned to Hawaii by the first steamer, and as soon as it could be managed he was wedded to Kokua, and carried her up the mountain side to the Bright House.

Now it was so with these two, that when they were together, Keawe's heart was stilled; but so soon as he was alone he fell into a brooding horror, and heard the flames crackle, and saw the red fire burn in the bottomless pit. The girl, indeed, had come to him wholly; her heart leapt in her side at sight of him, her hand clung to his; and she was so fashioned from the hair upon her head to the nails upon her toes that none could see her without joy. She was pleasant in her nature. She had the good word always. Full of song she was, and went to and fro in the Bright House, the brightest thing in its three storeys, carolling like the birds. And Keawe beheld and heard her with delight, and then must shrink upon one side, and weep and groan to think upon the price that he had paid for her; and then he must dry his eyes, and wash his face, and go and sit with her on the broad balconies, joining in her songs, and, with a sick spirit, answering her smiles.

There came a day when her feet began to be heavy and her songs more rare; and now it was not Keawe only that would weep apart, but each would sunder from the other and sit in opposite balconies with the whole width of the Bright House betwixt. Keawe was so sunk in his despair, he scarce observed the change, and was only glad he had more hours to sit alone and brood upon his destiny, and was not so frequently condemned to pull a smiling face on a sick heart. But one day, coming softly through the house, he heard the sound of a child sobbing, and there was Kokua rolling her face upon the balcony floor, and weeping like the lost.

'You do well to weep in this house, Kokua,' he said. 'And yet I would give the head off my body that you (at least) might have been happy.'

'Happy!' she cried. 'Keawe, when you lived alone in your Bright House, you were the word of the island for a happy man; laughter and song were in your mouth, and your face was as bright as the sunrise. Then you wedded poor Kokua; and the good God knows what is amiss in her—but from that day you have not smiled. Oh!' she cried, 'what ails me? I thought I was pretty, and I knew I loved him. What ails me that I throw this cloud upon my husband?'

'Poor Kokua,' said Keawe. He sat down by her side, and sought to take her hand; but that she plucked away. 'Poor Kokua,' he said, again. 'My poor child—my pretty. And I had thought all this while to spare you! Well, you shall know all. Then, at least, you will pity poor Keawe; then you will understand how much he loved you in the past—that he dared hell for your possession—and how much he loves you still (the poor condemned one), that he can yet call up a smile when he beholds you.'

With that, he told her all, even from the beginning.

'You have done this for me?' she cried. 'Ah, well, then what do I care!'—and she clasped and wept upon him.

'Ah, child!' said Keawe, 'and yet, when I consider of the fire of hell, I care a good deal!'

'Never tell me,' said she; 'no man can be lost because he loved Kokua, and no other fault. I tell you, Keawe, I shall save you with these hands, or perish in your company. What! you loved me, and gave your soul, and you think I will not die to save you in return?'

'Ah, my dear! you might die a hundred times, and what

difference would that make?' he cried, 'except to leave me lonely till the time comes of my damnation?'

'You know nothing,' said she. 'I was educated in a school in Honolulu; I am no common girl. And I tell you, I shall save my lover. What is this you say about a cent? But all the world is not American.* In England they have a piece they call a farthing, which is about half a cent. Ah! sorrow!' she cried, 'that makes it scarcely better, for the buyer must be lost, and we shall find none so brave as my Keawe! But, then, there is France; they have a small coin there which they call a centime, and these go five to the cent or thereabout. We could not do better. Come, Keawe, let us go to the French islands; let us go to Tahiti, as fast as ships can bear us. There we have four centimes, three centimes, two centimes, one centime; four possible sales to come and go on; and two of us to push the bargain. Come, my Keawe! kiss me, and banish care. Kokua will defend you.'

'Gift of God!' he cried. 'I cannot think that God will punish me for desiring aught so good! Be it as you will, then; take me where you please: I put my life and my salvation in your hands.'

Early the next day Kokua was about her preparations. She took Keawe's chest that he went with sailoring; and first she put the bottle in a corner; and then packed it with the richest of their clothes and the bravest of the knick-knacks in the house. 'For,' said she, 'we must seem to be rich folks, or who will believe in the bottle?' All the time of her preparation she was as gay as a bird; only when she looked upon Keawe, the tears would spring in her eye, and she must run and kiss him. As for Keawe, a weight was off his soul; now that he had his secret shared, and some hope in front of him, he seemed like a new man, his feet went lightly on the earth, and his breath was good to him again. Yet was terror still at his elbow; and ever and again, as the wind blows out a taper, hope died in him, and he saw the flames toss and the red fire burn in hell.

It was given out in the country they were gone pleasuring to the States, which was thought a strange thing, and yet not so strange as the truth, if any could have guessed it. So they went to Honolulu in the *Hall*, and thence in the *Umatilla** to San

Francisco with a crowd of Haoles, and at San Francisco took their passage by the mail brigantine, the *Tropic Bird*,* for Papeete,* the chief place of the French in the south islands. Thither they came, after a pleasant voyage, on a fair day of the Trade Wind,* and saw the reef with the surf breaking, and Motuiti* with its palms, and the schooner riding within-side, and the white houses of the town low down along the shore among green trees, and overhead the mountains and the clouds of Tahiti, the wise island.

It was judged the most wise to hire a house, which they did accordingly, opposite the British Consul's,* to make a great parade of money, and themselves conspicuous with carriages and horses. This it was very easy to do, so long as they had the bottle in their possession; for Kokua was more bold than Keawe, and, whenever she had a mind, called on the imp for twenty or a hundred dollars. At this rate they soon grew to be remarked in the town; and the strangers from Hawaii, their riding and their driving, the fine holokus and the rich lace of Kokua, became the matter of much talk.

They got on well after the first with the Tahitian language, which is indeed like to the Hawaiian, with a change of certain letters;* and as soon as they had any freedom of speech, began to push the bottle. You are to consider it was not an easy subject to introduce; it was not easy to persuade people you were in earnest, when you offered to sell them for four centimes the spring of health and riches inexhaustible. It was necessary besides to explain the dangers of the bottle; and either people disbelieved the whole thing and laughed, or they thought the more of the darker part, became overcast with gravity, and drew away from Keawe and Kokua, as from persons who had dealings with the devil. So far from gaining ground, these two began to find they were avoided in the town; the children ran away from them screaming, a thing intolerable to Kokua; Catholics crossed themselves as they went by; and all persons began with one accord to disengage themselves from their advances.

Depression fell upon their spirits. They would sit at night in their new house, after a day's weariness, and not exchange one word, or the silence would be broken by Kokua bursting suddenly into sobs. Sometimes they would pray together; sometimes they would have the bottle out upon the floor, and sit all evening watching how the shadow hovered in the midst. At such times they would be afraid to go to rest. It was long ere slumber came to them, and, if either dozed off, it would be to wake and find the other silently weeping in the dark, or, perhaps, to wake alone, the other having fled from the house and the neighbourhood of that bottle, to pace under the bananas in the little garden, or to wander on the beach by moonlight.

One night it was so when Kokua awoke. Keawe was gone. She felt in the bed and his place was cold. Then fear fell upon her, and she sat up in bed. A little moonshine filtered through the shutters. The room was bright, and she could spy the bottle on the floor. Outside it blew high, the great trees of the avenue cried aloud, and the fallen leaves rattled in the verandah. In the midst of this Kokua was aware of another sound; whether of a beast or of a man she could scarce tell, but it was as sad as death, and cut her to the soul. Softly she arose, set the door ajar, and looked forth into the moonlit yard. There, under the bananas, lay Keawe, his mouth in the dust, and as he lay he moaned.

It was Kokua's first thought to run forward and console him; her second potently withheld her. Keawe had borne himself before his wife like a brave man; it became her little in the hour of weakness to intrude upon his shame. With the thought she drew back into the house.

'Heaven!' she thought, 'how careless have I been—how weak! It is he, not I, that stands in this eternal peril; it was he, not I, that took the curse upon his soul. It is for my sake, and for the love of a creature of so little worth and such poor help, that he now beholds so close to him the flames of hell—ay, and smells the smoke of it, lying without there in the wind and moonlight. Am I so dull of spirit that never till now I have surmised my duty, or have I seen it before and turned aside? But now, at least, I take up my soul in both the hands of my affection; now I say farewell to the white steps of heaven and the waiting faces of my friends. A love for a love, and let mine be equalled with Keawe's! A soul for a soul, and be it mine to perish!'

She was a deft woman with her hands, and was soon apparelled. She took in her hands the change—the precious centimes they kept ever at their side; for this coin is little used, and they had made provision at a Government office. When she was forth in the avenue clouds came on the wind, and the moon was blackened. The town slept, and she knew not whither to turn till she heard one coughing in the shadow of the trees.

'Old man,' said Kokua, 'what do you here abroad in the cold night?'

The old man could scarce express himself for coughing, but she made out that he was old and poor, and a stranger in the island.

'Will you do me a service?' said Kokua. 'As one stranger to another, and as an old man to a young woman, will you help a daughter of Hawaii?'

'Ah,' said the old man. 'So you are the witch from the eight islands,* and even my old soul you seek to entangle. But I have heard of you, and defy your wickedness.'

'Sit down here,' said Kokua, 'and let me tell you a tale.' And she told him the story of Keawe from the beginning to the end.

'And now,' said she, 'I am his wife, whom he bought with his soul's welfare. And what should I do? If I went to him myself and offered to buy it, he would refuse. But if you go, he will sell it eagerly; I will await you here; you will buy it for four centimes, and I will buy it again for three. And the Lord strengthen a poor girl!'

'If you meant falsely,' said the old man, 'I think God would strike you dead.'

'He would!' cried Kokua. 'Be sure he would. I could not be so treacherous—God would not suffer it.'

'Give me the four centimes and await me here,' said the old man.

Now, when Kokua stood alone in the street, her spirit died. The wind roared in the trees, and it seemed to her the rushing of the flames of hell; the shadows tossed in the light of the street lamp, and they seemed to her the snatching hands of evil ones. If she had had the strength, she must have run away, and if she had had the breath she must have screamed aloud;

but, in truth, she could do neither, and stood and trembled in the avenue, like an affrighted child.

Then she saw the old man returning, and he had the bottle in his hand.

'I have done your bidding,' said he. 'I left your husband weeping like a child; tonight he will sleep easy.' And he held the bottle forth.

'Before you give it me,' Kokua panted, 'take the good with the evil—ask to be delivered from your cough.'

'I am an old man,' replied the other, 'and too near the gate of the grave to take a favour from the devil. But what is this? Why do you not take the bottle? Do you hesitate?'

'Not hesitate!' cried Kokua. 'I am only weak. Give me a moment. It is my hand resists, my flesh shrinks back from the accursed thing. One moment only!'

The old man looked upon Kokua kindly. 'Poor child!' said he, 'you fear; your soul misgives you. Well, let me keep it. I am old, and can never more be happy in this world, and as for the next—'

'Give it me!' gasped Kokua. 'There is your money. Do you think I am so base as that? Give me the bottle.'

'God bless you, child,' said the old man.

Kokua concealed the bottle under her holoku, said farewell to the old man, and walked off along the avenue, she cared not whither. For all roads were now the same to her, and led equally to hell. Sometimes she walked, and sometimes ran; sometimes she screamed out loud in the night, and sometimes lay by the wayside in the dust and wept. All that she had heard of hell came back to her; she saw the flames blaze, and she smelt the smoke, and her flesh withered on the coals.

Near day she came to her mind again, and returned to the house. It was even as the old man said—Keawe slumbered like a child. Kokua stood and gazed upon his face.

'Now, my husband,' said she, 'it is your turn to sleep. When you wake it will be your turn to sing and laugh. But for poor Kokua, alas! that meant no evil—for poor Kokua no more sleep, no more singing, no more delight, whether in earth or heaven.'

With that she lay down in the bed by his side, and her

misery was so extreme that she fell in a deep slumber instantly.

Late in the morning her husband woke her and gave her the good news. It seemed he was silly with delight, for he paid no heed to her distress, ill though she dissembled it. The words stuck in her mouth, it mattered not; Keawe did the speaking. She ate not a bite, but who was to observe it? for Keawe cleared the dish. Kokua saw and heard him, like some strange thing in a dream; there were times when she forgot or doubted, and put her hands to her brow; to know herself doomed and hear her husband babble, seemed so monstrous.

All the while Keawe was eating and talking, and planning the time of their return, and thanking her for saving him, and fondling her, and calling her the true helper after all.* He laughed at the old man that was fool enough to buy that bottle.

'A worthy old man he seemed,' Keawe said. 'But no one can judge by appearances. For why did the old reprobate require the bottle?'

'My husband,' said Kokua, humbly, 'his purpose may have been good.'

Keawe laughed like an angry man.

'Fiddle-de-dee!' cried Keawe. 'An old rogue, I tell you; and an old ass to boot. For the bottle was hard enough to sell at four centimes; and at three it will be quite impossible. The margin is not broad enough, the thing begins to smell of scorching—brrr!' said he, and shuddered. 'It is true I bought it myself at a cent, when I knew not there were smaller coins. I was a fool for my pains; there will never be found another: and whoever has that bottle now will carry it to the pit.'

'O my husband!' said Kokua. 'Is it not a terrible thing to save oneself by the eternal ruin of another? It seems to me I could not laugh. I would be humbled. I would be filled with melancholy. I would pray for the poor holder.'

Then Keawe, because he felt the truth of what she said, grew the more angry. 'Heighty-teighty!' cried he. 'You may be filled with melancholy if you please. It is not the mind of a good wife. If you thought at all of me, you would sit shamed.'

Thereupon he went out, and Kokua was alone.

What chance had she to sell that bottle at two centimes? None, she perceived. And if she had any, here was her husband hurrying her away to a country where there was nothing lower than a cent. And here—on the morrow of her sacrifice—was her husband leaving her and blaming her.

She would not even try to profit by what time she had, but sat in the house, and now had the bottle out and viewed it with unutterable fear, and now, with loathing, hid it out of sight.

By-and-by, Keawe came back, and would have her take a drive.

'My husband, I am ill,' she said. 'I am out of heart. Excuse me, I can take no pleasure.'

Then was Keawe more wroth than ever. With her, because he thought she was brooding over the case of the old man; and with himself, because he thought she was right, and was ashamed to be so happy.

'This is your truth,' cried he, 'and this your affection! Your husband is just saved from eternal ruin, which he encountered for the love of you—and you can take no pleasure! Kokua, you have a disloyal heart.'

He went forth again furious, and wandered in the town all day. He met friends, and drank with them; they hired a carriage and drove into the country, and there drank again. All the time Keawe was ill at ease, because he was taking this pastime while his wife was sad, and because he knew in his heart that she was more right than he; and the knowledge made him drink the deeper.

Now there was an old brutal Haole drinking with him, one that had been a boatswain of a whaler, a runaway, a digger in gold mines, a convict in prisons. He had a low mind and a foul mouth; he loved to drink and to see others drunken; and he pressed the glass upon Keawe. Soon there was no more money in the company.

'Here, you!' says the boatswain, 'you are rich, you have been always saying. You have a bottle or some foolishness.'

'Yes,' says Keawe, 'I am rich; I will go back and get some money from my wife, who keeps it.'

'That's a bad idea, mate,' said the boatswain. 'Never you trust a petticoat with dollars. They're all as false as water; you keep an eye on her.'

Now, this word struck in Keawe's mind; for he was muddled with what he had been drinking.

'I should not wonder but she was false, indeed,' thought he. 'Why else should she be so cast down at my release? But I will show her I am not the man to be fooled. I will catch her in the act.'

Accordingly, when they were back in town, Keawe bade the boatswain wait for him at the corner, by the old calaboose,* and went forward up the avenue alone to the door of his house. The night had come again; there was a light within, but never a sound; and Keawe crept about the corner, opened the back door softly, and looked in.

There was Kokua on the floor, the lamp at her side; before her was a milk-white bottle, with a round belly and a long neck; and as she viewed it, Kokua wrung her hands.

A long time Keawe stood and looked in the doorway. At first he was struck stupid; and then fear fell upon him that the bargain had been made amiss, and the bottle had come back to him as it came at San Francisco; and at that his knees were loosened, and the fumes of the wine departed from his head like mists off a river in the morning. And then he had another thought; and it was a strange one, that made his cheeks to burn.

'I must make sure of this,' thought he.

So he closed the door, and went softly round the corner again, and then came noisily in, as though he were but now returned. And, lo! by the time he opened the front door no bottle was to be seen; and Kokua sat in a chair and started up like one awakened out of sleep.

'I have been drinking all day and making merry,' said Keawe. 'I have been with good companions, and now I only come back for money, and return to drink and carouse with them again.'

Both his face and voice were as stern as judgment, but Kokua was too troubled to observe.

'You do well to use your own, my husband,' said she, and her words trembled.

'O, I do well in all things,' said Keawe, and he went straight to the chest and took out money. But he looked besides in the corner where they kept the bottle, and there was no bottle there.

At that the chest heaved upon the floor like a sea-billow, and the house span about him like a wreath of smoke, for he saw he was lost now, and there was no escape. 'It is what I feared,' he thought. 'It is she who has bought it.'

And then he came to himself a little and rose up; but the sweat streamed on his face as thick as the rain and as cold as the well-water.

'Kokua,' said he, 'I said to you today what ill became me. Now I return to carouse with my jolly companions,' and at that he laughed a little quietly. 'I will take more pleasure in the cup if you forgive me.'

She clasped his knees in a moment; she kissed his knees with flowing tears.

'O,' she cried, 'I asked but a kind word!'

'Let us never one think hardly of the other,' said Keawe, and was gone out of the house.

Now, the money that Keawe had taken was only some of that store of centime pieces they had laid in at their arrival. It was very sure he had no mind to be drinking. His wife had given her soul for him, now he must give his for hers; no other thought was in the world with him.

At the corner, by the old calaboose, there was the boatswain waiting.

'My wife has the bottle,' said Keawe, 'and, unless you help me to recover it, there can be no more money and no more liquor tonight.'

'You do not mean to say you are serious about that bottle?' cried the boatswain.

'There is the lamp,' said Keawe. 'Do I look as if I was jesting?'

'That is so,' said the boatswain. 'You look as serious as a ghost.'

'Well, then,' said Keawe, 'here are two centimes; you must

go to my wife in the house, and offer her these for the bottle, which (if I am not much mistaken) she will give you instantly. Bring it to me here, and I will buy it back from you for one; for that is the law with this bottle, that it still must be sold for a less sum. But whatever you do, never breathe a word to her that you have come from me.'

'Mate, I wonder are you making a fool of me?' asked the boatswain.

'It will do you no harm if I am,' returned Keawe.

'That is so, mate,' said the boatswain.

'And if you doubt me,' added Keawe, 'you can try. As soon as you are clear of the house, wish to have your pocket full of money, or a bottle of the best rum, or what you please, and you will see the virtue of the thing.'

'Very well, Kanaka,' says the boatswain. 'I will try; but if you are having your fun out of me, I will take my fun out of you with a belaying pin.'*

So the whaler-man went off up the avenue; and Keawe stood and waited. It was near the same spot where Kokua had waited the night before; but Keawe was more resolved, and never faltered in his purpose; only his soul was bitter with despair.

It seemed a long time he had to wait before he heard a voice singing in the darkness of the avenue. He knew the voice to be the boatswain's; but it was strange how drunken it appeared upon a sudden.

Next, the man himself came stumbling into the light of the lamp. He had the devil's bottle buttoned in his coat; another bottle was in his hand; and even as he came in view he raised it to his mouth and drank.

'You have it,' said Keawe. 'I see that.'

'Hands off!' cried the boatswain, jumping back. 'Take a step near me, and I'll smash your mouth. You thought you could make a cat's-paw of me, did you?'

'What do you mean?' cried Keawe.

'Mean?' cried the boatswain. 'This is a pretty good bottle, this is; that's what I mean. How I got it for two centimes I can't make out; but I'm sure you shan't have it for one.'

'You mean you won't sell?' gasped Keawe.

'No, *sir*!' cried the boatswain. 'But I'll give you a drink of the rum, if you like.'

'I tell you,' said Keawe, 'the man who has that bottle goes to hell.'

'I reckon I'm going anyway,' returned the sailor; 'and this bottle's the best thing to go with I've struck yet. No, sir!' he cried again, 'this is my bottle now, and you can go and fish for another.'

'Can this be true?' Keawe cried. 'For your own sake, I beseech you, sell it me!'

'I don't value any of your talk,' replied the boatswain. 'You thought I was a flat;* now you see I'm not; and there's an end. If you won't have a swallow of the rum, I'll have one myself. Here's your health, and good-night to you!'

So off he went down the avenue towards town, and there goes the bottle out of the story.

But Keawe ran to Kokua light as the wind; and great was their joy that night; and great, since then, has been the peace of all their days in the Bright House.

THE ISLE OF VOICES

KEOLA was married with Lehua, daughter of Kalamake,* the wise man of Molokai,* and he kept his dwelling with the father of his wife. There was no man more cunning than that prophet; he read the stars, he could divine by the bodies of the dead, and by the means of evil creatures: he could go alone into the highest parts of the mountain, into the region of the hobgoblins, and there he would lay snares to entrap the spirits of ancient.

For this reason no man was more consulted in all the Kingdom of Hawaii.* Prudent people bought, and sold, and married, and laid out their lives by his counsels; and the King had him twice to Kona to seek the treasures of Kamehameha.* Neither was any man more feared: of his enemies, some had dwindled in sickness by the virtue of his incantations, and some had been spirited away, the life and the clay both, so that folk looked in vain for so much as a bone of their bodies. It was rumoured that he had the art or the gift of the old heroes. Men had seen him at night upon the mountains, stepping from one cliff to the next; they had seen him walking in the high forest, and his head and shoulders were above the trees.

This Kalamake was a strange man to see. He was come of the best blood in Molokai and Maui,* of a pure descent; and yet he was more white to look upon than any foreigner: his hair the colour of dry grass, and his eyes red and very blind, so that 'Blind as Kalamake, that can see across tomorrow,' was a byword in the islands.

Of all these doings of his father-in-law, Keola knew a little by the common repute, a little more he suspected, and the rest he ignored. But there was one thing troubled him. Kalamake was a man that spared for nothing, whether to eat or to drink, or to wear; and for all he paid in bright new dollars. 'Bright as Kalamake's dollars,' was another saying in the Eight Isles.* Yet he neither sold, nor planted, nor took hire—only now and then from his sorceries—and there was no source conceivable for so much silver coin.

It chanced one day Keola's wife was gone upon a visit to Kaunakakai,* on the lee side of the island, and the men were forth at the sea-fishing. But Keola was an idle dog, and he lay in the verandah and watched the surf beat on the shore and the birds fly about the cliff. It was a chief thought with him always—the thought of the bright dollars. When he lay down to bed he would be wondering why they were so many, and when he woke at morn he would be wondering why they were all new; and the thing was never absent from his mind. But this day of all days he made sure in his heart of some discovery. For it seems he had observed the place where Kalamake kept his treasure, which was a lock-fast desk against the parlour wall, under the print of Kamehameha the Fifth, and a photograph of Queen Victoria with her crown; and it seems again that, no later than the night before, he found occasion to look in, and behold! the bag lay there empty. And this was the day of the steamer; he could see her smoke off Kalaupapa;* and she must soon arrive with a month's goods, tinned salmon and gin, and all manner of rare luxuries for Kalamake.

'Now if he can pay for his goods today,' Keola thought, 'I shall know for certain that the man is a warlock, and the dollars come out of the Devil's pocket.'

While he was so thinking, there was his father-in-law behind him, looking vexed.

'Is that the steamer?' he asked.

'Yes,' said Keola. 'She has but to call at Pelekunu,* and then she will be here.'

'There is no help for it then,' returned Kalamake, 'and I must take you in my confidence, Keola, for the lack of anyone better. Come here within the house.'

So they stepped together into the parlour, which was a very fine room, papered and hung with prints, and furnished with a rocking-chair, and a table and a sofa in the European style. There was a shelf of books besides, and a family Bible in the midst of the table, and the lock-fast writing desk against the wall; so that anyone could see it was the house of a man of substance.*

Kalamake made Keola close the shutters of the windows, while he himself locked all the doors and set open the lid of the desk. From this be brought forth a pair of necklaces hung with charms and shells, a bundle of dried herbs, and the dried leaves of trees, and a green branch of palm.

'What I am about,' said he, 'is a thing beyond wonder. The men of old were wise; they wrought marvels, and this among the rest; but that was at night, in the dark, under the fit stars and in the desert. The same will I do here in my own house and under the plain eye of day.'

So saying, he put the bible under the cushion of the sofa so that it was all covered, brought out from the same place a mat of a wonderfully fine texture, and heaped the herbs and leaves on sand in a tin pan. And then he and Keola put on the necklaces and took their stand upon the opposite corners of the mat.

'The time comes,' said the warlock; 'be not afraid.'

With that he set flame to the herbs, and began to mutter and wave the branch of palm. At first the light was dim because of the closed shutters; but the herbs caught strongly afire, and the flames beat upon Keola, and the room glowed with the burning; and next the smoke rose and made his head swim and his eyes darken, and the sound of Kalamake muttering ran in his ears. And suddenly, to the mat on which they were standing came a snatch or twitch, that seemed to be more swift than lightning. In the same wink the room was gone and the house, the breath all beaten from Keola's body. Volumes of light rolled upon his eyes and head, and he found himself transported to a beach of the sea, under a strong sun, with a great surf roaring: he and the warlock standing there on the same mat, speechless, gasping and grasping at one another, and passing their hands before their eyes.

'What was this?' cried Keola, who came to himself the first, because he was the younger. 'The pang of it was like death.'

'It matters not,' panted Kalamake. 'It is now done.'

'And, in the name of God, where are we?' cried Keola.

'That is not the question,' replied the sorcerer. 'Being here, we have matter in our hands, and that we must attend to. Go, while I recover my breath, into the borders of the wood, and bring me the leaves of such and such a herb, and such and such a tree, which you will find to grow there plentifully—three handfuls of each. And be speedy. We must be home again before the steamer comes; it would seem strange if we had disappeared.' And he sat on the sand and panted.

Keola went up the beach, which was of shining sand and coral, strewn with singular shells; and he thought in his heart—

'How do I not know this beach? I will come here again and gather shells.'

In front of him was a line of palms against the sky; not like the palms of the Eight Islands, but tall and fresh and beautiful, and hanging out withered fans like gold among the green, and he thought in his heart—

'It is strange I should not have found this grove. I will come here again, when it is warm, to sleep.' And he thought, 'How warm it has grown suddenly!' For it was winter in Hawaii, and the day had been chill. And he thought also, 'Where are the grey mountains? And where is the high cliff with the hanging forest and the wheeling birds?' And the more he considered, the less he might conceive in what quarter of the islands he was fallen.

In the border of the grove, where it met the beach, the herb was growing, but the tree further back. Now, as Keola went toward the tree, he was aware of a young woman who had nothing on her body but a belt of leaves.

'Well!' thought Keola, 'they are not very particular about their dress in this part of the country.' And he paused, supposing she would observe him and escape; and seeing that she still looked before her, stood and hummed aloud. Up she leaped at the sound. Her face was ashen; she looked this way and that, and her mouth gaped with the terror of her soul. But it was a strange thing that her eyes did not rest upon Keola.

'Good day,' said he. 'You need not be so frightened; I will not eat you.' And he had scarce opened his mouth before the young woman fled into the bush.

'These are strange manners,' thought Keola. And, not thinking what he did, ran after her.

As she ran, the girl kept crying in some speech that was not practised in Hawaii, yet some of the words were the same,* and he knew she kept calling and warning others. And presently he saw more people running—men, women and children, one with another, all running and crying like people at a fire. And with that he began to grow afraid himself, and returned to Kalamake bringing the leaves. Him he told what he had seen.

'You must pay no heed,' said Kalamake, 'All this is like a dream and shadows. All will disappear and be forgotten.'

'It seemed none saw me,' said Keola.

'And none did,' replied the sorcerer. 'We walk here in the broad sun invisible by reason of these charms. Yet they hear us; and therefore it is well to speak softly, as I do.'

With that he made a circle round the mat with stones, and in the midst he set the leaves.

'It will be your part,' said he, 'to keep the leaves alight, and feed the fire slowly. While they blaze (which is but for a little moment) I must do my errand; and before the ashes blacken, the same power that brought us carries us away. Be ready now with the match; and do you call me in good time lest the flames burn out and I be left.'

As soon as the leaves caught, the sorcerer leaped like a deer out of the circle, and began to race along the beach like a hound that has been bathing. As he ran, he kept stooping to snatch shells; and it seemed to Keola that they glittered as he took them. The leaves blazed with a clear flame that consumed them swiftly; and presently Keola had but a handful left, and the sorcerer was far off, running and stopping.

'Back!' cried Keola. 'Back! The leaves are near done.'

At that Kalamake turned, and if he had run before, now he flew. But fast as he ran, the leaves burned faster. The flame was ready to expire when, with a great leap, he bounded on the mat. The wind of his leaping blew it out; and with that the beach was gone, and the sun and the sea, and they stood once more in the dimness of the shuttered parlour, and were once more shaken and blinded; and on the mat betwixt them lay a pile of shining dollars. Keola ran to the shutters; and there was the steamer tossing in the swell close in.

The same night Kalamake took his son-in-law apart, and gave him five dollars in his hand.

'Keola,' said he, 'if you are a wise man (which I am doubtful of) you will think you slept this afternoon on the verandah, and dreamed as you were sleeping. I am a man of few words, and I have for my helpers people of short memories.'

Never a word more said Kalamake, nor referred again to that affair. But it ran all the while in Keola's head—if he were lazy before, he would now do nothing.

'Why should I work,' thought he, 'when I have a father-in-law who makes dollars of sea-shells?'

Presently his share was spent. He spent it all upon fine clothes. And then he was sorry:

'For,' thought he, 'I had done better to have bought a concertina, with which I might have entertained myself all day long.' And then he began to grow vexed with Kalamake.

'This man has the soul of a dog,' thought he. 'He can gather dollars when he pleases on the beach, and he leaves me to pine for a concertina! Let him beware: I am no child, I am as cunning as he, and hold his secret.' With that he spoke to his wife Lehua, and complained of her father's manners.

'I would let my father be,' said Lehua. 'He is a dangerous man to cross.'

'I care that for him!' cried Keola; and snapped his fingers. 'I have him by the nose. I can make him do what I please.' And he told Lehua the story.

But she shook her head.

'You may do what you like,' said she; 'but as sure as you thwart my father, you will be no more heard of. Think of this person, and that person; think of Hua, who was a noble of the House of Representatives,* and went to Honolulu every year; and not a bone or a hair of him was found. Remember Kamau, and how he wasted to a thread, so that his wife lifted him with one hand. Keola, you are a baby in my father's hands; he will take you with his thumb and finger and eat you like a shrimp.'

Now Keola was truly afraid of Kalamake, but he was vain too; and these words of his wife's incensed him.

'Very well,' said he, 'if that is what you think of me, I will show how much you are deceived.' And he went straight to where his father-in-law was sitting in the parlour.

'Kalamake,' said he, 'I want a concertina.'

'Do you, indeed?' said Kalamake.

'Yes,' said he, 'and I may as well tell you plainly, I mean to have it. A man who picks up dollars on the beach can certainly afford a concertina.'

'I had no idea you had so much spirit,' replied the sorcerer. 'I thought you were a timid, useless lad, and I cannot describe how much pleased I am to find I was mistaken. Now I begin to think I may have found an assistant and successor in my difficult business. A concertina? You shall have the best in Honolulu. And tonight, as soon as it is dark, you and I will go and find the money.'

'Shall we return to the beach?' asked Keola.

'No, no!' replied Kalamake; 'you must begin to learn more of my secrets. Last time I taught you to pick shells; this time I shall teach you to catch fish. Are you strong enough to launch Pili's boat?'

'I think I am,' returned Keola. 'But why should we not take your own, which is afloat already?'

'I have a reason which you will understand thoroughly before tomorrow,' said Kalamake. 'Pili's boat is the better suited for my purpose. So, if you please, let us meet there as soon as it is dark; and in the meanwhile, let us keep our own counsel, for there is no cause to let the family into our business.'

Honey is not more sweet than was the voice of Kalamake, and Keola could scarce contain his satisfaction.

'I might have had my concertina weeks ago,' thought he, 'and there is nothing needed in this world but a little courage.'

Presently after he spied Lehua weeping, and was half in a mind to tell her all was well.

'But no,' thinks he; 'I shall wait till I can show her the concertina; we shall see what the chit will do then. Perhaps she will understand in the future that her husband is a man of some intelligence.'

As soon as it was dark father and son-in-law launched Pili's boat and set the sail. There was a great sea, and it blew strong from the leeward; but the boat was swift and light and dry, and skimmed the waves. The wizard had a lantern, which he lit and held with his finger through the ring; and the two sat in the stern and smoked cigars, of which Kalamake had always a provision, and spoke like friends of magic and the great sums of money which they could make by its exercise, and what they should buy first, and what second; and Kalamake talked like a father.

Presently he looked all about, and above him at the stars, and back at the island, which was already three parts sunk under the sea, and he seemed to consider ripely his position.

'Look!' says he, 'there is Molokai already far behind us, and Maui like a cloud; and by the bearing of these three stars I know I am come where I desire. This part of the sea is called the Sea of the Dead. It is in this place extraordinarily deep, and the floor is all covered with the bones of men, and in the holes of this part gods and goblins keep their habitation. The flow of the sea is to the north, stronger than a shark can swim, and any man who shall here be thrown out of a ship it bears away like a wild horse into the uttermost ocean. Presently he is spent and goes down, and his bones are scattered with the rest, and the gods devour his spirit.'

Fear came on Keola at the words, and he looked, and by the light of the stars and the lantern, the warlock seemed to change.

'What ails you?' cried Keola, quick and sharp.

'It is not I who am ailing,' said the wizard; 'but there is one here very sick.'

With that he changed his grasp upon the lantern, and, behold! as he drew his finger from the ring, the finger stuck and the ring was burst, and his hand was grown to be of the bigness of three.

At that sight Keola screamed and covered his face.

But Kalamake held up the lantern. 'Look rather at my face!' said he—and his head was huge as a barrel; and still he grew and grew as a cloud grows on a mountain, and Keola sat before him screaming, and the boat raced on the great seas.

'And now,' said the wizard, 'what do you think about that

concertina? and are you sure you would not rather have a flute? No?' says he; 'that is well, for I do not like my family to be changeable of purpose. But I begin to think I had better get out of this paltry boat, for my bulk swells to a very unusual degree, and if we are not the more careful, she will presently be swamped.'

With that he threw his legs over the side. Even as he did so, the greatness of the man grew thirty-fold and forty-fold as swift as sight or thinking, so that he stood in the deep seas to the armpits, and his head and shoulders rose like a high isle, and the swell beat and burst upon his bosom, as it beats and breaks against a cliff.* The boat ran still to the north, but he reached out his hand, and took the gunwale by the finger and thumb, and broke the side like a biscuit, and Keola was spilled into the sea. And the pieces of the boat the sorcerer crushed in the hollow of his hand and flung miles away into the night.

'Excuse me taking the lantern,' said he; 'for I have a long wade before me, and the land is far, and the bottom of the sea uneven, and I feel the bones under my toes.'

And he turned and went off walking with great strides; and as often as Keola sank in the trough he could see him no longer; but as often as he was heaved upon the crest, there he was striding and dwindling, and he held the lamp high over his head, and the waves broke white about him as he went.

Since first the islands were fished out of the sea,* there was never a man so terrified as this Keola. He swam indeed, but he swam as puppies swim when they are cast in to drown, and knew not wherefore. He could but think of the hugeness of the swelling of the warlock, of that face which was great as a mountain, of those shoulders that were broad as an isle, and of the seas that beat on them in vain. He thought, too, of the concertina, and shame took hold upon him; and of the dead men's bones, and fear shook him.

Of a sudden he was aware of something dark against the stars that tossed, and a light below, and a brightness of the cloven sea; and he heard speech of men. He cried out aloud and a voice answered; and in a twinkling the bows of a ship hung above him on a wave like a thing balanced, and swooped down. He caught with his two hands in the chains of her, and the next moment was buried in the rushing seas, and the next hauled on board by seamen.

They gave him gin and biscuit and dry clothes, and asked him how he came where they found him, and whether the light which they had seen was the lighthouse, Lae o Ka Laau.* But Keola knew white men are like children and only believe their own stories; so about himself he told them what he pleased, and as for the light (which was Kalamake's lantern) he vowed he had seen none.

This ship was a schooner bound for Honolulu, and then to trade in the low islands;* and by a very good chance for Keola she had lost a man off the bowsprit in a squall. It was no use talking. Keola durst not stay in the Eight Islands. Word goes so quickly, and all men are so fond to talk and carry news, that if he hid in the north end of Kauai or in the south end of Kaū,* the wizard would have wind of it before a month, and he must perish. So he did what seemed the most prudent, and shipped sailor in the place of the man who had been drowned.

In some ways the ship was a good place. The food was extraordinarily rich and plenty, with biscuits and salt beef every day, and pea-soup and puddings made of flour and suet twice a week, so that Keola grew fat. The captain also was a good man, and the crew no worse than other whites. The trouble was the mate, who was the most difficult man to please Keola had ever met with, and beat and cursed him daily, both for what he did and what he did not. The blows that he dealt were very sore, for he was strong; and the words he used were very unpalatable, for Keola was come of a good family and accustomed to respect. And what was the worst of all, whenever Keola found a chance to sleep, there was the mate awake and stirring him up with a rope's end. Keola saw it would never do; and he made up his mind to run away.

They were about a month out from Honolulu when they made the land. It was a fine starry night, the sea was smooth as well as the sky fair; it blew a steady trade;* and there was the island on their weather bow,* a ribbon of palm trees lying flat along the sea. The captain and the mate looked at it with the night glass, and named the name of it, and talked of it, beside the wheel where Keola was steering. It seemed it was an isle where no traders came. By the captain's way, it was an isle besides where no man dwelt; but the mate thought otherwise.

'I don't give a cent for the directory,'* said he. 'I've been past here one night in the schooner *Eugenie*;* it was just such a night as this; they were fishing with torches, and the beach was thick with lights like a town.'

'Well, well,' says the captain, 'it's steep-to,* that's the great point; and there ain't any outlying dangers by the chart, so we'll just hug the lee side of it. Keep her romping full, don't I tell you!' he cried to Keola, who was listening so hard that he forgot to steer.

And the mate cursed him, and swore that Kanaka* was for no use in the world, and if he got started after him with a belaying pin,* it would be a cold day for Keola.

And so the captain and mate lay down on the house together, and Keola was left to himself.

'This island will do very well for me,' he thought; 'if no traders deal there, the mate will never come. And as for Kalamake, it is not possible he can ever get as far as this.'

With that he kept edging the schooner nearer in. He had to do this quietly, for it was the trouble with these white men, and above all with the mate, that you could never be sure of them; they would all be sleeping sound, or else pretending, and if a sail shook, they would jump to their feet and fall on you with a rope's end. So Keola edged her up little by little, and kept all drawing. And presently the land was close on board, and the sound of the sea on the sides of it grew loud.

With that, the mate sat up suddenly upon the house.

'What are you doing?' he roars. 'You'll have the ship ashore!'

And he made one bound for Keola, and Keola made another clean over the rail and plump into the starry sea. When he came up again, the schooner had payed off on her true course, and the mate stood by the wheel himself, and Keola heard him cursing. The sea was smooth under the lee of the island; it was warm besides, and Keola had his sailor's knife, so he had no fear of sharks. A little way before him the trees stopped; there was a break in the line of the land like the mouth of a harbour; and the tide, which was then flowing, took him up and carried him through. One minute he was without, and the next within: had floated there in a wide shallow water, bright with ten thousand stars, and all about him was the ring of the land, with its string of palm trees. And he was amazed, because this was a kind of island he had never heard of.

The time of Keola in that place was in two periods—the period when he was alone, and the period when he was there with the tribe. At first he sought everywhere and found no man; only some houses standing in a hamlet, and the marks of fires. But the ashes of the fires were cold and the rains had washed them away; and the winds had blown, and some of the huts were overthrown. It was here he took his dwelling; and he made a fire drill, and a shell hook, and fished and cooked his fish, and climbed after green cocoanuts, the juice of which he drank, for in all the isle there was no water. The days were long to him, and the nights terrifying. He made a lamp of cocoa-shell, and drew the oil of the ripe nuts, and made a wick of fibre; and when evening came he closed up his hut, and lit his lamp, and lay and trembled till morning. Many a time he thought in his heart he would have been better in the bottom of the sea, his bones rolling there with the others.

All this while he kept by the inside of the island, for the huts were on the shore of the lagoon, and it was there the palms grew best, and the lagoon itself abounded with good fish. And to the outer side he went once only, and he looked but the once at the beach of the ocean, and came away shaking. For the look of it, with its bright sand, and strewn shells, and strong sun and surf, went sore against his inclination.

'It cannot be,' he thought, 'and yet it is very like. And how do I know? These white men, although they pretend to know where they are sailing, must take their chance like other people. So that after all we may have sailed in a circle, and I may be quite near to Molokai, and this may be the very beach where my father-in-law gathers his dollars.'

So after that he was prudent, and kept to the land side.

It was perhaps a month later, when the people of the place arrived—the fill of six great boats. They were a fine race of men, and spoke a tongue that sounded very different from the tongue of Hawaii, but so many of the words were the same that it was not difficult to understand. The men besides were very courteous, and the women very towardly; and they made Keola welcome, and built him a house, and gave him a wife; and what surprised him the most, he was never sent to work with the young men.

And now Keola had three periods. First he had a period of being very sad, and then he had a period when he was pretty merry. Last of all came the third, when he was the most terrified man in the four oceans.

The cause of the first period was the girl he had to wife. He was in doubt about the island, and he might have been in doubt about the speech, of which he had heard so little when he came there with the wizard on the mat. But about his wife there was no mistake conceivable, for she was the same girl that ran from him crying in the wood. So he had sailed all this way, and might as well have stayed in Molokai; and had left home and wife and all his friends for no other cause but to escape his enemy, and the place he had come to was that wizard's hunting ground, and the shore where he walked invisible. It was at this period when he kept the most close to the lagoon side, and as far as he dared, abode in the cover of his hut.

The cause of the second period was talk he heard from his wife and the chief islanders. Keola himself said little. He was never so sure of his new friends, for he judged they were too civil to be wholesome, and since he had grown better acquainted with his father-in-law the man had grown more cautious. So he told them nothing of himself, but only his name and descent, and that he came from the Eight Islands, and what fine islands they were; and about the king's palace in Honolulu, and how he was a chief friend of the king and the missionaries.* But he put many questions and learned much. The island where he was was called the Isle of Voices; it belonged to the tribe, but they made their home upon another, three hours' sail to the southward. There they lived and had their permanent houses, and it was a rich island, where were eggs and chickens and pigs, and ships came trading with rum and tobacco. It was there the schooner had gone after Keola deserted; there, too, the mate had died, like the fool of a white man as he was. It seems, when the ship came, it was the beginning of the sickly season in that isle, when the fish of the lagoon are poisonous, and all who eat of them swell up and die. The mate was told of it; he saw the boats preparing, because in that season the people leave that island and sail to the Isle of Voices; but he was a fool of a white man, who would believe no stories but his own, and he caught one of these fish, cooked it and ate it, and swelled up and died, which was good news to Keola. As for the Isle of Voices, it lay solitary the most part of the year; only now and then a boat's crew came for copra, and in the bad season, when the fish at the main isle were poisonous, the tribe dwelt there in a body. It had its name from a marvel, for it seemed the seaside of it was all beset with invisible devils; day and night you heard them talking one with another in strange tongues; day and night little fires blazed up and were extinguished on the beach; and what was the cause of these doings no man might conceive. Keola asked them if it were the same in their own island where they stayed, and they told him no, not there; nor yet in any other of some hundred isles that lay all about them in that sea; but it was a thing peculiar to the Isle of Voices. They told him also that these fires and voices were ever on the seaside and in the seaward fringes of the wood, and a man might dwell by the lagoon two thousand years (if he could live so long) and never be any way troubled;* and even on the seaside the devils did no harm if let alone. Only once a chief had cast a spear at one of the voices, and the same night he fell out of a cocoanut palm and was killed.

Keola thought a good bit with himself. He saw he would be all right when the tribe returned to the main island, and right enough where he was, if he kept by the lagoon, yet he had a mind to make things righter if he could. So he told the high chief he had once been in an isle that was pestered the same way, and the folk had found a means to cure that trouble.

'There was a tree growing in the bush there,' says he, 'and it seems these devils came to get the leaves of it. So the people of the isle cut down the tree wherever it was found, and the devils came no more.'

They asked what kind of tree this was, and he showed them the tree of which Kalamake burned the leaves. They found it hard to believe, yet the idea tickled them. Night after night the old men debated it in their councils, but the high chief (though he was a brave man) was afraid of the matter, and reminded them daily of the chief who cast a spear against the voices and was killed, and the thought of that brought all to a stand again.

Though he could not yet bring about the destruction of the trees, Keola was well enough pleased, and began to look about him and take pleasure in his days; and, among other things, he was the kinder to his wife, so that the girl began to love him greatly. One day he came to the hut, and she lay on the ground lamenting.

'Why,' said Keola, 'what is wrong with you now?'

She declared it was nothing.

The same night she woke him. The lamp burned very low, but he saw by her face she was in sorrow.

'Keola,' she said, 'put your ear to my mouth that I may whisper, for no one must hear us. Two days before the boats begin to be got ready, go you to the sea-side of the isle and lie in a thicket. We shall choose that place beforehand, you and I; and hide food; and every night I shall come near by there singing. So when a night comes and you do not hear me, you shall know we are clean gone out of the island, and you may come forth again in safety.'

The soul of Keola died within him.

'What is this?' he cried. 'I cannot live among devils. I will not be left behind upon this isle. I am dying to leave it.'

'You will never leave it alive, my poor Keola,' said the girl; 'for to tell you the truth, my people are eaters of men; but this they keep secret. And the reason they will kill you before we leave is because in our island ships come, and Donat-Rimarau* comes and talks for the French, and there is a white trader there in a house with a verandah, and a catechist. Oh, that is a fine place indeed! The trader has barrels filled with flour; and a French warship once came in the lagoon and gave everybody wine and biscuit. Ah, my poor Keola, I wish I could take you there, for great is my love to you, and it is the finest place in the seas except Papeete.'

So now Keola was the most terrified man in the four oceans. He had heard tell of eaters of men in the south islands,* and the thing had always been a fear to him; and here it was knocking at his door. He had heard besides, by travellers, of their practices, and how when they are in a mind to eat a man, they cherish and fondle him like a mother with a favourite baby. And he saw this must be his own case; and that was why he had been housed, and fed, and wived, and liberated from all work; and why the old men and the chiefs discoursed with him like a person of weight. So he lay on his bed and railed upon his destiny; and the flesh curdled on his bones.

The next day the people of the tribe were very civil, as their way was. They were elegant speakers, and they made beautiful poetry, and jested at meals, so that a missionary must have died laughing. It was little enough Keola cared for their fine ways; all he saw was the white teeth shining in their mouths, and his gorge rose at the sight; and when they were done eating, he went and lay in the bush like a dead man.

The next day it was the same, and then his wife followed him.

'Keola,' she said, 'if you do not eat, I tell you plainly you will be killed and cooked tomorrow. Some of the old chiefs are murmuring already. They think you are fallen sick and must lose flesh.'

With that Keola got to his feet, and anger burned in him.

'It is little I care one way or the other,' said he. 'I am between the devil and the deep sea.* Since die I must, let me die the quickest way; and since I must be eaten at the best of it, let me rather be eaten by hobgoblins than by men. Farewell,' said he, and he left her standing, and walked to the seaside of that island.

It was all bare in the strong sun; there was no sign of man, only the beach was trodden, and all about him as he went, the voices talked and whispered, and the little fires sprang up and burned down. All tongues of the earth were spoken there; the French, the Dutch, the Russian, the Tamil, the Chinese. Whatever land knew sorcery, there were some of its people whispering in Keola's ear. That beach was thick as a cried fair, yet no man seen; and as he walked he saw the shells vanish before him, and no man to pick them up. I think the devil would have been afraid to be alone in such a company; but Keola was past fear and courted death. When the fires sprang up, he charged for them like a bull. Bodiless voices called to and fro; unseen hands poured sand upon the flames; and they were gone from the beach before he reached them.

'It is plain Kalamake is not here,' he thought, 'or I must have been killed long since.'

With that he sat him down in the margin of the wood, for he was tired, and put his chin upon his hands. The business before his eyes continued: the beach babbled with voices, and the fires sprang up and sank, and the shells vanished and were renewed again even while he looked.

'It was a by-day when I was here before,' he thought, 'for it was nothing to this.'

And his head was dizzy with the thought of these millions and millions of dollars, and all these hundreds and hundreds of persons culling them upon the beach and flying in the air higher and swifter than eagles.

'And to think how they have fooled me with their talk of mints,' says he, 'and that money was made there, when it is clear that all the new coin in all the world is gathered on these sands! But I will know better the next time!' said he.

And at last, he knew not very well how or when, sleep fell on Keola, and he forgot the island and all his sorrows.

Early the next day, before the sun was yet up, a bustle woke him. He awoke in fear, for he thought the tribe had caught him napping; but it was no such matter. Only, on the beach in front of him, the bodiless voices called and shouted one upon another, and it seemed they all passed and swept beside him up the coast of the island.

'What is afoot now?' thinks Keola. And it was plain to him it was something beyond ordinary, for the fires were not lighted nor the shells taken, but the bodiless voices kept posting up the beach,* and hailing and dying away; and others following, and by the sound of them these wizards should be angry.

'It is not me they are angry at,' thought Keola, 'for they pass me close.'

As when hounds go by, or horses in a race, or city folk coursing to a fire, and all men join and follow after, so it was now with Keola; and he knew not what he did, nor why he did it, but there, lo and behold! he was running with the voices.

So he turned one point of the island, and this brought him in view of a second; and there he remembered the wizard trees to have been growing by the score together in a wood. From this point there went up a hubbub of men crying not to be described; and by the sound of them, those that he ran with shaped their course for the same quarter. A little nearer, and there began to mingle with the outcry the crash of many axes. And at this a thought came at last into his mind that the high chief had consented; that the men of the tribe had set-to cutting down these trees; that word had gone about the isle from sorcerer to sorcerer, and these were all now assembling to defend their trees. Desire of strange things swept him on. He posted with the voices, crossed the beach, and came into the borders of the wood, and stood astonished. One tree had fallen, others were part hewed away. There was the tribe clustered. They were back to back, and bodies lay, and blood flowed among their feet. The hue of fear was on all their faces; their voices went up to heaven shrill as a weasel's cry.

Have you seen a child when he is all alone and has a wooden sword, and fights, leaping and hewing with the empty air? Even so the man-eaters huddled back to back, and heaved up their axes, and laid on, and screamed as they laid on, and behold! no man to contend with them! only here and there Keola saw an axe swinging over against them without hands; and time and again a man of the tribe would fall before it, clove in twain or burst asunder, and his soul sped howling.

For awhile Keola looked upon this prodigy like one that dreams, and then fear took him by the midst as sharp as death, that he should behold such doings. Even in that same flash the high chief of the clan espied him standing, and pointed and called out his name. Thereat the whole tribe saw him also, and their eyes flashed, and their teeth clashed.

'I am too long here,' thought Keola, and ran further out of the wood and down the beach, not caring whither.

'Keola!' said a voice close by upon the empty sand.

'Lehua! is that you?' he cried, and gasped, and looked in vain for her; but by the eyesight he was stark alone.

'I saw you pass before,' the voice answered; 'but you would not hear me. Quick! get the leaves and the herbs, and let us flee.'

'You are there with the mat?' he asked.

'Here, at your side,' said she. And he felt her arms about him. 'Quick! the leaves and the herbs, before my father can get back!'

So Keola ran for his life, and fetched the wizard fuel; and Lehua guided him back, and set his feet upon the mat, and made the fire. All the time of its burning, the sound of the battle towered out of the wood; the wizards and the man-eaters hard at fight; the wizards, the viewless ones, roaring out aloud like bulls upon a mountain, and the men of the tribe replying shrill and savage out of the terror of their souls. And all the time of the burning, Keola stood there and listened, and shook, and watched how the unseen hands of Lehua poured the leaves. She poured them fast, and the flame burned high, and scorched Keola's hands; and she speeded and blew the burning with her breath. The last leaf was eaten, the flame fell, and the shock followed, and there were Keola and Lehua in the room at home.

Now, when Keola could see his wife at last he was mighty pleased, and he was mighty pleased to be home again in Molokai and sit down beside a bowl of poi*—for they make no poi on board ships, and there was none in the Isle of Voices—and he was out of the body with pleasure to be clean escaped out of the hands of the eaters of men. But there was another matter not so clear, and Lehua and Keola talked of it all night and were troubled. There was Kalamake left upon the isle. If, by the blessing of God, he could but stick there, all were well; but should he escape and return to Molokai, it would be an ill day for his daughter and her husband. They spoke of his gift of swelling, and whether he could wade that distance in the seas. But Keola knew by this time where that island was—and that is to say, in the Low or Dangerous Archipelago.* So they fetched the atlas and looked upon the distance in the map, and by what they could make of it, it seemed a far way for an old gentleman to walk. Still, it would not do to make too sure of a warlock like Kalamake, and they determined at last to take counsel of a white missionary.

So the first one that came by Keola told him everything. And the missionary was very sharp on him for taking the second wife in the low island; but for all the rest, he vowed he could make neither head nor tail of it.

'However,' says he, 'if you think this money of your father's ill gotten, my advice to you would be, give some of it to the lepers* and some to the missionary fund. And as for this extraordinary rigmarole, you cannot do better than keep it to yourselves.'

But he warned the police at Honolulu that, by all he could make out, Kalamake and Keola had been coining false money, and it would not be amiss to watch them.

Keola and Lehua took his advice, and gave many dollars to the lepers and the fund. And no doubt the advice must have been good, for from that day to this, Kalamake has never more been heard of. But whether he was slain in the battle by the trees, or whether he is still kicking his heels upon the Isle of Voices, who shall say?

THE EBB-TIDE

A Trio and Quartette

BY

ROBERT LOUIS STEVENSON AND LLOYD OSBOURNE

*'There is a tide in the affairs of men'**

PART I · THE TRIO

CHAPTER I

NIGHT ON THE BEACH

THROUGHOUT the island world of the Pacific, scattered men of many European races and from almost every grade of society carry activity and disseminate disease. Some prosper, some vegetate. Some have mounted the steps of thrones and owned islands and navies. Others again must marry for a livelihood; a strapping, merry, chocolate-coloured dame supports them in sheer idleness; and, dressed like natives, but still retaining some foreign element of gait or attitude, still perhaps with some relic (such as a single eye-glass) of the officer and gentleman, they sprawl in palm-leaf verandahs and entertain an island audience with memoirs of the music-hall. And there are still others, less pliable, less capable, less fortunate, perhaps less base, who continue, even in these isles of plenty, to lack bread.

At the far end of the town of Papeete,* three such men were seated on the beach under a *purao*-tree.*

It was late. Long ago the band had broken up and marched musically home, a motley troop of men and women, merchant clerks and navy officers, dancing in its wake, arms about waist and crowned with garlands. Long ago darkness and silence had gone from house to house about the tiny pagan city. Only the street lamps shone on, making a glow-worm halo in the umbrageous alleys or drawing a tremulous image on the waters of the port. A sound of snoring ran among the piles of lumber by the Government pier. It was wafted ashore from the graceful clipper-bottomed schooners, where they lay moored close in like dinghies, and their crews were stretched upon the deck under the open sky or huddled in a rude tent amidst the disorder of merchandise.

But the men under the *purao* had no thought of sleep. The same temperature in England would have passed without remark in summer; but it was bitter cold for the South Seas. Inanimate nature knew it, and the bottle of cocoanut oil stood frozen in every bird-cage house about the island; and the men knew it, and shivered. They wore flimsy cotton clothes, the same they had sweated in by day and run the gauntlet of the tropic showers; and to complete their evil case, they had no breakfast to mention, less dinner, and no supper at all.

In the telling South Sea phrase, these three men were *on the beach.** Common calamity had brought them acquainted, as the three most miserable English-speaking creatures in Tahiti; and beyond their misery, they knew next to nothing of each other, not even their true names. For each had made a long apprenticeship in going downward; and each, at some stage of the descent, had been shamed into the adoption of an *alias.* And yet not one of them had figured in a court of justice; two were men of kindly virtues; and one, as he sat and shivered under the *purao,* had a tattered Virgil in his pocket.

Certainly, if money could have been raised upon the book, Robert Herrick would long ago have sacrificed that last possession; but the demand for literature, which is so marked a feature in some parts of the South Seas, extends not so far as the dead tongues; and the Virgil, which he could not exchange against a meal, had often consoled him in his hunger. He would study it, as he lay with tightened belt on the floor of the old calaboose,* seeking favourite passages and finding new ones only less beautiful because they lacked the consecration of remembrance. Or he would pause on random country walks; sit on the path side, gazing over the sea on the mountains of Eimeo;* and dip into the *Aeneid,* seeking *sortes.** And if the oracle (as is the way of oracles) replied with no very certain nor encouraging voice, visions of England at least would throng upon the exile's memory: the busy schoolroom, the green playing-fields, holidays at home, and the perennial roar of London, and the fireside, and the white head of his father. For it is the destiny of those grave, restrained and classic writers, with whom we make enforced and often painful acquaintanceship at school, to pass into the blood and become native in the memory; so that a phrase of Virgil speaks not so much of Mantua or Augustus, but of English places and the student's own irrevocable youth.

Robert Herrick was the son of an intelligent, active, and ambitious man, small partner in a considerable London house. Hopes were conceived of the boy; he was sent to a good school, gained there an Oxford scholarship, and proceeded in course to the Western University. With all his talent and taste (and he had much of both) Robert was deficient in consistency and intellectual manhood, wandered in bypaths of study, worked at music or at metaphysics when he should have been at Greek, and took at last a paltry degree. Almost at the same time, the London house was disastrously wound up; Mr Herrick must begin the world again as a clerk in a strange office, and Robert relinquish his ambitions and accept with gratitude a career that he detested and despised. He had no head for figures, no interest in affairs, detested the constraint of hours, and despised the aims and the success of merchants. To grow rich was none of his ambitions; rather to do well. A worse or a more bold young man would have refused the destiny; perhaps tried his future with his pen; perhaps enlisted. Robert, more prudent, possibly more timid, consented to embrace that way of life in which he could most readily assist his family. But he did so with a mind divided; fled the neighbourhood of former comrades; and chose, out of several positions placed at his disposal, a clerkship in New York.

His career thenceforth was one of unbroken shame. He did not drink, he was exactly honest, he was never rude to his employers, yet was everywhere discharged. Bringing no interest to his duties, he brought no attention; his day was a tissue of things neglected and things done amiss; and from place to place and from town to town, he carried the character of one thoroughly incompetent. No man can bear the word applied to him without some flush of colour, as indeed there is none other that so emphatically slams in a man's face the door of self-respect. And to Herrick, who was conscious of talents and acquirements, who looked down upon those humble duties in which he was found wanting, the pain was the more exquisite. Early in his fall, he had ceased to be able to make remittances; shortly after, having nothing but failure to communicate, he ceased writing home; and about a year before this tale begins, turned suddenly upon the streets of San Francisco by a vulgar and infuriated German Jew, he had broken the last bonds of self-respect, and upon a sudden impulse, changed his name and invested his last dollar in a passage on the mail brigantine, the *City of Papeete*. With what expectation he had trimmed his flight for the South Seas, Herrick perhaps scarcely knew. Doubtless there were fortunes to be made in pearl and copra;* doubtless others not more gifted than himself had climbed in the island world to be queen's consorts and king's ministers. But if Herrick had gone there with any manful purpose, he would have kept his father's name: the *alias* betrayed his moral bankruptcy; he had struck his flag; he entertained no hope to reinstate himself or help his straitened family; and he came to the islands (where he knew the climate to be soft, bread cheap, and manners easy) a skulker from life's battle and his own immediate duty. Failure, he had said, was his portion; let it be a pleasant failure.

It is fortunately not enough to say 'I will be base.' Herrick continued in the islands his career of failure; but in the new scene and under the new name, he suffered no less sharply than before. A place was got, it was lost in the old style; from the long-suffering of the keepers of restaurants he fell to more open charity upon the wayside; as time went on, good-nature became weary, and after a repulse or two, Herrick became shy. There were women enough who would have supported a far worse and a far uglier man; Herrick never met or never knew them: or if he did both, some manlier feeling would revolt, and he preferred starvation. Drenched with rains, broiling by day, shivering by night, a disused and ruinous prison for a bedroom, his diet begged or pilfered out of rubbish heaps, his associates two creatures equally outcast with himself, he had drained for months the cup of penitence. He had known what it was to be resigned, what it was to break forth in a childish fury of rebellion against fate, and what it was to sink into the coma of despair. The time had changed him. He told himself no longer tales of an easy and perhaps agreeable declension; he read his nature otherwise; he had proved himself incapable of rising, and he now learned by experience that he could not stoop to fall. Something that was scarcely pride or strength, that was perhaps only refinement, withheld him from capitulation; but he looked on upon his own misfortune with a growing rage, and sometimes wondered at his patience.

It was now the fourth month completed, and still there was no change or sign of change. The moon, racing through a world of flying clouds of every size and shape and density, some black as inkstains, some delicate as lawn, threw the marvel of her Southern brightness over the same lovely and detested scene: the island mountains crowned with the perennial island cloud, the embowered city studded with rare lamps, the masts in the harbour, the smooth mirror of the lagoon, and the mole* of the barrier reef on which the breakers whitened. The moon shone too, with bull's-eye sweeps, on his companions; on the stalwart frame of the American who called himself Brown, and was known to be a master-mariner in some disgrace; and on the dwarfish person, the pale eyes and toothless smile of a vulgar and bad-hearted cockney clerk. Here was society for Robert Herrick! The Yankee skipper was a man at least: he had sterling qualities of tenderness and resolution; he was one whose hand you could take without a blush. But there was no redeeming grace about the other, who called himself sometimes Hay and sometimes Tomkins, and laughed at the discrepancy; who had been employed in every store in Papeete, for the creature was able in his way; who had been discharged from each in turn, for he was wholly vile; who had alienated all his old employers so that they passed him in the street as if he were a dog, and all his old comrades so that they shunned him as they would a creditor.

Not long before, a ship from Peru had brought an influenza, and it now raged in the island, and particularly in Papeete. From all round the *purao* arose and fell a dismal sound of men coughing, and strangling as they coughed. The sick natives, with the islander's impatience of a touch of fever, had crawled from their houses to be cool, and squatting on the shore or on the beached canoes, painfully expected the new day. Even as the crowing of cocks goes about the country in the night from farm to farm, accesses of coughing arose, and spread, and died in the distance, and sprang up again. Each miserable shiverer caught the suggestion from his neighbour, was torn for some minutes by that cruel ecstasy, and left spent and without voice or courage when it passed. If a man had pity to spend, Papeete beach, in that cold night and in that infected season, was a place to spend it on. And of all the sufferers, perhaps the least deserving, but surely the most pitiable, was the London clerk. He was used to another life, to houses, beds, nursing, and the dainties of the sick-room; he lay here now, in the cold open, exposed to the gusting of the wind, and with an empty belly. He was besides infirm; the disease shook him to the vitals; and his companions watched his endurance with surprise. A profound commiseration filled them, and contended with and conquered their abhorrence. The disgust attendant on so ugly a sickness magnified this dislike; at the same time, and with more than compensating strength, shame for a sentiment so inhuman bound them the more straitly to his service; and even the evil they knew of him swelled their solicitude, for the thought of death is always the least supportable when it draws near to the merely sensual and selfish. Sometimes they held him up; sometimes, with mistaken helpfulness, they beat him between the shoulders; and when the poor wretch lay back ghastly and spent after a paroxysm of coughing, they would sometimes peer into his face, doubtfully exploring it for any mark of life. There is no one but has some virtue: that of the clerk was courage; and he would make haste to reassure them in a pleasantry not always decent.

'I'm all right, pals,' he gasped once: 'this is the thing to strengthen the muscles of the larynx.'

'Well, you take the cake!' cried the captain.

'O, I'm good plucked enough,' pursued the sufferer with a broken utterance. 'But it do seem bloomin' hard to me, that I should be the only party down with this form of vice, and the only one to do the funny business. I think one of you other parties might wake up. Tell a fellow something.'

'The trouble is we've nothing to tell, my son,' returned the captain.

'I'll tell you, if you like, what I was thinking,' said Herrick.

'Tell us anything,' said the clerk, 'I only want to be reminded that I ain't dead.'

Herrick took up his parable, lying on his face and speaking slowly and scarce above his breath, not like a man who has anything to say, but like one talking against time.

'Well, I was thinking this,' he began: 'I was thinking I lay on Papeete beach one night—all moon and squalls and fellows coughing—and I was cold and hungry, and down in the mouth, and was about ninety years of age, and had spent two hundred and twenty of them on Papeete beach. And I was thinking I wished I had a ring to rub, or had a fairy godmother, or could raise Beelzebub. And I was trying to remember how you did it. I knew you made a ring of skulls, for I had seen that in the *Freischütz*:* and that you took off your coat and turned up your sleeves, for I had seen Formes do that when he was playing Kaspar,* and you could see (by the way he went about it) it was a business he had studied; and that you ought to have something to kick up a smoke and a bad smell, I daresay a cigar might do, and that you ought to say the Lord's Prayer backwards. Well, I wondered if I could do that; it seemed rather a feat, you see. And then I wondered if I would say it forward, and I thought I did. Well, no sooner had I got to *world without end*, than I saw a man in a *pariu*,* and with a mat under his arm, come along the beach from the town. He was rather a hard-favoured old party, and he limped and crippled, and all the time he kept coughing. At first I didn't cotton to his looks, I thought, and then I got sorry for the old soul because he coughed so hard. I remembered that we had some of that cough mixture the American consul gave the captain for Hay. It never did Hay a ha'porth of service, but I thought it might do the old gentleman's business for him, and stood up. "*Yorana!*"* says I. "*Yorana!*" says he. "Look here," I said, "I've got some first-rate stuff in a bottle; it'll fix your cough, savvy? *Harry my*[1] and I'll measure you a table-spoonful in the palm of my hand, for all our plate is at the bankers." So I thought the old party came up, and the nearer he came, the less I took to him. But I had passed my word, you see.'

'Wot is this bloomin' drivel?' interrupted the clerk. 'It's like the rot there is in tracts.'

'It's a story; I used to tell them to the kids at home,' said Herrick. 'If it bores you, I'll drop it.'

'O, cut along!' returned the sick man, irritably, 'It's better than nothing.'

'Well,' continued Herrick, 'I had no sooner given him the cough mixture than he seemed to straighten up and change, and I saw he wasn't a Tahitian after all, but some kind of Arab, and had a long beard on his chin. "One good turn deserves another," says he. "I am a magician out of the *Arabian Nights*, and this mat that I have under my arm is the original carpet of Mohammed Ben Somebody-or-other. Say the word, and you can have a cruise upon the carpet." "You don't mean to say this is the Travelling Carpet?" I cried. "You bet I do," said he. "You've been to America since last I read the *Arabian Nights*," said I, a little suspicious. "I should think so," said he. "Been everywhere. A man with a carpet like this isn't going to moulder in a semi-detached villa." Well, that struck me as reasonable. "All right," I said; "and do you mean to tell me I can get on that carpet and go straight to London, England?" I said, "London, England," captain, because he seemed to have been so long in your part of the world. "In the crack of a whip," said he. I figured up the time. What is the difference between Papeete and London, captain?'

'Taking Greenwich and Point Venus,* nine hours, odd minutes and seconds,' replied the mariner.

[1] Come here.

'Well, that's about what I made it,' resumed Herrick, 'about nine hours. Calling this three in the morning, I made out I would drop into London about noon; and the idea tickled me immensely. "There's only one bother," I said, "I haven't a copper cent. It would be a pity to go to London and not buy the morning *Standard*." "O!" said he, "you don't realize the conveniences of this carpet. You see this pocket? you've only got to stick your hand in, and you pull it out filled with sovereigns."'

'Double-eagles,* wasn't it?' inquired the captain.

'That was what it was!' cried Herrick. 'I thought they seemed unusually big, and I remember now I had to go to the money-changers at Charing Cross and get English silver.'

'O, you went there?' said the clerk. 'Wot did you do? Bet you had a B.-and-S.!'*

'Well, you see, it was just as the old boy said—like the cut of a whip,' said Herrick. 'The one minute I was here on the beach at three in the morning, the next I was in front of the Golden Cross at midday. At first I was dazzled, and covered my eyes, and there didn't seem the smallest change; the roar of the Strand and the roar of the reef were like the same: hark to it now, and you can hear the cabs and buses rolling and the streets resound! And then at last I could look about, and there was the old place, and no mistake! With the statues in the square, and St Martin's-in-the-Fields, and the bobbies, and the sparrows, and the hacks; and I can't tell you what I felt like. I felt like crying, I believe, or dancing, or jumping clean over the Nelson Column. I was like a fellow caught up out of Hell and flung down into the dandiest part of Heaven. Then I spotted for a hansom with a spanking horse. "A shilling for yourself, if you're there in twenty minutes!" said I to the jarvey.* He went a good pace, though of course it was a trifle to the carpet; and in nineteen minutes and a half I was at the door.'

'What door?' asked the captain.

'Oh, a house I know of,' returned Herrick.

'Bet it was a public-house!' cried the clerk,—only these were not his words. 'And w'y didn't you take the carpet there instead of trundling in a growler?'*

'I didn't want to startle a quiet street,' said the narrator. 'Bad form. And besides, it was a hansom.'

'Well, and what did you do next?' inquired the captain.

'Oh, I went in,' said Herrick.

'The old folks?' asked the captain.

'That's about it,' said the other, chewing a grass.

'Well, I think you are about the poorest 'and at a yarn!' cried the clerk. 'Crikey, it's like *Ministering Children*!* I can tell you there would be more beer and skittles about my little jaunt. I would go and have a B.-and-S. for luck. Then I would get a big ulster with astracan fur,* and take my cane and do the la-de-dạ down Piccadilly. Then I would go to a slap-up restaurant, and have green peas, and a bottle of fizz, and a chump chop—Oh! and I forgot, I'd 'ave some devilled whitebait first—and green gooseberry tart, and 'ot coffee, and some of that form of vice in big bottles with a seal—Benedictine—that's the bloomin' nyme! Then I'd drop into a theatre, and pal on with some chappies, and do the dancing rooms and bars, and that, and wouldn't go 'ome till morning, till daylight doth appear. And the next day I'd have watercresses, 'am, muffin, and fresh butter; wouldn't I just, O my!'

The clerk was interrupted by a fresh attack of coughing.

'Well, now, I'll tell you what I would do,' said the captain: 'I would have none of your fancy rigs with the man driving from the mizzen cross-trees, but a plain fore-and-aft hack cab of the highest registered tonnage. First of all, I would bring up at the market and get a turkey and a sucking-pig. Then I'd go to a wine-merchant's and get a dozen of champagne, and a dozen of some sweet wine, rich and sticky and strong, something in the port or madeira line, the best in the store. Then I'd bear up for a toy-store, and lay out twenty dollars in assorted toys for the piccaninies; and then to a confectioner's and take in cakes and pies and fancy bread, and that stuff with the plums in it; and then to a news-agency and buy all the papers, all the picture ones for the kids, and all the story papers for the old girl about the Earl discovering himself to Anna-Mariar and the escape of the Lady Maude from the private madhouse; and then I'd tell the fellow to drive home.'

'There ought to be some syrup for the kids,' suggested Herrick; 'they like syrup.'

'Yes, syrup for the kids, red syrup at that!' said the captain. 'And those things they pull at, and go pop, and have measly poetry inside. And then I tell you we'd have a thanksgiving-day and Christmas-tree combined. Great Scott, but I would like to see the kids! I guess they would light right out of the house, when they saw daddy driving up. My little Adar—'

The captain stopped sharply.

'Well, keep it up!' said the clerk.

'The damned thing is, I don't know if they ain't starving!' cried the captain.

'They can't be worse off than we are, and that's one comfort,' returned the clerk. 'I defy the devil to make me worse off.'

It seemed as if the devil heard him. The light of the moon had been some time cut off and they had talked in darkness. Now there was heard a roar, which drew impetuously nearer; the face of the lagoon was seen to whiten; and before they had staggered to their feet, a squall burst in rain upon the outcasts. The rage and volume of that avalanche one must have lived in the tropics to conceive; a man panted in its assault, as he might pant under a shower-bath; and the world seemed whelmed in night and water.

They fled, groping for their usual shelter—it might be almost called their home—in the old calaboose; came drenched into its empty chambers; and lay down, three sops of humanity on the cold coral floors, and presently, when the squall was overpast, the others could hear in the darkness the chattering of the clerk's teeth.

'I say, you fellows,' he wailed, 'for God's sake, lie up and try to warm me. I'm blymed if I don't think I'll die else!'

So the three crept together into one wet mass, and lay until day came, shivering and dozing off, and continually reawakened to wretchedness by the coughing of the clerk.

CHAPTER II

MORNING ON THE BEACH—THE THREE LETTERS

THE clouds were all fled, the beauty of the tropic day was spread upon Papeete; and the wall of breaking seas upon the reef, and the palms upon the islet, already trembled in the heat. A French man-of-war was going out, homeward bound; she lay in the middle distance of the port, an ant-heap for activity. In the night a schooner had come in, and now lay far out, hard by the passage; and the yellow flag, the emblem of pestilence, flew on her. From up the coast, a long procession of canoes headed round the point and towards the market, bright as a scarf with the many-coloured clothing of the natives and the piles of fruit. But not even the beauty and the welcome warmth of the morning, not even these naval movements, so interesting to sailors and to idlers, could engage the attention of the outcasts. They were still cold at heart, their mouths sour from the want of sleep, their steps rambling from the lack of food; and they strung like lame geese along the beach in a disheartened silence. It was towards the town they moved; towards the town whence smoke arose, where happier folk were breakfasting; and as they went, their hungry eyes were upon all sides, but they were only scouting for a meal.

A small and dingy schooner lay snug against the quay, with which it was connected by a plank. On the forward deck, under a spot of awning, five Kanakas* who made up the crew, were squatted round a basin of fried feis,[2] and drinking coffee from tin mugs.

'Eight bells: knock off for breakfast!' cried the captain with a miserable heartiness. 'Never tried this craft before; positively my first appearance; guess I'll draw a bumper house.'

He came close up to where the plank rested on the grassy quay; turned his back upon the schooner, and began to

[2] *Fei* is the hill banana.

whistle that lively air, 'The Irish Washerwoman.' It caught the ears of the Kanaka seamen like a preconcerted signal; with one accord they looked up from their meal and crowded to the ship's side, fei in hand and munching as they looked. Even as a poor brown Pyrenean bear dances in the streets of English towns under his master's baton; even so, but with how much more of spirit and precision, the captain footed it in time to his own whistling, and his long morning shadow capered beyond him on the grass. The Kanakas smiled on the performance; Herrick looked on heavy-eyed, hunger for the moment conquering all sense of shame; and a little farther off, but still hard by, the clerk was torn by the seven devils of the influenza.

The captain stopped suddenly, appeared to perceive his audience for the first time, and represented the part of a man surprised in his private hour of pleasure.

'Hello!' said he.

The Kanakas clapped hands and called upon him to go on.

'No, *sir*!' said the captain. 'No eat, no dance. Savvy?'

'Poor old man!' returned one of the crew. 'Him no eat?'

'Lord, no!' said the captain. 'Like-um too much eat. No got.'

'All right. Me got,' said the sailor; 'you tome here. Plenty toffee, plenty fei. Nutha man him tome too.'

'I guess we'll drop right in,' observed the captain; and he and his companions hastened up the plank. They were welcomed on board with the shaking of hands; place was made for them about the basin; a sticky demijohn of molasses was added to the feast in honour of company, and an accordion brought from the forecastle and significantly laid by the performer's side.

'*Ariana*,'[3] said he lightly, touching the instrument as he spoke; and he fell to on a long savoury fei, made an end of it, raised his mug of coffee, and nodded across at the spokesman of the crew. 'Here's your health, old man; you're a credit to the South Pacific,' said he.

With the unsightly greed of hounds they glutted themselves

[3] By-and-bye.

with the hot food and coffee; and even the clerk revived and the colour deepened in his eyes. The kettle was drained, the basin cleaned; their entertainers, who had waited on their wants throughout with the pleased hospitality of Polynesians, made haste to bring forward a dessert of island tobacco and rolls of pandanus leaf to serve as paper; and presently all sat about the dishes puffing like Indian Sachems.*

'When a man 'as breakfast every day, he don't know what it is,' observed the clerk.

'The next point is dinner,' said Herrick; and then with a passionate utterance: 'I wish to God I was a Kanaka!'

'There's one thing sure,' said the captain. 'I'm about desperate, I'd rather hang than rot here much longer.' And with the word he took the accordion and struck up 'Home, sweet home.'

'O, drop that!' cried Herrick, 'I can't stand that.'

'No more can I,' said the captain. 'I've got to play something though: got to pay the shot, my son.' And he struck up 'John Brown's Body' in a fine sweet baritone: 'Dandy Jim of Carolina', came next; 'Rorin the Bold', 'Swing low, Sweet Chariot', and 'The Beautiful Land' followed. The captain was paying his shot with usury, as he had done many a time before; many a meal had he bought with the same currency from the melodious-minded natives, always, as now, to their delight.

He was in the middle of 'Fifteen Dollars in the Inside Pocket', singing with dogged energy, for the task went sore against the grain, when a sensation was suddenly to be observed among the crew.

'*Tapena Tom harry my*,'[4] said the spokesman, pointing.

And the three beachcombers,* following his indication, saw the figure of a man in pyjama trousers and a white jumper approaching briskly from the town.

'That's Tapena Tom, is it?' said the captain, pausing in his music. 'I don't seem to place the brute.'

'We'd better cut,' said the clerk. ''E's no good.'

'Well,' said the musician deliberately, 'one can't most

[4] 'Captain Tom is coming.'

generally always tell. I'll try it on, I guess. Music has charms to soothe the savage Tapena, boys. We might strike it rich; it might amount to iced punch in the cabin.'

'Hiced punch? O my!' said the clerk. 'Give him something 'ot, captain. "Way down the Swannee River"; try that.'

'No, *sir*! Looks Scotch,' said the captain; and he struck, for his life, into 'Auld Lang Syne'.

Captain Tom continued to approach with the same business-like alacrity; no change was to be perceived in his bearded face as he came swinging up the plank: he did not even turn his eyes on the performer.

> 'We twa hae paidled in the burn
> Frae morning tide till dine,'*

went the song.

Captain Tom had a parcel under his arm, which he laid on the house roof, and then turning suddenly to the strangers: 'Here, you!' he bellowed, 'be off out of that!'

The clerk and Herrick stood not on the order of their going, but fled incontinently by the plank. The performer, on the other hand, flung down the instrument and rose to his full height slowly.

'What's that you say?' he said. 'I've half a mind to give you a lesson in civility.'

'You set up any more of your gab to me,' returned the Scotchman, 'and I'll show ye the wrong side of a jyle. I've heard tell of the three of ye. Ye're not long for here, I can tell ye that. The Government has their eyes upon ye. They make short work of damned beachcombers, I'll say that for the French.'

'You wait till I catch you off your ship!' cried the captain: and then, turning to the crew, 'Good-bye, you fellows!' he said. 'You're gentlemen, anyway! The worst nigger among you would look better upon a quarter-deck than that filthy Scotchman.'

Captain Tom scorned to reply; he watched with a hard smile the departure of his guests; and as soon as the last foot was off the plank, turned to the hands to work cargo.

The beachcombers beat their inglorious retreat along the shore; Herrick first, his face dark with blood, his knees trembling under him with the hysteria of rage. Presently, under the same *purao* where they had shivered the night before, he cast himself down, and groaned aloud, and ground his face into the sand.

'Don't speak to me, don't speak to me. I can't stand it,' broke from him.

The other two stood over him perplexed.

'Wot can't he stand now?' said the clerk. ''Asn't he 'ad a meal? *I'm* lickin' my lips.'

Herrick reared up his wild eyes and burning face. 'I can't beg!' he screamed, and again threw himself prone.

'This thing's got to come to an end,' said the captain with an intake of the breath.

'Looks like signs of an end, don't it?' sneered the clerk.

'He's not so far from it, and don't you deceive yourself,' replied the captain. 'Well,' he added in a livelier voice, 'you fellows hang on here, and I'll go and interview my representative.'

Whereupon he turned on his heel, and set off at a swinging sailor's walk towards Papeete.

It was some half-hour later when he returned. The clerk was dozing with his back against the tree: Herrick still lay where he had flung himself; nothing showed whether he slept or waked.

'See, boys!' cried the captain, with that artificial heartiness of his which was at times so painful, 'here's a new idea.' And he produced note-paper, stamped envelopes, and pencils, three of each. 'We can all write home by the mail brigantine; the consul says I can come over to his place and ink up the addresses.'

'Well, that's a start, too,' said the clerk. 'I never thought of that.'

'It was that yarning last night about going home that put me up to it,' said the captain.

'Well, 'and over,' said the clerk. 'I'll 'ave a shy,' and he retired a little distance to the shade of a canoe.

The others remained under the *purao*. Now they would

write a word or two, now scribble it out; now they would sit biting at the pencil end and staring seaward; now their eyes would rest on the clerk, where he sat propped on the canoe, leering and coughing, his pencil racing glibly on the paper.

'I can't do it,' said Herrick suddenly. 'I haven't got the heart.'

'See here,' said the captain, speaking with unwonted gravity; 'it may be hard to write, and to write lies at that; and God knows it is; but it's the square thing. It don't cost anything to say you're well and happy, and sorry you can't make a remittance this mail; and if you don't, I'll tell you what I think it is—I think it's about the high-water mark of being a brute beast.'

'It's easy to talk,' said Herrick. 'You don't seem to have written much yourself, I notice.'

'What do you bring in me for?' broke from the captain. His voice was indeed scarce raised above a whisper, but emotion clanged in it. 'What do you know about me? If you had commanded the finest barque that ever sailed from Portland;* if you had been drunk in your berth when she struck the breakers in Fourteen Island Group, and hadn't had the wit to stay there and drown, but came on deck, and given drunken orders, and lost six lives—I could understand your talking then! There,' he said more quietly, 'that's my yarn, and now you know it. It's a pretty one for the father of a family. Five men and a woman murdered. Yes, there was a woman on board, and hadn't no business to be either. Guess, I sent her to Hell, if there is such a place. I never dared go home again; and the wife and the little ones went to England to her father's place. I don't know what's come to them,' he added, with a bitter shrug.

'Thank you, captain,' said Herrick. 'I never liked you better.'

They shook hands, short and hard, with eyes averted, tenderness swelling in their bosoms.

'Now, boys! to work again at lying!' said the captain.

'I'll give my father up,' returned Herrick with a writhen smile. 'I'll try my sweetheart instead for a change of evils.'

And here is what he wrote:—

'Emma, I have scratched out the beginning to my father, for I think I can write more easily to you. This is my last farewell to all, the last you will ever hear or see of an unworthy friend and son. I have failed in life; I am quite broken down and disgraced. I pass under a false name; you will have to tell my father that with all your kindness. It is my own fault. I know, had I chosen, that I might have done well; and yet I swear to you I tried to choose. I could not bear that you should think I did not try. For I loved you all; you must never doubt me in that, you least of all. I have always unceasingly loved, but what was my love worth? and what was I worth? I had not the manhood of a common clerk, I could not work to earn you; I have lost you now, and for your sake I could be glad of it. When you first came to my father's house—do you remember those days?—I want you to, you saw the best of me then, all that was good in me. Do you remember the day I took your hand and would not let it go—and the day on Battersea Bridge, when we were looking at a barge, and I began to tell you one of my silly stories, and broke off to say I loved you? That was the beginning, and now here is the end. When you have read this letter, you will go round and kiss them all good-bye, my father and mother, and the children, one by one, and poor uncle; and tell them all to forget me, and forget me yourself. Turn the key in the door; let no thought of me return; be done with the poor ghost that pretended he was a man and stole your love. Scorn of myself grinds in me as I write. I should tell you I am well and happy, and want for nothing. I do not exactly make money, or I should send a remittance; but I am well cared for, have friends, live in a beautiful place and climate, such as we have dreamed of together, and no pity need be wasted on me. In such places, you understand, it is easy to live, and live well, but often hard to make sixpence in money. Explain this to my father, he will understand. I have no more to say; only linger, going out, like an unwilling guest. God in heaven bless you. Think of me at the last, here, on a bright beach, the sky and sea immoderately blue, and the great breakers roaring outside on a barrier reef, where a little isle sits green with palms. I am well and strong. It is a more pleasant way to die than if you were crowding about me on a sick-bed. And yet I am dying. This is my last kiss. Forgive, forget the unworthy.'

So far he had written, his paper was all filled, when there returned a memory of evenings at the piano, and that song, the masterpiece of love, in which so many have found the expression of their dearest thoughts. '*Einst, O wunder!*'* he added. More was not required; he knew that in his love's heart the context would spring up, escorted with fair images and harmony; of how all through life her name should tremble in his ears, her name be everywhere repeated in the sounds of nature; and when death came, and he lay dissolved, her memory lingered and thrilled among his elements.

> 'Once, O wonder! once from the ashes of my heart
> Arose a blossom—'

Herrick and the captain finished their letters about the same time; each was breathing deep, and their eyes met and were averted as they closed the envelopes.

'Sorry I write so big,' said the captain gruffly. 'Came all of a rush, when it did come.'

'Same here,' said Herrick. 'I could have done with a ream when I got started; but it's long enough for all the good I had to say.'

They were still at the addresses when the clerk strolled up, smirking and twirling his envelope, like a man well pleased. He looked over Herrick's shoulder.

'Hullo,' he said, 'you ain't writing 'ome.'

'I am, though,' said Herrick; 'she lives with my father. Oh, I see what you mean,' he added. 'My real name is Herrick. No more Hay,'—they had both used the same *alias*—'no more Hay than yours, I daresay.'

'Clean bowled in the middle stump!' laughed the clerk. 'My name's 'Uish if you want to know. Everybody has a false nyme in the Pacific. Lay you five to three the captain 'as.'

'So I have too,' replied the captain; 'and I've never told my own since the day I tore the title-page out of my Bowditch* and flung the damned thing into the sea. But I'll tell it to you, boys. John Davis is my name. I'm Davis of the *Sea Ranger*.'

'Dooce you are!' said Huish. 'And what was she? a pirate or a slyver?'

'She was the fastest barque out of Portland, Maine,' replied the captain; 'and for the way I lost her, I might as well have bored a hole in her side with an auger.'

'Oh, you lost her, did you?' said the clerk. ''Ope she was insured?'

No answer being returned to this sally, Huish, still

brimming over with vanity and conversation, struck into another subject.

'I've a good mind to read you my letter,' said he. 'I've a good fist with a pen when I choose, and this is a prime lark. She was a barmaid I ran across in Northampton; she was a spanking fine piece, no end of style; and we cottoned at first sight like parties in the play. I suppose I spent the chynge of a fiver on that girl. Well, I 'appened to remember her nyme, so I wrote to her, and told her 'ow I had got rich, and married a queen in the Hislands, and lived in a blooming palace. Such a sight of crammers! I must read you one bit about my opening the nigger parliament in a cocked 'at. It's really prime.'

The captain jumped to his feet. 'That's what you did with the paper that I went and begged for you?' he roared.

It was perhaps lucky for Huish—it was surely in the end unfortunate for all—that he was seized just then by one of his prostrating accesses of cough; his comrades would have else deserted him, so bitter was their resentment. When the fit had passed, the clerk reached out his hand, picked up the letter, which had fallen to the earth, and tore it into fragments, stamp and all.

'Does that satisfy you?' he asked sullenly.

'We'll say no more about it,' replied Davis.

CHAPTER III

THE OLD CALABOOSE—DESTINY AT THE DOOR

THE old calaboose, in which the waifs had so long harboured, is a low, rectangular enclosure of building at the corner of a shady western avenue and a little townward of the British consulate. Within was a grassy court, littered with wreckage and the traces of vagrant occupation. Six or seven cells opened from the court: the doors, that had once been locked on mutinous whalermen, rotting before them in the grass. No mark remained of their old destination, except the rusty bars upon the windows.

The floor of one of the cells had been a little cleared; a bucket (the last remaining piece of furniture of the three caitiffs) stood full of water by the door, a half cocoanut-shell beside it for a drinking-cup; and on some ragged ends of mat Huish sprawled asleep, his mouth open, his face deathly. The glow of the tropic afternoon, the green of sunbright foliage, stared into that shady place through door and window; and Herrick, pacing to and fro on the coral floor, sometimes paused and laved his face and neck with tepid water from the bucket. His long arrears of suffering, the night's vigil, the insults of the morning, and the harrowing business of the letter, had strung him to that point when pain is almost pleasure, time shrinks to a mere point, and death and life appear indifferent. To and fro he paced like a caged brute; his mind whirling through the universe of thought and memory; his eyes, as he went, skimming the legends on the wall. The crumbling whitewash was all full of them: Tahitian names, and French, and English, and rude sketches of ships under sail and men at fisticuffs.

It came to him of a sudden that he too must leave upon these walls the memorial of his passage. He paused before a clean space, took the pencil out, and pondered. Vanity, so hard to dislodge, awoke in him. We call it vanity at least; perhaps unjustly. Rather it was the bare sense of his existence prompted him; the sense of his life, the one thing wonderful, to which he scarce clung with a finger. From his jarred nerves, there came a strong sentiment of coming change; whether good or ill he could not say: change, he knew no more—change, with inscrutable veiled face, approaching noiseless. With the feeling, came the vision of a concert room, the rich hues of instruments, the silent audience, and the loud voice of the symphony. 'Destiny knocking at the door,' he thought; drew a stave on the plaster, and wrote in the famous phrase from the Fifth Symphony.* 'So,' thought he, 'they will know that I loved music and had classical tastes. They? He, I suppose: the unknown, kindred spirit that shall come some day and read my *memor querela*.* Ha, he shall have Latin too!' And he added: *terque quaterque beati Queis ante ora patrum*.*

He turned again to his uneasy pacing, but now with an irrational and supporting sense of duty done. He had dug his grave that morning; now he had carved his epitaph; the folds of the toga were composed, why should he delay the insignificant trifle that remained to do? He paused and looked long in the face of the sleeping Huish, drinking disenchantment and distaste of life. He nauseated himself with that vile countenance. Could the thing continue? What bound him now? Had he no rights?—only the obligation to go on, without discharge or furlough, bearing the unbearable? *Ich trage unerträgliches*,* the quotation rose in his mind; he repeated the whole piece, one of the most perfect of the most perfect of poets; and a phrase struck him like a blow: *Du, stolzes Herz, du hast es ja gewollt*.* Where was the pride of his heart? And he raged against himself, as a man bites on a sore tooth, in a heady sensuality of scorn. 'I have no pride, I have no heart, no manhood,' he thought, 'or why should I prolong a life more shameful than the gallows? Or why should I have fallen to it? No pride, no capacity, no force. Not even a bandit! and to be starving here with worse than banditti—with this trivial hell-hound!' His rage against his comrade rose and flooded him, and he shook a trembling fist at the sleeper.

A swift step was audible. The captain appeared upon the threshold of the cell, panting and flushed, and with a foolish face of happiness. In his arms he carried a loaf of bread and bottles of beer; the pockets of his coat were bulging with cigars. He rolled his treasures on the floor, grasped Herrick by both hands, and crowed with laughter.

'Broach the beer!' he shouted. 'Broach the beer, and glory hallelujah!'

'Beer?' repeated Huish, struggling to his feet.

'Beer it is!' cried Davis. 'Beer and plenty of it. Any number of persons can use it (like Lyon's tooth-tablet) with perfect propriety and neatness. Who's to officiate?'

'Leave me alone for that,' said the clerk. He knocked the necks off with a lump of coral, and each drank in succession from the shell.

'Have a weed,' said Davis. 'It's all in the bill.'

'What is up?' asked Herrick.

The captain fell suddenly grave. 'I'm coming to that,' said he. 'I want to speak with Herrick here. You, Hay—or Huish, or whatever your name is—you take a weed and the other bottle, and go and see how the wind is down by the *purao*. I'll call you when you're wanted!'

'Hey? Secrets? That ain't the ticket,' said Huish.

'Look here, my son,' said the captain, 'this is business, and don't you make any mistake about it. If you're going to make trouble, you can have it your own way and stop right here. Only get the thing right: if Herrick and I go, we take the beer. Savvy?'

'Oh, I don't want to shove my oar in,' returned Huish. 'I'll cut right enough. Give me the swipes. You can jaw till you're blue in the face for what I care. I don't think it's the friendly touch: that's all.' And he shambled grumbling out of the cell into the staring sun.

The captain watched him clear of the courtyard; then turned to Herrick.

'What is it?' asked Herrick thickly.

'I'll tell you,' said Davis. 'I want to consult you. It's a chance we've got. What's that?' he cried, pointing to the music on the wall.

'What?' said the other. 'Oh, that! It's music; it's a phrase of Beethoven's I was writing up. It means Destiny knocking at the door.'

'Does it?' said the captain, rather low; and he went near and studied the inscription; 'and this French?' he asked, pointing to the Latin.

'O, it just means I should have been luckier if I had died at home,' returned Herrick impatiently. 'What is this business?'

'Destiny knocking at the door,' repeated the captain; and then, looking over his shoulder, 'Well, Mr Herrick, that's about what it comes to,' he added.

'What do you mean? Explain yourself,' said Herrick.

But the captain was again staring at the music. 'About how long ago since you wrote up this truck?' he asked.

'What does it matter?' exclaimed Herrick. 'I daresay half-an-hour.'

'My God, it's strange!' cried Davis. 'There's some men would call that accidental: not me. That—'and he drew his thick finger under the music—'that's what I call Providence.'

'You said we had a chance,' said Herrick.

'Yes, *sir*!' said the captain, wheeling suddenly face to face with his companion. 'I did so. If you're the man I take you for, we have a chance.'

'I don't know what you take me for,' was the reply. 'You can scarce take me too low.'

'Shake hands, Mr Herrick,' said the captain. 'I know you. You're a gentleman and a man of spirit. I didn't want to speak before that bummer there; you'll see why. But to you I'll rip it right out. I got a ship.'

'A ship?' cried Herrick. 'What ship?'

'That schooner we saw this morning off the passage.'

'The schooner with the hospital flag?'

'That's the hooker,' said Davis. 'She's the *Farallone*, hundred and sixty tons register, out of 'Frisco for Sydney, in California champagne. Captain, mate, and one hand all died of the small-pox, same as they had round in the Paumotus,* I guess. Captain and mate were the only white men; all the hands Kanakas; seems a queer kind of outfit from a Christian port. Three of them left and a cook; didn't know where they were; I can't think where they were either, if you come to that; Wiseman must have been on the booze, I guess, to sail the course he did. However, there *he* was, dead; and here are the Kanakas as good as lost. They bummed around at sea like the babes in the wood; and tumbled end-on upon Tahiti. The consul here took charge. He offered the berth to Williams; Williams had never had the small-pox and backed down. That was when I came in for the letter-paper; I thought there was something up when the consul asked me to look in again; but I never let on to you fellows, so 's you'd not be disappointed. Consul tried M'Neil; scared of small-pox. He tried Capirati, that Corsican, and Leblue, or whatever his name is, wouldn't lay a hand on it; all too fond of their sweet lives. Last of all, when there wasn't nobody else left to offer it to, he offers it to me. "Brown, will you ship captain and take her to Sydney?" says he. "Let me choose my own mate and another white hand," says I, "for I don't hold with this Kanaka crew racket; give us all two months' advance to get our clothes and instruments out of pawn, and I'll take stock tonight, fill up stores, and get to sea tomorrow before dark!" That's what I said. "That's good enough," says the consul, "and you can count yourself damned lucky, Brown," says he. And he said it pretty meaningful-appearing, too. However, that's all one now. I'll ship Huish before the mast*—of course I'll let him berth aft—and I'll ship you mate at seventy-five dollars and two months' advance.'

'Me mate? Why, I'm a landsman!' cried Herrick.

'Guess you've got to learn,' said the captain. 'You don't fancy I'm going to skip and leave you rotting on the beach perhaps? I'm not that sort, old man. And you're handy anyway; I've been shipmates with worse.'

'God knows I can't refuse,' said Herrick. 'God knows I thank you from my heart.'

'That's all right,' said the captain. 'But it ain't all.' He turned aside to light a cigar.

'What else is there?' asked the other, with a pang of undefinable alarm.

'I'm coming to that,' said Davis, and then paused a little. 'See here,' he began, holding out his cigar between his finger and thumb, 'suppose you figure up what this'll amount to.

You don't catch on? Well, we get two months' advance; we can't get away from Papeete—our creditors wouldn't let us go—for less; it'll take us along about two months to get to Sydney; and when we get there, I just want to put it to you squarely: What the better are we?'

'We're off the beach at least,' said Herrick.

'I guess there's a beach at Sydney,' returned the captain; 'and I'll tell you one thing, Mr Herrick—I don't mean to try. No, *sir*! Sydney will never see me.'

'Speak out plain,' said Herrick.

'Plain Dutch,' replied the captain. 'I'm going to own that schooner. It's nothing new; it's done every year in the Pacific. Stephens stole a schooner the other day, didn't he? Hayes and Pease* stole vessels all the time. And it's the making of the crowd of us. See here—you think of that cargo. Champagne! why, it's like as if it was put up on purpose. In Peru we'll sell that liquor off at the pier-head, and the schooner after it, if we can find a fool to buy her; and then light out for the mines. If you'll back me up, I stake my life I carry it through.'

'Captain,' said Herrick, with a quailing voice, 'don't do it!'

'I'm desperate,' returned Davis. 'I've got a chance; I may never get another. Herrick, say the word; back me up; I think we've starved together long enough for that.'

'I can't do it. I'm sorry. I can't do it. I've not fallen as low as that,' said Herrick, deadly pale.

'What did you say this morning?' said Davis. 'That you couldn't beg? It's the one thing or the other, my son.'

'Ah, but this is the jail!' cried Herrick. 'Don't tempt me. It's the jail.'

'Did you hear what the skipper said on board that schooner?' pursued the captain. 'Well, I tell you he talked straight. The French have let us alone for a long time; it can't last longer; they've got their eye on us; and as sure as you live, in three weeks you'll be in jail whatever you do. I read it in the consul's face.'

'You forget, captain,' said the young man. 'There is another way. I can die; and to say truth, I think I should have died three years ago.'

The captain folded his arms and looked the other in the face. 'Yes,' said he, 'yes, you can cut your throat; that's a frozen fact; much good may it do you! And where do I come in?'

The light of a strange excitement came in Herrick's face. 'Both of us,' said he, 'both of us together. It's not possible you can enjoy this business. Come,' and he reached out a timid hand, 'a few strokes in the lagoon—and rest!'

'I tell you, Herrick, I'm 'most tempted to answer you the way the man does in the Bible, and say, "*Get thee behind me, Satan!*"'* said the captain. 'What! you think I would go drown myself, and I got children starving? Enjoy it? No, by God, I do not enjoy it! but it's the row I've got to hoe, and I'll hoe it till I drop right here. I have three of them, you see, two boys and the one girl, Adar. The trouble is that you are not a parent yourself. I tell you, Herrick, I love you,' the man broke out; 'I didn't take to you at first, you were so anglified and tony, but I love you now; it's a man that loves you stands here and wrestles with you. I can't go to sea with the bummer alone; it's not possible. Go drown yourself, and there goes my last chance—the last chance of a poor miserable beast, earning a crust to feed his family. I can't do nothing but sail ships, and I've no papers. And here I get a chance, and you go back on me! Ah, you've no family, and that's where the trouble is!'

'I have indeed,' said Herrick.

'Yes, I know,' said the captain, 'you think so. But no man's got a family till he's got children. It's only the kids count. There's something about the little shavers . . . I can't talk of them. And if you thought a cent about this father that I hear you talk of, or that sweetheart you were writing to this morning, you would feel like me. You would say, What matter laws, and God, and that? My folks are hard up, I belong to them, I'll get them bread, or, by God! I'll get them wealth, if I have to burn down London for it. That's what you would say. And I'll tell you more: your heart is saying so this living minute. I can see it in your face. You're thinking, Here's poor friendship for the man I've starved along of, and as for the girl that I set up to be in love with, here's a mighty limp kind of a love that won't carry me as far as 'most any man would go for a demijohn of whisky. There's not much *ro*mance to that love, anyway; it's not the kind they carry on about in song-books. But what's the good of my carrying on talking, when it's all in your inside as plain as print? I put the question to you once for all. Are you going to desert me in my hour of need?—you know if I've deserted you—or will you give me your hand, and try a fresh deal, and go home (as like as not) a millionaire? Say no, and God pity me! Say yes, and I'll make the little ones pray for you every night on their bended knees. "God bless Mr Herrick!" that's what they'll say, one after the other, the old girl sitting there holding stakes at the foot of the bed, and the damned little innocents . . .' he broke off. 'I don't often rip out about the kids,' he said; 'but when I do, there's something fetches loose.'

'Captain,' said Herrick faintly, 'is there nothing else?'

'I'll prophesy if you like,' said the captain with renewed vigour. 'Refuse this, because you think yourself too honest, and before a month's out you'll be jailed for a sneak-thief. I give you the word fair. I can see it, Herrick, if you can't; you're breaking down. Don't think, if you refuse this chance, that you'll go on doing the evangelical; you're about through with your stock; and before you know where you are, you'll be right out on the other side. No, it's either this for you; or else it's Caledonia.* I bet you never were there, and saw those white, shaved men, in their dust clothes and straw hats, prowling around in gangs in the lamplight at Noumea;* they look like wolves, and they look like preachers, and they look like the sick; Huish is a daisy to the best of them. Well, there's your company. They're waiting for you, Herrick, and you got to go; and that's a prophecy.'

And as the man stood and shook through his great stature, he seemed indeed like one in whom the spirit of divination worked and might utter oracles. Herrick looked at him, and looked away; it seemed not decent to spy upon such agitation; and the young man's courage sank.

'You talk of going home,' he objected. 'We could never do that.'

'*We* could,' said the other. 'Captain Brown couldn't, nor Mr Hay, that shipped mate with him couldn't. But what's that to do with Captain Davis or Mr Herrick, you galoot?'

'But Hayes had these wild islands where he used to call,' came the next fainter objection.

'We have the wild islands of Peru,' retorted Davis. 'They were wild enough for Stephens, no longer agone than just last year. I guess they'll be wild enough for us.'

'And the crew?'

'All Kanakas. Come, I see you're right, old man. I see you'll stand by.' And the captain once more offered his hand.

'Have it your own way then,' said Herrick. 'I'll do it: a strange thing for my father's son. But I'll do it. I'll stand by you, man, for good or evil.'

'God bless you!' cried the captain, and stood silent. 'Herrick,' he added with a smile, 'I believe I'd have died in my tracks, if you'd said, No!'

And Herrick, looking at the man, half believed so also.

'And now we'll go break it to the bummer,' said Davis.

'I wonder how he'll take it,' said Herrick.

'Him? Jump at it!' was the reply.

CHAPTER IV

THE YELLOW FLAG

THE schooner *Farallone* lay well out in the jaws of the pass, where the terrified pilot had made haste to bring her to her moorings and escape. Seen from the beach through the thin line of shipping, two objects stood conspicuous to seaward: the little isle, on the one hand, with its palms and the guns and batteries raised forty years before in defence of Queen Pomare's capital;* the outcast *Farallone,* upon the other, banished to the threshold of the port, rolling there to her scuppers, and flaunting the plague-flag as she rolled. A few sea-birds screamed and cried about the ship; and within easy range, a man-of-war guard-boat hung off and on and glittered with the weapons of marines. The exuberant daylight and the blinding heaven of the tropics picked out and framed the pictures.

A neat boat, manned by natives in uniform, and steered by the doctor of the port, put from shore towards three of the afternoon, and pulled smartly for the schooner. The foresheets were heaped with sacks of flour, onions, and potatoes, perched among which was Huish dressed as a foremast hand; a heap of chests and cases impeded the action of the oarsmen; and in the stern, by the left hand of the doctor, sat Herrick, dressed in a fresh rig of slops,* his brown beard trimmed to a point, a pile of paper novels on his lap, and nursing the while between his feet a chronometer, for which they had exchanged that of the *Farallone,* long since run down and the rate lost.

They passed the guard-boat, exchanging hails with the boatswain's mate in charge, and drew near at last to the forbidden ship. Not a cat stirred, there was no speech of man; and the sea being exceeding high outside, and the reef close to where the schooner lay, the clamour of the surf hung round her like the sound of battle.

'*Ohé la goëlette!*'* sang out the doctor, with his best voice.

Instantly, from the house where they had been stowing away stores, first Davis, and then the ragamuffin, swarthy crew made their appearance.

'Hullo, Hay, that you?' said the captain, leaning on the rail. 'Tell the old man to lay her alongside, as if she was eggs. There's a hell of a run of sea here, and his boat's brittle.'

The movement of the schooner was at that time more than usually violent. Now she heaved her side as high as a deep-sea steamer's, and showed the flashing of her copper; now she swung swiftly toward the boat until her scuppers gurgled.

'I hope you have sea-legs,' observed the doctor. 'You will require them.'

Indeed, to board the *Farallone,* in that exposed position where she lay, was an affair of some dexterity. The less precious goods were hoisted roughly in; the chronometer, after repeated failures, was passed gently and successfully from hand to hand; and there remained only the more difficult business of embarking Huish. Even that piece of dead weight (shipped A.B.* at eighteen dollars, and described by the captain to the consul as an invaluable man) was at last hauled on board without mishap; and the doctor, with civil salutations, took his leave.

The three co-adventurers looked at each other, and Davis heaved a breath of relief.

'Now let's get this chronometer fixed,' said he, and led the way into the house. It was a fairly spacious place; two staterooms and a good-sized pantry opened from the main cabin; the bulk-heads were painted white, the floor laid with waxcloth. No litter, no sign of life remained; for the effects of the dead men had been disinfected and conveyed on shore. Only on the table, in a saucer, some sulphur burned, and the fumes set them coughing as they entered. The captain peered into the starboard stateroom, where the bed-clothes still lay tumbled in the bunk, the blanket flung back as they had flung it back from the disfigured corpse before its burial.

'Now, I told these niggers to tumble that truck overboard,' grumbled Davis. 'Guess they were afraid to lay hands on it. Well, they've hosed the place out; that's as much as can be expected, I suppose. Huish, lay on to these blankets.'

'See you blooming well far enough first,' said Huish, drawing back.

'What's that?' snapped the captain. 'I'll tell you, my young friend, I think you make a mistake. I'm captain here.'

'Fat lot I care,' returned the clerk.

'That so?' said Davis. 'Then you'll berth forward with the niggers! Walk right out of this cabin.'

'Oh, I dessay!' said Huish. 'See any green in my eye? A lark's a lark.'

'Well, now, I'll explain this business, and you'll see (once for all) just precisely how much lark there is to it,' said Davis. 'I'm captain, and I'm going to be it. One thing of three. First, you take my orders here as cabin steward, in which case you mess with us. Or second, you refuse, and I pack you forward—and you get as quick as the word's said. Or, third and last, I'll signal that man-of-war and send you ashore under arrest for mutiny.'

'And, of course, I wouldn't blow the gaff? O no!' replied the jeering Huish.

'And who's to believe you, my son?' inquired the captain. 'No, *sir*! There ain't no lark about my captainizing. Enough said. Up with these blankets.'

Huish was no fool, he knew when he was beaten; and he was no coward either, for he stepped to the bunk, took the infected bed-clothes fairly in his arms, and carried them out of the house without a check or tremor.

'I was waiting for the chance,' said Davis to Herrick. 'I needn't do the same with you, because you understand it for yourself.'

'Are you going to berth here?' asked Herrick, following the captain into the stateroom, where he began to adjust the chronometer in its place at the bed-head.

'Not much!' replied he. 'I guess I'll berth on deck. I don't know as I'm afraid, but I've no immediate use for confluent smallpox.'

'I don't know that I'm afraid either,' said Herrick. 'But the thought of these two men sticks in my throat; that captain and mate dying here, one opposite to the other. It's grim. I wonder what they said last?'

'Wiseman and Wishart?' said the captain. 'Probably mighty small potatoes. That's a thing a fellow figures out for himself one way, and the real business goes quite another. Perhaps Wiseman said, "Here, old man, fetch up the gin, I'm feeling powerful rocky." And perhaps Wishart said, "Oh, hell!"'

'Well, that's grim enough,' said Herrick.

'And so it is,' said Davis. 'There; there's that chronometer fixed. And now it's about time to up anchor and clear out.'

He lit a cigar and stepped on deck.

'Here, you! What's *your* name?' he cried to one of the hands, a lean-flanked, clean-built fellow from some far western island, and of a darkness almost approaching to the African.

'Sally Day,'* replied the man.

'Devil it is,' said the captain. 'Didn't know we had ladies on board. Well, Sally, oblige me by hauling down that rag there. I'll do the same for you another time.' He watched the yellow bunting as it was eased past the cross-trees and handed down on deck. 'You'll float no more on this ship,' he observed. 'Muster the people aft, Mr Hay,' he added, speaking unnecessarily loud, 'I've a word to say to them.'

It was with a singular sensation that Herrick prepared for the first time to address a crew. He thanked his stars indeed, that they were natives. But even natives, he reflected, might be critics too quick for such a novice as himself; they might perceive some lapse from that precise and cut-and-dry English which prevails on board a ship; it was even possible they understood no other; and he racked his brain, and overhauled his reminiscences of sea romance for some appropriate words.

'Here, men! tumble aft!' he said. 'Lively now! all hands aft!'

They crowded in the alleyway like sheep.

'Here they are, sir,' said Herrick.

For some time the captain continued to face the stern; then turned with ferocious suddenness on the crew, and seemed to enjoy their shrinking.

'Now,' he said, twisting his cigar in his mouth and toying with the spokes of the wheel, 'I'm Captain Brown. I command this ship. This is Mr Hay, first officer. The other white man is cabin steward, but he'll stand watch and do his trick. My orders shall be obeyed smartly. You savvy, "*smartly*"? There shall be no growling about the kaikai,* which will be above allowance. You'll put a handle to the mate's name, and tack on "sir" to every order I give you. If you're smart and quick, I'll make this ship comfortable for all hands.' He took the cigar out of his mouth. 'If you're not,' he added, in a roaring voice, 'I'll make it a floating hell. Now, Mr Hay, we'll pick watches, if you please.'

'All right,' said Herrick.

'You will please use "sir" when you address me, Mr Hay,' said the captain. 'I'll take the lady. Step to starboard, Sally.' And then he whispered in Herrick's ear: 'take the old man.'

'I'll take you, there,' said Herrick.

'What's your name?' said the captain. 'What's that you say? Oh, that's not English; I'll have none of your highway gibberish on my ship. We'll call you old Uncle Ned, because you've got no wool on the top of your head, just the place where the wool ought to grow. Step to port, Uncle. Don't you hear Mr Hay has picked you? Then I'll take the white man. White Man, step to starboard. Now which of you two is the cook? You? Then Mr Hay takes your friend in the blue dungaree. Step to port, Dungaree. There, we know who we all are: Dungaree, Uncle Ned, Sally Day, White Man, and Cook. All F.F.V.'s* I guess. And now, Mr Hay, we'll up anchor, if you please.'

'For heaven's sake, tell me some of the words,' whispered Herrick.

An hour later, the *Farallone* was under all plain sail, the rudder hard a-port, and the cheerfully-clanking windlass had brought the anchor home.

'All clear, sir,' cried Herrick from the bow.

The captain met her with the wheel, as she bounded like a stag from her repose, trembling and bending to the puffs. The guard-boat gave a parting hail, the wake whitened and ran out; the *Farallone* was under weigh.

Her berth had been close to the pass. Even as she forged ahead Davis slewed her for the channel between the pier ends of the reef, the breakers sounding and whitening to either hand. Straight through the narrow band of blue, she shot to seaward: and the captain's heart exulted as he felt her tremble underfoot, and (looking back over the taffrail) beheld the roofs of Papeete changing position on the shore and the island mountains rearing higher in the wake.

But they were not yet done with the shore and the horror of the yellow flag. About midway of the pass, there was a cry and a scurry, a man was seen to leap upon the rail, and, throwing his arms over his head, to stoop and plunge into the sea.

'Steady as she goes,' the captain cried, relinquishing the wheel to Huish.

The next moment he was forward in the midst of the Kanakas, belaying-pin* in hand.

'Anybody else for shore?' he cried, and the savage trumpeting of his voice, no less than the ready weapon in his hand, struck fear in all. Stupidly they stared after their escaped companion, whose black head was visible upon the water, steering for the land. And the schooner meanwhile slipt like a racer through the pass, and met the long sea of the open ocean with a souse of spray.

'Fool that I was, not to have a pistol ready!' exclaimed Davies. 'Well, we go to sea short-handed, we can't help that. You have a lame watch of it, Mr Hay.'

'I don't see how we are to get along,' said Herrick.

'Got to,' said the captain. 'No more Tahiti for me.'

Both turned instinctively and looked astern. The fair island was unfolding mountain-top on mountain-top; Eimeo, on the port board, lifted her splintered pinnacles; and still the schooner raced to the open sea.

'Think!' cried the captain with a gesture, 'yesterday morning I danced for my breakfast like a poodle dog.'

CHAPTER V

THE CARGO OF CHAMPAGNE

THE ship's head was laid to clear Eimeo to the north, and the captain sat down in the cabin, with a chart, a ruler, and an epitome.

'East a half no'the,' said he, raising his face from his labours. 'Mr Hay, you'll have to watch your dead reckoning;* I want every yard she makes on every hair's-breadth of a course. I'm going to knock a hole right straight through the Paumotus, and that's always a near touch. Now, if this South East Trade* ever blew out of the S.E., which it don't, we might hope to lie within half a point of our course. Say we lie within a point of it. That'll just about weather Fakarava.* Yes, sir, that's what we've got to do, if we tack for it. Brings us through this slush of little islands in the cleanest place: see?' And he showed where his ruler intersected the wide-lying labyrinth of the Dangerous Archipelago.* 'I wish it was night, and I could put her about right now; we're losing time and easting. Well, we'll do our best. And if we don't fetch Peru, we'll bring up to Ecuador. All one, I guess. Depreciated dollars down, and no questions asked. A remarkable fine institootion, the South American don.'

Tahiti was already some way astern, the Diadem* rising from among broken mountains—Eimeo was already close aboard, and stood black and strange against the golden splendour of the west—when the captain took his departure from the two islands, and the patent log was set.

Some twenty minutes later, Sally Day, who was continually leaving the wheel to peer in at the cabin clock, announced in a shrill cry 'Fo' bell,' and the cook was to be seen carrying the soup into the cabin.

'I guess I'll sit down and have a pick with you,' said Davis to Herrick. 'By the time I've done, it'll be dark, and we'll clap the hooker on the wind for South America.'

In the cabin at one corner of the table, immediately below

the lamp, and on the lee side of a bottle of champagne, sat Huish.

'What's this? Where did that come from?' asked the captain.

'It's fizz, and it came from the after-'old, if you want to know,' said Huish, and drained his mug.

'This'll never do,' exclaimed Davis, the merchant seaman's horror of breaking into cargo showing incongruously forth on board that stolen ship. 'There was never any good came of games like that.'

'You byby!' said Huish. 'A fellow would think (to 'ear him) we were on the square! And look 'ere, you've put this job up 'ansomely for me, 'aven't you? I'm to go on deck and steer while you two sit and guzzle, and I'm to go by a nickname, and got to call you "sir" and "mister". Well, you look here, my bloke: I'll have fizz *ad lib.*, or it won't wash. I tell you that. And you know mighty well, you ain't got any man-of-war to signal now.'

Davis was staggered. 'I'd give fifty dollars this had never happened,' he said weakly.

'Well, it '*as* 'appened, you see,' returned Huish. 'Try some; it's devilish good.'

The Rubicon was crossed without another struggle. The captain filled a mug and drank.

'I wish it was beer,' he said with a sigh. 'But there's no denying it's the genuine stuff and cheap at the money. Now, Huish, you clear out and take your wheel.'

The little wretch had gained a point, and he was gay. 'Ay, ay, sir,' said he, and left the others to their meal.

'Pea soup!' exclaimed the captain. 'Blamed if I thought I should taste pea soup again!'

Herrick sat inert and silent. It was impossible after these months of hopeless want to smell the rough, high-spiced sea victuals without lust, and his mouth watered with desire of the champagne. It was no less impossible to have assisted at the scene between Huish and the captain, and not to perceive, with sudden bluntness, the gulf where he had fallen. He was a thief among thieves. He said it to himself. He could not touch the soup. If he had moved at all, it must have been to leave the table, throw himself overboard, and drown—an honest man.

'Here,' said the captain, 'you look sick, old man; have a drop of this.'

The champagne creamed and bubbled in the mug; its bright colour, its lively effervescence, seized his eye. 'It is too late to hesitate,' he thought; his hand took the mug instinctively; he drank, with unquenchable pleasure and desire of more; drained the vessel dry, and set it down with sparkling eyes.

'There is something in life after all!' he cried. 'I had forgot what it was like. Yes, even this is worth while. Wine, food, dry clothes—why, they're worth dying, worth hanging for! Captain, tell me one thing: why aren't all the poor folk foot-pads?'

'Give it up,' said the captain.

'They must be damned good,' cried Herrick. 'There's something here beyond me. Think of that calaboose! Suppose we were sent suddenly back.' He shuddered as stung by a convulsion, and buried his face in his clutching hands.

'Here, what's wrong with you?' cried the captain. There was no reply; only Herrick's shoulders heaved, so that the table was shaken. 'Take some more of this. Here, drink this. I order you to. Don't start crying when you're out of the wood.'

'I'm not crying,' said Herrick, raising his face and showing his dry eyes. 'It's worse than crying. It's the horror of that grave that we've escaped from.'

'Come now, you tackle your soup; that'll fix you,' said Davis kindly. 'I told you you were all broken up. You couldn't have stood out another week.'

'That's the dreadful part of it!' cried Herrick. 'Another week and I'd have murdered some one for a dollar! God! and I know that? And I'm still living? It's some beastly dream.'

'Quietly, quietly! Quietly does it, my son. Take your pea soup. Food, that's what you want,' said Davis.

The soup strengthened and quieted Herrick's nerves; another glass of wine, and a piece of pickled pork and fried banana completed what the soup began; and he was able once more to look the captain in the face.

'I didn't know I was so much run down,' he said.

'Well,' said Davis, 'you were as steady as a rock all day: now you've had a little lunch, you'll be as steady as a rock again.'

'Yes,' was the reply, 'I'm steady enough now, but I'm a queer kind of a first officer.'

'Shucks!' cried the captain. 'You've only got to mind the ship's course, and keep your slate to half a point. A babby could do that, let alone a college graduate like you. There ain't nothing *to* sailoring, when you come to look it in the face. And now we'll go and put her about. Bring the slate; we'll have to start our dead reckoning right away.'

The distance run since the departure was read off the log by the binnacle light* and entered on the slate.

'Ready about,' said the captain. 'Give me the wheel, White Man, and you stand by the mainsheet. Boom tackle, Mr Hay, please, and then you can jump forward and attend head sails.'

'Ay, ay, sir,' responded Herrick.

'All clear forward?' asked Davis.

'All clear, sir.'

'Hard a-lee!' cried the captain. 'Haul in your slack as she comes,' he called to Huish. 'Haul in your slack, put your back into it; keep your feet out of the coils.' A sudden blow sent Huish flat along the deck, and the captain was in his place. 'Pick yourself up and keep the wheel hard over!' he roared. 'You wooden fool, you wanted to get killed, I guess. Draw the jib,' he cried a moment later; and then to Huish, 'Give me the wheel again, and see if you can coil that sheet.'

But Huish stood and looked at Davis with an evil countenance. 'Do you know you struck me?' said he.

'Do you know I saved your life?' returned the other, not deigning to look at him, his eyes travelling instead between the compass and the sails. 'Where would you have been, if that boom had swung out and you bundled in the slack? No, *sir*, we'll have no more of you at the mainsheet. Seaport towns are full of mainsheet-men; they hop upon one leg, my son, what's left of them, and the rest are dead. (Set your boom tackle, Mr Hay.) Struck you, did I? Lucky for you I did.'

'Well,' said Huish slowly, 'I dessay there may be somethink in that. 'Ope there is.' He turned his back elaborately on the captain, and entered the house, where the speedy explosion of a champagne cork showed he was attending to his comfort.

Herrick came aft to the captain. 'How is she doing now?' he asked.

'East and by no'the a half no'the,' said Davis. 'It's about as good as I expected.'

'What'll the hands think of it?' said Herrick.

'Oh, they don't think. They ain't paid to,' says the captain.

'There was something wrong, was there not? between you and—' Herrick paused.

'That's a nasty little beast, that's a biter,' replied the captain, shaking his head. 'But so long as you and me hang in, it don't matter.'

Herrick lay down in the weather alleyway; the night was cloudless, the movement of the ship cradled him, he was oppressed besides by the first generous meal after so long a time of famine; and he was recalled from deep sleep by the voice of Davis singing out: 'Eight bells!'

He rose stupidly and staggered aft, where the captain gave him the wheel.

'By the wind,' said the captain. 'It comes a little puffy; when you get a heavy puff, steal all you can to windward, but keep her a good full.'

He stepped towards the house, paused and hailed the forecastle.

'Got such a thing as a concertina forward?' said he. 'Bully for you, Uncle Ned. Fetch it aft, will you?'

The schooner steered very easy; and Herrick, watching the moon-whitened sails, was overpowered by drowsiness. A sharp report from the cabin startled him; a third bottle had been opened; and Herrick remembered the *Sea Ranger* and Fourteen Island Group. Presently the notes of the accordion sounded, and then the captain's voice:

> 'O honey, with our pockets full of money,
> We will trip, trip, trip, we will trip it on the quay,
> And I will dance with Kate, and Tom will dance with Sall,
> When we're all back from South Amerikee.'*

So it went to its quaint air; and the watch below lingered and listened by the forward door, and Uncle Ned was to be seen in the moonlight nodding time; and Herrick smiled at the wheel, his anxieties a while forgotten. Song followed song; another cork exploded; there were voices raised, as though the pair in the cabin were in disagreement; and presently it seemed the breach was healed; for it was now the voice of Huish that struck up, to the captain's accompaniment—

'Up in a balloon, boys,
Up in a balloon,
All among the little stars
And round about the moon.'*

A wave of nausea overcame Herrick at the wheel. He wondered why the air, the words (which were yet written with a certain knack), and the voice and accent of the singer, should all jar his spirit like a file on a man's teeth. He sickened at the thought of his two comrades drinking away their reason upon stolen wine, quarrelling and hiccupping and waking up, while the doors of a prison yawned for them in the near future. 'Shall I have sold my honour for nothing?' he thought; and a heat of rage and resolution glowed in his bosom—rage against his comrades—resolution to carry through this business if it might be carried; pluck profit out of shame, since the shame at least was now inevitable; and come home, home from South America—how did the song go?—'with his pockets full of money'.

'O honey, with our pockets full of money,
We will trip, trip, trip, we will trip it on the quay:'

so the words ran in his head; and the honey took on visible form, the quay rose before him and he knew it for the lamplit Embankment, and he saw the lights of Battersea bridge bestride the sullen river. All through the remainder of his trick, he stood entranced, reviewing the past. He had been always true to his love, but not always sedulous to recall her. In the growing calamity of his life, she had swum more distant, like the moon in mist. The letter of farewell, the dishonourable hope that had surprised and corrupted him in his distress, the changed scene, the sea, the night and the music—all stirred him to the roots of manhood. 'I *will* win her,' he thought, and ground his teeth. 'Fair or foul, what matters if I win her?'

'Fo' bell, matey. I think um fo' bell'—he was suddenly recalled by these words in the voice of Uncle Ned.

'Look in at the clock, Uncle,' said he. He would not look himself, from horror of the tipplers.

'Him past, matey,' repeated the Hawaiian.

'So much the better for you, Uncle,' he replied; and he gave up the wheel, repeating the directions as he had received them.

He took two steps forward and remembered his dead reckoning. 'How has she been heading?' he thought; and he flushed from head to foot. He had not observed or had forgotten; here was the old incompetence; the slate must be filled up by guess. 'Never again!' he vowed to himself in silent fury, 'never again. It shall be no fault of mine if this miscarry.' And for the remainder of his watch, he stood close by Uncle Ned, and read the face of the compass as perhaps he had never read a letter from his sweetheart.

All the time, and spurring him to the more attention, song, loud talk, fleering laughter and the occasional popping of a cork, reached his ears from the interior of the house; and when the port watch was relieved at midnight, Huish and the captain appeared upon the quarter-deck with flushed faces and uneven steps, the former laden with bottles, the latter with two tin mugs. Herrick silently passed them by. They hailed him in thick voices, he made no answer, they cursed him for a churl, he paid no heed although his belly quivered with disgust and rage. He closed-to the door of the house behind him, and cast himself on a locker in the cabin—not to sleep he thought—rather to think and to despair. Yet he had scarce turned twice on his uneasy bed, before a drunken voice hailed him in the ear, and he must go on deck again to stand the morning watch.

The first evening set the model for those that were to follow. Two cases of champagne scarce lasted the four-and-twenty hours, and almost the whole was drunk by Huish and the captain. Huish seemed to thrive on the excess; he was never sober, yet never wholly tipsy; the food and the sea air had soon healed him of his disease, and he began to lay on flesh. But with Davis things went worse. In the drooping, unbuttoned figure that sprawled all day upon the lockers, tippling and reading novels; in the fool who made of the evening watch a public carouse on the quarter-deck, it would have been hard to recognize the vigorous seaman of Papeete roads. He kept himself reasonably well in hand till he had taken the sun and yawned and blotted through his calculations; but from the moment he rolled up the chart, his hours were passed in slavish self-indulgence or in hoggish slumber. Every other branch of his duty was neglected, except maintaining a stern discipline about the dinner-table. Again and again Herrick would hear the cook called aft, and see him running with fresh tins, or carrying away again a meal that had been totally condemned. And the more the captain became sunk in drunkenness, the more delicate his palate showed itself. Once, in the forenoon, he had a bo'sun's chair rigged over the rail, stripped to his trousers, and went overboard with a pot of paint. 'I don't like the way this schooner's painted,' said he, 'and I taken a down upon her name.' But he tired of it in half an hour, and the schooner went on her way with an incongruous patch of colour on the stern, and the word *Farallone* part obliterated and part looking through. He refused to stand either the middle or the morning watch. It was fine-weather sailing, he said; and asked, with a laugh, 'Who ever heard of the old man standing watch himself?' To the dead reckoning which Herrick still tried to keep, he would pay not the least attention nor afford the least assistance.

'What do we want of dead reckoning?' he asked. 'We get the sun all right, don't we?'

'We mayn't get it always though,' objected Herrick. 'And you told me yourself you weren't sure of the chronometer.'

'Oh, there ain't no flies in the chronometer!' cried Davis.

'Oblige me so far, captain,' said Herrick stiffly. 'I am anxious to keep this reckoning, which is a part of my duty; I do not know what to allow for current, nor how to allow for it. I am too inexperienced; and I beg of you to help me.'

'Never discourage zealous officer,' said the captain, unrolling the chart again, for Herrick had taken him over his day's work and while he was still partly sober. 'Here it is: look for yourself; anything from west to west no' the-west, and anyways from 5 to 25 miles. That's what the A'm'ralty chart says; I guess you don't expect to get on ahead of your own Britishers?'

'I am trying to do my duty, Captain Brown,' said Herrick, with a dark flush, 'and I have the honour to inform you that I don't enjoy being trifled with.'

'What in thunder do you want?' roared Davis. 'Go and look at the blamed wake. If you're trying to do your duty, why don't you go and do it? I guess it's no business of mine to go and stick my head over the ship's rump? I guess it's yours. And I'll tell you what it is, my fine fellow, I'll trouble you not to come the dude* over me. You're insolent, that's what's wrong with you. Don't you crowd me, Mr Herrick, Esquire.'

Herrick tore up his papers, threw them on the floor, and left the cabin.

'He's turned a bloomin' swot, ain't he?' sneered Huish.

'He thinks himself too good for his company, that's what ails Herrick, Esquire,' raged the captain. 'He thinks I don't understand when he comes the heavy swell. Won't sit down with us, won't he? won't say a civil word? I'll serve the son of a gun as he deserves. By God, Huish, I'll show him whether he's too good for John Davis!'

'Easy with the names, cap',' said Huish, who was always the more sober. 'Easy over the stones, my boy!'

'All right, I will. You're a good sort, Huish. I didn't take to you at first, but I guess you're right enough. Let's open another bottle,' said the captain; and that day, perhaps because he was excited by the quarrel, he drank more recklessly, and by four o'clock was stretched insensible upon the locker.

Herrick and Huish supped alone, one after the other, opposite his flushed and snorting body. And if the sight killed Herrick's hunger, the isolation weighed so heavily on the clerk's spirit, that he was scarce risen from table ere he was currying favour with his former comrade.

Herrick was at the wheel when he approached, and Huish leaned confidentially across the binnacle.

'I say, old chappie,' he said, 'you and me don't seem to be such pals somehow.'

Herrick gave her a spoke or two in silence; his eye, as it skirted from the needle to the luff* of the foresail, passed the man by without speculation. But Huish was really dull, a thing he could support with difficulty, having no resources of his own. The idea of a private talk with Herrick, at this stage of their relations, held out particular inducements to a person of his character. Drink besides, as it renders some men hypersensitive, made Huish callous. And it would almost have required a blow to make him quit his purpose.

'Pretty business, ain't it?' he continued; 'Dyvis on the lush? Must say I thought you gave it 'im A1 today. He didn't like it a bit; took on hawful after you were gone.—"'Ere," says I, "'old on, easy on the lush," I says. "'Errick was right, and you know it. Give 'im a chanst," I says.—"'Uish," sezee, "don't you gimme no more of your jaw, or I'll knock your bloomin' eyes out." Well, wot can I do, 'Errick? But I tell you, I don't 'arf like it. It looks to me like the *Sea Rynger* over again.'

Still Herrick was silent.

'Do you 'ear me speak?' asked Huish sharply. 'You're pleasant, ain't you?'

'Stand away from that binnacle,' said Herrick.

The clerk looked at him, long and straight and black; his figure seemed to writhe like that of a snake about to strike; then he turned on his heel, went back to the cabin and opened a bottle of champagne. When eight bells were cried, he slept on the floor beside the captain on the locker; and of the whole starboard watch, only Sally Day appeared upon the summons. The mate proposed to stand the watch with him, and let Uncle Ned lie down; it would make twelve hours on deck, and probably sixteen, but in this fair-weather sailing, he might safely sleep between his tricks of wheel, leaving orders to be called on any sign of squalls. So far he could trust the men, between whom and himself a close relation had sprung up. With Uncle Ned he held long nocturnal conversations, and the old man told him his simple and hard story of exile, suffering, and injustice among cruel whites. The cook, when he found Herrick messed alone, produced for him unexpected and sometimes unpalatable dainties, of which he forced himself to eat. And one day, when he was forward, he was surprised to feel a caressing hand run down his shoulder, and to hear the voice of Sally Day crooning in his ear: 'You gootch man!' He turned, and, choking down a sob, shook hands with the negrito. They were kindly, cheery, childish souls. Upon the Sunday each brought forth his separate Bible—for they were all men of alien speech even to each other, and Sally Day communicated with his mates in English only, each read or made believe to read his chapter, Uncle Ned with spectacles on his nose; and they would all join together in the singing of missionary hymns. It was thus a cutting reproof to compare the islanders and the whites aboard the *Farallone*. Shame ran in Herrick's blood to remember what employment he was on, and to see these poor souls—and even Sally Day, the child of cannibals, in all likelihood a cannibal himself—so faithful to what they knew of good. The fact that he was held in grateful favour by these innocents served like blinders to his conscience, and there were times when he was inclined, with Sally Day, to call himself a good man. But the height of his favour was only now to appear. With one voice, the crew protested; ere Herrick knew what they were doing, the cook was aroused and came a willing volunteer; all hands clustered about their mate with expostulations and caresses; and he was bidden to lie down and take his customary rest without alarm.

'He tell you tlue,' said Uncle Ned. 'You sleep. Evely man hea he do all light. Evely man he like you too much.'

Herrick struggled, and gave way; choked upon some trivial words of gratitude; and walked to the side of the house, against which he leaned, struggling with emotion.

Uncle Ned presently followed him and begged him to lie down.

'It's no use, Uncle Ned,' he replied. 'I couldn't sleep. I'm knocked over with all your goodness.'

'Ah, no call me Uncle Ned no mo'!' cried the old man. 'No my name! My name Taveeta,* all-e-same Taveeta King of Islael. Wat for he call that Hawaii? I think no savvy nothing—all-e-same Wise-a-mana.'

It was the first time the name of the late captain had been mentioned, and Herrick grasped the occasion. The reader shall be spared Uncle Ned's unwieldy dialect, and learn in less embarrassing English, the sum of what he now communicated. The ship had scarce cleared the Golden Gates before the captain and mate had entered on a career of drunkenness, which was scarcely interrupted by their malady and only closed by death. For days and weeks they had encountered neither land nor ship; and seeing themselves lost on the huge deep with their insane conductors, the natives had drunk deep of terror.

At length they made a low island,* and went in; and Wiseman and Wishart landed in the boat.

There was a great village, a very fine village, and plenty Kanakas in that place; but all mighty serious; and from every here and there in the back parts of the settlement, Taveeta heard the sounds of island lamentation. 'I no savvy *talk* that island,' said he. 'I savvy hear um *cly.* I think, Hum! too many people die here!' But upon Wiseman and Wishart the significance of that barbaric keening was lost. Full of bread and drink, they rollicked along unconcerned, embraced the girls who had scarce energy to repel them, took up and joined (with drunken voices) in the death wail, and at last (on what they took to be an invitation) entered under the roof of a house in which was a considerable concourse of people sitting silent. They stooped below the eaves, flushed and laughing; within a minute they came forth again with changed faces and silent tongues; and as the press severed to make way for them, Taveeta was able to perceive, in the deep shadow of the house, the sick man raising from his mat a head already defeatured by disease. The two tragic triflers fled without hesitation for their boat, screaming on Taveeta to make haste; they came aboard with all speed of oars, raised anchor and crowded sail upon the ship with blows and curses, and were at sea again—and again drunk—before sunset. A week after, and the last of the two had been committed to the deep. Herrick asked Taveeta where that island was, and he replied that, by what he gathered of folks' talk as they went up together from the beach, he supposed it must be one of the Paumotus. This was in itself probable enough, for the Dangerous Archipelago had been swept that year from east to west by devastating smallpox; but Herrick thought it a strange course to lie from Sydney. Then he remembered the drink.

'Were they not surprised when they made the island?' he asked.

'Wise-a-mana he say "dam! what this?"' was the reply.

'O, that's it then,' said Herrick. 'I don't believe they knew where they were.'

'I think so too,' said Uncle Ned. 'I think no savvy. This one mo' betta,' he added, pointing to the house where the drunken captain slumbered: 'Take-a-sun all-e-time.'

The implied last touch completed Herrick's picture of the life and death of his two predecessors; of their prolonged, sordid, sodden sensuality as they sailed, they knew not whither, on their last cruise. He held but a twinkling and unsure belief in any future state; the thought of one of punishment he derided; yet for him (as for all) there dwelt a horror about the end of the brutish man. Sickness fell upon him at the image thus called up; and when he compared it with the scene in which himself was acting, and considered the doom that seemed to brood upon the schooner, a horror that was almost superstitious fell upon him. And yet the strange thing was, he did not falter. He who had proved his incapacity in so many fields, being now falsely placed amid duties which he did not understand, without help, and it might be said without countenance, had hitherto surpassed expectation; and even the shameful misconduct and shocking disclosures of that night seemed but to nerve and strengthen him. He had sold his honour; he vowed it should not be in vain; 'it shall be no fault of mine if this miscarry,' he repeated. And in his heart he wondered at himself. Living rage no doubt supported him; no doubt also, the sense of the last cast, of the ships burned, of all doors closed but one, which is so strong a tonic to the merely weak, and so deadly a depressent to the merely cowardly.

For some time the voyage went otherwise well. They weathered Fakarava with one board; and the wind holding well to the southward and blowing fresh, they passed between Raraka and Katiu, and ran some days north-east by east-half-east under the lee of Takume and Honden,* neither of which they made. In about 14° South and between 134° and 135° West, it fell a dead calm with rather a heavy sea. The captain refused to take in sail, the helm was lashed, no watch was set, and the *Farallone* rolled and banged for three days, according to observation, in almost the same place. The fourth morning, a little before day, a breeze sprang up and rapidly freshened. The captain had drunk hard the night before; he was far from sober when he was roused; and when he came on deck for the first time at half-past eight, it was plain he had already drunk deep again at breakfast. Herrick avoided his eye; and resigned the deck with indignation to a man more than half-seas over.

By the loud commands of the captain and the singing out of fellows at the ropes, he could judge from the house that sail was being crowded on the ship; relinquished his half-eaten breakfast; and came on deck again, to find the main and the jib topsails set, and both watches and the cook turned out to hand the staysail. The *Farallone* lay already far over; the sky was obscured with misty scud; and from the windward an ominous squall came flying up, broadening and blackening as it rose.

Fear thrilled in Herrick's vitals. He saw death hard by; and if not death, sure ruin. For if the *Farallone* lived through the coming squall, she must surely be dismasted. With that their enterprise was at an end, and they themselves bound prisoners to the very evidence of their crime. The greatness of the peril and his own alarm sufficed to silence him. Pride, wrath, and shame raged without issue in his mind; and he shut his teeth and folded his arms close.

The captain sat in the boat to windward, bellowing orders and insults, his eyes glazed, his face deeply congested; a bottle set between his knees, a glass in his hand half empty. His back was to the squall, and he was at first intent upon the setting of the sail. When that was done, and the great trapezium of canvas had begun to draw and to trail the lee-rail of the *Farallone* level with the foam, he laughed out an empty laugh, drained his glass, sprawled back among the lumber in the boat, and fetched out a crumpled novel.

Herrick watched him, and his indignation glowed red-hot. He glanced to windward where the squall already whitened the near sea and heralded its coming with a singular and dismal sound. He glanced at the steersman, and saw him clinging to the spokes with a face of a sickly blue. He saw the crew were running to their stations without orders. And it seemed as if something broke in his brain; and the passion of anger, so long restrained, so long eaten in secret, burst suddenly loose and shook him like a sail. He stepped across to the captain and smote his hand heavily on the drunkard's shoulder.

'You brute,' he said, in a voice that tottered, 'look behind you!'

'Wha's that?' cried Davis, bounding in the boat and upsetting the champagne.

'You lost the *Sea Ranger* because you were a drunken sot,' said Herrick. 'Now you're going to lose the *Farallone.* You're going to drown here the same way as you drowned others, and be damned. And your daughter shall walk the streets, and your sons be thieves like their father.'

For the moment, the words struck the captain white and foolish. 'My God!' he cried, looking at Herrick as upon a ghost; 'my God, Herrick!'

'Look behind you, then!' reiterated the assailant.

The wretched man, already partly sobered, did as he was told, and in the same breath of time leaped to his feet. 'Down staysail!' he trumpeted. The hands were thrilling for the order, and the great sail came with a run, and fell half overboard among the racing foam. 'Jib topsail-halyards! Let the stays'l be,' he said again.

But before it was well uttered, the squall shouted aloud and fell, in a solid mass of wind and rain commingled, on the *Farallone*; and she stooped under the blow, and lay like a thing dead. From the mind of Herrick reason fled; he clung in the weather rigging, exulting; he was done with life, and he gloried in the release; he gloried in the wild noises of the wind and the choking onslaught of the rain; he gloried to die so, and now, amid this coil of the elements. And meanwhile, in the waist up to his knees in water—so low the schooner lay—the captain was hacking at the foresheet with a pocket-knife. It was a question of seconds, for the *Farallone* drank deep of the encroaching seas. But the hand of the captain had the advance; the foresail boom tore apart the last strands of the sheet and crashed to leeward; the *Farallone* leaped up into the wind and righted; and the peak and throat halyards, which had long been let go, began to run at the same instant.

For some ten minutes more she careered under the impulse of the squall; but the captain was now master of himself and of his ship, and all danger at an end. And then, sudden as a trick-change upon the stage, the squall blew by, the wind dropped into light airs, the sun beamed forth again upon the tattered schooner; and the captain, having secured the foresail boom and set a couple of hands to the pump, walked aft, sober, a little pale, and with the sodden end of a cigar still stuck between his teeth even as the squall had found it. Herrick followed him; he could scarce recall the violence of his late emotions, but he felt there was a scene to go through, and he was anxious and even eager to go through with it.

The captain, turning at the house end, met him face to face, and averted his eyes. 'We've lost the two tops'ls and the stays'l,' he gabbled. 'Good business, we didn't lose any sticks. I guess you think we're all the better without the kites.'

'That's not what I'm thinking,' said Herrick, in a voice strangely quiet, that yet echoed confusion in the captain's mind.

'I know that,' he cried, holding up his hand. 'I know what you're thinking. No use to say it now. I'm sober.'

'I have to say it, though,' returned Herrick.

'Hold on, Herrick; you've said enough,' said Davis. 'You've said what I would take from no man breathing but yourself; only I know it's true.'

'I have to tell you, Captain Brown,' pursued Herrick, 'that I resign my position as mate. You can put me in irons or shoot me, as you please; I will make no resistance, only, I decline in any way to help or to obey you; and I suggest you should put Mr Huish in my place. He will make a worthy first officer to your captain, sir.' He smiled, bowed, and turned to walk forward.

'Where are you going, Herrick?' cried the captain, detaining him by the shoulder.

'To berth forward with the men, sir,' replied Herrick, with

the same hateful smile. 'I've been long enough aft here with you—gentlemen.'

'You're wrong there,' said Davis. 'Don't you be too quick with me; there ain't nothing wrong but the drink—it's the old story, man! Let me get sober once, and then you'll see,' he pleaded.

'Excuse me, I desire to see no more of you,' said Herrick.

The captain groaned aloud. 'You know what you said about my children?' he broke out.

'By rote. In case you wish me to say it you again?' asked Herrick.

'Don't!' cried the captain, clapping his hands to his ears. 'Don't make me kill a man I care for! Herrick, if you see me put a glass to my lips again till we're ashore, I give you leave to put a bullet through me; I beg you to it! You're the only man aboard whose carcase is worth losing; do you think I don't know that? do you think I ever went back on you? I always knew you were in the right of it—drunk or sober, I knew that. What do you want?—an oath? Man, you're clever enough to see that this is sure-enough earnest.'

'Do you mean there shall be no more drinking?' asked Herrick, 'neither by you nor Huish? that you won't go on stealing my profits and drinking my champagne that I gave my honour for? and that you'll attend to your duties, and stand watch and watch,* and bear your proper share of the ship's work, instead of leaving it all on the shoulders of a landsman, and making yourself the butt and scoff of native seamen? Is that what you mean? If it is, be so good as say it categorically.'

'You put these things in a way hard for a gentleman to swallow,' said the captain. 'You wouldn't have me say I was ashamed of myself? Trust me this once; I'll do the square thing, and there's my hand on it.'

'Well, I'll try it once,' said Herrick. 'Fail me again . . .'

'No more now!' interrupted Davis. 'No more, old man! Enough said. You've a riling tongue when your back's up, Herrick. Just be glad we're friends again, the same as what I am; and go tender on the raws; I'll see as you don't repent it. We've been mighty near death this day—don't say whose fault it was!—pretty near hell, too, I guess. We're in a mighty bad line of life, us two, and ought to go easy with each other.'

He was maundering; yet it seemed as if he were maundering with some design, beating about the bush of some communication that he feared to make, or perhaps only talking against time in terror of what Herrick might say next. But Herrick had now spat his venom; his was a kindly nature, and, content with his triumph, he had now begun to pity. With a few soothing words, he sought to conclude the interview, and proposed that they should change their clothes.

'Not right yet,' said Davis. 'There's another thing I want to tell you first. You know what you said about my children? I want to tell you why it hit me so hard; I kind of think you'll feel bad about it too. It's about my little Adar. You hadn't ought to have quite said that—but of course I know you didn't know. She—she's dead, you see.'

'Why, Davis!' cried Herrick. 'You've told me a dozen times she was alive! Clear your head, man! This must be the drink.'

'No, *sir*,' said Davis. 'She's dead. Died of a bowel complaint. That was when I was away in the brig *Oregon*. She lies in Portland, Maine. "Adar, only daughter of Captain John Davis and Mariar his wife, aged five." I had a doll for her on board. I never took the paper off'n that doll, Herrick; it went down the way it was with the *Sea Ranger*, that day I was damned.'

The Captain's eyes were fixed on the horizon, he talked with an extraordinary softness but a complete composure; and Herrick looked upon him with something that was almost terror.

'Don't think I'm crazy neither,' resumed Davis. 'I've all the cold sense that I know what to do with. But I guess a man that's unhappy's like a child; and this is a kind of a child's game of mine. I never could act up to the plain-cut truth, you see; so I pretend. And I warn you square; as soon as we're through with this talk, I'll start in again with the pretending. Only, you see, she can't walk no streets,' added the captain, 'couldn't even make out to live and get that doll!'

Herrick laid a tremulous hand upon the captain's shoulder.

'Don't do that!' cried Davis, recoiling from the touch.

'Can't you see I'm all broken up the way it is? Come along, then; come along, old man; you can put your trust in me right through; come along and get dry clothes.'

They entered the cabin, and there was Huish on his knees prising open a case of champagne.

''Vast, there!' cried the captain. 'No more of that. No more drinking on this ship.'

'Turned teetotal, 'ave you?' inquired Huish. 'I'm agreeable. About time, eh? Bloomin' nearly lost another ship, I fancy.' He took out a bottle and began calmly to burst the wire with the spike of a corkscrew.

'Do you hear me speak?' cried Davis.

'I suppose I do. You speak loud enough,' said Huish. 'The trouble is that I don't care.'

Herrick plucked the captain's sleeve. 'Let him free now,' he said. 'We've had all we want this morning.'

'Let him have it then,' said the captain. 'It's his last.'

By this time the wire was open, the string was cut, the head of gilded paper was torn away; and Huish waited, mug in hand, expecting the usual explosion. It did not follow. He eased the cork with his thumb; still there was no result. At last he took the screw and drew it. It came out very easy and with scarce a sound.

''Illo!' said Huish. ''Ere's a bad bottle.'

He poured some of the wine into the mug; it was colourless and still. He smelt and tasted it.

'W'y, wot's this?' he said. 'It's water!'

If the voice of trumpets had suddenly sounded about the ship in the midst of the sea, the three men in the house could scarcely have been more stunned than by this incident. The mug passed round; each sipped, each smelt of it; each stared at the bottle in its glory of gold paper as Crusoe may have stared at the footprint;* and their minds were swift to fix upon a common apprehension. The difference between a bottle of champagne and a bottle of water is not great; between a shipload of one or of the other lay the whole scale from riches to ruin.

A second bottle was broached. There were two cases standing ready in a stateroom; these two were brought out, broken open, and tested. Still with the same result: the contents were still colourless and tasteless, and dead as the rain in a beached fishing-boat.

'Crikey!' said Huish.

'Here, let's sample the hold!' said the captain, mopping his brow with a back-handed sweep; and the three stalked out of the house, grim and heavy-footed.

All hands were turned out; two Kanakas were sent below, another stationed at a purchase; and Davis, axe in hand, took his place beside the coamings.

'Are you going to let the men know?' whispered Herrick.

'Damn the men!' said Davis. 'It's beyond that. We've got to know ourselves.'

Three cases were sent on deck and sampled in turn; from each bottle, as the captain smashed it with the axe, the champagne ran bubbling and creaming.

'Go deeper, can't you?' cried Davis to the Kanakas in the hold.

The command gave the signal for a disastrous change. Case after case came up, bottle after bottle was burst, and bled mere water. Deeper yet, and they came upon a layer where there was scarcely so much as the intention to deceive; where the cases were no longer branded, the bottles no longer wired or papered, where the fraud was manifest and stared them in the face.

'Here's about enough of this foolery!' said Davis. 'Stow back the cases in the hold, Uncle, and get the broken crockery overboard. Come with me,' he added to his co-adventurers, and led the way back into the cabin.

CHAPTER VI

THE PARTNERS

EACH took a side of the fixed table; it was the first time they had sat down at it together; but now all sense of incongruity, all memory of differences, was quite swept away by the presence of the common ruin.

'Gentlemen,' said the captain, after a pause, and with very much the air of a chairman opening a board-meeting, 'we're sold.'

Huish broke out in laughter. 'Well, if this ain't the 'ighest old rig!' he cried. 'And Dyvis 'ere, who thought he had got up so bloomin' early in the mornin'! We've stolen a cargo of spring water! Oh, my crikey!' and he squirmed with mirth.

The captain managed to screw out a phantom smile.

'Here's Old Man Destiny again,' said he to Herrick, 'but this time I guess he's kicked the door right in.'

Herrick only shook his head.

'O Lord, it's rich!' laughed Huish. 'It would really be a scrumptious lark if it 'ad 'appened to somebody else! And wot are we to do next? Oh, my eye! with this bloomin' schooner, too?'

'That's the trouble,' said Davis. 'There's only one thing certain: it's no use carting this old glass and ballast to Peru. No, *sir*, we're in a hole.'

'O my, and the merchant!' cried Huish; 'the man that made this shipment! He'll get the news by the mail brigantine; and he'll think of course we're making straight for Sydney.'

'Yes, he'll be a sick merchant,' said the captain. 'One thing: this explains the Kanaka crew. If you're going to lose a ship, I would ask no better myself than a Kanaka crew. But there's one thing it don't explain; it don't explain why she came down Tahiti ways.'

'W'y, to lose her, you byby!' said Huish.

'A lot you know,' said the captain. 'Nobody wants to lose a

schooner; they want to lose her *on her course*, you skeericks! You seem to think underwriters haven't got enough sense to come in out of the rain.'

'Well,' said Herrick, 'I can tell you (I am afraid) why she came so far to the eastward. I had it of Uncle Ned. It seems these two unhappy devils, Wiseman and Wishart, were drunk on the champagne from the beginning—and died drunk at the end.'

The captain looked on the table.

'They lay in their two bunks, or sat here in this damned house,' he pursued, with rising agitation, 'filling their skins with the accursed stuff, till sickness took them. As they sickened and the fever rose, they drank the more. They lay here howling and groaning, drunk and dying, all in one. They didn't know where they were, they didn't care. They didn't even take the sun, it seems.'

'Not take the sun?' cried the captain, looking up. 'Sacred Billy! what a crowd!'.

'Well, it don't matter to Joe!' said Huish. 'Wot are Wiseman and the t'other buffer to us?'

'A good deal, too,' says the captain. 'We're their heirs, I guess.'

'It is a great inheritance,' said Herrick.

'Well, I don't know about that,' returned Davis. 'Appears to me as if it might be worse. 'Tain't worth what the cargo would have been of course, at least not money down. But I'll tell you what it appears to figure up to. Appears to me as if it amounted to about the bottom dollar of the man in 'Frisco.'

''Old on,' said Huish. 'Give a fellow time; 'ow's this, umpire?'

'Well, my sons,' pursued the captain, who seemed to have recovered his assurance, 'Wiseman and Wishart were to be paid for casting away this old schooner and its cargo. We're going to cast away the schooner right enough; and I'll make it my private business to see that we get paid. What were W. and W. to get? That's more'n I can tell. But W. and W. went into this business themselves, they were on the crook. Now *we're* on the square, *we* only stumbled into it; and that merchant has just got to squeal, and I'm the man to see that he squeals good. No, *sir*! there's some stuffing to this *Farallone* racket after all.'

'Go it, cap!' cried Huish. 'Yoicks! Forrard! 'Old 'ard! There's your style for the money! Blow me if I don't prefer this to the hother.'

'I do not understand,' said Herrick. 'I have to ask you to excuse me; I do not understand.'

'Well now, see here, Herrick,' said Davis, 'I'm going to have a word with you anyway upon a different matter, and it's good that Huish should hear it too. We're done with this boozing business, and we ask your pardon for it right here and now. We have to thank you for all you did for us while we were making hogs of ourselves; you'll find me turn-to all right in future; and as for the wine, which I grant we stole from you, I'll take stock and see you paid for it. That's good enough, I believe. But what I want to point out to you is this. The old game was a risky game. The new game's as safe as running a Vienna Bakery. We just put this *Farallone* before the wind, and run till we're well to looard of our port of departure and reasonably well up with some other place, where they have an American Consul. Down goes the *Farallone*, and good bye to her! A day or so in the boat; the consul packs us home, at Uncle Sam's expense, to 'Frisco; and if that merchant don't put the dollars down, you come to me!'

'But I thought,' began Herrick; and then broke out: 'oh, let's get on to Peru!'

'Well, if you're going to Peru for your health, I won't say no!' replied the captain. 'But for what other blame' shadow of a reason you should want to go there, gets me clear. We don't want to go there with this cargo; I don't know as old bottles is a lively article anywheres; leastways, I'll go my bottom cent, it ain't Peru. It was always a doubt if we could sell the schooner; I never rightly hoped to, and now I'm sure she ain't worth a hill of beans; what's wrong with her, I don't know; I only know it's something, or she wouldn't be here with this truck in her inside. Then again, if we lose her, and land in Peru, where are we? We can't declare the loss, or how did we get to Peru? In that case the merchant can't touch the insurance; most likely he'll go bust; and don't you think you see the three of us on the beach of Callao?'*

'There's no extradition there,' said Herrick.

'Well, my son, and we want to be extraded,' said the captain. 'What's our point? We want to have a consul extrade us as far as San Francisco and that merchant's office door. My idea is that Samoa would be found an eligible business centre. It's dead before the wind; the States have a consul there, and 'Frisco steamers call, so's we could skip right back and interview the merchant.'

'Samoa?' said Herrick. 'It will take us for ever to get there.'

'Oh, with a fair wind!' said the captain.

'No trouble about the log, eh?' asked Huish.

'No, *sir,*' said Davis. '*Light airs and baffling winds. Squalls and calms. D.R.: five miles. No obs. Pumps attended.* And fill in the barometer and thermometer off of last year's trip. "Never saw such a voyage," says you to the consul. "Thought I was going to run short . . ."' He stopped in mid career. ''Say,' he began again, and once more stopped. 'Beg your pardon, Herrick,' he added with undisguised humility, 'but did you keep the run of the stores?'

'Had I been told to do so, it should have been done, as the rest was done, to the best of my little ability,' said Herrick. 'As it was, the cook helped himself to what he pleased.'

Davis looked at the table.

'I drew it rather fine, you see,' he said at last. 'The great thing was to clear right out of Papeete before the consul could think better of it. Tell you what: I guess I'll take stock.'

And he rose from table and disappeared with a lamp in the lazarette.

''Ere's another screw loose,' observed Huish.

'My man,' said Herrick, with a sudden gleam of animosity, 'it is still your watch on deck, and surely your wheel also?'

'You come the 'eavy swell, don't you, ducky?' said Huish. 'Stand away from that binnacle. Surely your w'eel, my man. Yah.'

He lit a cigar ostentatiously, and strolled into the waist with his hands in his pockets.

In a surprisingly short time, the captain reappeared; he did not look at Herrick, but called Huish back and sat down.

'Well,' he began, 'I've taken stock—roughly.' He paused as if for somebody to help him out; and none doing so, both gazing on him instead with manifest anxiety, he yet more heavily resumed. 'Well, it won't fight. We can't do it; that's the bed-rock. I'm as sorry as what you can be, and sorrier. But the game's up. We can't look near Samoa. I don't know as we could get to Peru.'

'Wot-ju mean?' asked Huish brutally.

'I can't 'most tell myself,' replied the captain. 'I drew it fine; I said I did; but what's been going on here gets me! Appears as if the devil had been around. That cook must be the holiest kind of fraud. Only twelve days, too! Seems like craziness. I'll own up square to one thing: I seem to have figured too fine upon the flour. But the rest—my land! I'll never understand it! There's been more waste on this twopenny ship than what there is to an Atlantic Liner.' He stole a glance at his companions; nothing good was to be gleaned from their dark faces; and he had recourse to rage. 'You wait till I interview that cook!' he roared and smote the table with his fist. 'I'll interview the son of a gun so's he's never been spoken to before. I'll put a bead upon the——!'

'You will not lay a finger on the man,' said Herrick. 'The fault is yours and you know it. If you turn a savage loose in your storeroom, you know what to expect. I will not allow the man to be molested.'

It is hard to say how Davis might have taken this defiance; but he was diverted to a fresh assailant.

'Well!' drawled Huish, 'you're a plummy captain, ain't you? You're a blooming captain! Don't you set up any of your chat to me, John Dyvis: I know you now, you ain't any more use than a bloomin' dawl! Oh, you "don't know", don't you? Oh, it "gets you", do it? Oh, I dessay! W'y, weren't you 'owling for fresh tins every blessed day? 'Ow often 'ave I 'eard you send the 'ole bloomin' dinner off and tell the man to chuck it in the swill-tub? And breakfast? Oh, my crikey! breakfast for ten, and you 'ollerin' for more! And now you "can't 'most tell"! Blow me, if it ain't enough to make a man write an insultin' letter to Gawd! You dror it mild, John Dyvis; don't 'andle me; I'm dyngerous.'

Davis sat like one bemused; it might even have been doubted if he heard, but the voice of the clerk rang about the cabin like that of a cormorant among the ledges of the cliff.

'That will do, Huish,' said Herrick.

'Oh, so you tyke his part, do you? you stuck-up sneerin' snob! Tyke it then. Come on, the pair of you. But as for John Dyvis, let him look out! He struck me the first night aboard, and I never took a blow yet but wot I gave as good. Let him knuckle down on his marrow bones and beg my pardon. That's my last word.'

'I stand by the Captain,' said Herrick. 'That makes us two to one, both good men; and the crew will all follow me. I hope I shall die very soon; but I have not the least objection to killing you before I go. I should prefer it so; I should do it with no more remorse than winking. Take care—take care, you little cad!'

The animosity with which these words were uttered was so marked in itself, and so remarkable in the man who uttered them, that Huish stared, and even the humiliated Davis reared up his head and gazed at his defender. As for Herrick, the successive agitations and disappointments of the day had left him wholly reckless; he was conscious of a pleasant glow, an agreeable excitement; his head seemed empty, his eyeballs burned as he turned them, his throat was dry as a biscuit; the least dangerous man by nature, except in so far as the weak are always dangerous, at that moment he was ready to slay or to be slain with equal unconcern.

Here at least was the gage thrown down, and battle offered; he who should speak next would bring the matter to an issue there and then; all knew it to be so and hung back; and for many seconds by the cabin clock, the trio sat motionless and silent.

Then came an interruption, welcome as the flowers in May.

'Land ho!' sang out a voice on deck. 'Land a weatha bow!'

'Land!' cried Davis, springing to his feet. 'What's this? There ain't no land here.'

And as men may run from the chamber of a murdered

corpse, the three ran forth out of the house and left their quarrel behind them, undecided.

The sky shaded down at the sea-level to the white of opals; the sea itself, insolently, inkily blue, drew all about them the uncompromising wheel of the horizon. Search it as they pleased, not even the practised eye of Captain Davis could descry the smallest interruption. A few filmy clouds were slowly melting overhead; and about the schooner, as around the only point of interest, a tropic bird,* white as a snowflake, hung, and circled, and displayed, as it turned, the long vermilion feather of its tail. Save the sea and the heaven, that was all.

'Who sang out land?' asked Davis. 'If there's any boy playing funny-dog with me, I'll teach him skylarking!'

But Uncle Ned contentedly pointed to a part of the horizon, where a greenish, filmy iridescence could be discerned floating like smoke on the pale heavens.

Davis applied his glass to it, and then looked at the Kanaka. 'Call that land?' said he. 'Well, it's more than I do.'

'One time long ago,' said Uncle Ned, 'I see Anaa* all-e-same that, four five hours befo' we come up. Capena he say sun go down, sun go up again; he say lagoon all-e-same milla.'

'All-e-same *what*?' asked Davis.

'Milla, sah,' said Uncle Ned.

'Oh, ah! mirror,' said Davis. 'I see; reflection from the lagoon. Well, you know, it is just possible, though it's strange I never heard of it. Here, let's look at the chart.'

They went back to the cabin, and found the position of the schooner well to windward of the archipelago in the midst of a white field of paper.

'There! you see for yourselves,' said Davis.

'And yet I don't know,' said Herrick, 'I somehow think there's something in it. I'll tell you one thing too, captain; that's all right about the reflection; I heard it in Papeete.'

'Fetch up that Findlay,* then!' said Davis. 'I'll try it all ways. An island wouldn't come amiss, the way we're fixed.'

The bulky volume was handed up to him, broken-backed as is the way with Findlay; and he turned to the place and began to run over the text, muttering to himself and turning over the pages with a wetted finger.

'Hullo!' he exclaimed. 'How's this?' And he read aloud. '*New Island.** According to M. Delille this island, which from private interests would remain unknown, lies, it is said, in lat. 12°49′10″ S. long. 133°6′ W. In addition to the position above given, Commander Matthews H.M.S. *Scorpion*, states that an island exists in lat. 12°0′ S. long. 133°16′ W. This must be the same, if such an island exists, which is very doubtful, and totally disbelieved in by South Sea traders.'

'Golly!' said Huish.

'It's rather in the conditional mood,' said Herrick.

'It's anything you please,' cried Davis, 'only there it is! That's our place, and don't you make any mistake.'

'"Which from private interests would remain unknown,"' read Herrick, over his shoulder. 'What may that mean?'

'It should mean pearls,' said Davis. 'A pearling island the government don't know about? That sounds like real estate. Or suppose it don't mean anything. Suppose it's just an island; I guess we could fill up with fish, and cocoanuts, and native stuff, and carry out the Samoa scheme hand over fist. How long did he say it was before they raised Anaa? Five hours, I think?'

'Four or five,' said Herrick.

Davis stepped to the door. 'What breeze had you that time you made Anaa, Uncle Ned?' said he.

'Six or seven knots,' was the reply.

'Thirty or thirty-five miles,' said Davis. 'High time we were shortening sail, then. If it is an island, we don't want to be butting our head against it in the dark; and if it isn't an island, we can get through it just as well by daylight. Ready about!' he roared.

And the schooner's head was laid for that elusive glimmer in the sky, which began already to pale in lustre and diminish in size, as the stain of breath vanishes from a window pane. At the same time she was reefed close down.

PART II · THE QUARTETTE

CHAPTER VII

THE PEARL-FISHER

ABOUT four in the morning, as the captain and Herrick sat together on the rail, there arose from the midst of the night in front of them the voice of breakers. Each sprang to his feet and stared and listened. The sound was continuous, like the passing of a train; no rise or fall could be distinguished; minute by minute the ocean heaved with an equal potency against the invisible isle; and as time passed, and Herrick waited in vain for any vicissitude in the volume of that roaring, a sense of the eternal weighed upon his mind. To the expert eye the isle itself was to be inferred from a certain string of blots along the starry heaven. And the schooner was laid to and anxiously observed till daylight.

There was little or no morning bank. A brightening came in the east; then a wash of some ineffable, faint, nameless hue between crimson and silver; and then coals of fire. These glimmered a while on the sea-line, and seemed to brighten and darken and spread out, and still the night and the stars reigned undisturbed; it was as though a spark should catch and glow and creep along the foot of some heavy and almost incombustible wall-hanging, and the room itself be scarce menaced. Yet a little after, and the whole east glowed with gold and scarlet, and the hollow of heaven was filled with the daylight.

The isle—the undiscovered, the scarce-believed in—now lay before them and close aboard; and Herrick thought that never in his dreams had he beheld anything more strange and delicate. The beach was excellently white, the continuous barrier of trees inimitably green; the land perhaps ten feet high, the trees thirty more. Every here and there, as the schooner coasted northward, the wood was intermitted; and he could see clear over the inconsiderable strip of land (as a man looks over a wall) to the lagoon within—and clear over that again to where the far side of the atoll prolonged its pencilling of trees against the morning sky. He tortured himself to find analogies. The isle was like the rim of a great vessel sunken in the waters; it was like the embankment of an annular railway grown upon with wood: so slender it seemed amidst the outrageous breakers, so frail and pretty, he would scarce have wondered to see it sink and disappear without a sound, and the waves close smoothly over its descent.

Meanwhile the captain was in the four cross-trees, glass in hand, his eyes in every quarter, spying for an entrance, spying for signs of tenancy. But the isle continued to unfold itself in joints, and to run out in indeterminate capes, and still there was neither house nor man, nor the smoke of fire. Here a multitude of sea-birds soared and twinkled, and fished in the blue waters; and there, and for miles together, the fringe of cocoa-palm and pandanus extended desolate, and made desirable green bowers for nobody to visit, and the silence of death was only broken by the throbbing of the sea.

The airs were very light, their speed was small; the heat intense. The decks were scorching underfoot, the sun flamed overhead, brazen, out of a brazen sky; the pitch bubbled in the seams, and the brains in the brain-pan. And all the while the excitement of the three adventurers glowed about their bones like a fever. They whispered, and nodded, and pointed, and put mouth to ear, with a singular instinct of secrecy, approaching that island under-hand like eavesdroppers and thieves; and even Davis from the cross-trees gave his orders mostly by gestures. The hands shared in this mute strain, like dogs, without comprehending it; and through the roar of so many miles of breakers, it was a silent ship that approached an empty island.

At last they drew near to the break in that interminable gangway. A spur of coral sand stood forth on the one hand; on the other a high and thick tuft of trees cut off the view; between was the mouth of the huge laver. Twice a day the ocean crowded in that narrow entrance and was heaped between these frail walls; twice a day, with the return of the ebb, the mighty surplusage of water must struggle to escape. The hour in which the *Farallone* came there was the hour of flood. The sea turned (as with the instinct of the homing pigeon) for the vast receptacle, swept eddying through the gates, was transmuted, as it did so, into a wonder of watery and silken hues, and brimmed into the inland sea beyond. The schooner looked up close-hauled, and was caught and carried away by the influx like a toy. She skimmed; she flew; a momentary shadow touched her decks from the shoreside trees; the bottom of the channel showed up for a moment and was in a moment gone; the next, she floated on the bosom of the lagoon, and below, in the transparent chamber of waters, a myriad of many-coloured fishes were sporting, a myriad pale flowers of coral diversified the floor.

Herrick stood transported. In the gratified lust of his eye, he forgot the past and the present; forgot that he was menaced by a prison on the one hand and starvation on the other; forgot that he was come to that island, desperately foraging, clutching at expedients. A drove of fishes, painted like the rainbow and billed like parrots, hovered up in the shadow of the schooner, and passed clear of it, and glinted in the submarine sun. They were beautiful, like birds, and their silent passage impressed him like a strain of song.

Meanwhile, to the eye of Davis in the cross-trees, the lagoon continued to expand its empty waters, and the long succession of the shore-side trees to be paid out like fishing-line off a reel. And still there was no mark of habitation. The schooner, immediately on entering, had been kept away to the nor'ard where the water seemed to be the most deep; and she was now skimming past the tall grove of trees, which stood on that side of the channel and denied further view. Of the whole of the low shores of the island, only this bight remained to be revealed. And suddenly the curtain was raised; they began to open out a haven, snugly elbowed there, and beheld, with an astonishment beyond words, the roofs of men.

The appearance, thus 'instantaneously disclosed'* to those on the deck of the *Farallone*, was not that of a city, rather of a substantial country farm with its attendant hamlet: a long line of sheds and store-houses; apart, upon the one side, a deep-veranda'ed dwelling-house; on the other, perhaps a dozen native huts; a building with a belfry and some rude offer at architectural features that might be thought to mark it out for a chapel; on the beach in front some heavy boats drawn up, and a pile of timber running forth into the burning shallows of the lagoon. From a flagstaff at the pierhead, the red ensign of England was displayed. Behind, about, and over, the same tall grove of palms, which had masked the settlement in the beginning, prolonged its roof of tumultuous green fans, and turned and ruffled overhead, and sang its silver song all day in the wind. The place had the indescribable but unmistakable appearance of being in commission; yet there breathed from it a sense of desertion that was almost poignant, no human figure was to be observed going to and fro about the houses, and there was no sound of human industry or enjoyment. Only, on the top of the beach and hard by the flagstaff, a woman of exorbitant stature and as white as snow was to be seen beckoning with uplifted arm. The second glance identified her as a piece of naval sculpture, the figure-head of a ship that had long hovered and plunged into so many running billows, and was now brought ashore to be the ensign and presiding genius of that empty town.*

The *Farallone* made a soldier's breeze* of it; the wind, besides, was stronger inside than without under the lee of the land; and the stolen schooner opened out successive objects with the swiftness of a panorama, so that the adventurers stood speechless. The flag spoke for itself; it was no frayed and weathered trophy that had beaten itself to pieces on the post, flying over desolation; and to make assurance stronger, there was to be descried in the deep shade of the veranda, a glitter of crystal and the fluttering of white napery. If the figure-head at the pier-end, with its perpetual gesture and its leprous whiteness, reigned alone in that hamlet as it seemed to do, it would not have reigned long. Men's hands had been busy, men's feet stirring there, within the circuit of the clock. The *Farallones* were sure of it; their eyes dug in the deep shadow of the palms for some one hiding; if intensity of looking might have prevailed, they would have pierced the walls of houses; and there came to them, in these pregnant seconds, a sense of being watched and played with, and of a blow impending, that was hardly bearable.

The extreme point of palms they had just passed enclosed a creek, which was thus hidden up to the last moment from the eyes of those on board; and from this, a boat put suddenly and briskly out, and a voice hailed.

'Schooner ahoy!' it cried. 'Stand in for the pier! In two cables' lengths you'll have twenty fathoms water and good holding-ground.'

The boat was manned with a couple of brown oarsmen in scanty kilts of blue. The speaker, who was steering, wore white clothes, the full dress of the tropics; a wide hat shaded his face; but it could be seen that he was of stalwart size, and his voice sounded like a gentleman's. So much could be made out. It was plain, besides, that the *Farallone* had been descried some time before at sea, and the inhabitants were prepared for its reception.

Mechanically the orders were obeyed, and the ship berthed; and the three adventurers gathered aft beside the house and waited, with galloping pulses and a perfect vacancy of mind, the coming of the stranger who might mean so much to them. They had no plan, no story prepared; there was no time to make one; they were caught red-handed and must stand their chance. Yet this anxiety was chequered with hope. The island being undeclared, it was not possible the man could hold any office or be in a position to demand their papers. And beyond that, if there was any truth in Findlay, as it now seemed there should be, he was the representative of the 'private reasons', he must see their coming with a profound disappointment; and perhaps (hope whispered) he would be willing and able to purchase their silence.

The boat was by that time forging alongside, and they were able at last to see what manner of man they had to do with. He was a huge fellow, six feet four in height, and of a build proportionately strong, but his sinews seemed to be dissolved in a listlessness that was more than languor. It was only the eye that corrected this impression; an eye of an unusual mingled brilliancy and softness, sombre as coal and with lights that outshone the topaz; an eye of unimpaired health and virility;

an eye that bid you beware of the man's devastating anger. A complexion, naturally dark, had been tanned in the island to a hue hardly distinguishable from that of a Tahitian; only his manners and movements, and the living force that dwelt in him, like fire in flint, betrayed the European. He was dressed in white drill, exquisitely made; his scarf and tie were of tender-coloured silks; on the thwart beside him there leaned a Winchester rifle.*

'Is the doctor on board?' he cried as he came up. 'Dr Symonds, I mean? You never heard of him? Nor yet of the *Trinity Hall*? Ah!'

He did not look surprised, seemed rather to affect it in politeness; but his eye rested on each of the three white men in succession with a sudden weight of curiosity that was almost savage. 'Ah, *then*!' said he, 'there is some small mistake, no doubt, and I must ask you to what I am indebted for this pleasure?'

He was by this time on the deck, but he had the art to be quite unapproachable; the friendliest vulgarian, three parts drunk, would have known better than take liberties; and not one of the adventurers so much as offered to shake hands.

'Well,' said Davis, 'I suppose you may call it an accident. We had heard of your island, and read that thing in the Directory about the *Private Reasons*, you see; so when we saw the lagoon reflected in the sky, we put her head for it at once, and so here we are.'

''Ope we don't intrude!' said Huish.

The stranger looked at Huish with an air of faint surprise, and looked pointedly away again. It was hard to be more offensive in dumb show.

'It may suit me, your coming here,' he said. 'My own schooner is overdue, and I may put something in your way in the meantime. Are you open to a charter?'

'Well, I guess so,' said Davis; 'it depends.'

'My name is Attwater,' continued the stranger. 'You, I presume, are the captain?'

'Yes, sir. I am the captain of this ship: Captain Brown,' was the reply.

'Well, see 'ere!' said Huish, 'better begin fair! 'E's skipper on deck right enough, but not below. Below, we're all equal, all got a lay in the adventure; when it comes to business, I'm as good as 'e; and what I say is, let's go into the 'ouse and have a lush, and talk it over among pals. We've some prime fizz,' he said, and winked.

The presence of the gentleman lighted up like a candle the vulgarity of the clerk; and Herrick instinctively, as one shields himself from pain, made haste to interrupt.

'My name is Hay,' said he, 'since introductions are going. We shall be very glad if you will step inside.'

Attwater leaned to him swiftly. 'University man?' said he.

'Yes, Merton,' said Herrick, and the next moment blushed scarlet at his indiscretion.

'I am of the other lot,' said Attwater: 'Trinity Hall, Cambridge, I called my schooner after the old shop. Well! this is a queer place and company for us to meet in, Mr Hay,' he pursued, with easy incivility to the others. 'But do you bear out . . . I beg this gentleman's pardon, I really did not catch his name.'

'My name is 'Uish, sir,' returned the clerk, and blushed in turn.

'Ah!' said Attwater. And then turning again to Herrick, 'Do you bear out Mr Whish's description of your vintage? or was it only the unaffected poetry of his own nature bubbling up?'

Herrick was embarrassed; the silken brutality of their visitor made him blush; that he should be accepted as an equal, and the others thus pointedly ignored, pleased him in spite of himself, and then ran through his veins in a recoil of anger.

'I don't know,' he said. 'It's only California; it's good enough, I believe.'

Attwater seemed to make up his mind. 'Well then, I'll tell you what: you three gentlemen come ashore this evening and bring a basket of wine with you; I'll try and find the food,' he said. 'And by the by, here is a question I should have asked you when I came on board: have you had smallpox?'

'Personally, no,' said Herrick. 'But the schooner had it.'

'Deaths?' from Attwater.

'Two,' said Herrick.

'Well, it is a dreadful sickness,' said Attwater.

''Ad you any deaths?' asked Huish, ''ere on the island?'

'Twenty-nine,' said Attwater. 'Twenty-nine deaths and thirty-one cases, out of thirty-three souls upon the island.—That's a strange way to calculate, Mr Hay, is it not? Souls! I never say it but it startles me.'

'Oh, so that's why everything's deserted?' said Huish.

'That is why, Mr Whish,' said Attwater; 'that is why the house is empty and the graveyard full.'

'Twenty-nine out of thirty-three!' exclaimed Herrick. 'Why, when it came to burying—or did you bother burying?'

'Scarcely,' said Attwater; 'or there was one day at least when we gave up. There were five of the dead that morning, and thirteen of the dying, and no one able to go about except the sexton and myself. We held a council of war, took the . . . empty bottles . . . into the lagoon, and . . . buried them.' He looked over his shoulder, back at the bright water. 'Well, so you'll come to dinner, then? Shall we say half-past six? *So* good of you!'

His voice, in uttering these conventional phrases, fell at once into the false measure of society; and Herrick unconsciously followed the example.

'I am sure we shall be very glad,' he said. 'At half-past six? Thank you so very much.'

'"For my voice has been tuned to the note of the gun
That startles the deep when the combat's begun,"'*

quoted Attwater, with a smile, which instantly gave way to an air of funereal solemnity. 'I shall particularly expect Mr Whish,' he continued. 'Mr Whish, I trust you understand the invitation?'

'I believe you, my boy!' replied the genial Huish.

'That is right then; and quite understood, is it not?' said Attwater. 'Mr Whish and Captain Brown at six thirty without fault—and you, Hay, at four sharp.'

And he called his boat.

During all this talk, a load of thought or anxiety had weighed upon the captain. There was no part for which nature had so liberally endowed him as that of the genial ship-captain. But today he was silent and abstracted. Those who knew him could see that he hearkened close to every syllable, and seemed to ponder and try it in balances. It would have been hard to say what look there was, cold, attentive, and sinister, as of a man maturing plans, which still brooded over the unconscious guest; it was here, it was there, it was nowhere; it was now so little that Herrick chid himself for an idle fancy; and anon it was so gross and palpable that you could say every hair on the man's head talked mischief.

He woke up now, as with a start. 'You were talking of a charter,' said he.

'Was I?' said Attwater. 'Well, let's talk of it no more at present.'

'Your own schooner is overdue, I understand?' continued the captain.

'You understand perfectly, Captain Brown,' said Attwater; 'thirty-three days overdue at noon today.'

'She come and goes, eh? plies between here and . . . ?' hinted the captain.

'Exactly; every four months; three trips in the year,' said Attwater.

'You go in her, ever?' asked Davis.

'No, one stops here,' said Attwater, 'one has plenty to attend to.'

'Stop here, do you?' cried Davis. 'Say, how long?'

'How long, O Lord,'* said Attwater with perfect, stern gravity. 'But it does not seem so,' he added, with a smile.

'No, I daresay not,' said Davis. 'No, I suppose not. Not with all your gods about you, and in as snug a berth as this. For it is a pretty snug berth,' said he, with a sweeping look.

'The spot, as you are good enough to indicate, is not entirely intolerable,' was the reply.

'Shell, I suppose?' said Davis.

'Yes, there was shell,' said Attwater.

'This is a considerable big beast of a lagoon, sir,' said the captain. 'Was there a—was the fishing—would you call the fishing anyways *good*?'

'I don't know that I would call it anyways anything,' said Attwater, 'if you put it to me direct.'

'There were pearls too?' said Davis.

'Pearls, too,' said Attwater.

'Well, I give out!' laughed Davis, and his laughter rang cracked like a false piece. 'If you're not going to tell, you're not going to tell, and there's an end to it.'

'There can be no reason why I should affect the least degree of secrecy about my island,' returned Attwater; 'that came wholly to an end with your arrival; and I am sure, at any rate, that gentlemen like you and Mr Whish, I should have always been charmed to make perfectly at home. The point on which we are now differing—if you can call it a difference—is one of times and seasons. I have some information which you think I might impart, and I think not. Well, we'll see tonight! By-by, Whish!' He stepped into his boat, and shoved off. 'All understood, then?' said he. 'The captain and Mr Whish at six thirty, and you, Hay, at four precise. You understand that, Hay? Mind, I take no denial. If you're not there by the time named, there will be no banquet; no song, no supper, Mr Whish!'

White birds whisked in the air above, a shoal of particoloured fishes in the scarce denser medium below; between, like Mahomet's coffin,* the boat drew away briskly on the surface, and its shadow followed it over the glittering floor of the lagoon. Attwater looked steadily back over his shoulders as he sat; he did not once remove his eyes from the *Farallone* and the group on her quarter-deck beside the house, till his boat ground upon the pier. Thence, with an agile pace, he hurried ashore, and they saw his white clothes shining in the chequered dusk of the grove until the house received him.

The captain, with a gesture and a speaking countenance, called the adventurers into the cabin.

'Well,' he said to Herrick, when they were seated, 'there's one good job at least. He's taken to you in earnest.'

'Why should that be a good job?' said Herrick.

'Oh, you'll see how it pans out presently,' returned Davis. 'You go ashore and stand in with him, that's all! You'll get lots of pointers; you can find out what he has, and what the charter is, and who's the fourth man—for there's four of them, and we're only three.'

'And suppose I do, what next?' cried Herrick. 'Answer me that!'

'So I will, Robert Herrick,' said the captain. 'But first, let's see all clear. I guess you know,' he said with an imperious solemnity, 'I guess you know the bottom is out of this *Farallone* speculation? I guess you know it's *right* out? and if this old island hadn't been turned up right when it did, I guess you know where you and I and Huish would have been?'

'Yes, I know that,' said Herrick. 'No matter who's to blame, I know it. And what next?'

'No matter who's to blame, you know it, right enough,' said the captain, 'and I'm obliged to you for the reminder. Now here's this Attwater: what do you think of him?'

'I do not know,' said Herrick. 'I am attracted and repelled. He was insufferably rude to you.'

'And you, Huish?' said the captain.

Huish sat cleaning a favourite briar-root; he scarce looked up from that engrossing task. 'Don't ast me what I think of him!' he said. 'There's a day comin', I pray Gawd, when I can tell it him myself.'

'Huish means the same as what I do,' said Davis, 'When that man came stepping around, and saying "Look here, I'm Attwater"—and you knew it was so, by God!—I sized him right straight up. Here's the real article, I said, and I don't like it; here's the real, first-rate, copper-bottomed aristocrat. "*Aw! don't know ye, do I? God damn ye, did God make ye?*" No, that couldn't be nothing but genuine; a man got to be born to that, and notice! smart as champagne and hard as nails; no kind of a fool; no, *sir*! not a pound of him! Well, what's he here upon this beastly island for? I said. *He's* not here collecting eggs. He's a palace at home, and powdered flunkies; and if he don't stay there, you bet he knows the reason why! Follow?'

'O yes, I 'ear you,' said Huish.

'He's been doing good business here, then,' continued the captain. 'For ten years, he's been doing a great business. It's pearl and shell, of course; there couldn't be nothing else in such a place, and no doubt the shell goes off regularly by this *Trinity Hall*, and the money for it straight into the bank, so that's no use to us. But what else is there? Is there nothing else he would be likely to keep here? Is there nothing else he would be bound to keep here? Yes, sir; the pearls! First, because they're too valuable to trust out of his hands. Second, because pearls want a lot of handling and matching; and the man who sells his pearls as they come in, one here, one there, instead of hanging back and holding up—well, that man's a fool, and it's not Attwater.'

'Likely,' said Huish, 'that's w'at it is; not proved, but likely.'

'It's proved,' said Davis bluntly.

'Suppose it was?' said Herrick. 'Suppose that was all so, and he had these pearls—a ten years' collection of them?—Suppose he had? There's my question.'

The captain drummed with his thick hands on the board in front of him; he looked steadily in Herrick's face, and Herrick as steadily looked upon the table and the pattering fingers; there was a gentle oscillation of the anchored ship, and a big patch of sunlight travelled to and fro between the one and the other.

'Hear me!' Herrick burst out suddenly.

'No, you better hear me first,' said Davis. 'Hear me and understand me. *We*'ve got no use for that fellow, whatever you may have. He's your kind, he's not ours; he's took to you, and he's wiped his boots on me and Huish. Save him if you can!'

'Save him?' repeated Herrick.

'Save him, if you're able!' reiterated Davis, with a blow of his clenched fist. 'Go ashore, and talk him smooth; and if you get him and his pearls aboard, I'll spare him. If you don't, there's going to be a funeral. Is that so, Huish? does that suit you?'

'I ain't a forgiving man,' said Huish, 'but I'm not the sort to spoil business neither. Bring the bloke on board and bring his pearls along with him, and you can have it your own way; maroon him where you like,—I'm agreeable.'

'Well, and if I can't?' cried Herrick, while the sweat streamed upon his face. 'You talk to me as if I was God Almighty, to do this and that! But if I can't?'

'My son,' said the captain, 'you better do your level best, or you'll see sights!'

'O yes,' said Huish. 'O crikey, yes!' He looked across at Herrick with a toothless smile that was shocking in its savagery; and his ear caught apparently by the trivial expression he had used, broke into a piece of the chorus of a comic song which he must have heard twenty years before in London: meaningless gibberish that, in that hour and place, seemed hateful as a blasphemy: 'Hikey, pikey, crikey, fikey, chillinga-wallaba dory.'

The captain suffered him to finish; his face was unchanged.

'The way things are, there's many a man that wouldn't let you go ashore,' he resumed. 'But I'm not that kind. I know you'd never go back on me, Herrick! Or if you choose to,—go, and do it, and be damned!' he cried, and rose abruptly from the table.

He walked out of the house; and as he reached the door, turned and called Huish, suddenly and violently, like the barking of a dog. Huish followed, and Herrick remained alone in the cabin.

'Now, see here!' whispered Davis. 'I know that man. If you open your mouth to him again, you'll ruin all.'

CHAPTER VIII

BETTER ACQUAINTANCE

THE boat was gone again, and already halfway to the *Farallone,* before Herrick turned and went unwillingly up the pier. From the crown of the beach, the figure-head confronted him with what seemed irony, her helmeted head tossed back, her formidable arm apparently hurling something, whether shell or missile, in the direction of the anchored schooner. She seemed a defiant deity from the island, coming forth to its threshold with a rush as of one about to fly, and perpetuated in that dashing attitude. Herrick looked up at her, where she towered above him head and shoulders, with singular feelings of curiosity and romance, and suffered his mind to travel to and fro in her life-history. So long she had been the blind conductress of a ship among the waves; so long she had stood here idle in the violent sun, that yet did not avail to blister her; and was even this the end of so many adventures? he wondered, or was more behind? And he could have found it in his heart to regret that she was not a goddess, nor yet he a pagan, that he might have bowed down before her in that hour of difficulty.

When he now went forward, it was cool with the shadow of many well-grown palms; draughts of the dying breeze swung them together overhead; and on all sides, with a swiftness beyond dragon-flies or swallows, the spots of sunshine flitted, and hovered, and returned. Underfoot, the sand was fairly solid and quite level, and Herrick's steps fell there noiseless as in new-fallen snow. It bore the marks of having been once weeded like a garden alley at home; but the pestilence had done its work, and the weeds were returning. The buildings of the settlement showed here and there through the stems of the colonnade, fresh painted, trim and dandy, and all silent as the grave. Only, here and there in the crypt, there was a rustle and scurry and some crowing of poultry; and from behind the house with the verandahs, he saw smoke arise and heard the crackling of a fire.

The store-houses* were nearest him upon his right. The first was locked; in the second, he could dimly perceive, through a window, a certain accumulation of pearl-shell piled in the far end; the third, which stood gaping open on the afternoon, seized on the mind of Herrick with its multiplicity and disorder of romantic things. Therein were cables, windlasses and blocks of every size and capacity; cabin windows and ladders; rusty tanks, a companion hutch; a binnacle with its brass mountings and its compass idly pointing, in the confusion and dusk of that shed, to a forgotten pole; ropes, anchors, harpoons, a blubber-dipper of copper, green with years, a steering-wheel, a tool-chest with the vessel's name upon the top, the *Asia*: a whole curiosity-shop of sea-curios, gross and solid, heavy to lift, ill to break, bound with brass and shod with iron. Two wrecks at the least must have contributed to this random heap of lumber; and as Herrick looked upon it, it seemed to him as if the two ships' companies were there on guard, and he heard the tread of feet and whisperings, and saw with the tail of his eye the commonplace ghosts of sailor men.

This was not merely the work of an aroused imagination, but had something sensible to go upon; sounds of a stealthy approach were no doubt audible; and while he still stood staring at the lumber, the voice of his host sounded suddenly, and with even more than the customary softness of enunciation, from behind.

'Junk,' it said, 'only old junk! And does Mr Hay find a parable?'

'I find at least a strong impression,' replied Herrick, turning quickly, lest he might be able to catch, on the face of the speaker, some commentary on the words.

Attwater stood in the doorway, which he almost wholly filled; his hands stretched above his head and grasping the architrave. He smiled when their eyes met, but the expression was inscrutable.

'Yes, a powerful impression. You are like me; nothing so affecting as ships!' said he. 'The ruins of an empire would leave me frigid, when a bit of an old rail that an old shellback leaned on in the middle watch, would bring me up all standing. But come, let's see some more of the island. It's all sand and coral and palm trees; but there's a kind of a quaintness in the place.'

'I find it heavenly,' said Herrick, breathing deep, with head bared in the shadow.

'Ah, that's because you're new from sea,' said Attwater. 'I daresay too, you can appreciate what one calls it. It's a lovely name. It has a flavour, it has a colour, it has a ring and fall to it; it's like its author—it's half Christian! Remember your first view of the island, and how it's only woods and woods and water; and suppose you had asked somebody for the name, and he had answered—*nemorosa Zacynthos*.'

'*Jam medio apparet fluctu!*'* exclaimed Herrick. 'Ye gods, yes, how good!'

'If it gets upon the chart, the skippers will make nice work of it,' said Attwater. 'But here, come and see the diving-shed.'

He opened a door, and Herrick saw a large display of apparatus neatly ordered: pumps and pipes, and the leaded boots, and the huge snouted helmets shining in rows along the wall; ten complete outfits.

'The whole eastern half of my lagoon is shallow, you must understand,' said Attwater; 'so we were able to get in the dress to great advantage. It paid beyond belief, and was a queer sight when they were at it, and these marine monsters'—tapping the nearest of the helmets—'kept appearing and reappearing in the midst of the lagoon.* Fond of parables?' he asked abruptly.

'O yes!' said Herrick.

'Well, I saw these machines come up dripping and go down again, and come up dripping and go down again, and all the while the fellow inside as dry as toast!' said Attwater; 'and I thought we all wanted a dress to go down into the world in, and come up scatheless. What do you think the name was?' he inquired.

'Self-conceit,' said Herrick.

'Ah, but I mean seriously!' said Attwater.

'Call it self-respect, then!' corrected Herrick, with a laugh.

'And why not Grace? Why not God's Grace, Hay?' asked Attwater. 'Why not the grace of your Maker and Redeemer, He who died for you, He who upholds you, He whom you daily crucify afresh? There is nothing here,'—striking on his bosom—'nothing there'—smiting the wall—'and nothing there'—stamping—'nothing but God's Grace! We walk upon it, we breathe it; we live and die by it; it makes the nails and axles of the universe; and a puppy in pyjamas prefers self-conceit!' The huge dark man stood over against Herrick by the line of the diver's helmets, and seemed to swell and glow; and the next moment the life had gone from him. 'I beg your pardon,' said he; 'I see you don't believe in God?'

'Not in your sense, I am afraid,' said Herrick.

'I never argue with young atheists or habitual drunkards,' said Attwater flippantly. 'Let us go across the island to the outer beach.'

It was but a little way, the greatest width of that island scarce exceeding a furlong, and they walked gently. Herrick was like one in a dream. He had come there with a mind divided; come prepared to study that ambiguous and sneering mask, drag out the essential man from underneath, and act accordingly; decision being till then postponed. Iron cruelty, an iron insensibility to the suffering of others, the uncompromising pursuit of his own interests, cold culture, manners without humanity; these he had looked for, these he still thought he saw. But to find the whole machine thus glow with the reverberation of religious zeal, surprised him beyond words; and he laboured in vain, as he walked, to piece together into any kind of whole his odds and ends of knowledge—to adjust again into any kind of focus with itself, his picture of the man beside him.

'What brought you here to the South Seas?' he asked presently.

'Many things,' said Attwater. 'Youth, curiosity, romance, the love of the sea, and (it will surprise you to hear) an interest in missions. That has a good deal declined, which will surprise you less. They go the wrong way to work; they are too parsonish, too much of the old wife, and even the old apple-wife. *Clothes, clothes,* are their idea; but clothes are not

Christianity, any more than they are the sun in heaven, or could take the place of it! They think a parsonage with roses, and church bells, and nice old women bobbing in the lanes, are part and parcel of religion. But religion is a savage thing, like the universe it illuminates; savage, cold, and bare, but infinitely strong.'

'And you found this island by an accident?' said Herrick.

'As you did!' said Attwater. 'And since then I have had a business, and a colony, and a mission of my own. I was a man of the world before I was a Christian; I'm a man of the world still, and I made my mission pay. No good ever came of coddling. A man has to stand up in God's sight and work up to his weight avoirdupois; then I'll talk to him, but not before. I gave these beggars what they wanted: a judge in Israel, the bearer of the sword and scourge; I was making a new people here; and behold, the angel of the Lord smote them and they were not!'

With the very uttering of the words, which were accompanied by a gesture, they came forth out of the porch of the palm wood by the margin of the sea and full in front of the sun which was near setting. Before them the surf broke slowly. All around, with an air of imperfect wooden things inspired with wicked activity, the crabs trundled and scuttled into holes. On the right, whither Attwater pointed and abruptly turned, was the cemetery of the island, a field of broken stones from the bigness of a child's hand to that of his head, diversified by many mounds of the same material, and walled by a rude rectangular enclosure. Nothing grew there but a shrub or two with some white flowers; nothing but the number of the mounds, and their disquieting shape, indicated the presence of the dead.

'"The rude forefathers of the hamlet lie!"'*

quoted Attwater as he entered by the open gateway into that unholy close. 'Coral to coral, pebbles to pebbles,' he said, 'this has been the main scene of my activity in the South Pacific. Some were good, and some bad, and the majority (of course and always) null. Here was a fellow, now, that used to frisk like a dog; if you had called him he came like an arrow from a bow; if you had not, and he came unbidden, you should have seen the deprecating eye and the little intricate dancing step. Well, his trouble is over now, he has lain down with kings and councillors;* the rest of his acts, are they not written in the book of the chronicles? That fellow was from Penrhyn;* like all the Penrhyn islanders he was ill to manage; heady, jealous, violent: the man with the nose! He lies here quiet enough. And so they all lie.

'"And darkness was the burier of the dead!"'*

He stood, in the strong glow of the sunset, with bowed head; his voice sounded now sweet and now bitter with the varying sense.

'You loved these people?' cried Herrick, strangely touched.

'I?' said Attwater. 'Dear no! Don't think me a philanthropist. I dislike men, and hate women. If I like the islanders at all, it is because you see them here plucked of their lendings, their dead birds and cocked hats, their petticoats and coloured hose. Here was one I liked though,' and he set his foot upon a mound. 'He was a fine savage fellow; he had a dark soul; yes, I liked this one. I am fanciful,' he added, looking hard at Herrick, 'and I take fads. I like you.'

Herrick turned swiftly and looked far away to where the clouds were beginning to troop together and amass themselves round the obsequies of day. 'No one can like me,' he said.

'You are wrong there,' said the other, 'as a man usually is about himself. You are attractive, very attractive.'

'It is not me,' said Herrick; 'no one can like me. If you knew how I despised myself—and why!' His voice rang out in the quiet graveyard.

'I knew that you despised yourself,' said Attwater. 'I saw the blood come into your face today when you remembered Oxford. And I could have blushed for you myself, to see a man, a gentleman, with these two vulgar wolves.'

Herrick faced him with a thrill. 'Wolves?' he repeated.

'I said wolves and vulgar wolves,' said Attwater. 'Do you know that today, when I came on board, I trembled?'

'You concealed it well,' stammered Herrick.

'A habit of mine,' said Attwater. 'But I was afraid, for all that: I was afraid of the two wolves.' He raised his hand slowly. 'And now, Hay, you poor lost puppy, what do you do with the two wolves?'

'What do I do? I don't do anything,' said Herrick. 'There is nothing wrong; all is above-board; Captain Brown is a good soul; he is a . . . he is . . .' The phantom voice of Davis called in his ear: 'There's going to be a funeral;' and the sweat burst forth and streamed on his brow. 'He is a family man,' he resumed again, swallowing; 'he has children at home—and a wife.'

'And a very nice man?' said Attwater. 'And so is Mr Whish, no doubt?'

'I won't go so far as that,' said Herrick. 'I do not like Huish. And yet . . . he has his merits too.'

'And, in short, take them for all in all, as good a ship's company as one would ask?' said Attwater.

'O yes,' said Herrick, 'quite.'

'So then we approach the other point of why you despise yourself?' said Attwater.

'Do we not all despise ourselves?' cried Herrick. 'Do not you?'

'Oh, I say I do. But do I?' said Attwater. 'One thing I know at least: I never gave a cry like yours. Hay! it came from a bad conscience! Ah, man, that poor diving-dress of self-conceit is sadly tattered! Today, if ye will hear my voice. Today, now, while the sun sets, and here in this burying-place of brown innocents, fall on your knees and cast your sins and sorrows on the Redeemer. Hay—'

'Not Hay!' interrupted the other, strangling. 'Don't call me that! I mean . . . For God's sake, can't you see I'm on the rack?'

'I see it, I know it, I put and keep you there, my fingers are on the screws!' said Attwater. 'Please God, I will bring a penitent this night before His throne. Come, come to the mercy-seat! He waits to be gracious, man—waits to be gracious!'

He spread out his arms like a crucifix; his face shone with the brightness of a seraph's; in his voice, as it rose to the last word, the tears seemed ready.

Herrick made a vigorous call upon himself. 'Attwater,' he said, 'you push me beyond bearing. What am I to do? I do not believe. It is living truth to you; to me, upon my conscience, only folk-lore. I do not believe there is any form of words under heaven, by which I can lift the burthen from my shoulders. I must stagger on to the end with the pack of my responsibility; I cannot shift it; do you suppose I would not, if I thought I could? I cannot—cannot—cannot—and let that suffice.'

The rapture was all gone from Attwater's countenance; the dark apostle had disappeared; and in his place there stood an easy, sneering gentleman, who took off his hat and bowed. It was pertly done, and the blood burned in Herrick's face.

'What do you mean by that?' he cried.

'Well, shall we go back to the house?' said Attwater. 'Our guests will soon be due.'

Herrick stood his ground a moment with clenched fists and teeth; and as he so stood, the fact of his errand there slowly swung clear in front of him, like the moon out of clouds. He had come to lure that man on board; he was failing, even if it could be said that he had tried; he was sure to fail now, and knew it, and knew it was better so. And what was to be next?

With a groan he turned to follow his host, who was standing with polite smile, and instantly and somewhat obsequiously led the way in the now darkened colonnade of palms. There they went in silence, the earth gave up richly of her perfume, the air tasted warm and aromatic in the nostrils; and from a great way forward in the wood, the brightness of lights and fire marked out the house of Attwater.

Herrick meanwhile resolved and resisted an immense temptation to go up, to touch him on the arm and breathe a word in his ear: 'Beware, they are going to murder you.' There would be one life saved; but what of the two others? The three lives went up and down before him like buckets in a well, or like the scales of balances. It had come to a choice, and one that must be speedy. For certain invaluable minutes, the wheels of life ran before him, and he could still divert them with a touch to the one side or the other, still choose who was to live and who was to die. He considered the men. Attwater intrigued, puzzled, dazzled, enchanted and revolted him; alive, he seemed but a doubtful good; and the thought of him lying dead was so unwelcome that it pursued him, like a vision, with every circumstance of colour and sound. Incessantly, he had before him the image of that great mass of man stricken down in varying attitudes and with varying wounds; fallen prone, fallen supine, fallen on his side; or clinging to a doorpost with the changing face and the relaxing fingers of the death-agony. He heard the click of the trigger, the thud of the ball, the cry of the victim; he saw the blood flow. And this building up of circumstance was like a consecration of the man, till he seemed to walk in sacrificial fillets. Next he considered Davis, with his thick-fingered, coarse-grained, oat-bread commonness of nature, his indomitable valour and mirth in the old days of their starvation, the endearing blend of his faults and virtues, the sudden shining forth of a tenderness that lay too deep for tears; his children, Ada and her bowel complaint, and Ada's doll. No, death could not be suffered to approach that head even in fancy; with a general heat and a bracing of his muscles, it was borne in on Herrick that Ada's father would find in him a son to the death. And even Huish showed a little in that sacredness; by the tacit adoption of daily life they were become brothers; there was an implied bond of loyalty in their cohabitation of the ship and their passed miseries, to which Herrick must be a little true or wholly dishonoured. Horror of sudden death for horror of sudden death, there was here no hesitation possible: it must be Attwater. And no sooner was the thought formed (which was a sentence) than his whole mind of man ran in a panic to the other side: and when he looked within himself, he was aware only of turbulence and inarticulate outcry.

In all this there was no thought of Robert Herrick. He had complied with the ebb-tide in man's affairs, and the tide had carried him away; he heard already the roaring of the maelstrom that must hurry him under. And in his bedevilled and dishonoured soul there was no thought of self.

For how long he walked silent by his companion Herrick had no guess. The clouds rolled suddenly away; the orgasm was over; he found himself placid with the placidity of despair; there returned to him the power of commonplace speech; and he heard with surprise his own voice say: 'What a lovely evening!'

'Is it not?' said Attwater. 'Yes, the evenings here would be very pleasant if one had anything to do. By day, of course, one can shoot.'

'You shoot?' asked Herrick.

'Yes, I am what you would call a fine shot,' said Attwater. 'It is faith; I believe my balls will go true; if I were to miss once, it would spoil me for nine months.'

'You never miss, then?' said Herrick.

'Not unless I mean to,' said Attwater. 'But to miss nicely is the art. There was an old king one knew in the western islands,* who used to empty a Winchester all round a man, and stir his hair or nick a rag out of his clothes with every ball except the last; and that went plump between the eyes. It was pretty practice.'

'You could do that?' asked Herrick, with a sudden chill.

'Oh, I can do anything,' returned the other. 'You do not understand: what must be, must.'

They were now come near to the back part of the house. One of the men was engaged about the cooking fire, which burned with the clear, fierce, essential radiance of cocoanut-shells. A fragrance of strange meats was in the air. All round in the verandahs lamps were lighted, so that the place shone abroad in the dusk of the trees with many complicated patterns of shadow.

'Come and wash your hands,' said Attwater, and led the way into a clean, matted room with a cot bed, a safe, a shelf or two of books in a glazed case, and an iron washing-stand. Presently he cried in the native, and there appeared for a moment in the doorway a plump and pretty young woman with a clean towel.

'Hullo!' cried Herrick, who now saw for the first time the fourth survivor of the pestilence, and was startled by the recollection of the captain's orders.

'Yes,' said Attwater, 'the whole colony lives about the house, what's left of it. We are all afraid of devils, if you please! and Taniera and she sleep in the front parlour, and the other boy on the verandah.'

'She is pretty,' said Herrick.

'Too pretty,' said Attwater. 'That was why I had her married. A man never knows when he may be inclined to be a fool about women; so when we were left alone, I had the pair of them to the chapel and performed the ceremony. She made a lot of fuss. I do not take at all the romantic view of marriage,' he explained.

'And that strikes you as a safeguard?' asked Herrick with amazement.

'Certainly. I am a plain man and very literal. *Whom God hath joined together*, are the words, I fancy. So one married them, and respects the marriage,' said Attwater.

'Ah!' said Herrick.

'You see, I may look to make an excellent marriage when I go home,' began Attwater, confidentially. 'I am rich. This safe alone'—laying his hand upon it—'will be a moderate fortune, when I have the time to place the pearls upon the market. Here are ten years' accumulation from a lagoon, where I have had as many as ten divers going all day long; and I went further than people usually do in these waters, for I rotted a lot of shell, and did splendidly. Would you like to see them?'

This confirmation of the captain's guess hit Herrick hard, and he contained himself with difficulty. 'No, thank you, I think not,' said he. 'I do not care for pearls. I am very indifferent to all these . . .'

'Gewgaws?' suggested Attwater. 'And yet I believe you ought to cast an eye on my collection, which is really unique, and which—oh! it is the case with all of us and everything about us!—hangs by a hair. Today it groweth up and flourisheth; tomorrow it is cut down and cast into the oven.* Today it is here and together in this safe; tomorrow—tonight!—it may be scattered. Thou fool, this night thy soul shall be required of thee.'*

'I do not understand you,' said Herrick.

'Not?' said Attwater.

'You seem to speak in riddles,' said Herrick, unsteadily. 'I do not understand what manner of man you are, nor what you are driving at.'

Attwater stood with his hands upon his hips, and his head

bent forward. 'I am a fatalist,' he replied, 'and just now (if you insist on it) an experimentalist. Talking of which, by the bye, who painted out the schooner's name?' he said, with mocking softness, 'because, do you know? one thinks it should be done again. It can still be partly read; and whatever is worth doing, is surely worth doing well. You think with me? That is so nice! Well, shall we step on the veranda? I have a dry sherry that I would like your opinion of.'

Herrick followed him forth to where, under the light of the hanging lamps, the table shone with napery and crystal; followed him as the criminal goes with the hangman, or the sheep with the butcher; took the sherry mechanically, drank it, and spoke mechanical words of praise. The object of his terror had become suddenly inverted; till then he had seen Attwater trussed and gagged, a helpless victim, and had longed to run in and save him; he saw him now tower up mysterious and menacing, the angel of the Lord's wrath, armed with knowledge and threatening judgment. He set down his glass again, and was surprised to see it empty.

'You go always armed?' he said, and the next moment could have plucked his tongue out.

'Always,' said Attwater. 'I have been through a mutiny here; that was one of my incidents of missionary life.'

And just then the sound of voices reached them, and looking forth from the veranda they saw Huish and the captain drawing near.

CHAPTER IX

THE DINNER PARTY

THEY sat down to an island dinner, remarkable for its variety and excellence: turtle-soup and steak, fish, fowls, a sucking pig, a cocoanut salad, and sprouting cocoanut roasted for dessert. Not a tin had been opened; and save for the oil and vinegar in the salad, and some green spears of onion which Attwater cultivated and plucked with his own hand, not even the condiments were European. Sherry, hock, and claret succeeded each other, and the *Farallone* champagne brought up the rear with the dessert.

It was plain that, like so many of the extremely religious in the days before teetotalism, Attwater had a dash of the epicure. For such characters it is softening to eat well; doubly so to have designed and had prepared an excellent meal for others; and the manners of their host were agreeably mollified in consequence. A cat of huge growth sat on his shoulder purring, and occasionally, with a deft paw, capturing a morsel in the air. To a cat he might be likened himself, as he lolled at the head of his table, dealing out attentions and innuendos, and using the velvet and the claw indifferently. And both Huish and the captain fell progressively under the charm of his hospitable freedom.

Over the third guest, the incidents of the dinner may be said to have passed for long unheeded. Herrick accepted all that was offered him, ate and drank without tasting, and heard without comprehension. His mind was singly occupied in contemplating the horror of the circumstances in which he sat. What Attwater knew, what the captain designed, from which side treachery was to be first expected, these were the ground of his thoughts. There were times when he longed to throw down the table and flee into the night. And even that was debarred him; to do anything, to say anything, to move at all, were only to precipitate the barbarous tragedy; and he sat spell-bound, eating with white lips. Two of his companions observed him narrowly, Attwater with raking, sidelong glances that did not interrupt his talk, the captain with a heavy and anxious consideration.

'Well, I must say this sherry is a really prime article,' said Huish, ' 'Ow much does it stand you in, if it's a fair question?'

'A hundred and twelve shillings in London, and the freight to Valparaiso, and on again,' said Attwater. 'It strikes one as really not a bad fluid.'

'A 'undred and twelve!' murmured the clerk, relishing the wine and the figures in a common ecstasy: 'O my!'

'So glad you like it,' said Attwater. 'Help yourself, Mr Whish, and keep the bottle by you.'

'My friend's name is Huish and not Whish, sir,' said the captain with a flush.

'I beg your pardon, I am sure. Huish and not Whish; certainly,' said Attwater. 'I was about to say that I have still eight dozen,' he added, fixing the captain with his eye.

'Eight dozen what?' said Davis.

'Sherry,' was the reply. 'Eight dozen excellent sherry. Why, it seems almost worth it in itself; to a man fond of wine.'

The ambiguous words struck home to guilty consciences, and Huish and the captain sat up in their places and regarded him with a scare.

'Worth what?' said Davis.

'A hundred and twelve shillings,' replied Attwater.

The captain breathed hard for a moment. He reached out far and wide to find any coherency in these remarks; then, with a great effort, changed the subject.

'I allow we are about the first white men upon this island, sir,' said he.

Attwater followed him at once, and with entire gravity, to the new ground. 'Myself and Dr Symonds excepted, I should say the only ones,' he returned. 'And yet who can tell? In the course of the ages some one may have lived here, and we sometimes think that some one must. The cocoa-palms grow all round the island, which is scarce like nature's planting. We found besides, when we landed, an unmistakable cairn upon the beach; use unknown; but probably erected in the hope of gratifying some mumbo-jumbo whose very name is forgotten, by some thick-witted gentry whose very bones are lost. Then the island (witness the *Directory*) has been twice reported; and since my tenancy, we have had two wrecks, both derelict. The rest is conjecture.'

'Dr Symonds is your partner, I guess?' said Davis.

'A dear fellow, Symonds! How he would regret it, if he knew you had been here!' said Attwater.

''E's on the *Trinity 'All*, ain't he?' asked Huish.

'And if you could tell me where the *Trinity 'All* was, you would confer a favour, Mr Whish!' was the reply.

'I suppose she has a native crew?' said Davis.

'Since the secret has been kept ten years, one would suppose she had,' replied Attwater.

'Well, now, see 'ere!' said Huish. 'You have everythink about you in no end style, and no mistake, but I tell you it wouldn't do for me. Too much of "the old rustic bridge by the mill"; too retired, by 'alf. Give me the sound of Bow Bells!'

'You must not think it was always so,' replied Attwater. 'This was once a busy shore, although now, hark! you can hear the solitude. I find it stimulating. And talking of the sound of bells, kindly follow a little experiment of mine in silence.' There was a silver bell at his right hand to call the servants; he made them a sign to stand still, struck the bell with force, and leaned eagerly forward. The note rose clear and strong; it rang out clear and far into the night and over the deserted island; it died into the distance until there only lingered in the porches of the ear a vibration that was sound no longer. 'Empty houses, empty sea, solitary beaches!' said Attwater. 'And yet God hears the bell! And yet we sit in this veranda on a lighted stage with all heaven for spectators! And you call that solitude?'

There followed a bar of silence, during which the captain sat mesmerized.

Then Attwater laughed softly. 'These are the diversions of a lonely man,' he resumed, 'and possibly not in good taste. One tells oneself these little fairy tales for company. If there *should* happen to be anything in folk-lore, Mr Hay? But here comes the claret. One does not offer you Lafitte, captain, because I believe it is all sold to the railroad dining-cars in your great country; but this Brâne-Mouton is of a good year, and Mr Whish will give me news of it.'

'That's a queer idea of yours!' cried the captain, bursting with a sigh from the spell that had bound him. 'So you mean to tell me now, that you sit here evenings and ring up . . . well, ring on the angels . . . by yourself?'

'As a matter of historic fact, and since you put it directly, one does not,' said Attwater. 'Why ring a bell, when there flows out from oneself and everything about one a far more momentous silence? the least beat of my heart and the least thought in my mind echoing into eternity for ever and for ever and for ever.'

'O look 'ere,' said Huish, 'turn down the lights at once, and the Band of 'Ope will oblige! This ain't a spiritual séance.'

'No folk-lore about Mr Whish—I beg your pardon, captain: Huish not Whish, of course,' said Attwater.

As the boy was filling Huish's glass, the bottle escaped from his hand and was shattered, and the wine spilt on the veranda floor. Instant grimness as of death appeared in the face of Attwater; he smote the bell imperiously, and the two brown natives fell into the attitude of attention and stood mute and trembling. There was just a moment of silence and hard looks; then followed a few savage words in the native; and, upon a gesture of dismissal, the service proceeded as before.

None of the party had as yet observed upon the excellent bearing of the two men. They were dark, undersized, and well set-up; stepped softly, waited deftly, brought on the wines and dishes at a look, and their eyes attended studiously on their master.

'Where do you get your labour from anyway?' asked Davis.

'Ah, where not?' answered Attwater.

'Not much of a soft job, I suppose?' said the captain.

'If you will tell me where getting labour is!' said Attwater with a shrug. 'And of course, in our case, as we could name no destination, we had to go far and wide and do the best we could. We have gone as far west as the Kingsmills and as far south as Rapa-iti.* Pity Symonds isn't here! He is full of yarns. That was his part, to collect them. Then began mine, which was the educational.'

'You mean to run them?' said Davis.

'Ay! to run them,' said Attwater.

'Wait a bit,' said Davis, 'I'm out of my depth. How was this? Do you mean to say you did it single-handed?'

'One did it single-handed,' said Attwater, 'because there was nobody to help one.'

'By God, but you must be a holy terror!' cried the captain, in a glow of admiration.

'One does one's best,' said Attwater.

'Well, now!' said Davis, 'I have seen a lot of driving in my time and been counted a good driver myself; I fought my way, third mate, round the Cape Horn with a push of packet-rats that would have turned the devil out of hell and shut the door on him; and I tell you, this racket of Mr Attwater's takes the cake. In a ship, why, there ain't nothing to it! You've got the law with you, that's what does it. But put me down on this blame' beach alone, with nothing but a whip and a mouthful of bad words, and ask me to . . . no, *sir*! it's not good enough! I haven't got the sand for that!' cried Davis. 'It's the law behind,' he added; 'it's the law does it, every time!'

'The beak ain't as black as he's sometimes pynted,' observed Huish, humorously.

'Well, one got the law after a fashion,' said Attwater. 'One had to be a number of things. It was sometimes rather a bore.'

'I should smile!' said Davis. 'Rather lively, I should think!'

'I daresay we mean the same thing,' said Attwater. 'However, one way or another, one got it knocked into their heads that they *must* work, and they *did* . . . until the Lord took them!'

''Ope you made 'em jump,' said Huish.

'When it was necessary, Mr Whish, I made them jump,' said Attwater.

'You bet you did,' cried the captain. He was a good deal flushed, but not so much with wine as admiration; and his eyes drank in the huge proportions of the other with delight. 'You bet you did, and you bet that I can see you doing it! By God, you're a man, and you can say I said so.'

'Too good of you, I'm sure,' said Attwater.

'Did you—did you ever have crime here?' asked Herrick, breaking his silence with a pungent voice.

'Yes,' said Attwater, 'we did.'

'And how did you handle that, sir?' cried the eager captain.

'Well, you see, it was a queer case,' replied Attwater. 'It was a case that would have puzzled Solomon. Shall I tell it you? yes?'

The captain rapturously accepted.

'Well,' drawled Attwater, 'here is what it was. I daresay you know two types of natives, which may be called the obsequious and the sullen? Well, one had them, the types themselves, detected in the fact; and one had them together. Obsequiousness ran out of the first like wine out of a bottle, sullenness congested in the second. Obsequiousness was all smiles; he ran to catch your eye, he loved to gabble; and he had about a dozen words of beach English,* and an eighth-of-an-inch veneer of Christianity. Sullens was industrious; a big down-looking bee. When he was spoken to, he answered with a black look and a shrug of one shoulder, but the thing would be done. I don't give him to you for a model of manners; there was nothing showy about Sullens; but he was strong and steady, and ungraciously obedient. Now Sullens got into trouble; no matter how; the regulations of the place were broken, and he was punished accordingly—without effect. So, the next day, and the next, and the day after, till I began to be weary of the business, and Sullens (I am afraid) particularly so. There came a day when he was in fault again, for the—oh, perhaps the thirtieth time; and he rolled a dull eye upon me, with a spark in it, and appeared to speak. Now the regulations of the place are formal upon one point: we allow no explanations; none are received, none allowed to be offered. So one stopped him instantly, but made a note of the circumstance. The next day, he was gone from the settlement. There could be nothing more annoying; if the labour took to running away, the fishery was wrecked. There are sixty miles of this island, you see, all in length like the Queen's Highway; the idea of pursuit in such a place was a piece of single-minded childishness, which one did not entertain. Two days later, I made a discovery; it came in upon me with a flash that Sullens had been unjustly punished from beginning to end, and the real culprit throughout had been Obsequiousness. The native who talks, like the woman who hesitates, is lost. You set him talking and lying; and he talks, and lies, and watches your face to see if he has pleased you; till at last, out comes the truth! It came out of Obsequiousness in the regular course. I said nothing to him; I dismissed him; and late as it was, for it was already night, set off to look for Sullens. I had not far to go: about two hundred yards up the island, the moon showed him to me. He was hanging in a cocoa-palm—I'm not botanist enough to tell you how—but it's the way, in nine cases out of ten, these natives commit suicide. His tongue was out, poor devil, and the birds had got at him; I spare you details, he was an ugly sight! I gave the business six good hours of thinking in this veranda. My justice had been made a fool of; I don't suppose that I was ever angrier. Next day, I had the conch sounded and all hands out before sunrise. One took one's gun, and led the way, with Obsequiousness. He was very talkative; the beggar supposed that all was right now he had confessed; in the old schoolboy phrase, he was plainly 'sucking up' to me; full of protestations of good-will and good behaviour; to which one answered one really can't remember what. Presently the tree came in sight, and the hanged man. They all burst out lamenting for their comrade in the island way, and Obsequiousness was the loudest of the mourners. He was quite genuine; a noxious creature, without any consciousness of guilt. Well, presently—to make a long story short—one told him to go up the tree. He stared a bit, looked at one with a trouble in his eye, and had rather a sickly smile; but went. He was obedient to the last; he had all the pretty virtues, but the truth was not in him. So soon as he was up, he looked down, and there was the rifle covering him; and at that he gave a whimper like a dog. You could hear a pin drop; no more keening now. There they all crouched upon the ground, with bulging eyes; there was he in the tree-top, the colour of lead; and between was the dead man, dancing a bit in the air. He was obedient to the last, recited his crime, recommended his soul to God. And then . . .'

Attwater paused, and Herrick, who had been listening attentively, made a convulsive movement which upset his glass.

'And then?' said the breathless captain.

'Shot,' said Attwater. 'They came to ground together.'

Herrick sprang to his feet with a shriek and an insensate gesture.

'It was a murder,' he screamed. 'A cold-hearted, bloody-minded murder! You monstrous being! Murderer and hypocrite—murderer and hypocrite—murderer and hypocrite—' he repeated, and his tongue stumbled among the words.

The captain was by him in a moment. 'Herrick!' he cried, 'behave yourself! Here, don't be a blame' fool!'

Herrick struggled in his embrace like a frantic child, and suddenly bowing his face in his hands, choked into a sob, the first of many, which now convulsed his body silently, and now jerked from him indescribable and meaningless sounds.

'Your friend appears over-excited,' remarked Attwater, sitting unmoved but all alert at table.

'It must be the wine,' replied the captain. 'He ain't no drinking man, you see. I—I think I'll take him away. A walk'll sober him up, I guess.'

He led him without resistance out of the veranda and into the night, in which they soon melted; but still for some time, as they drew away, his comfortable voice was to be heard soothing and remonstrating, and Herrick answering, at intervals, with the mechanical noises of hysteria.

''E's like a bloomin' poultry yard!' observed Huish, helping himself to wine (of which he spilled a good deal) with gentlemanly ease. 'A man should learn to beyave at table,' he added.

'Rather bad form, is it not?' said Attwater. 'Well, well, we are left *tête-à-tête*. A glass of wine with you, Mr Whish!'

CHAPTER X

THE OPEN DOOR

THE captain and Herrick meanwhile turned their back upon the lights in Attwater's veranda, and took a direction towards the pier and the beach of the lagoon.

The isle, at this hour, with its smooth floor of sand, the pillared roof overhead, and the prevalent illumination of the lamps, wore an air of unreality like a deserted theatre or a public garden at midnight. A man looked about him for the statues and tables. Not the least air of wind was stirring among the palms, and the silence was emphasized by the continuous clamour of the surf from the sea-shore, as it might be of traffic in the next street.

Still talking, still soothing him, the captain hurried his patient on, brought him at last to the lagoon side, and leading him down the beach, laved his head and face with the tepid water. The paroxysm gradually subsided, the sobs became less convulsive and then ceased; by an odd but not quite unnatural conjunction, the captain's soothing current of talk died away at the same time and by proportional steps, and the pair remained sunk in silence. The lagoon broke at their feet in petty wavelets, and with a sound as delicate as a whisper; stars of all degrees looked down on their own images in that vast mirror; and the more angry colour of the *Farallone*'s riding lamp burned in the middle distance. For long they continued to gaze on the scene before them, and hearken anxiously to the rustle and tinkle of that miniature surf, or the more distant and loud reverberations from the outer coast. For long speech was denied them; and when the words came at last, they came to both simultaneously.

'Say, Herrick . . .' the captain was beginning.

But Herrick, turning swiftly towards his companion, bent him down with the eager cry: 'Let's up anchor, captain, and to sea!'

'Where to, my son?' said the captain. 'Up anchor's easy saying. But where to?'

'To sea,' responded Herrick. 'The sea's big enough! To sea—away from this dreadful island and that, oh! that sinister man!'

'Oh, we'll see about that,' said Davis. 'You brace up, and we'll see about that. You're all run down, that's what's wrong with you; you're all nerves, like Jemimar; you've got to brace up good and be yourself again, and then we'll talk.'

'To sea,' reiterated Herrick, 'to sea tonight—now—this moment!'

'It can't be, my son,' replied the captain firmly. 'No ship of mine puts to sea without provisions, you can take that for settled.'

'You don't seem to understand,' said Herrick. 'The whole thing is over, I tell you. There is nothing to do here, when he knows all. That man there with the cat knows all; can't you take it in?'

'All what?' asked the captain, visibly discomposed. 'Why, he received us like a perfect gentleman and treated us real handsome, until you began with your foolery—and I must say I seen men shot for less, and nobody sorry! What more do you expect anyway?'

Herrick rocked to and fro upon the sand, shaking his head.

'Guying us,' he said, 'he was guying us—only guying us; it's all we're good for.'

'There was one queer thing, to be sure,' admitted the captain, with a misgiving of the voice; 'that about the sherry. Damned if I caught on to that. Say, Herrick, you didn't give me away?'

'Oh! give you away!' repeated Herrick with weary, querulous scorn. 'What was there to give away? We're transparent; we've got rascal branded on us: detected rascal—detected rascal! Why, before he came on board, there was the name painted out, and he saw the whole thing. He made sure we would kill him there and then, and stood guying you and Huish on the chance. He calls that being frightened! Next he had me ashore; a fine time I had! *The two wolves,* he calls you and Huish.—*What is the puppy doing with the two wolves?* he asked. He showed me his pearls; he said they might be dispersed before morning, and *all hung by a hair*—and smiled as he said it, such a smile! O, it's no use, I tell you! He knows all, he sees through all; we only make him laugh with our pretences—he looks at us and laughs like God!'

There was a silence. Davis stood with contorted brows, gazing into the night.

'The pearls?' he said suddenly. 'He showed them to you? he has them?'

'No, he didn't show them; I forgot: only the safe they were in,' said Herrick. 'But you'll never get them!'

'I've two words to say to that,' said the captain.

'Do you think he would have been so easy at table, unless he was prepared?' cried Herrick. 'The servants were both armed. He was armed himself; he always is; he told me. You will never deceive his vigilance. Davis, I know it! It's all up, I tell you, and keep telling you and proving it. All up; all up. There's nothing for it, there's nothing to be done: all gone: life, honour, love. Oh, my God, my God, why was I born?'

Another pause followed upon this outburst.

The captain put his hands to his brow.

'Another thing!' he broke out. 'Why did he tell you all this? Seems like madness to me!'

Herrick shook his head with gloomy iteration. 'You wouldn't understand if I were to tell you,' said he.

'I guess I can understand any blame' thing that you can tell me,' said the captain.

'Well, then, he's a fatalist,' said Herrick.

'What's that, a fatalist?' said Davis.

'Oh, it's a fellow that believes a lot of things,' said Herrick, 'believes that his bullets go true; believes that all falls out as God chooses, do as you like to prevent it; and all that.'

'Why, I guess I believe right so myself,' said Davis.

'You do?' said Herrick.

'You bet I do!' says Davis.

Herrick shrugged his shoulders. 'Well, you must be a fool,' said he, and he leaned his head upon his knees.

The captain stood biting his hands.

'There's one thing sure,' he said at last. 'I must get Huish out of that. *He's* not fit to hold his end up with a man like you describe.'

And he turned to go away. The words had been quite simple; not so the tone; and the other was quick to catch it.

'Davis!' he cried, 'no! Don't do it. Spare *me*, and don't do it—spare yourself, and leave it alone—for God's sake, for your children's sake!'

His voice rose to a passionate shrillness; another moment, and he might be overheard by their not distant victim. But Davis turned on him with a savage oath and gesture; and the miserable young man rolled over on his face on the sand, and lay speechless and helpless.

The captain meanwhile set out rapidly for Attwater's house. As he went, he considered with himself eagerly, his thoughts racing. The man had understood, he had mocked them from the beginning; he would teach him to make a mockery of John Davis! Herrick thought him a god; give him a second to aim in, and the god was overthrown. He chuckled as he felt the butt of his revolver. It should be done now, as he went in. From behind? It was difficult to get there. From across the table? No, the captain preferred to shoot standing, so as you could be sure to get your hand upon your gun. The best would be to summon Huish, and when Attwater stood up and turned—Ah, then would be the moment. Wrapped in this ardent prefiguration of events, the captain posted towards the house with his head down.

'Hands up! Halt!' cried the voice of Attwater.

And the captain, before he knew what he was doing, had obeyed. The surprise was complete and irremediable. Coming on the top crest of his murderous intentions, he had walked straight into an ambuscade, and now stood, with his hands impotently lifted, staring at the veranda.

The party was now broken up. Attwater leaned on a post, and kept Davis covered with a Winchester. One of the servants was hard by with a second at the port arms,* leaning a little forward, round-eyed with eager expectancy. In the open space at the head of the stair, Huish was partly supported by the other native; his face wreathed in meaningless smiles, his mind seemingly sunk in the contemplation of an unlighted cigar.

'Well,' said Attwater, 'you seem to me to be a very twopenny pirate!'

The captain uttered a sound in his throat for which we have no name; rage choked him.

'I am going to give you Mr Whish—or the wine-sop that remains of him,' continued Attwater. 'He talks a great deal when he drinks, Captain Davis of the *Sea Ranger*. But I have quite done with him—and return the article with thanks. Now,' he cried sharply. 'Another false movement like that, and your family will have to deplore the loss of an invaluable parent; keep strictly still, Davis.'

Attwater said a word in the native, his eye still undeviatingly fixed on the captain; and the servant thrust Huish smartly forward from the brink of the stair. With an extraordinary simultaneous dispersion of his members, that gentleman bounded forth into space, struck the earth, ricochetted, and brought up with his arms about a palm. His mind was quite a stranger to these events; the expression of anguish that deformed his countenance at the moment of the leap was probably mechanical; and he suffered these convulsions in silence; clung to the tree like an infant; and seemed, by his dips, to suppose himself engaged in the pastime of bobbing for apples. A more finely sympathetic mind or a more observant eye might have remarked, a little in front of him on the sand, and still quite beyond reach, the unlighted cigar.

'There is your Whitechapel carrion!' said Attwater. 'And now you might very well ask me why I do not put a period to you at once, as you deserve. I will tell you why, Davis. It is because I have nothing to do with the *Sea Ranger* and the people you drowned, or the *Farallone* and the champagne that you stole. That is your account with God; He keeps it, and He will settle it when the clock strikes. In my own case, I have nothing to go on but suspicion, and I do not kill on suspicion, not even vermin like you. But understand! if ever I see any of you again, it is another matter, and you shall eat a bullet. And now take yourself off. March! and as you value what you call your life, keep your hands up as you go!'

The captain remained as he was, his hands up, his mouth open: mesmerized with fury.

'March!' said Attwater. 'One—two—three!'

And Davis turned and passed slowly away. But even as he went, he was meditating a prompt, offensive return. In the twinkling of an eye, he had leaped behind a tree; and was crouching there, pistol in hand, peering from either side of his place of ambush with bared teeth; a serpent already poised to strike. And already he was too late. Attwater and his servants had disappeared; and only the lamps shone on the deserted table and the bright sand about the house, and threw into the night in all directions the strong and tall shadows of the palms.

Davis ground his teeth. Where were they gone, the cowards? to what hole had they retreated beyond reach? It was in vain he should try anything, he, single and with a second-hand revolver, against three persons, armed with Winchesters, and who did not show an ear out of any of the apertures of that lighted and silent house. Some of them might have already ducked below it from the rear, and be drawing a bead upon him at that moment from the low-browed crypt, the receptacle of empty bottles and broken crockery. No, there was nothing to be done but to bring away (if it were still possible) his shattered and demoralized forces.

'Huish,' he said, 'come along.'

''S lose my ciga',' said Huish, reaching vaguely forward.

The captain let out a rasping oath. 'Come right along here,' said he.

''S all righ'. Sleep here 'th Atty-Attwa. Go boar' t'morr',' replied the festive one.

'If you don't come, and come now, by the living God, I'll shoot you!' cried the captain.

It is not to be supposed that the sense of these words in any way penetrated to the mind of Huish; rather that, in a fresh attempt upon the cigar, he over-balanced himself and came flying erratically forward: a course which brought him within reach of Davis.

'Now you walk straight,' said the captain, clutching him, 'or I'll know why not!'

''S lose my ciga',' replied Huish.

The captain's contained fury blazed up for a moment. He

twisted Huish round, grasped him by the neck of the coat, ran him in front of him to the pier-end, and flung him savagely forward on his face.

'Look for your cigar then, you swine!' said he, and blew his boat-call till the pea in it ceased to rattle.

An immediate activity responded on board the *Farallone*; far-away voices, and soon the sound of oars, floated along the surface of the lagoon; and at the same time, from nearer hand, Herrick aroused himself and strolled languidly up. He bent over the insignificant figure of Huish, where it grovelled, apparently insensible, at the base of the figure-head.

'Dead?' he asked.

'No, he's not dead,' said Davis.

'And Attwater?' asked Herrick.

'Now you just shut your head!' replied Davis. 'You can do that, I fancy, and by God, I'll show you how! I'll stand no more of your drivel.'

They waited accordingly in silence till the boat bumped on the furthest piers; then raised Huish, head and heels, carried him down the gangway, and flung him summarily in the bottom. On the way out he was heard murmuring of the loss of his cigar; and after he had been handed up the side like baggage, and cast down in the alleyway to slumber, his last audible expression was: 'Splen'l fl' Attwa'!' This the expert construed into 'Splendid fellow, Attwater'; with so much innocence had this great spirit issued from the adventures of the evening.

The captain went and walked in the waist with brief, irate turns; Herrick leaned his arms on the taffrail; the crew had all turned in. The ship had a gentle, cradling motion; at times a block piped like a bird. On shore, through the colonnade of palm stems, Attwater's house was to be seen shining steadily with many lamps. And there was nothing else visible, whether in the heaven above or in the lagoon below, but the stars and their reflexions. It might have been minutes or it might have been hours, that Herrick leaned there, looking in the glorified water and drinking peace. 'A bath of stars,' he was thinking; when a hand was laid at last on his shoulder.

'Herrick,' said the captain, 'I've been walking off my trouble.'

A sharp jar passed through the young man, but he neither answered nor so much as turned his head.

'I guess I spoke a little rough to you on shore,' pursued the captain; 'the fact is, I was real mad; but now it's over, and you and me have to turn to and think.'

'I will *not* think,' said Herrick.

'Here, old man!' said Davis, kindly; 'this won't fight, you know! You've got to brace up and help me get things straight. You're not going back on a friend? That's not like you, Herrick!'

'O yes, it is,' said Herrick.

'Come, come!' said the captain, and paused as if quite at a loss. 'Look here,' he cried, 'you have a glass of champagne. *I* won't touch it, so that'll show you if I'm in earnest. But it's just the pick-me-up for you; it'll put an edge on you at once.'

'O, you leave me alone!' said Herrick, and turned away.

The captain caught him by the sleeve; and he shook him off and turned on him, for the moment, like a demoniac.

'Go to hell in your own way!' he cried.

And he turned away again, this time unchecked, and stepped forward to where the boat rocked alongside and ground occasionally against the schooner. He looked about him. A corner of the house was interposed between the captain and himself; all was well; no eye must see him in that last act. He slid silently into the boat; thence, silently, into the starry water. Instinctively he swam a little; it would be time enough to stop by and by.

The shock of the immersion brightened his mind immediately. The events of the ignoble day passed before him in a frieze of pictures, and he thanked 'whatever Gods there be'* for that open door of suicide. In such a little while he would be done with it, the random business at an end, the prodigal son come home. A very bright planet shone before him and drew a trenchant wake along the water. He took that for his line and followed it. That was the last earthly thing that he should look upon; that radiant speck, which he had soon magnified into a City of Laputa,* along whose terraces there walked men and women of awful and benignant features, who viewed him with distant commiseration. These imaginary spectators consoled him; he told himself their talk, one to another; it was of himself and his sad destiny.

From such flights of fancy, he was aroused by the growing coldness of the water. Why should he delay? Here, where he was now, let him drop the curtain, let him seek the ineffable refuge, let him lie down with all races and generations of men in the house of sleep. It was easy to say, easy to do. To stop swimming: there was no mystery in that, if he could do it. Could he? And he could not. He knew it instantly. He was aware instantly of an opposition in his members, unanimous and invincible, clinging to life with a single and fixed resolve, finger by finger, sinew by sinew; something that was at once he and not he—at once within and without him; the shutting of some miniature valve in his brain, which a single manly thought should suffice to open—and the grasp of an external fate ineluctable as gravity. To any man there may come at times a consciousness that there blows, through all the articulations of his body, the wind of a spirit not wholly his; that his mind rebels; that another girds him and carries him whither he would not. It came now to Herrick, with the authority of a revelation. There was no escape possible. The open door was closed in his recreant face. He must go back into the world and amongst men without illusion. He must stagger on to the end with the pack of his responsibility and his disgrace, until a cold, a blow, a merciful chance ball, or the more merciful hangman, should dismiss him from his infamy. There were men who could commit suicide; there were men who could not; and he was one who could not.

For perhaps a minute, there raged in his mind the coil of this discovery; then cheerless certitude followed; and, with an incredible simplicity of submission to ascertained fact, he turned round and struck out for shore. There was a courage in this which he could not appreciate; the ignobility of his cowardice wholly occupying him. A strong current set against him like a wind in his face; he contended with it heavily, wearily, without enthusiasm, but with substantial advantage;

marking his progress the while, without pleasure, by the outline of the trees. Once he had a moment of hope. He heard to the southward of him, towards the centre of the lagoon, the wallowing of some great fish, doubtless a shark, and paused for a little, treading water. Might not this be the hangman? he thought. But the wallowing died away; mere silence succeeded; and Herrick pushed on again for the shore, raging as he went at his own nature. Ay, he would wait for the shark; but if he had heard him coming! . . . His smile was tragic. He could have spat upon himself.

About three in the morning, chance, and the set of the current, and the bias of his own right-handed body, so decided it between them that he came to shore upon the beach in front of Attwater's. There he sat down, and looked forth into a world without any of the lights of hope. The poor diving-dress of self-conceit was sadly tattered! With the fairy tale of suicide, of a refuge always open to him, he had hitherto beguiled and supported himself in the trials of life; and behold! that also was only a fairy tale, that also was folk-lore. With the consequences of his acts he saw himself implacably confronted for the duration of life: stretched upon a cross, and nailed there with the iron bolts of his own cowardice. He had no tears; he told himself no stories. His disgust with himself was so complete, that even the process of apologetic mythology had ceased. He was like a man cast down from a pillar, and every bone broken. He lay there, and admitted the facts, and did not attempt to rise.

Dawn began to break over the far side of the atoll, the sky brightened, the clouds became dyed with gorgeous colours, the shadows of the night lifted. And, suddenly, Herrick was aware that the lagoon and the trees wore again their daylight livery; and he saw, on board the *Farallone,* Davis extinguishing the lantern, and smoke rising from the galley.

Davis, without doubt, remarked and recognized the figure on the beach; or perhaps hesitated to recognize it; for after he had gazed a long while from under his hand, he went into the house and fetched a glass. It was very powerful; Herrick had often used it. With an instinct of shame, he hid his face in his hands.

'And what brings you here, Mr Herrick-Hay, or Mr Hay-Herrick?' asked the voice of Attwater. 'Your back view from my present position is remarkably fine, and I would continue to present it. We can get on very nicely as we are, and if you were to turn round, do you know? I think it would be awkward.'

Herrick slowly rose to his feet; his heart throbbed hard, a hideous excitement shook him, but he was master of himself. Slowly he turned, and faced Attwater and the muzzle of a pointed rifle. 'Why could I not do that last night?' he thought.

'Well, why don't you fire?' he said aloud, with a voice that trembled.

Attwater slowly put his gun under his arm, then his hands in his pockets.

'What brings you here?' he repeated.

'I don't know,' said Herrick; and then, with a cry: 'Can you do anything with me?'

'Are you armed?' said Attwater. 'I ask for the form's sake.'

'Armed? No!' said Herrick. 'O yes, I am, too!'

And he flung upon the beach a dripping pistol.

'You are wet,' said Attwater.

'Yes, I am wet,' said Herrick. 'Can you do anything with me?'

Attwater read his face attentively.

'It would depend a good deal upon what you are,' said he.

'What I am? A coward!' said Herrick.

'There is very little to be done with that,' said Attwater. 'And yet the description hardly strikes one as exhaustive.'

'Oh, what does it matter?' cried Herrick. 'Here I am. I am broken crockery; I am a burst drum; the whole of my life is gone to water; I have nothing left that I believe in, except my living horror of myself. Why do I come to you? I don't know; you are cold, cruel, hateful; and I hate you, or I think I hate you. But you are an honest man, an honest gentleman. I put myself, helpless, in your hands. What must I do? If I can't do anything, be merciful and put a bullet through me; it's only a puppy with a broken leg!'

'If I were you, I would pick up that pistol, come up to the house, and put on some dry clothes,' said Attwater.

'If you really mean it?' said Herrick. 'You know they—we—they . . . But you know all.'

'I know quite enough,' said Attwater. 'Come up to the house.'

And the captain, from the deck of the *Farallone*, saw the two men pass together under the shadow of the grove.

CHAPTER XI

DAVID AND GOLIATH

HUISH had bundled himself up from the glare of the day—his face to the house, his knees retracted. The frail bones in the thin tropical raiment seemed scarce more considerable than a fowl's; and Davis, sitting on the rail with his arm about a stay, contemplated him with gloom, wondering what manner of counsel that insignificant figure should contain. For since Herrick had thrown him off and deserted to the enemy, Huish, alone of mankind, remained to him to be a helper and oracle.

He considered their position with a sinking heart. The ship was a stolen ship; the stores, whether from initial carelessness or ill administration during the voyage, were insufficient to carry them to any port except back to Papeete; and there retribution waited in the shape of a gendarme, a judge with a queer-shaped hat, and the horror of distant Noumea. Upon that side, there was no glimmer of hope. Here, at the island, the dragon was roused; Attwater with his men and his Winchesters watched and patrolled the house; let him who dare approach it. What else was then left but to sit there, inactive, pacing the decks—until the *Trinity Hall* arrived and they were cast into irons, or until the food came to an end, and the pangs of famine succeeded? For the *Trinity Hall* Davis was prepared; he would barricade the house, and die there defending it, like a rat in a crevice. But for the other? The cruise of the *Farallone*, into which he had plunged, only a fortnight before, with such golden expectations, could this be the nightmare end of it? The ship rotting at anchor, the crew stumbling and dying in the scuppers? It seemed as if any extreme of hazard were to be preferred to so grisly a certainty; as if it would be better to up-anchor after all, put to sea at a venture, and, perhaps, perish at the hands of cannibals on one of the more obscure Paumotus. His eye roved swiftly over sea and sky in quest of any promise of wind, but the fountains of the Trade were empty. Where it had run yesterday and for weeks before, a roaring blue river charioting clouds, silence now reigned; and the whole height of the atmosphere stood balanced. On the endless ribbon of island that stretched out to either hand of him its array of golden and green and silvery palms, not the most volatile frond was to be seen stirring; they drooped to their stable images in the lagoon like things carved of metal, and already their long line began to reverberate heat. There was no escape possible that day, none probable on the morrow. And still the stores were running out!

Then came over Davis, from deep down in the roots of his being, or at least from far back among his memories of childhood and innocence, a wave of superstition. This run of ill luck was something beyond natural; the chances of the game were in themselves more various; it seemed as if the devil must serve the pieces. The devil? He heard again the clear note of Attwater's bell ringing abroad into the night, and dying away. How if God . . . ?

Briskly, he averted his mind. Attwater: that was the point. Attwater had food and a treasure of pearls; escape made possible in the present, riches in the future. They must come to grips with Attwater; the man must die. A smoky heat went over his face, as he recalled the impotent figure he had made last night, and the contemptuous speeches he must bear in silence. Rage, shame, and the love of life, all pointed the one way; and only invention halted: how to reach him? had he strength enough? was there any help in that misbegotten packet of bones against the house?

His eyes dwelled upon him with a strange avidity, as though he would read into his soul; and presently the sleeper moved, stirred uneasily, turned suddenly round, and threw him a blinking look. Davis maintained the same dark stare, and Huish looked away again and sat up.

'Lord, I've an 'eadache on me!' said he. 'I believe I was a bit swipey* last night. W'ere's that cry-byby, 'Errick?'

'Gone,' said the captain.

'Ashore?' cried Huish. 'Oh, I say! I'd 'a gone, too.'

'Would you?' said the captain.

'Yes, I would,' replied Huish. 'I like Attwater. 'E's all right;

we got on like one o'clock when you were gone. And ain't his sherry in it, rather? It's like Spiers and Ponds' Amontillado! I wish I 'ad a drain of it now.' He sighed.

'Well, you'll never get no more of it—that's one thing,' said Davis, gravely.

''Ere! wot's wrong with you, Dyvis? Coppers 'ot?* Well, look at *me*! *I* ain't grumpy,' said Huish; 'I'm as plyful as a canary-bird, I am.'

'Yes,' said Davis, 'you're playful; I own that; and you were playful last night, I believe, and a damned fine performance you made of it.'

''Allo!' said Huish. ''Ow's this? Wot performance?'

'Well, I'll tell you,' said the captain, getting slowly off the rail.

And he did: at full length, with every wounding epithet and absurd detail repeated and emphasized; he had his own vanity and Huish's upon the grill, and roasted them; and as he spoke, he inflicted and endured agonies of humiliation. It was a plain man's masterpiece of the sardonic.

'What do you think of it?' said he, when he had done, and looked down at Huish, flushed and serious, and yet jeering.

'I'll tell you wot it is,' was the reply, 'you and me cut a pretty dicky figure.'

'That's so,' said Davis, 'a pretty measly figure, by God! And, by God, I want to see that man at my knees.'

'Ah!' said Huish. ''Ow to get him there?'

'That's it!' cried Davis. 'How to get hold of him! They're four to two; though there's only one man among them to count, and that's Attwater. Get a bead on Attwater, and the others would cut and run and sing out like frightened poultry—and old man Herrick would come round with his hat for a share of the pearls. No, *sir*! it's how to get hold of Attwater! And we daren't even go ashore; he would shoot us in the boat like dogs.'

'Are you particular about having him dead or alive?' asked Huish.

'I want to see him dead,' said the captain.

'Ah, well!' said Huish, 'then I believe I'll do a bit of breakfast.'

And he turned into the house.

The captain doggedly followed him.

'What's this?' he asked. 'What's your idea, anyway?'

'Oh, you let me alone, will you?' said Huish, opening a bottle of champagne. 'You'll 'ear my idea soon enough. Wyte till I pour some cham on my 'ot coppers.' He drank a glass off, and affected to listen. ''Ark!' said he, ''ear it fizz. Like 'am fryin', I declyre. 'Ave a glass, do, and look sociable.'

'No!' said the captain, with emphasis; 'no, I will not! there's business.'

'You p'ys your money and you tykes your choice, my little man,' returned Huish. 'Seems rather a shyme to me to spoil your breakfast for wot's really ancient 'istory.'

He finished three parts of a bottle of champagne, and nibbled a corner of biscuit, with extreme deliberation; the captain sitting opposite and champing the bit like an impatient horse. Then Huish leaned his arms on the table and looked Davis in the face.

'W'en you're ready!' said he.

'Well, now, what's your idea?' said Davis, with a sigh.

'Fair play!' said Huish. 'What's yours?'

'The trouble is that I've got none,' replied Davis; and wandered for some time in aimless discussion of the difficulties in their path, and useless explanations of his own fiasco.

'About done?' said Huish.

'I'll dry up right here,' replied Davis.

'Well, then,' said Huish, 'you give me your 'and across the table, and say, "Gawd strike me dead if I don't back you up."'

His voice was hardly raised, yet it thrilled the hearer. His face seemed the epitome of cunning, and the captain recoiled from it as from a blow.

'What for?' said he.

'Luck,' said Huish. 'Substantial guarantee demanded.'

And he continued to hold out his hand.

'I don't see the good of any such tomfoolery,' said the other.

'I do, though,' returned Huish. 'Gimme your 'and and say the words; then you'll 'ear my view of it. Don't, and you don't.'

The captain went through the required form, breathing short, and gazing on the clerk with anguish. What to fear, he knew not; yet he feared slavishly what was to fall from the pale lips.

'Now, if you'll excuse me 'alf a second,' said Huish, 'I'll go and fetch the byby.'

'The baby?' said Davis. 'What's that?'

'Fragile. With care. This side up,' replied the clerk with a wink, as he disappeared.

He returned, smiling to himself, and carrying in his hand a silk handkerchief. The long stupid wrinkles ran up Davis's brow, as he saw it. What should it contain? He could think of nothing more recondite than a revolver.

Huish resumed his seat.

'Now,' said he, 'are you man enough to take charge of 'Errick and the niggers? Because I'll take care of Hattwater.'

'How?' cried Davis. 'You can't!'

'Tut, tut!' said the clerk. 'You gimme time. Wot's the first point? The first point is that we can't get ashore, and I'll make you a present of that for a 'ard one. But 'ow about a flag of truce? Would that do the trick, d'ye think? or would Attwater simply blyze aw'y at us in the bloomin' boat like dawgs?'

'No,' said Davis, 'I don't believe he would.'

'No more do I,' said Huish; 'I don't believe he would either; and I'm sure I 'ope he won't! So then you can call us ashore. Next point is to get near the managin' direction. And for that I'm going to 'ave you write a letter, in w'ich you s'y you're ashymed to meet his eye, and that the bearer, Mr J. L. 'Uish, is empowered to represent you. Armed with w'ich seemin'ly simple expedient, Mr J. L. 'Uish will proceed to business.'

He paused, like one who had finished, but still held Davis with his eye.

'How?' said Davis. 'Why?'

'Well, you see, you're big,' returned Huish; ''e knows you 'ave a gun in your pocket, and anybody can see with 'alf an eye that you ain't the man to 'esitate about usin' it. So it's no go with you, and never was; you're out of the runnin', Dyvis. But he won't be afryde of me, I'm such a little un! I'm unarmed—

no kid about that—and I'll hold my 'ands up right enough.' He paused. 'If I can manage to sneak up nearer to him as we talk,' he resumed, 'you look out and back me up smart. If I don't, we go aw'y again, and nothink to 'urt. See?'

The captain's face was contorted by the frenzied effort to comprehend.

'No, I don't see,' he cried, 'I can't see. What do you mean?'

'I mean to do for the Beast!' cried Huish, in a burst of venomous triumph, 'I'll bring the 'ulkin' bully to grass. He's 'ad his larks out of me; I'm goin' to 'ave my lark out of 'im, and a good lark too!'

'What is it?' said the captain, almost in a whisper.

'Sure you want to know?' asked Huish.

Davis rose and took a turn in the house.

'Yes, I want to know,' he said at last with an effort.

'W'en your back's at the wall, you do the best you can, don't you?' began the clerk. 'I s'y that, because I 'appen to know there's a prejudice against it; it's considered vulgar, awf'ly vulgar.' He unrolled the handkerchief and showed a four-ounce jar. 'This 'ere's vitriol, this is,' said he.

The captain stared upon him with a whitening face.

'This is the stuff!' he pursued, holding it up. 'This'll burn to the bone; you'll see it smoke upon 'im like 'ell fire! One drop upon 'is bloomin' heyesight, and I'll trouble you for Attwater!'

'No, no, by God!' exclaimed the captain.

'Now, see 'ere, ducky,' said Huish, 'this is my bean feast, I believe? I'm goin' up to that man single-'anded, I am. 'E's about seven foot high, and I'm five foot one. 'E's a rifle in his 'and, 'e's on the look out, 'e wasn't born yesterday. This is Dyvid and Goliar, I tell you! If I'd ast you to walk up and face the music I could understand. But I don't. I on'y ast you to stand by and spifflicate* the niggers. It'll all come in quite natural; you'll see, else! Fust thing you know, you'll see him running round and 'owling like a good un. . . .'

'Don't!' said Davis. 'Don't talk of it!'

'Well, you *are* a juggins!' exclaimed Huish. 'What did you want? You wanted to kill him, and tried to last night. You wanted to kill the 'ole lot of them and tried to, and 'ere I show you 'ow; and because there's some medicine in a bottle you kick up this fuss!'

'I suppose that's so,' said Davis. 'It don't seem someways reasonable, only there it is.'

'It's the happlication of science, I suppose?' sneered Huish.

'I don't know what it is,' cried Davis, pacing the floor; 'it's there! I draw the line at it. I can't put a finger to no such piggishness. It's too damned hateful!'

'And I suppose it's all your fancy pynted it,' said Huish, 'w'en you take a pistol and a bit o' lead, and copse a man's brains all over him? No accountin' for tystes.'

'I'm not denying it,' said Davis, 'it's something here, inside of me. It's foolishness; I daresay it's dam foolishness. I don't argue, I just draw the line. Isn't there no other way?'

'Look for yourself,' said Huish. 'I ain't wedded to this, if you think I am; I ain't ambitious; I don't make a point of playin' the lead; I offer to, that's all, and if you can't show me better, by Gawd, I'm goin' to!'

'Then the risk!' cried Davis.

'If you ast me straight, I should say it was a case of seven to one and no takers,' said Huish. 'But that's my look-out, ducky, and I'm gyme. Look at me, Dyvis, there ain't any shilly-shally about me. I'm gyme, that's wot I am: gyme all through.'

The captain looked at him. Huish sat there, preening his sinister vanity, glorying in his precedency in evil; and the villainous courage and readiness of the creature shone out of him like a candle from a lantern. Dismay and a kind of respect seized hold on Davis in his own despite. Until that moment, he had seen the clerk always hanging back, always listless, uninterested, and openly grumbling at a word of anything to do; and now, by the touch of an enchanter's wand, he beheld him sitting girt and resolved, and his face radiant. He had raised the devil, he thought; and asked who was to control him? and his spirits quailed.

'Look as long as you like,' Huish was going on. 'You don't see any green in my eye! I ain't afryde of Attwater, I ain't afryde of you, and I ain't afryde of words. You want to kill people, that's wot *you* want; but you want to do it in kid gloves, and it can't be done that w'y. Murder ain't genteel, it ain't easy, it ain't safe, and it tykes a man to do it. 'Ere's the man.'

'Huish!' began the captain with energy; and then stopped, and remained staring at him with corrugated brows.

'Well, hout with it!' said Huish. ''Ave you anythink else to put up? Is there any other chanst to try?'

The captain held his peace.

'There you are then!' said Huish with a shrug.

Davis fell again to his pacing.

'Oh, you may do sentry-go till you're blue in the mug, you won't find anythink else,' said Huish.

There was a little silence; the captain, like a man launched on a swing, flying dizzily among extremes of conjecture and refusal.

'But see,' he said, suddenly pausing. 'Can you? Can the thing be done? It—it can't be easy.'

'If I get within twenty foot of 'im it'll be done; so you look out,' said Huish, and his tone of certainty was absolute.

'How can you know that?' broke from the captain in a choked cry. 'You beast, I believe you've done it before!'

'Oh, that's private affyres,' returned Huish, 'I ain't a talking man.'

A shock of repulsion struck and shook the captain; a scream rose almost to his lips; had he uttered it, he might have cast himself at the same moment on the body of Huish, might have picked him up, and flung him down, and wiped the cabin with him, in a frenzy of cruelty that seemed half moral. But the moment passed; and the abortive crisis left the man weaker. The stakes were so high—the pearls on the one hand—starvation and shame on the other. Ten years of pearls! the imagination of Davis translated them into a new, glorified existence for himself and his family. The seat of this new life must be in London; there were deadly reasons against Portland, Maine; and the pictures that came to him were of English manners. He saw his boys marching in the procession of a school, with gowns on, an usher marshalling them and reading as he walked in a great book. He was installed in a villa, semi-detached; the name, *Rosemore,* on the gateposts. In a chair on the gravel walk, he seemed to sit smoking a cigar, a blue ribbon in his buttonhole,* victor over himself and circumstances, and the malignity of bankers. He saw the parlour with red curtains and shells on the mantelpiece—and with the fine inconsistency of visions, mixed a grog at the mahogany table ere he turned in. With that the *Farallone* gave one of the aimless and nameless movements which (even in an anchored ship and even in the most profound calm) remind one of the mobility of fluids; and he was back again under the cover of the house, the fierce daylight besieging it all round and glaring in the chinks, and the clerk in a rather airy attitude, awaiting his decision.

He began to walk again. He aspired after the realization of these dreams, like a horse nickering for water; the lust of them burned in his inside. And the only obstacle was Attwater, who had insulted him from the first. He gave Herrick a full share of the pearls, he insisted on it; Huish opposed him, and he trod the opposition down; and praised himself exceedingly. He was not going to use vitriol himself; was he Huish's keeper? It was a pity he had asked, but after all! . . . he saw the boys again in the school procession, with the gowns he had thought to be so 'tony' long since . . . And at the same time the incomparable shame of the last evening blazed up in his mind.

'Have it your own way!' he said hoarsely.

'Oh, I knew you would walk up,' said Huish. 'Now for the letter. There's paper, pens and ink. Sit down and I'll dictyte.'

The captain took a seat and the pen, looked a while helplessly at the paper, then at Huish. The swing had gone the other way; there was a blur upon his eyes. 'It's a dreadful business,' he said, with a strong twitch of his shoulders.

'It's rather a start, no doubt,' said Huish. 'Tyke a dip of ink. That's it. *William John Hattwater, Esq. Sir:*' he dictated.

'How do you know his name is William John?' asked Davis.

'Saw it on a packing case,' said Huish. 'Got that?'

'No,' said Davis. 'But there's another thing. What are we to write?'

'O my golly!' cried the exasperated Huish. 'Wot kind of man do *you* call yourself? *I'm* goin' to tell you wot to write; that's *my* pitch; if you'll just be so bloomin' condescendin' as to write it down! *William John Attwater, Esq., Sir:*' he reiterated. And the captain at last beginning half mechanically to move his pen, the dictation proceeded: '*It is with feelings of shyme and 'artfelt contrition that I approach you after the yumiliatin' events of last night. Our Mr 'Errick has left the ship, and will have doubtless communicated to you the nature of our 'opes. Needless to s'y, these are no longer possible: Fate 'as declyred against us, and we bow the 'ead. Well awyre as I am of the just suspicions with w'ich I am regarded, I do not venture to solicit the fyvour of an interview for myself, but in order to put an end to a situyation w'ich must be equally pyneful to all, I 'ave deputed my friend and partner, Mr J. L. Huish, to l'y before you my proposals, and w'ich by their moderytion, will, I trust, be found to merit your attention. Mr J. L. Huish is entirely unarmed, I swear to Gawd! and will 'old 'is 'ands over 'is 'ead from the moment he begins to approach you. I am your fytheful servant, John Dyvis.*'

Huish read the letter with the innocent joy of amateurs, chuckled gustfully to himself, and reopened it more than once after it was folded, to repeat the pleasure; Davis meanwhile sitting inert and heavily frowning.

Of a sudden he rose; he seemed all abroad. 'No!' he cried. 'No! it can't be! It's too much; it's damnation. God would never forgive it.'

'Well, and 'oo wants him to?' returned Huish, shrill with fury. 'You were damned years ago for the *Sea Rynger*, and said so yourself. Well then, be damned for something else, and 'old your tongue.'

The captain looked at him mistily. 'No,' he pleaded, 'no, old man! don't do it.'

''Ere now,' said Huish, 'I'll give you my ultimytum. Go or st'y w'ere you are; I don't mind; I'm goin' to see that man and chuck this vitriol in his eyes. If you st'y I'll go alone; the niggers will likely knock me on the 'ead, and a fat lot you'll be the better! But there's one thing sure: I'll 'ear no more of your moonin', mullygrubbin' rot, and tyke it stryte.'

The captain took it with a blink and a gulp. Memory, with phantom voices, repeated in his ears something similar, something he had once said to Herrick—years ago it seemed.

'Now, gimme over your pistol,' said Huish. 'I 'ave to see all clear. Six shots, and mind you don't wyste them.'

The captain, like a man in a nightmare, laid down his revolver on the table, and Huish wiped the cartridges and oiled the works.

It was close on noon, there was no breath of wind, and the heat was scarce bearable, when the two men came on deck, had the boat manned, and passed down, one after another, into the stern-sheets. A white shirt at the end of an oar served as flag of truce; and the men, by direction, and to give it the better chance to be observed, pulled with extreme slowness. The isle shook before them like a place incandescent; on the face of the lagoon blinding copper suns, no bigger than sixpences, danced and stabbed them in the eyeballs; there went up from sand and sea, and even from the boat, a glare of scathing brightness; and as they could only peer abroad from between closed lashes, the excess of light seemed to be changed into a sinister darkness, comparable to that of a thundercloud before it bursts.

The captain had come upon this errand for any one of a dozen reasons, the last of which was desire for its success. Superstition rules all men; semi-ignorant and gross natures, like that of Davis, it rules utterly. For murder he had been prepared; but this horror of the medicine in the bottle went beyond him, and he seemed to himself to be parting the last strands that united him to God. The boat carried him on to reprobation, to damnation; and he suffered himself to be carried passively consenting, silently bidding farewell to his better self and his hopes.

Huish sat by his side in towering spirits that were not wholly genuine. Perhaps as brave a man as ever lived, brave as a weasel, he must still reassure himself with the tones of his own voice; he must play his part to exaggeration, he must out-Herod Herod,* insult all that was respectable, and brave all that was formidable, in a kind of desperate wager with himself.

'Golly, but it's 'ot!' said he. 'Cruel 'ot, I call it. Nice d'y to get your gruel in! I s'y, you know, it must feel awf'ly peculiar to get bowled over on a d'y like this. I'd rather 'ave it on a cowld and frosty morning, wouldn't you? (Singing) "*'Ere we go round the mulberry bush on a cowld and frosty mornin'.*" (Spoken)

Give you my word, I 'aven't thought o' that in ten year; used to sing it at a hinfant school in 'Ackney, 'Ackney Wick it was. (Singing) "*This is the way the tyler does, the tyler does.*" (Spoken) Bloomin' 'umbug. 'Ow are you off now, for the notion of a future styte? Do you cotton to the tea-fight views, or the old red 'ot boguey business?'

'Oh, dry up!' said the captain.

'No, but I want to know,' said Huish. 'It's within the sp'ere of practical politics for you and me, my boy; we may both be bowled over, one up, t'other down, within the next ten minutes. It would be rather a lark, now, if you only skipped across, came up smilin' t'other side, and a hangel met you with a B.-and-S. under his wing. 'Ullo, you'd s'y: come, I tyke this kind.'

The captain groaned. While Huish was thus airing and exercising his bravado, the man at his side was actually engaged in prayer. Prayer, what for? God knows. But out of his inconsistent, illogical, and agitated spirit, a stream of supplication was poured forth, inarticulate as himself, earnest as death and judgment.

'Thou Gawd seest me!' continued Huish. 'I remember I had that written in my Bible. I remember the Bible too, all about Abinadab* and parties. Well, Gawd!' apostrophizing the meridian, 'you're goin' to see a rum start presently, I promise you that!'

The captain bounded.

'I'll have no blasphemy!' he cried, 'no blasphemy in my boat.'

'All right, cap,' said Huish. 'Anythink to oblige. Any other topic you would like to sudgest, the ryne-gyge, the lightnin' rod, Shykespeare, or the musical glasses?* 'Ere's conversation on tap. Put a penny in the slot, and . . . 'ullo! 'ere they are!' he cried. 'Now or never! is 'e goin' to shoot?'

And the little man straightened himself into an alert and dashing attitude, and looked steadily at the enemy.

But the captain rose half up in the boat with eyes protruding.

'What's that?' he cried.

'Wot's wot?' said Huish.

'Those—blamed things,' said the captain.

And indeed it was something strange. Herrick and Attwater, both armed with Winchesters, had appeared out of the grove behind the figure-head; and to either hand of them, the sun glistened upon two metallic objects, locomotory like men, and occupying in the economy of these creatures the places of heads—only the heads were faceless. To Davis between wind and water, his mythology appeared to have come alive, and Tophet* to be vomiting demons. But Huish was not mystified a moment.

'Diver's 'elmets, you ninny. Can't you see?' he said.

'So they are,' said Davis, with a gasp. 'And why? Oh, I see, it's for armour.'

'Wot did I tell you?' said Huish. 'Dyvid and Goliar all the w'y and back.'

The two natives (for they it was that were equipped in this unusual panoply of war) spread out to right and left, and at last lay down in the shade, on the extreme flank of the position. Even now that the mystery was explained, Davis was hatefully preoccupied, stared at the flame on their crests, and forgot, and then remembered with a smile, the explanation.

Attwater withdrew again into the grove, and Herrick, with his gun under his arm, came down the pier alone.

About half-way down he halted and hailed the boat.

'What do you want?' he cried.

'I'll tell that to Mr Attwater,' replied Huish, stepping briskly on the ladder. 'I don't tell it to you, because you played the trucklin' sneak. Here's a letter for him: tyke it, and give it, and be 'anged to you!'

'Davis, is this all right?' said Herrick.

Davis raised his chin, glanced swiftly at Herrick and away again, and held his peace. The glance was charged with some deep emotion, but whether of hatred or of fear, it was beyond Herrick to divine.

'Well,' he said, 'I'll give the letter.' He drew a score with his foot on the boards of the gangway. 'Till I bring the answer, don't move a step past this.'

And he returned to where Attwater leaned against a tree, and gave him the letter. Attwater glanced it through.

'What does that mean,' he asked, passing it to Herrick. 'Treachery?'

'Oh, I suppose so!' said Herrick.

'Well, tell him to come on,' said Attwater. 'One isn't a fatalist for nothing. Tell him to come on and to look out.'

Herrick returned to the figure-head. Half-way down the pier the clerk was waiting, with Davis by his side.

'You are to come along, Huish,' said Herrick. 'He bids you look out, no tricks.'

Huish walked briskly up the pier, and paused face to face with the young man.

'W'ere is 'e?' said he, and to Herrick's surprise, the low-bred, insignificant face before him flushed suddenly crimson and went white again.

'Right forward,' said Herrick, pointing. 'Now your hands above your head.'

The clerk turned away from him and towards the figure-head, as though he were about to address to it his devotions; he was seen to heave a deep breath; and raised his arms. In common with many men of his unhappy physical endowments, Huish's hands were disproportionately long and broad, and the palms in particular enormous; a four-ounce jar was nothing in that capacious fist. The next moment he was plodding steadily forward on his mission.

Herrick at first followed. Then a noise in his rear startled him, and he turned about to find Davis already advanced as far as the figure-head. He came, crouching and open-mouthed, as the mesmerized may follow the mesmerizer; all human considerations, and even the care of his own life, swallowed up in one abominable and burning curiosity.

'Halt!' cried Herrick, covering him with his rifle. 'Davis, what are you doing, man? *You* are not to come.'

Davis instinctively paused, and regarded him with a dreadful vacancy of eye.

'Put your back to that figure-head, do you hear me? and stand fast!' said Herrick.

The captain fetched a breath, stepped back against the figure-head, and instantly redirected his glances after Huish.

There was a hollow place of the sand in that part, and, as it were, a glade among the cocoa-palms in which the direct noonday sun blazed intolerably. At the far end, in the shadow, the tall figure of Attwater was to be seen leaning on a tree; towards him, with his hands over his head, and his steps smothered in the sand, the clerk painfully waded. The surrounding glare threw out and exaggerated the man's smallness; it seemed no less perilous an enterprise, this that he was gone upon, than for a whelp to besiege a citadel.

'There, Mr Whish. That will do,' cried Attwater. 'From that distance, and keeping your hands up, like a good boy, you can very well put me in possession of the skipper's views.'

The interval betwixt them was perhaps forty feet; and Huish measured it with his eye, and breathed a curse. He was already distressed with labouring in the loose sand, and his arms ached bitterly from their unnatural position. In the palm of his right hand, the jar was ready; and his heart thrilled, and his voice choked, as he began to speak.

'Mr Hattwater,' said he, 'I don't know if ever you 'ad a mother. . . .'

'I can set your mind at rest: I had,' returned Attwater; 'and henceforth, if I might venture to suggest it, her name need not recur in our communications. I should perhaps tell you that I am not amenable to the pathetic.'

'I am sorry, sir, if I 'ave seemed to tresparse on your private feelin's,' said the clerk, cringing and stealing a step. 'At least, sir, you will never pe'suade me that you are not a perfec' gentleman; I know a gentleman when I see him; and as such, I 'ave no 'esitation in throwin' myself on your merciful consideration. It *is* 'ard lines, no doubt; it's 'ard lines to have to hown yourself beat; it's 'ard lines to 'ave to come and beg to you for charity.'

'When, if things had only gone right, the whole place was as good as your own?' suggested Attwater. 'I can understand the feeling.'

'You are judging me, Mr Attwater,' said the clerk, 'and God knows how unjustly! *Thou Gawd seest me*, was the tex' I 'ad in my Bible, w'ich my father wrote it in with 'is own 'and upon the fly leaft.'

'I am sorry I have to beg your pardon once more,' said

Attwater; 'but, do you know, you seem to me to be a trifle nearer, which is entirely outside of our bargain. And I would venture to suggest that you take one—two—three—steps back; and stay there.'

The devil, at this staggering disappointment, looked out of Huish's face, and Attwater was swift to suspect. He frowned, he stared on the little man, and considered. Why should he be creeping nearer? The next moment, his gun was at his shoulder.

'Kindly oblige me by opening your hands. Open your hands wide—let me see the fingers spread, you dog—throw down that thing you're holding!' he roared, his rage and certitude increasing together.

And then, at almost the same moment, the indomitable Huish decided to throw, and Attwater pulled the trigger. There was scarce the difference of a second between the two resolves, but it was in favour of the man with the rifle; and the jar had not yet left the clerk's hand, before the ball shattered both. For the twinkling of an eye the wretch was in hell's agonies, bathed in liquid flames, a screaming bedlamite; and then a second and more merciful bullet stretched him dead.

The whole thing was come and gone in a breath. Before Herrick could turn about, before Davis could complete his cry of horror, the clerk lay in the sand, sprawling and convulsed.

Attwater ran to the body; he stooped and viewed it; he put his finger in the vitriol, and his face whitened and hardened with anger.

Davis had not yet moved; he stood astonished, with his back to the figure-head, his hands clutching it behind him, his body inclined forward from the waist.

Attwater turned deliberately and covered him with his rifle.

'Davis,' he cried, in a voice like a trumpet, 'I give you sixty seconds to make your peace with God!'

Davis looked, and his mind awoke. He did not dream of self-defence, he did not reach for his pistol. He drew himself up instead to face death, with a quivering nostril.

'I guess I'll not trouble the Old Man,' he said; 'considering the job I was on, I guess it's better business to just shut my face.'

Attwater fired; there came a spasmodic movement of the victim, and immediately above the middle of his forehead, a black hole marred the whiteness of the figure-head. A dreadful pause; then again the report, and the solid sound and jar of the bullet in the wood; and this time the captain had felt the wind of it along his cheek. A third shot, and he was bleeding from one ear; and along the levelled rifle Attwater smiled like a red Indian.

The cruel game of which he was the puppet was now clear to Davis; three times he had drunk of death, and he must look to drink of it seven times more before he was despatched. He held up his hand.

'Steady!' he cried; 'I'll take your sixty seconds.'

'Good!' said Attwater.

The captain shut his eyes tight like a child: he held his hands up at last with a tragic and ridiculous gesture.

'My God, for Christ's sake, look after my two kids,' he said; and then, after a pause and a falter, 'for Christ's sake, Amen.'

And he opened his eyes and looked down the rifle with a quivering mouth.

'But don't keep fooling me long!' he pleaded.

'That's all your prayer?' asked Attwater, with a singular ring in his voice.

'Guess so,' said Davis.

'So?' said Attwater, resting the butt of his rifle on the ground, 'is that done? Is your peace made with Heaven? Because it is with me. Go, and sin no more,* sinful father. And remember that whatever you do to others, God shall visit it again a thousandfold upon your innocents.'

The wretched Davis came staggering forward from his place against the figure-head, fell upon his knees, and waved his hands, and fainted.

When he came to himself again, his head was on Attwater's arm, and close by stood one of the men in diver's helmets, holding a bucket of water, from which his late executioner now laved his face. The memory of that dreadful passage returned upon him in a clap; again he saw Huish lying dead, again he seemed to himself to totter on the brink of an unplumbed eternity. With trembling hands he seized hold of the man whom he had come to slay; and his voice broke from him like that of a child among the nightmares of fever: 'O! isn't there no mercy? O! what must I do to be saved?'

'Ah!' thought Attwater, 'here is the true penitent.'

CHAPTER XII

A TAIL-PIECE

On a very bright, hot, lusty, strongly blowing noon, a fortnight after the events recorded, and a month since the curtain rose upon this episode, a man might have been spied, praying on the sand by the lagoon beach. A point of palm-trees isolated him from the settlement; and from the place where he knelt, the only work of man's hand that interrupted the expanse, was the schooner *Farallone,* her berth quite changed, and rocking at anchor some two miles to windward in the midst of the lagoon. The noise of the Trade ran very boisterous in all parts of the island; the nearer palm-trees crashed and whistled in the gusts, those farther off contributed a humming bass like the roar of cities; and yet, to any man less absorbed, there must have risen at times over this turmoil of the winds, the sharper note of the human voice from the settlement. There all was activity. Attwater, stripped to his trousers and lending a strong hand of help, was directing and encouraging five Kanakas; from his lively voice, and their more lively efforts, it was to be gathered that some sudden and joyful emergency had set them in this bustle; and the Union Jack floated once more on its staff. But the suppliant on the beach, unconscious of their voices, prayed on with instancy and fervour, and the sound of his voice rose and fell again, and his countenance brightened and was deformed with changing moods of piety and terror.

Before his closed eyes, the skiff had been for some time tacking towards the distant and deserted *Farallone*; and presently the figure of Herrick might have been observed to board her, to pass for a while into the house, thence forward to the forecastle, and at last to plunge into the main hatch. In all these quarters, his visit was followed by a coil of smoke; and he had scarce entered his boat again and shoved off, before flames broke forth upon the schooner. They burned gaily; kerosene had not been spared, and the bellows of the Trade incited the conflagration. About half way on the return voyage, when Herrick looked back, he beheld the *Farallone* wrapped to the topmasts in leaping arms of fire, and the voluminous smoke pursuing him along the face of the lagoon. In one hour's time, he computed, the waters would have closed over the stolen ship.

It so chanced that, as his boat flew before the wind with much vivacity, and his eyes were continually busy in the wake, measuring the progress of the flames, he found himself embayed to the northward of the point of palms, and here became aware at the same time, of the figure of Davis immersed in his devotion. An exclamation, part of annoyance, part of amusement, broke from him: and he touched the helm and ran the prow upon the beach not twenty feet from the unconscious devotee. Taking the painter in his hand, he landed, and drew near, and stood over him. And still the voluble and incoherent stream of prayer continued unabated. It was not possible for him to overhear the suppliant's petitions, which he listened to some while in a very mingled mood of humour and pity: and it was only when his own name began to occur and to be conjoined with epithets, that he at last laid his hand on the captain's shoulder.

'Sorry to interrupt the exercise,' said he; 'but I want you to look at the *Farallone.*'

The captain scrambled to his feet, and stood gasping and staring. 'Mr Herrick, don't startle a man like that!' he said. 'I don't seem someways rightly myself since . . .' he broke off. 'What did you say anyway? O, the *Farallone,*' and he looked languidly out.

'Yes,' said Herrick. 'There she burns! and you may guess from that what the news is.'

'The *Trinity Hall,* I guess,' said the captain.

'The same,' said Herrick; 'sighted half-an-hour ago, and coming up hand over fist.'

'Well, it don't amount to a hill of beans,' said the captain with a sigh.

'O, come, that's rank ingratitude!' cried Herrick.

'Well,' replied the captain, meditatively, 'you mayn't just see the way that I view it in, but I'd 'most rather stay here upon this island. I found peace here, peace in believing. Yes, I guess this island is about good enough for John Davis.'

'I never heard such nonsense!' cried Herrick. 'What! with all turning out in your favour the way it does, the *Farallone* wiped out, the crew disposed of, a sure thing for your wife and family, and you, yourself, Attwater's spoiled darling and pet penitent!'

'Now, Mr Herrick, don't say that,' said the captain gently; 'when you know he don't make no difference between us. But, O! why not be one of us? why not come to Jesus right away, and let's meet in yon beautiful land? That's just the one thing wanted; just say, Lord, I believe, help thou mine unbelief!* And He'll fold you in His arms. You see, I know! I been a sinner myself!'

THE CART-HORSES AND THE SADDLE-HORSE

TWO cart-horses, a gelding and a mare, were brought to Samoa, and put in the same field with a saddle-horse to run free on the island.* They were rather afraid to go near him, for they saw he was a saddle-horse, and supposed he would not speak to them. Now the saddle-horse had never seen creatures so big. 'These must be great chiefs,' thought he, and he approached them civilly. 'Lady and gentleman,' said he, 'I understand you are from the colonies.* I offer you my affectionate compliments, and make you heartily welcome to the islands.'

The colonials looked at him askance, and consulted with each other.

'Who can he be?' said the gelding.

'He seems suspiciously civil,' said the mare.

'I do not think he can be much account,' said the gelding.

'Depend upon it he is only a Kanaka,'* said the mare.

Then they turned to him.

'Go to the devil!' said the gelding.

'I wonder at your impudence, speaking to persons of our quality!' cried the mare.

The saddle-horse went away by himself. 'I was right,' said he, 'they are great chiefs.'

SOMETHING IN IT

THE natives told him many tales. In particular, they warned him of the house of yellow reeds tied with black sinnet,* how any one who touched it became instantly the prey of Akaänga, and was handed on to him by Miru the ruddy,* and hocussed with the kava* of the dead, and baked in the ovens and eaten by the eaters of the dead.

'There is nothing in it,' said the missionary.

There was a bay upon that island, a very fair bay to look upon; but, by the native saying, it was death to bathe there. 'There is nothing in that,' said the missionary; and he came to the bay, and went swimming. Presently an eddy took him and bore him towards the reef. 'Oho!' thought the missionary, 'it seems there is something in it after all.' And he swam the harder, but the eddy carried him away. 'I do not care about this eddy,' said the missionary; and even as he said it, he was aware of a house raised on piles above the sea; it was built of yellow reeds, one reed joined with another, and the whole bound with black sinnet; a ladder led to the door, and all about the house hung calabashes.* He had never seen such a house, nor yet such calabashes; and the eddy set for the ladder. 'This is singular,' said the missionary, 'but there can be nothing in it.' And he laid hold of the ladder and went up. It was a fine house; but there was no man there; and when the missionary looked back he saw no island, only the heaving of the sea. 'It is strange about the island,' said the missionary, 'but who's afraid? my stories are the true ones.' And he laid hold of a calabash, for he was one that loved curiosities. Now he had no sooner laid hand upon the calabash than that which he handled, and that which he saw and stood on, burst like a bubble and was gone; and night closed upon him, and the waters, and the meshes of the net; and he wallowed there like a fish.

'A body would think there was something in this,' said the

missionary. 'But if these tales are true, I wonder what about my tales!'

Now the flaming of Akaänga's torch drew near in the night; and the misshapen hands groped in the meshes of the net; and they took the missionary between the finger and the thumb, and bore him dripping in the night and silence to the place of the ovens of Miru. And there was Miru, ruddy in the glow of the ovens; and there sat her four daughters, and made the kava of the dead; and there sat the comers out of the islands of the living, dripping and lamenting.

This was a dread place to reach for any of the sons of men. But of all who ever came there, the missionary was the most concerned; and, to make things worse, the person next him was a convert of his own.

'Aha,' said the convert, 'so you are here like your neighbours? And how about all your stories?'

'It seems', said the missionary, with bursting tears, 'that there was nothing in them.'

By this the kava of the dead was ready, and the daughters of Miru began to intone in the old manner of singing. 'Gone are the green islands and the bright sea, the sun and the moon and the forty million stars, and life and love and hope. Henceforth is no more, only to sit in the night and silence, and see your friends devoured; for life is a deceit, and the bandage is taken from your eyes.'

Now when the singing was done, one of the daughters came with the bowl. Desire of that kava rose in the missionary's bosom; he lusted for it like a swimmer for the land, or a bridegroom for his bride; and he reached out his hand, and took the bowl, and would have drunk. And then he remembered, and put it back.

'Drink!' sang the daughter of Miru. 'There is no kava like the kava of the dead, and to drink of it once is the reward of living.'

'I thank you. It smells excellent,' said the missionary. 'But I am a blue-ribbon man* myself; and though I am aware there is a difference of opinion even in our own confession, I have always held kava to be excluded.'*

'What!' cried the convert. 'Are you going to respect a

taboo* at a time like this? And you were always so opposed to taboos when you were alive!'

'To other people's,' said the missionary. 'Never to my own.'

'But yours have all proved wrong,' said the convert.

'It looks like it,' said the missionary, 'and I can't help that. No reason why I should break my word.'

'I never heard the like of this!' cried the daughter of Miru. 'Pray, what do you expect to gain?'

'That is not the point,' said the missionary. 'I took this pledge for others, I am not going to break it for myself.'

The daughter of Miru was puzzled; she came and told her mother, and Miru was vexed; and they went and told Akaänga.

'I don't know what to do about this,' said Akaänga; and he came and reasoned with the missionary.

'But there *is* such a thing as right and wrong,' said the missionary; 'and your ovens cannot alter that.'

'Give the kava to the rest,' said Akaänga to the daughters of Miru. 'I must get rid of this sea-lawyer* instantly, or worse will come of it.'

The next moment the missionary came up in the midst of the sea, and there before him were the palm trees of the island. He swam to the shore gladly, and landed. Much matter of thought was in that missionary's mind.

'I seem to have been misinformed upon some points,' said he. 'Perhaps there is not much in it, as I supposed; but there is something in it after all. Let me be glad of that.'

And he rang the bell for service.

MORAL

The sticks break, the stones crumble,
The eternal altars tilt and tumble,
Sanctions and tales dislimn like mist
About the amazed evangelist.
He stands unshook from age to youth
Upon one pin-point of the truth.

EXPLANATORY NOTES

REFERENCES to works by Stevenson (other than those included in the present volume) are to the *Tusitala Edition* (1923–4) and are indicated by the abbreviation *Tusitala*; the abbreviation *Letters* i–v refers to volumes xxxi–xxxv of this edition. References to other frequently used sources are given using short title and page number only; full publication details of these works may be found in the 'Select Bibliography'.

The Beach of Falesá

3 *a low island near the line*: Pacific islands are either low (coral) or high (volcanic); 'the line' is a sailors' term for the equator.

binnacle lamp: the binnacle is the housing for the ship's compass; the binnacle lamp is an important light as it is necessary for reading the compass during the night.

4 *Pain-Killer and Kennedy's Discovery*: patent medicines. In *In the South Seas* Stevenson notes that '*pain-killer* in the islands is the generic name of medicine' (*Tusitala,* xx. 312). Fanny Stevenson mentions that the patent medicine 'Kennedy's White Discovery' was regularly administered to the crew of the *Equator*, the schooner on which the Stevensons made their second Pacific cruise ('Prefatory Note' to *The Wrecker, Tusitala,* vol. xii, p. xix).

copra: the dried meat of the coconut; prized primarily as a source of coconut oil, it was the main commercial interest of the South Seas in the later nineteenth century.

the beach: the place where whites lived and traded on Pacific islands; also taken metonymically to mean the whites themselves. See Marie Fraser, *In Stevenson's Samoa,* 124: ' "the beach"—*i.e.* the settlement of houses where the white men and half-castes have their stores, and where the ships touch'; and Stevenson, *Letters,* iii. 302: 'As for the white population of [Apia] (technically, "The Beach"), I don't suppose it is possible for any person not thoroughly conversant with the South Seas to form the smallest conception of such a society, with its grog-shops, its apparently unemployed hangers-on, its merchants of all degrees of respectability and the reverse.'

4 *Old Kafoozleum*: presumably the captain means Old Methuselah, the oldest man mentioned in the Bible, who is said to have died at the age of 969 years (Genesis 5: 27).

stern sheets: area in the stern of an open boat.

5 *getting tabooed*: becoming a proscribed person, with whom the islanders were forbidden to have dealings. As Stevenson wrote in *In the South Seas*, the taboo (properly 'tapu') was usually seen by Europeans as 'a meaningless or wanton prohibition' but was in fact an important institution regulating law, morals, and propriety, and implying 'that an act is criminal, immoral, against sound public policy, unbecoming or (as we say) "not in good form"' (*Tusitala*, xx. 43).

the Speak House: the building in which official audiences were granted and councils held in South Sea communities.

smart: MS 'smut'.

Kanaka: Polynesian word for man or mankind, taken up by Europeans to designate a native of the islands (male or female) and often used scornfully or pejoratively.

All the better part of the day: MS reads 'All the early part of the day', which makes more sense as we are told that Wiltshire and Case go on shore at 'high noon' (p. 6).

6 *in the islands*: at this point in the MS appears the following material, which was omitted from the serial and book versions of the story: 'I remember one bit of advice he gave me that morning, and one yarn he told. The bit of advice was this. "Whenever you get hold of any money," says he—"any christian money, I mean—the first thing to do is to fire it up to Sydney to the bank. It's only a temptation to a copra merchant; some day, he'll be in a row with the other traders, and he'll get his shirt out and buy copra with it. And the name of the man that buys copra with gold is Damfool," says he. That was the advice; and this was the yarn, which might have opened my eyes to the danger of that man for neighbour, if I had been anyway suspicious. It seems Case was trading somewhere in the Ellices. There was a man Miller a Dutchman there, who had a strong hold with the natives and handled the bulk of what there was. Well one fine day a schooner got wrecked in the lagoon, and Miller bought her (the way these things are usually managed) for an old song, which was the ruin of him. For having a lot of trade on hand that had cost him practically nothing, what does he do but begin cutting rates? Case went round to the other traders. "Wants to

lower prices?" says Case. "All right, then. He has five times the turn-over of any one of us; if buying at a loss is the game, he stands to lose five times more. Let's give him the bed rock; let's bilge the —!" And so they did, and five months after, Miller had to sell out his boat and station, and begin again somewhere in the Carolines.

All this talk suited me, and my new companion suited me, and I thought Falesá seemed . . .' (here the narrative resumes in the book version).

6 *a labour ship from up west*: a ship recruiting native labour from the western Pacific islands of Melanesia for work on plantations in Polynesia or Queensland. As most of the natives were taken by fraud or simply kidnapped, the term 'labour trade' was a euphemism for an effective slave trade.

Fiddler's Green: traditional sailor's paradise of unlimited music, dancing, women, drink, and tobacco.

Bashaw: a corruption of the Turkish word *pasha*, meaning a provincial governor or high official; thus, an arrogant or tyrannical man. The popular association of Turks with polygamy and harems is also suggested by Wiltshire's situation as a man with his pick of 'wives'.

7 *wetted through*: MS adds 'and a cutty sark at that'. A 'cutty sark' is a Scots expression for a short shirt.

shy: MS 'sly'. The sly side of Uma's character emerges on p. 28 when she tests Wiltshire's love by tempting him with copra, 'the same as you might offer candies to a child'.

cottoned to the cut of your jib: to 'cotton to' someone is, in American slang of the nineteenth century, to take a fancy to him, to stick to him as cotton would. The 'cut of your jib' is sea slang for an individual's appearance, deriving from the days when ships of different nationalities could be identified by the different cut of their jib sails.

9 *the trade*: i.e. the trade wind, so-called because its steadiness and constancy made it a reliable factor in trade in the days of sail. The trade winds blow in the lower latitudes from the north-east in the northern hemisphere and from the south-east in the southern hemisphere, as cold air flows from the poles to the equator, its path deflected to the west by the earth's rotation.

why I wanted to marry Uma: MS 'why in Hell I wanted to marry Uma'.

10 *Hard-shell Baptis'*: member of a strict group of Baptists in the United States, known for their extreme and inflexible Calvinistic views.

tapa: unwoven cloth made from the beaten bark of the paper mulberry or breadfruit tree; it was often decorated with intricate painted designs.

11 *it was the practice in these parts*: the original for Uma's marriage certificate is quoted in *In the South Seas*, where Stevenson discusses Gilbert Island women who had married white traders: 'It is true that the certificate of one, when she proudly showed it, proved to run thus, that she was "married for one night", and her gracious partner was at liberty to "send her to hell" the next morning; but she was none the wiser or the worse for the dastardly trick' (*Tusitala*, xx. 267). Apparently Wiltshire was not alone in choosing to honour the marriage rather than the certificate.

13 *luff*: the forward edge of a fore-and-aft sail, which trembles when the boat faces into the wind.

looked at me puzzled like: articulation of this puzzlement follows in the MS, but was omitted from the serial and book versions: ' "Why you do that?" she asked.'

Why you bring him?: in Beach-la-Mar (see note to p. 30), the masculine pronoun is used indiscriminately without reference to the gender of the noun, so that 'gin' and later 'wifie' are both referred to as 'he'.

14 *shipshape and Bristol fashion*: in good order and ready for business; the term derives from the reputation for efficiency enjoyed by the port of Bristol in its great commercial days.

15 *Devil a wink*: not a wink. Wiltshire is using a Scots idiom, in which 'devil a' means 'not a' or 'not any'.

16 *Dissenters*: members of Protestant sects which broke away from the established Church of England, attenders of 'chapel' rather than 'church'. They adopted forms of worship which tended to emphasize personal response rather than organized ritual; to those who took their religion more lightly or not at all, like Wiltshire, such displays of emotion were apt to be embarrassing.

fools of Kanakas: MS 'damfool kanakas'.

Ben: Ben Hird, supercargo on the *Janet Nichol*, on which Stevenson made his third Pacific cruise in 1890, and one of the dedicatees of *Island Nights' Entertainments.* As Graham Balfour (Stevenson's cousin and biographer) noted, 'In *The Beach of Falesa* [*sic*], also, Ben comes in once or twice without preface or explanation as part of the recognised machinery of island-existence'; see 'A South-Sea Trader', *Macmillan's Magazine*, 75 (1896), 66–7.

17 *regular Sydney style*: as Stevenson observed, Sydney was the 'metropolis' for the South Pacific (*Letters*, iii. 293). Wiltshire is aiming to make his store as good as a metropolitan one.

cant: a corner or angle.

French: MS 'Franch' (Stevenson's phonetic rendering of the priest's pronunciation).

18 *fussy-ocky*: Wiltshire's mispronunciation of the Samoan word 'fasioti', to kill.

19 *a cure*: an eccentric or odd person, probably an abbreviation of 'curious fellow'.

the horrors: delirium tremens.

a rare taking: MS 'a hell of a taking'.

22 *What we want is a man-of-war—a German, if we could—they know how to manage Kanakas*: Case probably has in mind the Samoan war of December 1888, when German men-of-war fired several times on native villages. In *A Footnote to History* Stevenson comments on 'the inefficacy of the war-ships' (*Tusitala*, xxi. 190) which either missed their targets or embroiled the Germans in disastrous skirmishes with the natives (particularly at Fangalii), and led to deteriorating relations with both the islanders and other foreign powers, especially the Americans. The Germans' decision to launch attacks from the men-of-war led to a loss of prestige by the Europeans. Earlier, 'No native would . . . have dreamed of defying these colossal ships, worked by mysterious powers, and laden with outlandish instruments of death' (*Tusitala*, xxi. 151). After the engagement with the Germans at Fangalii, 'Then, indeed, all Samoa drew a breath of wonder and delight. The invincible had fallen; the men of the vaunted war-ships had been met in the field . . . a superstition was no more' (*Tusitala*, xxi. 185). As a threat, the war-ships had a considerable mystique; in action that mystique was destroyed. Not only does Case's statement represent an attitude of belligerence and high-handedness towards the natives that Stevenson deplored, but it is also unintentionally ironic, as the episode of the men-of-

war showed that the Germans did not 'know how to manage Kanakas' at all, their actions leading to a decrease rather than an increase in their authority.

23 *sawder*: usually 'soft sawder'—flattery.

24 *put my monkey up*: made me angry.

27 *a hot temper*: MS 'a holy temper'.

28 *it may mean foreign, or extraordinary; or it might mean a mummy apple*: in George Pratt's *A Grammar and Dictionary of the Samoan Language*, 2nd edn., ed. S. J. Whitmee (London: Trübner, 1878), 'Ese' is translated as 'strange, different' and 'Esi' as the papaya or mummy apple. Pratt also gives the verb 'Esi', meaning 'to drive away', which seems the meaning most appropriate to Case, who drives all other white men away from Falesá.

such a hurry: MS 'such a blamed hurry'.

30 *Beach de Mar*: or Beach-la-Mar, a pidgin language of the Pacific region produced by contact between Europeans and islanders speaking mutually unintelligible languages. Often referred to as a 'trade jargon', it emerged from the need of nineteenth-century traders to communicate with islanders from whom they wished to obtain the sea-cucumber or beche-de-mer, from which the language takes its name. It was spread by the labour trade (see note to p. 6) as a means of communication, not only between Europeans and islanders, but between islanders speaking different languages. Strictly it should be identified with Melanesia rather than Polynesia (it formed the basis of Melanesian creole languages such as 'Bislama' in Vanuatu), but Stevenson seems to have regarded it as the *lingua franca* of the entire Pacific region, stating that 'it may be called, and will almost certainly become, the tongue of the Pacific' (*Tusitala*, xx. 10).

the Line Islands: a group of small, scattered islands, spanning the equator, to the north-east of Samoa; today part of the Republic of Kiribati.

in these parts: unlike Stevenson's other Pacific stories, 'The Beach of Falesá' does not use a real geographical location but is set on an imaginary island, which Stevenson planned to call Ulufanua, meaning a land of leaves (*Letters*, iv. 94), although he later dropped the name. Many of the place-names used in the story are similar to Samoan place-names and Stevenson drew extensively on his experience in Samoa in writing it, but the island is clearly not meant to be a part of Samoa, for Case's wife is identified as a 'Samoa woman' (p. 5) who goes 'home' (p. 70) at the end of the story.

30 *beachcomber*: contemptuous term for a white man with no visible means of support, existing on the fringes of white society and living by charity, odd jobs, or more disreputable means in Pacific ports. It could also denote a settler or ex-sailor who had 'gone native' and was being supported by a native woman or community.

Apia and Papeete and these flash towns: Apia and Papeete were the chief ports and seats of trade, white settlement, and colonial government in Samoa and Tahiti respectively.

Fale-alii: fictional place-name (although very similar to Falealili, a village and harbour on the island of Upolu in Samoa).

32 *Tonga-heart*: 'a term of reproach, equivalent to black-hearted' (Fanny Stevenson, *Our Samoan Adventure*, 133).

sweep: a disreputable, no-good person (from chimney-sweeps, who were made black and filthy by their work).

Misi: 'mister' in Beach-la-Mar—a term of respectful address.

33 *and set him up!*: in Scots idiom, an ironic or contemptuous expression directed at a person who gives himself airs; the Scots term 'set-up' means vain, conceited.

34 *queering me*: looking at me intently.

35 *Welsher*: a welsher is a swindler, one who fails to honour contracts and debts; Wiltshire's name 'on the beach' is an unflattering one for a trader.

Papa-Malulu: fictional place-name.

36 *that Blavatsky business in the papers*: Madame Blavatsky (1831–91), Ukrainian-born spiritualist, was one of the founders of the Theosophical Society, which was devoted to exploring aspects of nature and human faculties that could not be explained by empirical science. Her supposed powers as a psychic gained her a large following in the United States and England.

37 *taffy*: in America, a confection made of sugar, molasses, and butter, i.e. toffee; thence, a colloquial term for flattery, sweet words.

40 *the hateful scene*: the source for the story of Underhill's death was an anecdote told by Ben Hird (see note to p. 16), which Fanny Stevenson recorded: 'Speaking about the superstitions of Penrhyn, Mr Hird recalls the following grisly incident that occurred when he was stopping on the island. A man who was

paralysed on one side had a convulsion which caused spasmodic contractions on the other side. One of the sick man's family began at once to make a coffin. "But the man's not dead," said Mr Hird. "Oh yes," was the reply; "he's dead enough; it's the third time he has done this, so we are going to bury him." Mr Hird went to the native missionary, but his remonstrances had no effect; he kept on protesting until the last moment. "Why look," he said, "the man's limbs are quivering." "Oh that's only live flesh," was the reply, and some one fell to pommelling the poor wretch to quiet the "live flesh". The belief was that the man's spirit had departed long before and a devil who wished to use the body for his own convenience had been keeping the flesh alive. Mr Hird thinks that the man was insensible when buried and must soon have died' (*The Cruise of the 'Janet Nichol'*, 64).

41 *making clean the outside of the cup and platter*: Matthew 23: 25–6: 'Woe unto you, scribes and Pharisees, hypocrites! for ye make clean the outside of the cup and of the platter, but within they are full of extortion and excess. Thou blind Pharisee, cleanse first that which is within the cup and platter, that the outside of them may be clean also.'

preached from First Kings, nineteenth, on the fire, the earthquake, and the voice, distinguishing the true spiritual power: in 1 Kings 19, Elijah, an outcast among his people, goes into the wilderness and seeks guidance from God. 'And, behold, the Lord passed by, and a great and strong wind rent the mountains, and brake in pieces the rocks before the Lord; but the Lord was not in the wind: and after the wind an earthquake; but the Lord was not in the earthquake: And after the earthquake a fire; but the Lord was not in the fire: and after the fire a still small voice' (1 Kings 19: 11–12). Mr Tarleton's sermon attempts to persuade the villagers that 'true spiritual power' is found not in seemingly portentous signs, such as those manufactured by Case, but in the still, small voice of conscience.

44 *the big don and the funny dog*: a 'don' is a slang term for a pretentious person or 'swell', while 'dog' simply means 'fellow' in a playful or contemptuous sense. Black Jack is alternately giving himself airs and playing to his audience for laughs.

45 *obstropulous*: unruly, refractory (a corruption of 'obstreperous' in various Scottish, English, and American dialects).

cinnabar: mercury sulphide, a bright red or red-brown ore, metallic in lustre and crystalline in form, found in veins amongst volcanic rocks. With its steep mountains, black cliffs, and cinnabar streaks, the scenery described is the volcanic landscape of a 'high' island.

45 *the flying-fox (or vampire)*: Stevenson (or Wiltshire) is confusing two species of tropical bats. The flying fox, which feeds on fruit, is the largest of all bats, its wingspan extending in some instances up to five feet. The much smaller vampire bat feeds on the blood of mammals and birds.

48 *lianas*: woody vines, characteristic of tropical rainforests, which twine around other plants, often growing to great lengths and becoming tangled together to form dense curtains and knots.

50 *the thing was well known, and with handsome young men alone it was even common*: in his letters from Samoa, Stevenson recounts several stories, which correspond in detail to Uma's, of *aitu fafine* or women-devils supposed to haunt the woods; one 'appears as a lovely young lady, her bust particularly admired, to handsome young men; these die, her love being fatal' (*Letters*, iv. 41). The Samoans, he observes, 'believe the woods to be quite filled with spirits; some are like pigs, and some are like flying things; but others (and these are thought the most dangerous) come in the shape of beautiful young women and young men, beautifully dressed in the island manner, with fine kilts and fine necklaces and crowns of scarlet seeds and flowers. Woe betide he or she who gets to speak with one of these! They will be charmed out of their wits, and come home again quite silly, and go mad and die' (*Letters*, iv. 147).

51 *sensitive*: *mimosa pudica* or *la'aufefe*, an introduced plant prevalent in Samoa. Both its Latin and Samoan names mean 'modest' or 'fearful' and refer to the way the plant shrinks back on being touched, while its common native name, 'tuitui' or 'kuikui', means 'prickly' and refers to its thorns. Marie Fraser describes it as 'the noxious and ever-spreading sensitive plant, with its many prickles and pretty pink flowers' (*In Stevenson's Samoa*, 54–5). Stevenson became obsessed with this weed when clearing his property at Vailima, calling it 'our deadliest enemy', a 'singular, insidious thing, shrinking and biting like a weasel' (*Letters*, iv. 18).

it's a thing that's natural in the bush, and that's the end of it: the preceding paragraph represents the inspiration from which 'The Beach of Falesá' grew. Stevenson wrote in November 1890 that the new story 'just shot through me like a bullet in one of my moments of awe, alone in that tragic jungle' (*Letters*, iv. 20), and his description of an afternoon spent clearing a path in the woods closely resembles Wiltshire's account of his visit to the high bush: 'A strange business it was, and infinitely solitary; away above, the sun was in the high tree-tops; the lianas noosed and sought to hang me; the saplings struggled, and came up with that sob of death that one gets to know so well . . . Soon, toiling down in that pit of verdure, I heard blows on the far side, and then laughter. I confess a chill settled on my heart. Being so dead alone, in a place where by rights none should be beyond me, I was aware, upon interrogation, if those blows had drawn nearer, I should (of course quite unaffectedly) have executed a strategic movement to the rear; and only the other day I was lamenting my insensibility to superstition!' (*Letters*, iv. 16–17).

53 *a Tyrolean harp, whatever that may mean*: Wiltshire means an Aeolian harp, a musical instrument made of a wooden sound-box fitted with strings and placed to capture the wind which 'plays' it. It is named after Aeolus, the Greek god of the wind.

55 *luminous paint!*: the inspiration for Case's manufactured devil must have been the device adopted by Fanny Stevenson to prevent her pigs and fowls being stolen to feed the native chiefs visiting the district in December 1890. She wrote in her diary: 'I do not believe the missionaries will approve of my means of protection. I could think of nothing else so sure. I took the round top of a small meat cask and painted upon it a hideous head with great eyes and a wide, open mouth displaying a double row of pointed teeth. Instead of hair, flames radiate out from the head. These flames, the iris of the eyes, and the pointed teeth I have painted in luminous paint. It almost frightens me' (*Our Samoan Adventure*, 80).

bum: cry.

58 *the interpreter*: MS 'Uma for interpreter'.

59 *taking a header*: diving in, taking a plunge.

60 *a mechanics' debating society*: the establishment of Mechanics' Institutes was part of the early Victorian adult education movement which aimed to combine self-improvement with social discipline. Like many of the working-class men for whom they were intended, Wiltshire seems to have a poor opinion of the mechanics' societies; his simile identifies them with useless talk which prevents a man from getting on with the necessary work at hand.

60 *your Kanaka ignorance*: MS 'your blamed kanaka ignorance'.

the British and Foreign Bible Society, Blackfriars: a broadly evangelical, non-sectarian institution, founded in 1804 and devoted to making the Bible available as cheaply as possible to the largest number of readers in Britain and around the world.

62 *lucifer*: patent, and then generic, name for a match tipped with an inflammable substance and ignited by friction.

64 *clove hitch*: a knot used to lash objects together, or to secure bundles or bales; the more it is pulled upon, the more tightly it holds.

dead wood shine: cf. Stevenson, *Letters*, iv. 34–5, describing his rides home from Apia to Vailima at night: 'In the forest, the dead wood is phosphorescent; some nights the whole ground is strewn with it, so that it seems like a grating over a pale hell; doubtless this is one of the things that feed the night fears of the natives; and I am free to confess that in a night of trackless darkness where all else is void, these pallid *ignes suppositi* have a fantastic appearance, rather bogey even.'

66 *Winchester*: the famous repeating rifle, named after its manufacturer, Oliver Fisher Winchester.

67 *at the port-arms*: with the rifle held diagonally across and against the body—the position adopted in response to the military order 'Port arms!'.

a ship's hawser: any heavy line of rope or wire, generally over five inches in diameter, used for towing or other general ship's work. It would be 'taut' because of the tension to which it was subjected.

70 *full of one-handed men, like the parties in the 'Arabian Nights'*: a reference to the punishment for theft under Islamic law; in *The Arabian Nights* 'The Story Told by the Jewish Physician' features a young man whose right hand has been amputated for theft. Dynamite was routinely used in fishing in the Pacific islands and Fanny Stevenson writes in *Our Samoan Adventure* of 'Old Joe the boatman, who has lost one hand by dynamite in the usual South Sea fashion' (p. 224).

corroborree: Anglicized version of an Australian aboriginal word for a ceremonial or festive dance. It came to be used colloquially for any large social gathering or revelry.

71 *his trick being over*: 'trick' is a sailor's term for a spell of duty, as 'a trick at the wheel'.

71 *find the whites?*: MS 'find them whites?' (i.e. find whites for them).

The Bottle Imp

72 *the name and the root idea of a piece once rendered popular by the redoubtable O. Smith*: the source for Stevenson's story was 'The Bottle Imp', a melodrama by Richard Brinsley Peake (1792–1847), first performed at Covent Garden in 1828 featuring the actor Richard John 'Obi' Smith (1786–1855), commonly known as 'O. Smith'; Smith's performance in this piece sealed his reputation as a player of demons, monsters, and other villainous roles. Peake's play was itself based on a German folktale, and although Stevenson seems not to have encountered the prose source directly he acknowledged the story's generic origins when he spoke of 'The Bottle Imp' as 'the centre-piece of a volume of *Märchen*' he planned to write (*Letters*, v. 5).

designed and written for a Polynesian audience: it is unclear whether the story was written with translation in mind from the beginning, or whether Stevenson merely aimed to write a Polynesian-style tale which he later agreed to have translated. In any case, 'The Bottle Imp' was translated into the Samoan language by the Revd Arthur E. Claxton and appeared as 'O Le Fagu Aitu' from May to December 1891 in *O Le Sulu Samoa*, a Samoan-language newspaper published under the auspices of the London Missionary Society. In a letter of March 1891 Stevenson mentions 'going over the Samoan translation of my *Bottle Imp* with Claxton the missionary' (*Letters*, iv. 62). Fanny Stevenson wrote: 'I do not understand what civilising effect the story of *The Bottle Imp* was supposed to have on the natives, but I cannot think it quite fulfilled the expectations of the missionary who translated it'; nevertheless, she observed that 'Samoans are in the habit of speaking in parables; they found many different morals in *The Bottle Imp*, some very ingeniously extracted' ('Prefatory Note' to *Island Nights' Entertainments, Tusitala*, vol. xiii, pp. xii–xiii).

73 *the Island of Hawaii*: largest and most southerly of the eight islands comprising the Hawaiian Kingdom.

Honaunau, where the bones of Keawe the Great lie hidden in a cave: bay on the south-west coast of Hawaii, site of the Hale-o-Keawe, the royal mausoleum named after the semi-legendary Hawaiian ruling chief. Around 1829, as part of the push to modernize and Christianize the country, the sacred Hale-o-

Keawe was destroyed; the bones of Keawe and other kings were said to have been removed to a secret cave amongst the many which honeycombed the cliffs of this coastline. See *Tusitala*, xx. 195–6 for Stevenson's account of his visit to the Hale-o-Keawe in 1889.

73 *Hamakua coast*: north-east coast of Hawaii, known for its huge surf.

one hill which is covered with palaces: Nob Hill, where the rich of San Francisco built extravagant mansions in the 1870s.

75 *Captain Cook . . . slain upon Hawaii*: the death of Captain James Cook at Kealakekua Bay in 1779 marks a potent moment in the European imagination of the Pacific and the Pacific imagination of Europeans. The story that the Hawaiians had accepted Cook as the god Lono, and killed him when they realized he was merely human, may be a European myth; nevertheless, in this account Cook's death effectively symbolizes the shattering of the mystique of the white man and of his dream of undisputed authority in the Pacific. Stevenson links Cook to Napoleon through the motif of hubris and, perhaps with an eye to European expansionist ambitions as well as personal greed, warns that 'unless a man remain content with what he has, ill will befall him'.

Prester John: priest-king of medieval legend supposed to rule over a vast Christian kingdom in the East, a realm of riches and wonders.

76 *Chili piece*: in 1892, Stevenson's mother wrote that 5 Chili dollars were worth 15 shillings in Samoa (M. I. Stevenson, *Letters from Samoa*, 148); in the late nineteenth century 5 American dollars were roughly equal to a pound (20 shillings). Hence Keawe's comment on p. 77 that he bought the bottle for 'a little less' than 50 dollars, because one of his dollars was 'from Chili'.

78 *the Kona Coast*: the leeward (south-west) coast of the Island of Hawaii.

Kaü: district in the south of Hawaii.

Hookena: village on the Kona Coast, where Stevenson stayed in April–May 1889.

79 *ava*: also called 'kava'; the pepper plant *piper methysticum*, the root of which was used to prepare a drink of great social and ceremonial significance in Polynesia.

80 *the 'Hall'*: the *W. G. Hall*, an inter-island steamer which Stevenson took from Honolulu to Hawaii in 1889.

80 *cliffs, where the kings of old lay buried*: see note to p. 73.

82 *Nahinu*: a former judge, Stevenson's host at Hookena during his visit in 1889. Such references to real people and places Stevenson knew from his travels in Hawaii and Tahiti are what make the story, as Fanny Stevenson said, 'so circumstantial in its details', creating reality effects which seem to belie its fairy-tale status ('Prefatory Note' to *Island Nights' Entertainments, Tusitala,* vol. xiii, p. xii).

'Ka-Hale Nui'—the Great House: Keawe's house was no doubt inspired by one Stevenson saw in the Kona district: 'it stood on the immediate verge of a deep precipice: two stories high, with double balconies, painted white, and showing by my count fifteen windows . . . when we were home again at Hookena, and Nahinu was describing our itinerary to his wife, he mentioned we had baited at Ka-hale-nui—"the great house"' (*Tusitala,* xx. 191). Vailima, the Stevensons' home in Samoa, was also considered to be a 'great house' and in some minds Stevenson's (to the islanders) legendary wealth became mixed up with the legend of 'The Bottle Imp'; as his mother wrote, 'the house described in it somewhat resembles ours, and a good many of the natives suspect that Mr Stevenson has the "bottle" himself' (*Letters from Samoa,* 111); see also Fanny Stevenson's 'Prefatory Note' to *Island Nights' Entertainments, Tusitala,* vol. xiii, p. xii.

83 *Kailua*: part of the Kona district of Hawaii.

the night in which the dead of old days go abroad in the sides of Kona: 'Marchers of the night' or 'Spirit ranks', processions of gods and spirits of the dead, were believed by the Hawaiians to revisit sacred places on certain sacred nights; see Martha Beckwith, *Hawaiian Mythology* (1940; Honolulu: University of Hawaii Press, 1970), 164.

holoku: usually spelt 'holaku'; a long, loose gown, hanging from a yoke, usually worn over a flounced chemise. Fanny Stevenson wrote: 'The *holaku* is only the old-fashioned sacque, which happened, fortunately, to be the mode in England when the missionaries first came to the South Seas. It was loose, cool and graceful, and so well suited the natives that it became the regulation garment of the South Pacific' (*Our Samoan Adventure,* 170).

Kokua: the name means 'helper' in Hawaiian.

Oahu: island on which the Hawaiian capital, Honolulu, is situated.

85 *depart from all his friends to the north coast of Molokai between the mighty cliff and the sea-breakers*: in 1865 the Hawaiian government passed 'An Act to Prevent the Spread of Leprosy', which authorized the isolation and confinement of lepers in the interests of public health. For this purpose the government purchased land on the island of Molokai where a leper settlement was established. To many Hawaiians, banishment was more fearful than the disease itself, and they resented and often resisted the controversial law enforcing segregation. In 'The Lepers of Kona' Stevenson wrote in support of the segregation laws (*Tusitala*, xx. 205–10). He visited the Molokai leper settlement in May 1889.

Kalaupapa: site of the leper settlement at Molokai.

87 *Kanakas*: see note to p. 5.

Hilo: district on north-eastern (windward) side of the island of Hawaii.

Maui: the second largest of the Hawaiian islands.

Diamond Head: extinct volcano near Honolulu, named for the calcite crystals on its slopes which were thought to resemble diamonds.

Pola-Pola or Kahiki: Hawaiian forms of Bora-Bora (in the Society Islands) and Tahiti.

Waikiki: beach suburb of Honolulu.

88 *Beritania Street*: a fashionable street in downtown Honolulu.

90 *saw Berger beat the measure*: Henry Berger (1844–1929) came to Honolulu from Prussia in 1872 at the request of King Kamehameha V to direct the Royal Hawaiian Military Band, a post he filled until 1915. The largely native band's public concerts at the Royal Hawaiian Hotel, its performances at the harbour for arriving and departing steamers, and its tours of other islands, made it a major feature of Hawaiian social and cultural life. Berger's importance for Hawaiian music was enormous, as he collected, arranged, printed, and thereby preserved, a great deal of traditional music of the islands which would otherwise have been lost. He composed the music for 'Hawaii Ponoi', adopted as the national anthem in 1876.

92 *all the world is not American*: when Stevenson wrote 'The Bottle Imp' in 1889–90, Hawaii was still an independent kingdom; the US Congress did not pass its resolution to annex the islands until 1898. However, the islands were already dominated by

American commercial and political interests, which in 1893 would organize the revolution that ended the native monarchy and led first to the establishment of a republic run by American residents, and then to formal US annexation.

92 *Umatilla*: the ship on which Stevenson's mother sailed from Honolulu to San Francisco on 10 May 1889 (see McGaw, *Stevenson in Hawaii*, 78, 86).

93 *Tropic Bird*: this ship left San Francisco in June 1888 two days after the *Casco*, the yacht on which Stevenson and his family sailed for the South Seas (see Johnstone, *Recollections of Robert Louis Stevenson in the Pacific*, 21).

Papeete: see note to p. 30.

Trade Wind: see note to p. 9.

Motuiti: or Motu Uta, island in Papeete harbour.

opposite the British Consul's: Stevenson has placed Keawe and Kokua in the house he himself rented when he visited Papeete in 1888. His mother wrote: 'Louis's little house is just opposite the English consul's; next to that is the native church; and next that again the old prison, now in ruins, in which Herman Melville and the "long doctor" were confined, as you will remember, if you have read *Omua*' (*From Saranac to the Marquesas and Beyond*, 172). The prison (or 'calaboose') is mentioned later in the story; see note to p. 99.

like to the Hawaiian, with a change of certain letters: most of the Polynesian languages (that is, the languages of the eastern Pacific) are cognate; comparing words of the same meaning, one often finds that the consonants are changed, but the vowels and the arrangement of syllables are similar. Thus Stevenson wrote in *In the South Seas*: 'The impediment of tongues was one that I particularly over-estimated. The languages of Polynesia are easy to smatter, though hard to speak with elegance. And they are extremely similar, so that a person who has a tincture of one or two may risk, not without hope, an attempt upon the others' (*Tusitala*, xx. 10).

95 *the eight islands*: the Hawaiian islands.

97 *the true helper after all*: a reference to her name; see note to p. 83.

99 *the old calaboose*: 'calaboose' is an American word for a prison. The 'old calaboose' referred to here was the scene of Herman Melville's imprisonment in 1842; see notes to pp. 93 and 124.

101 *belaying pin*: a wooden or metal rod used for securing lines on sailing ships; it could be used as a weapon in disputes or as an instrument of punishment.

102 *a flat*: a dupe.

The Isle of Voices

103 *Lehua, daughter of Kalamake*: Lehua's name is that of a Hawaiian flower; according to Mary Pukui and Samuel Elbert in their *Hawaiian Dictionary* (Honolulu: University Press of Hawaii, 1971) it is an important image in Hawaiian songs and legends, and has several figurative meanings, including 'a beloved friend or relative' and 'a sweetheart'. Her father's name combines the words 'kala' (dollar, money) and 'make' (death), the two things with which he is most connected.

Molokai: one of the eight Hawaiian islands. The Hawaiian leper settlement was situated here (see note to p. 85), but 'The Isle of Voices' has nothing to do with that part of the island. As Stevenson wrote, 'The name of the whole large island of Molokai is sullied in the public mind, but [those settlements] which make up the leper territory, form an inconsiderable fraction of its surface, and the rest is a free country of clean folk' (*Tusitala*, xxi. 336).

the Kingdom of Hawaii: the Hawaiian Kingdom established by Kamehameha I (see next note) came to an end with the revolution of 1893 (see note to p. 92).

the King had him twice to Kona to seek the treasures of Kamehameha: Kamehameha was the first king to rule over the entire Hawaiian island group; a chief from the island of Hawaii, he conquered Oahu in 1795 and completed his conquest of the eight islands in 1810. According to legend, he had amassed an enormous fortune through his dealings with pirates, and had hidden it in the cliff caves at Kona, on the island of Hawaii; 'there . . . his reputed treasures, spoils of a buccaneer, lie, and are still vainly sought for, in one of the thousand caverns of the lava' (*Tusitala*, xx. 180). During his visit to Honolulu in 1889 Stevenson wrote that the present king, Kalakaua, was 'perpetually engaged on a treasure chase' for this hidden hoard (*Letters to Charles Baxter*, 246).

Maui: one of the Hawaiian islands, to the east of Molokai.

Eight Isles: the Hawaiian islands.

104 *Kaunakakai*: principal town on the southern coast of the island of Molokai.

Kalaupapa: peninsular on the north coast of Molokai, the site of the leper settlement.

Pelekunu: area in northern Molokai.

the house of a man of substance: Stevenson has modelled the furnishings and decorations of Kalamake's house, described on this page, on those of the house of the ex-judge, Nahinu, with whom he stayed during his visit to the Kona coast of Hawaii (see note to p. 82): 'it was on the European or, to be more descriptive, on the American plan. The parlour was fitted with the usual furniture and ornamented with the portraits of Kamehameha the third, [other Hawaiian royalty] and Queen Victoria. There was a Bible on the table, other books stood on a shelf' (*Tusitala*, xx. 183).

107 *some speech that was not practised in Hawaii, yet some of the words were the same*: see note to p. 93.

108 *a noble of the House of Representatives*: there is some confusion here; from 1840 the Hawaiian legislature consisted of two houses, the House of Representatives (elected) and the House of Nobles (of which membership was hereditary). Perhaps Stevenson's confusion was due to the fact that from 1864 the two houses sat together, as the Legislative Assembly.

111 *the swell beat and burst upon his bosom, as it beats and breaks against a cliff*: this part of the story is indebted to a Hawaiian legend associated with the deep ocean off the north coast of Molokai. Describing his sea journey from the Kalaupapa peninsular Stevenson commented: 'it was in these profound waters, where no ship may anchor, that the elastic Kana waded unembarrassed' (*Tusitala*, xxi. 336). The reference is to the legend of Hina, the 'Helen of Hawaii', who was abducted and held at the fortress of Haupo on the north coast of Molokai. Her son Kana led an attack on the fortress attempting to liberate her; when the attack failed he used his magical powers to swell to a great size and wade through the deep water assisting and rescuing his defeated warriors. The legend is recounted in King Kalakaua's *The Legends and Myths of Hawaii: The Fables and Folk-Lore of a Strange People* (New York: Webster, 1888), 67–94. Stevenson met the Hawaiian king many times during his stay in Honolulu in 1889, and according to his stepson, Lloyd Osbourne, 'Together they would pore for hours over the king's

notebooks, in which in his fine, slanting hand he had transcribed the legends of his dying people' ('Stevenson at Thirty-Nine', *Tusitala*, vol. xiv, p. ix).

111 *Since first the islands were fished out of the sea*: according to myth, the Hawaiian islands were fished out of the sea by the great fisherman Kapuhe'euanui. This fisherman of Tahiti caught a lump of coral on his hook and threw it back into the sea, whereupon it grew into the island of Hawaii; the process was repeated with each of the eight islands of the Hawaiian group; see Abraham Fornander, *An Account of the Polynesian Race, its Origin and Migrations*, 3 vols. (London: Trübner, 1878–85), ii. 18–19, and Martha Beckwith, *Hawaiian Mythology* (1940; Honolulu: University of Hawaii Press, 1970), 308–9. Cognate myths of the creation of islands by fishing them out of the sea are found throughout the Pacific, many featuring the demi-god Maui as the fisherman.

112 *the lighthouse, Lae o Ka Laau*: lighthouse at Ka-lae-o-ka-la'au point at the south-west extremity of the island of Molokai.

the low islands: there are several groups of 'low' islands (coral atolls) in the Pacific, the largest and most concentrated of which is the Low Archipelago or Paumotus (today the Tuamotus), to which the schooner takes Keola.

in the north end of Kauai or in the south end of Kaü: Kauai is the most northerly of the eight Hawaiian islands; Kaü is the most southern district of the most southerly island, Hawaii.

a steady trade: the trade wind; see note to p. 9.

their weather bow: the side of the bow facing the wind.

113 *the directory*: sailors in the Pacific in the nineteenth century depended for information on guides such as Alexander Findlay's *South Pacific Directory* (see note to p. 184) which collected the observations of earlier sailors. Especially with regard to the more remote and rarely visited regions of the Pacific, the directories did not offer authoritative information, but an aggregate of reports, sometimes conflicting with each other and constantly being revised, discredited, or updated. Stevenson exploited the uncertain or erroneous nature of information in the directories in several of his Pacific works, including *The Ebb-Tide* and *The Wrecker*; in the latter, various directories present conflicting reports, while the volumes of Findlay are described as 'all marked and scribbled over with corrections and additions' (*Tusitala*, xii. 214).

113 *the schooner 'Eugenie'*: Fanny Stevenson records that the schooner *Eugenie* was a slave-ship which had visited the Gilbert Islands in 1871 (*The Cruise of the 'Janet Nichol'*, 118); that the mate should have worked on a slave-ship adds another touch to his brutal, racist character.

steep-to: coast where the land rises steeply out of the water, and the water remains deep close to shore.

Kanaka: see note to p. 5.

belaying pin: see note to p. 101.

115 *the king and the missionaries*: these represented rival political factions in late nineteenth-century Hawaii. As Isobel Field (Stevenson's stepdaughter) wrote: 'I learned to my surprise that the word "missionary" had a political significance like Democrat or Republican. The leaders were the sons and grandsons of the original missionaries who came to Hawaii to convert the heathen. They were rich, prosperous American business men with one aim: to wrest the islands from the natives and have it [sic] taken over by the United States' (*This Life I've Loved*, 150). The 'palace' and the 'missionaries' also formed mutually exclusive social sets; Keola is outrageously claiming to be a 'chief friend' of both these dominant forces in Hawaiian politics and society.

116 *and never be any way troubled*: Stevenson found that this dread of the sea-shore was typical of low island societies; as he wrote in *In the South Seas*, 'the life of an atoll, unless it be enclosed, passes wholly on the shores of the lagoon; it is there the villages are seated, there the canoes ply and are drawn up; and the beach of the ocean is a place accursed and deserted, the fit scene only for wizardry and shipwreck, and in the native belief a haunting ground of murderous spectres' (*Tusitala*, xx. 130).

117 *Donat-Rimarau*: mistakenly printed as Donat-Kimaran (clearly from a misreading of Stevenson's handwriting) in *Island Nights' Entertainments*, this story having been set without Stevenson seeing proofs. M. Donat-Rimarau was the acting Vice-Resident or representative of the French government on the island of Fakarava in the Paumotus when the Stevensons visited in 1888 (*Tusitala*, xx. 160). Further details in this paragraph (the catechist, the visit of the French warship) are taken from the same visit and confirm that Stevenson had Fakarava in mind as the permanent home of the people of the Isle of Voices. In her note to the story Fanny Stevenson writes that Donat-Rimarau (whose name she spells 'Rimareau') had entertained the

Stevensons with supernatural stories of the Paumotus which she believed, together with the low island setting, had inspired 'The Isle of Voices' ('Prefatory Note' to *Island Nights' Entertainments*, *Tusitala*, vol. xiii, p. xiv).

118 *eaters of men in the south islands*: most historians believe that cannibalism was never or rarely practised in the Hawaiian Islands. At the time of European contact it was found in various island groups south of the equator, including the Low Archipelago.

between the devil and the deep sea: between two evils.

120 *posting up the beach*: to 'post' is to run or ride in haste.

121 *a bowl of poi*: Hawaiian staple food, 'a paste made from the boiled roots of the taro plant, mashed, mixed with water, and not served till slightly fermented' (Isobel Field, *This Life I've Loved*, 168). In other islands, such as the Marquesas, the more plentiful breadfruit was substituted for taro.

122 *Low or Dangerous Archipelago*: the variable winds and currents of the Low Archipelago, combined with its thickly clustered, poorly charted atolls and submerged reefs, constituted a notorious menace to ships; hence the alternative name, the Dangerous Archipelago.

the lepers: see note to p. 85.

The Ebb-Tide

123 *'There is a tide in the affairs of men'*: Shakespeare, *Julius Caesar*, IV. iii. 217.

Papeete: see note to p. 30.

purao-tree: 'a tree called the purao, something between the fig and mulberry in growth, and bearing a flower like a great yellow poppy with a maroon heart' (*Tusitala*, xx. 19).

124 *on the beach*: unemployed, destitute.

the old calaboose: see note to p. 99. Later in *The Ebb-Tide* we learn that the calaboose is 'at the corner of a shady western avenue and a little townward of the British consulate' and that its doors had 'once been locked on mutinous whalermen' (p. 143). This confirms that it is the same calaboose mentioned in 'The Bottle Imp', the 'Calabooza Beretanee' in which Herman Melville was held for some weeks in 1842; see Melville's *Omoo*, chapter 31.

Eimeo: also called Moorea, an extremely mountainous island to the west of Tahiti. Herrick was not the only visitor whose thoughts turned to scenes of Europe as he gazed on Eimeo. In Alexander Findlay's *A Directory for the Navigation of the South Pacific Ocean*, 5th edn. (London: Richard Holmes Laurie, 1884), which Stevenson used (see note to p. 184), Eimeo is described as 'a beautiful object in the view from Tahiti . . . its hills and mountains may, without any great stretch of imagination, be converted into battlements, spires and towers rising one above the other; their grey sides clothed here and there with verdure, which, at a distance, resembles ivy of the richest hue' (pp. 642–3).

124 *sortes*: (Latin) a casting of lots or an oracular response; *sortes Virgilianae* was the practice of seeking guidance or attempting to divine the future by randomly selecting passages from Virgil.

126 *copra*: see note to p. 4.

127 *mole*: breakwater.

129 *Freischütz*: *The Freeshooter* (1821), German Romantic opera by Carl Maria von Weber; a Faustian story in which the hunter Caspar sells his soul to 'the Black Huntsman' in return for magic bullets which always hit their mark. This is echoed later in *The Ebb-Tide* when the mysteriously powerful Attwater reveals that his bullets never miss their target.

Formes . . . when he was playing Kaspar: Karl Johann Formes (1815–89), German bass, made his Covent Garden debut as Caspar in *Der Freischütz*, which remained one of his most admired roles.

pariu: garment worn by both men and women in Polynesia, made of a rectangle of printed cotton wound around the waist; in *In the South Seas* Stevenson wrote admiringly of 'the gorgeous parti-coloured pariu, the Tahitian kilt' (*Tusitala*, xx. 158).

130 *Yorana*: Stevenson's phonetic spelling of the Tahitian greeting, ''Ia ora na'. A few lines further on the Tahitian 'A haere mai!' (come here!) is rendered by ear as 'Harry my!'

Point Venus: the northernmost point of Tahiti, to the east of Papeete, named after Cook's expedition in 1769 to observe the transit of Venus from this spot.

131 *Double-eagles*: United States gold coin worth twenty dollars, in circulation between 1850 and 1933, when it was the highest denomination US coin. Converted to sterling a double-eagle was worth about four pounds, and was thus much more valuable than a sovereign, the English gold coin worth a pound.

131 *B.-and-S.*: brandy and soda.

jarvey: colloquial term for a hackney-coachman.

growler: colloquial term for a four-wheeled cab.

132 *Ministering Children*: a devotional work for children by Maria Louisa Charlesworth (1819–80). First published in 1854, it had a huge circulation; a sequel was published in 1867.

ulster with astracan fur: an ulster was a long, loose, heavy overcoat; astracan (more usually spelled 'astrakhan' or 'astrachan') is a woven fabric with a curly surface, made in imitation of the fur-like woolly skins of young lambs from Astrakhan in Russia and used for trimming garments.

134 *Kanakas*: see note to p. 5.

136 *Indian Sachems*: native American chiefs.

beachcombers: see note to p. 30.

137 *'We twa hae paidled . . . till dine'*: misquotation from the fourth stanza of Robert Burns's 'Auld Lang Syne' (1788):

> We twa hae paidl'd in the burn,
> Frae morning sun till dine;
> But seas between us braid hae roar'd,
> Sin auld lang syne.

139 *Portland*: port in the American state of Maine.

140 *'Einst, O wunder!'*: from the song 'Adelaide', a poem by Friedrich von Matthisson, set to music by Beethoven in 1794–5. In his essay 'On Falling in Love', Stevenson called it 'the absolute expression of this midsummer spirit' of young love (*Tusitala*, XXV. 24).

141 *Bowditch*: *The American Practical Navigator* by Nathaniel Bowditch, first published 1802. It was revised by the US Navy Department and issued in 1882 as its standard guide to navigational practice and log-keeping procedures.

144 *the Fifth Symphony*: by Beethoven; the idea that the opening phrase represents fate knocking on the door originated with the composer himself.

memor querela: Horace, *Odes*, III. xi: 'et nostri memorem sepulcro scalpe querelam'—'and carve on our tomb a lament in our memory'.

terque quaterque beati Queis ante ora patrum: Virgil, *Aeneid*, i. 94–6: 'O terque quaterque beati, quis ante ora patrum Troiae sub moenibus altis contigit oppetere!'—'O thrice and four times blest, whose fate it was to die before their fathers' eyes beneath the high walls of Troy!'

144 *Ich trage unerträgliches*: 'I bear the unbearable', from Heinrich Heine's poem sequence of 1823–4, 'Die Heimkehr' ('The Homecoming'), poem 24, 'Ich unglücksel'ger Atlas! eine Welt'.

Du, stolzes Herz, du hast es ja gewollt: 'you, proud heart, you have what you desired'; from the same poem as the previous quotation.

146 *Paumotus*: see note to p. 112.

147 *before the mast*: where seamen were accommodated; officers were berthed aft.

148 *Hayes and Pease*: William ('Bully') Hayes and his sometime partner Ben Pease were buccaneers and slave-traders. Their fame in the South Seas was great, and a substantial body of gossip and legend accumulated around them as 'pirates of the Pacific'. They defrauded white men of their ships and cargoes and natives of their freedom (kidnapping and selling them into slavery on plantations). Although they were accused of many crimes, they were never convicted of any—hence, perhaps, their appeal to Davis as examples of successful perpetrators of frauds. Stephens, the other 'pirate' mentioned, seems to be a fictional figure.

149 *'Get thee behind me, Satan!'*: Christ's rebuke to Peter for tempting him to take the easy path; see Matthew 16: 23.

150 *Caledonia*: New Caledonia, French possession in Melanesia, site of French convict settlement.

Noumea: principal port of New Caledonia.

152 *the little isle . . . Queen Pomare's capital*: the island in Papeete harbour is Motuiti or Motu Uta, also mentioned in 'The Bottle Imp' (see note to p. 93). Melville described its appearance in 1842: 'Right in the middle of Papeetee harbor is a bright, green island, one circular grove of waving palms, and scarcely a hundred yards across . . . Commanding the harbor as it does, her majesty has done all she could to make a fortress of the island. The margin has been raised and leveled, and built up with a low parapet of hewn blocks of coral. Behind the parapet, are ranged at wide intervals, a number of rusty old cannon, of all fashions and calibres' (*Omoo: A Narrative of Adventures in the South Seas* (1847; Northwestern-Newberry Edition, 1968), 162–3). These guns were raised in symbolic rather than actual defence of the capital during the episode of gunboat diplomacy (at the same

time as Melville's visit) which forced the native ruler Queen Pomare IV to cede sovereignty of Tahiti to the French, under threat of bombardment from a French warship in Papeete harbour. The establishment of a French 'protectorate' was followed by French occupation which was resisted by most of the Tahitian people and led to three years of war (1844–7); however, again, armed resistance came not from the 'fortress' at Papeete (which was already in French hands), but from guerillas in the hills behind the town and in neighbouring islands.

152 *a fresh rig of slops*: cheap, ready-made garments supplied to sailors from ships' stores.

Ohé la goëlette!: schooner ahoy!

153 *A.B.*: Able Bodied, that is a fully qualified and experienced seaman, superior to an ordinary deck hand. The magnitude of the deception in describing Huish 'A.B.' is obvious.

155 *Sally Day*: the name of a member of the Melanesian crew on Stevenson's third Pacific cruise; see Fanny Stevenson, *The Cruise of the 'Janet Nichol'*, 167, 185.

156 *kaikai*: food (a Polynesian word, absorbed into Beach-la-Mar).

F.F.V.s: flying fish voyagers, i.e. sailors used to the fine weather and steady winds of the tropics (where flying fish were found); the term is derogatory, implying sailors who are only fit to deal with easy conditions.

157 *belaying-pin*: see note to p. 101.

158 *dead reckoning*: originally 'ded.' (from 'deduced') reckoning; estimating a ship's position using only speed and course steered from the last observed position.

South East Trade: see note to p. 9.

Fakarava: an atoll in the Paumotus or Dangerous Archipelago (now Tuamotus). Stevenson spent two weeks there in 1888, gaining much of the inspiration for 'The Isle of Voices'.

Dangerous Archipelago: see note to p. 122.

the Diadem: the highest peaks among the mountains of Tahiti.

161 *binnacle light*: see note to p. 3.

162 *'O honey . . . South Amerikee.'*: I have been unable to trace this song. It may be a traditional or ephemeral sailors' song, or Stevenson may have composed it in imitation thereof.

163 *'Up in a balloon, boys . . . moon.'*: chorus of a music-hall song by G. W. Hunt, published in 1868. The words are in fact:

Up in a balloon, up in a balloon,
All among the little stars sailing round the moon,
Up in a balloon, up in a balloon,
It's something awful jolly to be up in a balloon.

The complete words and music are given in John M. Garrett, *Sixty Years of British Music Hall* (London: Chappell, 1976).

166 *dude*: a dandy

167 *luff*: see note to p. 13.

168 *Taveeta*: Polynesian pronunciation of David.

169 *low island*: see note to p. 3.

170 *Raraka, Katiu, Takume, Honden*: atolls in the Paumotus (now Tuamotus). In the Heinemann edition (and subsequent editions) the first two islands are named 'Ranaka' and 'Ratiu', presumably from a misreading of Stevenson's handwriting; the confusion of 'R' and 'K' seems to have been a characteristic error (see note to p. 117). Subsequent editions have perpetuated the error; however, there are no atolls called 'Ranaka' and 'Ratiu', while Raraka and Katiu, neighbouring atolls to the east-north-east of Fakarava, lie exactly on the course of the *Farallone*.

174 *watch and watch*: schedule of duty where individuals or teams take alternate watches, i.e. four hours on and four hours off.

176 *as Crusoe may have stared at the footprint*: a reference to the crisis in Defoe's *Robinson Crusoe* when Crusoe, having long supposed himself to be the only inhabitant of his island, discovers a human footprint in the sand.

181 *Callao*: principal sea-port of Peru.

184 *tropic bird*: *phaethon rubricauda*, a sea-bird with two long scarlet tail feathers which were prized as personal decorations throughout the South Seas.

Anaa: island in the Low Archipelago (now the Tuamotus).

Findlay: Alexander George Findlay's first *Pacific Directory* was published in 1851. Stevenson owned his *Directory for the Navigation of the South Pacific Ocean*, 5th edn. (1884), and wrote to Charles Baxter: 'Persons with friends in the islands should purchase Findlay's *Pacific Directories*: they're the best of reading anyway, and may almost count as fiction' (*Letters to Charles Baxter*, 267).

185 *New Island*: apart from changing its position and the names of the informants and ship, Stevenson has transcribed the entry

for New Island word for word from the 1884 edition of Findlay, p. 531. This illustrates his contention that the directories of the still imperfectly known Pacific 'may almost count as fiction' (see above).

189 *'instantaneously disclosed'*: Wordsworth, *The Excursion*, ii. 834–5: 'The appearance, instantaneously disclosed, | Was of a mighty city . . .'

190 *presiding genius of that empty town*: cf. Stevenson's description of a visit to the pearl island of Penrhyn in 1890: 'the figurehead of the lost ship stood sentinel; a very white and haughty lady, Roman nosed and dressed in the costume of the Directory, contumeliously, with head thrown back, she gazed on the house and the crowding natives' (*Tusitala*, xxi. 310).

soldier's breeze: a favourable wind, usually a side wind.

192 *Winchester rifle*: see note to p. 66.

194 *'"For my voice has been tuned . . . combat's begun"'*: I have been unable to trace this quotation.

195 *'How long, O Lord'*: the lament of the Christian martyrs waiting for God to avenge them (Revelation 6: 10). Attwater's words may indicate simply the habit of biblical quotation, even in inappropriate situations, or may be meant to mock Davis and his intrusive questions, or may suggest Attwater's sense of his own possible imminent 'martyrdom' at the hands of the three criminals.

196 *Mahomet's coffin*: according to legend Mahomet's coffin was miraculously suspended in mid-air at Medina.

201 *store-houses*: the Heinemann edition has 'stone houses', but the buildings Herrick enters are used for storage, and 'store-houses' are mentioned on p. 189.

202 *nemorosa Zacynthos.' 'Jam medio apparet fluctu!'*: Virgil, *Aeneid*, iii. 270: 'now amid the waves appears wooded Zacynthus'.

these marine monsters . . . in the midst of the lagoon: cf. Stevenson's description, in 'The Education of an Engineer', of divers working in the bay of Wick: 'from time to time, a mailed dragon with a window-glass snout came dripping up the ladder' (*Tusitala*, xxx. 23). 'To go down in the diving-dress, that was my absorbing fancy', he wrote, and the essay recounts how the wish was gratified and Stevenson experienced the submarine world of the diver. 'It was one of the best things I got from my education as an engineer', he concluded (p. 26), and it provided him with one of the most important metaphors of *The Ebb-Tide.*

204 *'The rude forefathers of the hamlet lie!'*: a misquotation from the fourth stanza of Gray's *Elegy Written in a Country Churchyard* (1751): 'Each in his narrow cell for ever laid, | The rude forefathers of the hamlet sleep'. The misquotation has often been corrected by editors of the story.

205 *lain down with kings and councillors*: see Job 3: 13–14, where Job's troubles cause him to wish that he had died as soon as he was born: 'For now should I have lain still and been quiet, I should have slept: then had I been at rest, With kings and counsellors of the earth, which built desolate palaces for themselves'; the image of 'desolate palaces' suggests *The Ebb-Tide*'s concern with the vanity of human desire.

Penrhyn: also called Togarewa, a pearl island to the north-east of Samoa, now part of the Cook Islands. Stevenson was not much attracted by the island, which he visited in 1890, commenting on 'the rough and lawless manners of the race' (*Tusitala*, xxi. 311).

'And darkness was the burier of the dead!': misquotation of Shakespeare 2 *Henry IV*, I. i. 160: 'And darkness be the burier of the dead!'

209 *an old king one knew in the western islands*: Tembinok', the king of Apemama in the Gilbert Islands, under whose protection the Stevensons lived for about six weeks in 1889. The king dispensed summary justice with a Winchester rifle; Stevenson wrote 'I am told the king is a crack shot; that when he aims to kill, the grave may be got ready; and when he aims to miss, misses by so near a margin that the culprit tastes six times the bitterness of death' (*Tusitala*, xx. 301).

210 *Today it groweth up and flourisheth; tomorrow it is cut down and cast into the oven*: an amalgamation of two biblical quotations, Psalms 90: 5–6: 'in the morning they are like grass which groweth up. In the morning it flourisheth, and groweth up; in the evening it is cut down, and withereth', and Matthew 6: 30: 'the grass of the field, which to day is, and to morrow is cast into the oven'.

Thou fool, this night thy soul shall be required of thee: Luke 12: 20.

215 *as far west as the Kingsmills and as far south as Rapa-iti*: the Kingsmills, also known as the Gilbert Islands, in the western

Pacific, are now part of the Republic of Kiribati. Rapa-iti, an isolated volcanic island lying below the tropic of Capricorn, is one of the Austral or Tubuai Islands of French Polynesia.

217 *beach English*: see note to p. 30.

223 *at the port arms*: see note to p. 67.

227 *'whatever Gods there be'*: a misquotation from the poem 'Out of the night that covers me' (1875), popularly known as 'Invictus', by Stevenson's one-time friend and writing partner, W. E. Henley (1849–1903):

> Out of the night that covers me,
> Black as the Pit from pole to pole,
> I thank whatever gods may be
> For my unconquerable soul.
>
> In the fell clutch of circumstance
> I have not winced nor cried aloud.
> Under the bludgeonings of chance
> My head is bloody, but unbowed.

The poem ends with the declaration 'I am the master of my fate: | I am the captain of my soul'; Herrick's mental quotation of the poem is deeply ironic.

228 *City of Laputa*: flying island, visited by Gulliver in the third part of Swift's *Gulliver's Travels*; its inhabitants were so absorbed in abstract philosophical speculation that they failed to attend to practical matters of ordinary life.

233 *swipey*: tipsy.

234 *Coppers 'ot?*: 'hot coppers' is a slang term for the dry throat experienced after a drinking bout.

237 *spifflicate*: colloquial English term, meaning to disable or put out of action, to deal with (in a threatening sense).

240 *a blue ribbon in his buttonhole*: the blue ribbon denotes a teetotaller, after the practice of the Blue Ribbon Army, a nineteenth-century temperance union whose members wore a blue ribbon as a sign of membership. The 'fine inconsistency' of Davis's vision is that he both wears the blue ribbon and mixes a grog, a drink of spirits and water.

242 *out-Herod Herod*: to outdo in wickedness the tyrant Herod, whose evil acts included ordering the deaths of the innocent children of Bethlehem (Matthew 2: 16).

243 *Abinadab*: the name of several figures in the Bible, which Huish uses as an all-purpose term to denote biblical 'parties' in general.

Shykespeare, or the musical glasses: see Oliver Goldsmith, *The Vicar of Wakefield* (1766; Oxford: OUP, 1981), 46: 'The two ladies threw my girls quite into the shade; for they would talk of nothing but high life, and high lived company; with other fashionable topics, such as pictures, taste, Shakespear, and the musical glasses.' The phrase came to denote meaningless polite conversation.

244 *Tophet*: in the Old Testament, a place of fire and human sacrifice, symbolizing hell.

248 *Go, and sin no more*: Christ's injunction to the woman taken in adultery, whom he has refused to condemn; see John 8: 11.

252 *Lord, I believe, help thou mine unbelief!*: Mark 9: 24.

The Cart-Horses and the Saddle-Horse

253 *Two cart-horses, a gelding and a mare, were brought to Samoa, and put in the same field with a saddle-horse to run free on the island*: this fable is based on an episode at Vailima of which Fanny Stevenson gives the following account in her journal: 'The cart horses have arrived from Auckland, a couple of large, mild-eyed, gentle, dappled greys. It was pleasant to see them fall upon the grass after their tedious sea voyage, and amusing to watch Jack's [Stevenson's horse's] reception of them. He gazed at them in surprise at first, apparently thunderstruck at the great size of the two chiefs (for so he evidently regarded them) from the colonies. Then he began to show off before them, dancing and prancing and galloping around them in circles. The two big chiefs looked at him with mild curiosity. One said to the other, "That, I presume, is what is called a kanaka. Odd creature." And then they both returned to their luncheon and quite ignored poor Jack and his advances' (*Our Samoan Adventure*, 64–5). Presumably Stevenson and his wife both observed and shared an interpretation of the scene, which each then wrote up, Fanny in her journal and Stevenson as a fable.

the colonies: term by which the white settler societies of the Pacific, i.e. Australia and New Zealand, were distinguished from the islands.

Kanaka: see note to p. 5.

Something in It

255 *sinnet*: also sennit; flat cord formed by plaiting together strands of fibrous material such as ropeyarn, hemp, grass or fibre of the coconut husk.

Akaänga, Miru the ruddy: in Polynesian myth Miru was a spirit of the underworld, dedicated to the destruction of human souls; Johannes C. Andersen describes her as 'a fierce she-demon . . . whose favourite repast was the spirits of the unfortunate dead, whom she first stupefied with *kava*, then cooked in her oven and devoured' (*Myths and Legends of the Polynesians* (1928; Rutland, Vt.: Tuttle, 1969), 321). I have been unable to find any reference to the other demon, Akaänga.

kava: see note to p. 79.

calabashes: shells of gourds or pumpkins, used as vessels for liquids.

256 *blue-ribbon man*: see note to p. 240.

held kava to be excluded: kava is non-alcoholic, but has intoxicating and euphoria-producing effects, hence the difference of opinion about its status as an intoxicating liquor.

257 *taboo*: see note to p. 5. Stevenson pointed out that Europeans, who found the Polynesian idea of the taboo incomprehensible and meaningless, had their own taboos which were often no less, or even more, arbitrary (*Tusitala*, xx. 43). He also observed that where Polynesians generally exempted whites from their taboos, the concession was not returned: 'All the world must respect our tapus, or we gnash our teeth' (*Tusitala*, xx. 47).

sea-lawyer: one who cavils about rights and duties, questioning orders rather than obeying them; the term is of nautical origin, denoting an argumentative sailor.

The Oxford World's Classics Website

www.worldsclassics.co.uk

- Browse the full range of Oxford World's Classics online
- Sign up for our monthly e-alert to receive information on new titles
- Read extracts from the Introductions
- Listen to our editors and translators talk about the world's greatest literature with our Oxford World's Classics audio guides
- Join the conversation, follow us on Twitter at OWC_Oxford
- Teachers and lecturers can order inspection copies quickly and simply via our website

www.worldsclassics.co.uk